Praise for
THE ELEPHANT KEEPER

"Nicholson's light touch and sly humor ensure that the animal-human dialogue is entirely natural and intensely moving. (An) exceptional novel." —*Boston Globe*

"A sensitive boy suddenly becomes groom to Timothy and Jenny, the first pair of young elephants brought into England in the 1700s. This informative, engaging and moving book has clear insight into the impact of poverty, alienation and isolation that is as relevant today as it was then." —*San Francisco Chronicle Book Review*

"Bighearted and warm, with a slow-moving kind of grace, the book is very much like the two elephants that inhabit the world of the novel. Elegant and beautiful, the writing is precise and well-paced. *The Elephant Keeper* is a book that will stay with you long after you have read the last page. Jenny's ancient wisdom and Tom's fierce love and loyalty will, hopefully, inspire emulation." —*Raleigh News & Observer*

"An extended meditation on human needs and how our choices shape a better or lesser existence. [A] poignant, heartfelt novel." —*St. Louis Post-Dispatch*

"While deftly portraying 18th century village and estate life as well as the dark, fog-bound streets of London, *The Elephant Keeper* examines themes such as human choice, fate and the cruel British class system." —*Minneapolis Star Tribune*

"Christopher Nicholson takes readers to a time and place far removed from our own, and on an adventure they soon won't forget. This elegant story is not just for animal lovers. In it, readers see how the bonds of friendship go beyond time, age or species. Definitely one to put on your 'to read' list." —*Deseret Morning News*

"A tale by BBC radio documentary producer Nicholson about a man and an elephant canters along at a delightful pace, from the first meeting between the two on the quay in Bristol, England. Nicholson's elegiac alternate endings leave only the memory of their lasting bond—the elephant's legendary ability to 'never forget' is finally ours."
—*Publishers Weekly*

"An endearing account of a virtually telepathic relationship between man and animal."
—*Booklist*

"[A] remarkable debut. An unforgettable picture of an elephant/human relationship so close that, as the elephant learns to think like a human, she teaches her human to think like an elephant. This is one of the best books of the year."
—BookPage.com

"[Nicholson's] lush new novel of the late 18th century . . . Jenny is a magnificent character . . . She gives the book its weight, in every sense . . . the sheer richness of the story's texture. *The Elephant Keeper* evokes 18th-century village and estate life beautifully, and is stuffed with fascinating data from medical and veterinary history."
—*The Independent* (UK)

"Endearing . . . Like the elephant at its centre, Nicholson's book is gentle, profound and sweet-natured."
—*The Guardian*

"Christopher Nicholson traces the arc of Tom and Jenny's surprising journey with delicate empathy. He confronts sex, violence and power, but he does not shy away from less dramatic themes, such as gentleness and companionship, which help to make *The Elephant Keeper* such a rewarding book."
—*Times Literary Supplement* (London)

"A captivatingly original novel . . . This is a wonderful feat of storytelling, remarkable for its ability to wrench your heart without resorting to easy sentimentality."
—*Daily Mail* (London)

"A pleasingly ambling tale."
—*Financial Times*

About the Author

A prize-winning radio documentary producer who has worked for the BBC World Service, CHRISTOPHER NICHOLSON rode an elephant for the first time at Chitwan National Park in Nepal. He has been interested in natural history his entire life, and many of the programs he produced for the BBC centered on the connection between animals and humans. Because of a love for the novels of Thomas Hardy, Nicholson and his wife settled in Dorset, England, with their two children.

THE
ELEPHANT
KEEPER

THE ELEPHANT KEEPER

Christopher Nicholson

HARPER

NEW YORK · LONDON · TORONTO · SYDNEY

HARPER

A hardcover edition of this book was published in 2009 by William Morrow, an imprint of HarperCollins Publishers.

This book was originally published in 2009 in the United Kingdom by Fourth Estate.

HarperCollins books may be purchased for educational, business, or sales promotional use. For information please write: Special Markets Department, HarperCollins Publishers, 10 East 53rd Street, New York, NY 10022.

FIRST HARPER PAPERBACK PUBLISHED 2010.

Designed by Laura Kaeppel

The Library of Congress has catalogued the hardcover edition as follows:

Nicholson, Christopher, 1956–
  The elephant keeper / Christopher Nicholson.—1st ed.
    p. cm.
  ISBN 978-0-06-165160-1
  1. Elephants—Fiction. 2. Human-animal relationships—Fiction.
3. Stablehands—Fiction. 4. England social life and customs—18th century—Fiction. I. Title.
  PR6114.I29E44   2009
  823'.92—dc22
                                                              2009000852

ISBN 978-0-06-165161-8 (pbk.)

10 11 12 13 14   OV/RRD   10 9 8 7 6 5 4 3 2 1

To my mother

Part I

Sussex, 1773

April 24th

It was six days ago that Lord Bidborough, accompanied by another gentleman, came to the Elephant House and, after making the usual inquiries about my charge, who was, at that moment, quietly eating hay, asked whether it was true that, as he had heard, I was able to read. I replied that my parents had put in my way various books, which I had sat over, piecing together the letters until they began to make sense; whereupon his Lordship asked me which books, and I mentioned the Bible, *Pilgrim's Progress*, and *Gulliver's Travels*. This last work, I said, had so fascinated and enthralled me that I had formed the ambition of taking ship and travelling to remote parts of the globe in search of wealth and adventure, an ambition from which my father had dissuaded me, pointing out the dangers that lay in such travel, and recommending me to content myself with my lot. Lord Bidborough listened carefully. "Your father would appear to have been wise," he said, smiling. "Many lives have been squandered in the pursuit of adventure. Your parents could read and write, too?"—"They could read, my Lord, but scarcely write a word."—"But did you learn to write?" I replied that I had been taught to write at the village school, and had mastered the art tolerably well, although I had not written for a long time.

At this the other gentleman, whose name was Dr. Goldsmith, said: "Lord Bidborough reliably informs me that you are able to speak Elephant." I explained, cautiously, that I could communicate with the Elephant by making certain signs and sounds, and that I could also interpret certain signs and sounds made by the Elephant; but none of this was any more than a man might do with his most favoured hounds. Just as a hound would obey if told to beg, or sit, or leave the room, so, in the same fashion, I could command the Elephant to kneel down, to sit, to coil up her trunk, and to perform other tasks. Dr. Goldsmith here gave a glance to Lord Bidborough, who said, "Tom, Dr. Goldsmith would be most interested to see a demonstration of this communication at work." I readily complied, leading the Elephant out of her stable into the yard, where I bid her shake hands with Dr. Goldsmith; that is, to shake his hand with her trunk, which she proceeded to do, to his astonishment. At a word she knelt, very slowly and carefully, as is the way with Elephants, whereupon I made a sign with my hands and she rolled gently on to her side.

Lord Bidborough asked, if this was indeed not a form of language. Dr. Goldsmith answered, that it was certainly remarkable: "But," he went on, "is not the Elephant known as the half-reasoning Animal?" They discussed this for some minutes while the Elephant lay on the floor of the yard, her long-fringed eyes watching me for the signal to rise. From the slight twitches of her trunk I could tell that her patience was being tested, but she remained still and docile.

Presently the two gentlemen walked round her body and inspected her, poking her with their sticks and making further inquiries of her diet and her age. Dr. Goldsmith, who had pulled out a pocket-book and lead pencil, took notes on my answers. He was intrigued, as both ladies and gentlemen always are, with her trunk, which he called her probbossis. Having crouched to touch it, which he did with a certain caution, he asked me to explain its use and purpose. I replied that it had a double purpose: not only was it a breathing tube, like a human nose, in which respect it was highly sensitive, but also it served as an arm and a hand, in which respect it was both prodigiously strong, capable of tearing branches off trees and hurling rocks, and highly dextrous, enabling the Elephant to untie knotted ropes or to pick up objects as small as a piece of straw, or a pin, at will. I asked Dr. Goldsmith to put his pencil on the floor; next, having drawn the Elephant to her feet, I bid her pick it up and return it to him, which she did very courteously, and with a certain gleam of amusement in her eyes. Lord Bidborough gravely remarked that "the male of the human species also possesses an organ with a double purpose."

In order to demonstrate the Elephant's strength, I offered to command her to lift Dr. Goldsmith into the air, as she has often done in the past with his Lordship's acquaintances. Though obviously tempted, Dr. Goldsmith was concerned as to the possible dangers, and asked whether I could assure him that he would be perfectly safe. Was it possible that the beast would hurl him to the ground, or tighten her probbossis like a snake so that he would be unable to breathe? I said that I had no qualms whatever on the matter, and that I would stake my life on his safety; however, if he preferred, I would demonstrate by ordering the Elephant to lift me in his stead. Dr. Goldsmith was on the point of accepting my offer, when Lord Bidborough, with an arch smile, asked him if he was afraid. He seemed somewhat stung by this sally.

"Indeed, my Lord, I am not afraid in the least, but when it comes to my own life I generally exercise some prudence—however, in this instance, I am content to trust myself to your Lordship's guidance. If I should be squeezed to death, my affairs are in order—I am ready to meet my Maker."

So saying he took off his coat and stood arms extended, one arm holding his stick, the other his pencil and paper, while I gave the Elephant her instructions. Dr. Goldsmith is short in height, with a prominent forehead above a face that is deeply lined, and pitted from the Small Pox; and his expression, as the Elephant's trunk extended itself, coiled round his waist, gripped, and drew him without apparent effort from the ground, was such that Lord Bidborough laughed heartily. "Are you much squeezed?" he called. Dr. Goldsmith, some eight feet in the air, ignored his mirth, instead declaring in an affectedly calm voice that the prospect was d—ned excellent, and that he felt as comfortable as if he had been seated in a great chair; indeed, had he been equipped with a spyglass or a book, he would have been perfectly content to stay in the coils of the Elephant all afternoon. However, when I asked him whether he would care to be set upon the Elephant's back, or to be lowered to the ground, he replied that whenever it was convenient he would be most obliged if he could be replaced on terra firma. The Elephant lowered him to the ground and released him from her grip. Dr. Goldsmith was a trifle flushed, but not excessively so, and as I returned to him his coat, he thanked me very much for an experience that he would never forget.

I rewarded the Elephant's obedience with an apple that I kept in my pocket for such a purpose. Taking it eagerly with the end of her trunk, she swiftly placed it inside the cave of her mouth. Such a reward to an Elephant is as a sweet-meat is to a child.

It was then that Lord Bidborough asked me whether, if he were to supply me with pen, ink, and paper, I would be willing to write a history of the Elephant. He said that no one had ever written such a history before, and that an account describing the animal's characteristics, behaviour, habits, and intelligence, by someone such as myself, who had intimate knowledge of the creature, would be of immense interest to many important people in London and elsewhere. Dr. Goldsmith agreed, assuring me that I would be doing a service to Mankind to write about such a noble beast. I was much surprized and, for a moment, so daunted by the prospect, that I scarcely knew how to reply; at length I said that I feared that I would not have the skill.

"Tom, have no fear," said Lord Bidborough. "It need only be a simple account of particulars. In practice, writing is no different from talking—is that not so, Dr. Goldsmith?"

"Indeed, my Lord, writing is like talking; or, indeed, like riding a horse; once one is in the saddle, it is easy enough. A tap of the whip, and away you go. Of course, as there are good and bad riders, so there are good and bad writers, but everyone has the ability to write, provided he believes in his ability."

Although I had some doubts on the matter, it was clear to me that, his Lordship being my master, I had no choice but to agree to the request, which I did without further demur. He thanked me, and said that he would ask Mr. Bridge to arrange for writing materials to be brought to the Elephant House. Later that day one of the pages duly arrived with three quills, twenty sheets of paper, and a horn of ink.

I can scarcely describe the despair that I went through on the succeeding evening. I soon found a title, *The History of The Elephant. By Thomas Page*, to which I added, *Elephant Keeper to Lord Bidborough, of Easton, Sussex;* however, after this, I could not think how to proceed. Half-formed sentences drifted like down through my mind; when I reached out, they slid away. Why, I thought, do I have to write this history? Can anything written by a simple servant, the son of a groom, the keeper of an Elephant, be of interest to learned gentlemen in London? At one point, I remember, I had been gazing at the word *Elephant* for several minutes when the letters seemed to dissolve before my eyes, so that they became, not members of an alphabet, but lines and shapes without any meaning. Swimming in the candle-light, they seemed to make themselves into a single animal, a long, flattish beast with an E for a head and a t for a tail.

At length, remembering Lord Bidborough's "a simple account of particulars," I succeeded in writing a first sentence: *The Elephant is, without Dispute, the largest Creature in the World*—yet, before the ink had dried, I became filled with doubt. For (I thought), the Elephant is not the largest Creature in the world: there are creatures in the sea, whales and the Leviathan (which some people say is a kind of whale), which are far larger than Elephants. Thus I crossed out my first sentence, and instead wrote: *The Elephant is, without Dispute, the largest Creature in the entire terrestrial World,* which, on further reflection, I changed to: *There can be no Dispute that the Elephant is the largest and most stupendous Creature in the entire terrestrial World.* Then I found myself wondering whether even this was true. Who knows what the world contains? Who knows what may be disputed? I saw the gentlemen in London, shaking their heads and murmuring in disagreement. Crossing out again, I wrote: *It is generally believed that the Elephant is the largest and most stupendous Creature in the entire terrestrial World. When at its full Growth, it measures as much as sixteen Feet high, or higher.* Again, much doubt, but in desperation I plunged on: *While Nature has been generous to the Elephant in affording her such a great Size, it may be said that She has been careless as to Form: for the Elephant is commonly considered a most ugly Animal.* Here I checked, and re-wrote: *is commonly considered a most unwieldy Animal. Its most extraordinary Feature is the long Prottuberance which extends from its Nose, which is known as its Trunk.* I now crossed out *Trunk* and wrote *Probbossis,* which I thought would please Dr. Goldsmith and all the other learned gentlemen, but the word looked so odd that I resolved to have nothing to do with it and returned to *Trunk.* But a further doubt had struck me, as to whether I had been entirely accurate: for, it may be argued, the Trunk of the Elephant does not extend from, but is, its nose. Is a trunk any more than a very long and remarkable snout? However, I continued: *Its Ears are broad while its Skin is generally grey. It is said to be the most sagacious of Creatures and is known as the half-reasoning Animal. The Character of the Elephant is generally peaceful, yet they are renowned for their Bravery and Courage and will do battle with Lions and Tygers, if provoked.*

The pain which it cost me to produce these feeble sentences was enormous, and later in the night, I woke, and lay in the darkness, thinking to myself, Lord Bidborough expects me to write this History, therefore I must write it, for Lord Bidborough is my master: yet I know nothing of Elephants in the wild, in the Indies and the Cape. There are many stories about Elephants, some of which I heard from Mr. Coad, but I do not know whether they are true. I do not know whether it is true that, as Elephants grow older, their skins harden until they cannot be pierced by a sword, or whether it is true that Elephants have their own kings, who are attended by troops of servant Elephants, or whether it is true that Elephants worship the moon. I do not even know for certain that

Elephants fight with lions and tygers. How can I write outside my knowledge, except by a kind of guess-work, and what value is that? Besides (I went on, arguing with myself), whatever his Lordship says, writing is different from speaking; people do not write as they speak. In speech, they *use* ordinary, common words, the words which flow as easily out of their minds as water out of a spring, whereas, when they write, they *employ* a different vocabulary. In speech, a man *sees* an Elephant, but, once he has taken a pen into his hand, he *observes* it, or *regards* it. He does not *meet* an Elephant, but *encounters* it, and instead of *trying* to mount the same Elephant he *attempts*, or *strives*, or *endeavours*, to climb on its back. There is an entirely different language for writing, of which I am largely ignorant. I cannot write the History, I am incapable.

When I next met, that is, when I next *encountered* Lord Bidborough, I begged him to excuse me from the task. He read the page which I had written (to my shame, it was covered not only with crossings-out, but with numerous runs and blotches).

"Why, Tom," he said with a smile, "is she so very unwieldy? Is it that the Trunk is unwieldy, or the entire Creature?"

I stammered a reply: "My Lord, I do not think that she is unwieldy, however . . . I had originally written 'ugly.' Would 'ugly' be better?"

"Ugly? Tom, the Elephant is surely what Nature intended her to be. To me, she is a remarkable Beauty."

"To me also, my Lord. But, if I write that she is beautiful . . ." I stopped, confused.

Lord Bidborough looked at me in his kindly way. "Tom, forgive me—though I can see that you have laboured hard over this—it is not what I intended. I do not wish you to write a History of Elephants in general, but of this particular Elephant. I wish you to write a History of your Life together, in which you begin by relating how you first met the Elephant, and proceed from there. And if it is your opinion that she is beautiful, why, then, you should say so."

"Yes, my Lord," I said.

Again I stopped, unable to express the full extent of my reservations, except in my burning face.

"You know, Tom, so long as what you write is accurate and free from Invention—so long as it is faithful to the Truth—you cannot go far wrong," he told me.

"Yes, my Lord."

Having returned me the page, which I took very unwillingly, he went on: "By the by, Tom, though this is a small matter—with respect to style, there is no great need to employ capital letters quite so freely as you have done. In the past, I know, it was thought correct to lavish them on every possible occasion; but the fashion has changed, as fashions do."

"I will not use them at all, my Lord."

"No, no," said he, smiling, "you should use them for proper names, and at the beginning of sentences, and also, perhaps, if you wish to shew the importance of some thing or other—then they are valuable, and indeed necessary. For the rest, they may be left aside. But it is a small matter, scarcely worth mentioning."

"May I use a capital for the Elephant, my Lord?"

"Why—if you wish. After all, she is the subject of the History, is she not, and therefore very important. However, perhaps I should not have mentioned it. The simple Truth should be your aim, Tom. Fix yourself on that, and you will have no great difficulty."

"Yes, my Lord."

I find that I have therefore agreed to try again, that is to strive, to attempt, to endeavour again (*endeavour*, I think, being the largest and most imposing word, I am resolved to stick with *endeavour* as much as possible), though my doubts remain: for I have no skill in the art of composition, and I fear that, even if I succeed in writing the History, it will be a dull affair, since I am no Gulliver and have no adventures to fill up the pages.

The History of
The Elephant

Chapter I

I was born, the older of two children, in the village of Thornhill, Somersetshire, in the year of our Lord 1753. My father was head groom to Mr. John Harrington, a sugar merchant, who owned half a dozen ships trading out of the city of Bristol; these had brought him such wealth that he had acquired an estate, comprising some two thousand acres of farms and woodland. Mr. Harrington was very fond of riding over his land, and maintained a stable comprising some ten horses. From a very young age, it may be no more than two or three, I used to leave my mother's side and accompany my father as he walked from the village to the stables. I loved the warmth of the stables and the sweet smells of straw and dung, and I loved the horses, with their soft noses and large ears and intelligent eyes. I thought of the horses as my friends, and gave them names. There was one mare, a roan with a white blaze on her head, whom I named Star-light; I used to kiss her muzzle and talk to her, telling her stories that I supposed might amuse her, and she would prick her ears and appear to listen. I loved her greatly and persuaded myself that she loved me in return—imagining, even, that I was not a human being but a horse. One summer's evening, when I may have been six years of age, I fell asleep against her body in the straw, which caused a great alarm in my family, my mother and father passing a sleepless night in the belief that I had been stolen by gipsies, as happened occasionally in those days. When I was discovered, they did not know whether to be pleased or angry.

From this, you may draw the conclusion that I grew up a solitary boy, but I had the company of other children in Thornhill and Gillerton, and also of my younger brother, Jim, and we often played together round the stables. However, of the horses in Mr. Harrington's stables, six were cart-horses, two hunters, and two hackneys, that is, road-horses, and while the cart-horses were placid, heavy beasts, the hunters and hackneys had some thorough-bred in them and their tempers were far less certain. One of the hunters in particular, a big bay gelding, had a very nervous disposition, and one day he kicked out, and caught Jim a severe blow between the eyes. He was obliged to lie in darkness for more than a week, and, although he recovered, was left with the memory of the accident in the form of a scar on his forehead, and a plague of headaches; which I think, more than anything else, gave him his timid, retiring character and fitted him for his later life as a gardener. He developed a great fear of horses, and for ever after avoided the stables.

My father, who saw my love of horses, made it his business to teach me as much as he could on that subject. He would tell me how, if a horse were short of breath, and his flanks shivering, he might be suffering from the Strangles; if he were dim of sight, and lay down shivering, it was a sign of the Staggers; if his breath stank, or foul matter issued from the nostrils, he might have an Ulcer, unless the matter were white, in which case it was the Glanders, or black, when it was the Mourning of the Chine, which is a kind of consumption. He taught me to watch for the colour of a horse's urine, and the nature of his stool. Once, he led me up to a cart-horse which was suffering from worms. "Three different kinds of worms will attack a horse," he said, "the bot, the trunchion, and the red maw worm. Lift her tail." I did so, and I must have been very young, for my eyes were level with her fundament. "Now put in thy hand." I was afraid that she would kick out, but my father told me that she would not kick. So I stood on tip-toe and slid in my hand. "Further. To the elbow. Further. Now, what dost feel? With thy fingers. Dost feel something wriggling?" I said that I did, though I was not sure. "Pull him out." I did so, and found my wet fingers holding a little worm with a great head and small tail. "That is a bot," said my father. "He lives on the great gut and is easily pulled out. The trunchion and the maw worm live higher up. The trunchion is black and thick. The maw worm is long and thin and red."

I remember being amazed by the vast store of my father's knowledge, but he had learnt from his father, and in addition he owned a treasured copy of Gervase Markham's *Maister-Peece*, which has been called the Farrier's Bible. However, my father was his own man and did not agree with everything in Markham; for instance, in the matter of red worms, old Markham held that the first remedy was to bind human dung round the bit or snaffle, and, if that failed, thrust the guts of a hen down the horse's throat, whereas my father, on the contrary, believed a strong purge to be sufficient, though he purged only with great caution. Grooms in general think that a purge has worked only if it brings on a hurricane, but too strong a purge may kill a horse, especially if it is given to a horse which is weak or delicate, or which has an inflammation of the blood. However, there can be no doubt that purges are very valuable in cleansing impurities. Every groom has his favourite ingredients for purges, and while Markham preferred Nitre, my father used coarse Aloes and Rhuberb, or Cassia, rolled into balls the size of a pullet's egg, and given in spring and autumn.

I also learnt by watching my father at work, so that, by the age of eight or nine, I already knew the points of a good horse: that the mouth should be deep, the chest broad, the shoulders deep and the rump level with the withers, the tongue not too large, the neck not too long, the eye not too prottuberant. I knew how to bleed and purge, and how to cough a horse, that is, to try the soundness of his wind, by compressing the upper pipe of the wesand, or wind-pipe, between finger and thumb, and how to apply a glister, that is, lukewarm, and slowly. I knew how to tell a horse's age from the condition of his gums, from the gloss on his coat, and from a particular mark which appears on his front teeth, from the fifth to the ninth year, when it disappears; but I also knew how to detect the practice of bishoping, whereby the teeth are filed clean to make the animal seem younger; indeed, I remember that my father once shewed me a crone of a horse which, to judge from its hollowed cheeks and fading coat, must have been fully twenty years old, yet its teeth had been filed and cut to make it appear ten years the younger. My father's most important lesson, however, was one expressed not by his words, but in his acts: that horses are creatures with intelligence and emotions very like human beings, though to a lesser degree, and that when a horse is wayward, or rebellious, it is best to play the part not of a tyrant but of a lover, coaxing him gently into submission.

When I was twelve I became a groom in the stables at Harrington Hall, and as I took care of the horses—dressing, feeding, exercising, and performing a hundred other tasks for their benefit—I came to understand, or so I believe, something of their thoughts and feelings. Their disposition was greatly affected by the weather. On sunny days in spring and early summer, they would love to race round the fields and to roll on the ground, kicking their hooves in the air, but on sultry days when thunder was approaching they became nervous and irritable, especially if they were plagued by flies gathering round their eyes. I felt sorry for them, as I also felt sorry for them if they were ridden too hard, as often happened when they were taken hunting. In all my dealings with Mr. Harrington, I found him a very fair and generous employer, who never raised his voice in anger; yet, when he followed the hounds, he seemed to become a different man, and treated his mount with savagery. In a short morning's hunt, the same big bay that had kicked my brother, a handsome, prancing creature, would be whipped and wrenched by Mr. Harrington into a condition of great distress, panting and foaming, blood round the mouth and eyes starting from the sockets. It often fell to me to soothe this poor animal. I would lead him into his stable, which I had already prepared with a litter of fresh straw, and there lift off the bridle, loosen his girth, and throw a dry cloth over his loins; next, rub his face and throat and neck and give him a feed of hay. As he fed, I slowly washed his feet in soap and warm water, to the hocks, and last of all I took off the saddle, dried his back, and rubbed him down. All the while I would talk to him; for although my fellow grooms mocked me for this practice, horses like the sound of the human voice, and by degrees he would calm down, and recover his spirits.

Mr. Harrington had a young son, whose name was Joshua; he

frequently came into the stables by himself, and I was set the task of keeping him safe. After his fourth birthday, when Mr. Harrington bought him a short, shag-haired pony, I also became his riding master, and every day in the stable-yard would drill him in the art of riding; thus, for instance, his breast should be thrown out, with the arms bent at the elbows and the elbows resting on the hips; there should be a small hollow in the reins, which should be held with a light hand, and with the thumbs resting flat upon each rein, while the waist should be pushed toward the pommel, so uniting him with the motions of the pony. He was an eager pupil, though sometimes too impatient for his own good, or that of the pony, and often I had to remind him that the way in which the best rider communicates his wishes to his mount is through the mouth—the hands moving the reins, the reins operating on the branches of the bit, the branches upon the mouth-piece. For the most part, however, Joshua and I got on very well, and we became good friends. The one and only difference between us came over the use of the whip—for Mr. Harrington had given him a whip, and he became angry when I forbad him to use it. "My father whips his horse!" he objected, and was not pleased when I replied that no gentleman ever resorted to violence except when it was entirely necessary. On this subject I have been told that, in the Arab countries, which are known for their fine horses, the whip is scarcely ever used, and I wish that the same could be said here in England.

Mr. Harrington also owned a house in Bristol, and it was here that his family spent some months in the winter of 1765 to 1766. On account of my friendship with Joshua, I accompanied them, while my father stayed at Harrington Hall. I was greatly excited by the bustle and hubbub of Bristol, with its swarming streets, and soon began to entertain the notion that, instead of staying a humble groom, I might seek my fortune at sea. Mr. Harrington's house was off College Green, and thence it was but a short walk up Brandon Hill, from which I could trace the passage of the ships as they moved down the river's narrow channel and turned with spreading sails toward the open sea, like birds spreading their wings. Even nearer at hand was the quay itself, which I haunted and was haunted by, so that for hours at a stretch I would watch the ships as they swayed and jostled in the foul, filthy run of water, waiting their turn to unload their cargoes of sugar and rum, or tobacco and timber. The sailors were men with dark, weathered faces, and a swaggering gait which I envied and even tried to emulate; I would sidle into the taverns and eavesdrop on their conversations, and as I heard them talk about where they had been, and what they had seen, my imagination transported me into distant, exotick countries, and all kinds of improbable adventures.

Toward the end of that winter, I heard that a merchantman with an unusual cargo had landed at the quay after a long voyage to the East Indies. The rumour which ran like wild-fire through the city's taverns was that a mermaid had been caught, and was being offered for sale to the highest bidder. Eager to see such a curious creature, which was said to be very beautiful, with a snow-white skin and a tail somewhat like that of a Porpoise, I mentioned it to Joshua, who promptly ran to tell his father; whereupon Mr. Harrington appeared to ask whether I was certain that it was a true mermaid. I gave the honest answer that I had been told that it was, but had not seen it with my own eyes. Mr. Harrington said that travellers generally returned with a cargo of tales which proved to be false; however, given the number of tales concerning mermaids, he did not entirely discount the possibility that such creatures existed, and he therefore desired me to go to the quay with Joshua, and to find out what I could as to the truth or otherwise of the story.

Fearing that we might be too late, we hurried over the wooden bridge to the quay, where a throng of people had gathered by the great crane at the lower end of Princes Street. The ship in question, by name the *Dover*, lay alongside, and as its cargo, which consisted, for the most part, of spices and other goods from the Indies, was being hoist ashore, I called to one of the sailors and asked him whether the mermaid had yet been brought to land. He replied with a grin that, if I would give him a shilling, he would conduct me and Joshua to her quarters, where we could watch her combing her black hair. I was about to hand over the shilling when another tar told me that there was no such creature on board; although he and his ship-mates had seen several mermaids during the voyage along the coasts of Madagascar and round the Cape of Good Hope, it had proved impossible to catch any, owing to the cannibals who had attempted to board the ship in their insatiable hunger for human flesh. However, he went on, there were several exotick and fierce animals on the ship, but for safety's sake none of them could be landed until the tide was higher. I should here explain, for those who do not know Bristol well, that the tide in the city runs at a great speed and has a very great fall, amounting to as much as twenty or thirty feet; so that, when the tide is quite out, the ships wallow on the mud with their keels exposed, and the tops of their masts barely reaching above the level of the quay. This would be a great disadvantage to those wishing to load and unload their cargoes, but for the cranes which are placed along the quay and which can raise most cargoes like a feather. The tide now falling to a low ebb, it was judged safer to wait until the succeeding morning to land the animals. I asked the sailor what kinds of animals he meant, and he mentioned a Leopard, a striped horse, two Elephants, and a baboon with a white beard and blue testicles. "*Blue?*" I queried. "Blue as up there," he assured me, pointing at a patch of sky; which piece of improbable intelligence, I immediately discounted as false.

I asked the sailor what an Elephant looked like; he replied that it was like nothing on earth.

Joshua and I waited for more than two hours, hoping to get a glimpse of the animals, but as dusk began to fall I judged it best that we return to Mr. Harrington's house. I reported the sailor's account to Mr. Harrington, who said that he would be interested to see the creatures. Mrs. Harrington, who was present, said to her husband, "John, we do not want to start a menagery." This was the first time that I ever heard of a *menagery;* it is a French word, which means, a collection of animals. Mr. Harrington replied: "I have no intention of doing so, I assure you."

Early in the morning of the succeeding day, when we again went to the quay, Mr. Harrington accompanied us. With the tide now full, the deck of the *Dover* lay level with the quay; and we watched as, with many shouts, the great crane swung five sturdy crates on to the side of the quay. This took more than an hour, and, as the minutes passed, another crowd, almost as large as that of the day before, gathered to watch the spectacle unfold.

The Master of the *Dover* was one Captain Elias Hall, a stout, red-faced man who looked uneasy in a stiff suit. Taking a chisel, he prised two boards from the first crate, which had slipped its harness and landed heavily. It contained the striped horse, a creature known as a Zebra, and I saw at once that it had broken both its front legs and was very near death. Joshua was much distressed by its suffering, and the contents of the next crate to be opened were even more painful to behold, for the Leopard was long past all hope of recovery. This Leopard was evidently the prize trophy of the Captain, who had hoped, no doubt, to sell it for a large sum of money to some gentleman, and he did his best to rouse the poor

animal by kicking its body and pulling its tail, to no avail, since it
was utterly dead and had, indeed, begun to stink. The third crate,
rather smaller, held a ginger-coloured baboon with a neat white
beard and sky-blue testicles, just as the sailor had said; shivering
as if it were cold, and holding its head in its hands, it crouched in
a corner of the crate. Someone called for it to be brought forth, but
someone else told us that it was excessively dangerous and would
bite at will. Joshua now began to cry, saying that he wanted to go
home; however, Mr. Harrington dissuaded him.

The next crate to be opened contained a large grey animal,
lying on its side, deep in ordure, its hind legs in shackles. In my
ignorance I had no notion even whether it might be of the land
or sea, for in truth it did not resemble any creature that I had
ever seen or imagined, except perhaps a whale. I heard the word
Elephant, but scarcely registered its meaning in my astonishment.
It had two huge ear flaps, four thick legs, and a single snake-like
prottuberance dangling from the centre of its face. From a distance
it seemed hairless, although on closer inspection I saw thick wiry
hairs sprouting at intermittent intervals from the cracks and fis-
sures in its skin, which was the colour of ash. Its eyes were closed.
To me it looked nearly as dead as the Leopard, and Captain Hall
evidently feared as much, because he ordered two of his sailors
to throw sea-water over its body. At the shock of the water, the
creature's eyes remained closed, but it made a small stir with its
head, whereupon a party of sailors dragged it out of the crate and,
in spite of its great weight, endeavoured to set it on its feet. The
Elephant promptly collapsed, being unable to stand, very nearly
crushing one of the sailors beneath its weight. I was not surprised
that it could not stand for, as I was presently informed, it had been
confined in this tight space and virtual darkness for the entire
length of the voyage, a matter of some ninety-one days, during the

bulk of which it had been fed a meagre diet of biscuits and roots. It was easy to imagine the suffering that the creature must have endured, and the confusion in its mind; that it had survived the journey, was very near incredible.

When the final crate was opened we beheld another Elephant, in an even more desperate condition, a heap of grey skin.

Mr. Harrington and Captain Hall stepped aside and began to talk privately, while I learned more from the sailor. He told me that these two Elephants were mere children, barely half of the size that they might eventually achieve, something that I found privately incredible, but he assured me it was so. He said that another Elephant, a male, which had also been seized and brought on board ship, had been at least twice their bulk, and equipped with long tusks. When I asked where this prodigious creature now was the sailor told me that one night, at the height of a violent tempest, it had broken its shackles, burst out of its crate, and rampaged the length and breadth of the ship, bellowing and trumpeting. There were fears that, with its size and weight, it might charge through the side of the ship, but to re-capture it in such a temper, even in calm weather, would have been a most hazardous operation; during a storm, it was not to be contemplated. However, the Elephant soon slipped and fell groaning on the deck, whereupon it was secured with nets and ropes and shackles. It never stirred again, and refusing all food and water was dead within three days. Captain Hall, who had been hoping to sell it for a large sum, had been sorry at its end, but the crew was generally relieved to be rid of a dangerous animal, and glad of the flesh provided by the carcass. I asked the sailor what Elephant tasted like, and he answered that it was very palatable, similar in flavour to beef, though far tougher in texture. What remained of the carcass was cast overboard, though not before the tusks and teeth were removed and stored in Captain Hall's cabin.

Shewing my ignorance, I asked him what he meant by "tusks," whereupon he spread his arms and described two great scimitars of white horn, jutting not from the temples, as one would suppose, but from the sockets in the roof of the Elephant's mouth. The sailor said, it was a matter of regret that Nature had not supplied human beings with such weapons, which would have proved very useful. He also said that whoever bought these young Elephants would regret their purchase, for they would grow up full of rage and irritability, like the angry male.

Remembering Mr. Harrington's words about travellers' tales, I thought that this account of giant tusks might contain more invention than truth; however, both the tusks and teeth of the dead male were forthwith brought out of the ship. The teeth were well worn, testament to years of grinding, and reminded me of horses' teeth, though they were much larger, the two largest being as large as house-bricks, while the tusks were smooth and curved and long, though not quite as long as the sailor had told me. One tusk was somewhat longer than the other, and though the tip of the longer tusk was pointed, that of the shorter of the tusks had been blunted. Also, when he had compared them to scimitars, I had supposed that they had sharp edges, which would slice off a man's hand like the blade of a sword; whereas they were rounded. In colour, they were more cream than white.

Mr. Harrington now came to me. "Tom," said he, "is it your opinion that these miserable creatures are likely to live?"

I was a good deal flattered to be asked for my opinion, and also very uncertain how to reply. Both Elephants were breathing, but little more could be said in their favour; it seemed unlikely that either would survive for long. However, not wanting to answer entirely in the negative, I confidently suggested that they should be offered fresh water, and that if they drank it would be a sign that they might live. Pails of fresh water were promptly procured, and placed in front of the animals. Since their eyes were closed, they could scarcely be aware of what they were being offered; therefore, having received permission from Captain Hall, I cautiously crouched by the nearer of the Elephants, a female, and splashed a little water into her face. When she did not respond, I lifted her trunk, as I later learnt that it was called, and laid it across the back of my neck. This moment, when I touched an Elephant for the first time, when I felt the dry, wrinkled quality of its skin, when I felt the warmth of its skin, as warm as that of a human being, is one that I find hard to describe, but a great tenderness for the creature ran through me. By slowly straightening, I was able to lift the trunk and draw open the mouth of the Elephant, and into this dark cavern I poured a quantity of water. It vanished into the creature's throat like a stream vanishing into a hole in the ground. I poured off the entire contents of the pail, and was reaching for another pail when the Elephant's trunk seemed to slide off my neck, and to curl toward her mouth in search of further refreshment. At this sign of life I rejoiced greatly. After giving her the second pail, I turned my attention to the other Elephant, which I now saw to be a male, for two short tusks were poking from the skin above its mouth. I lifted its trunk, which was much heavier than that of the female, and laid it over my neck; but though I poured three full pails of water down its throat it failed to stir, and seemed past recovery. Mr. Harrington, who had watched all this, now turned to Captain Hall.

I had supposed that Mr. Harrington might purchase the tusks or some teeth; it never occurred to me that he would buy the Elephants. He was not, in general, the kind of man who acts out of a whim, or some passing caprice; his decisions were amply considered and based on Reason. In the end I believe that he bought the

Elephants partly out of compassion, partly to please Joshua, on whom he doted, and partly as a shrewd piece of business, which might end in a handsome profit. He paid, as I understand, the sum of fifty guineas for the pair. Captain Hall, stuffing the coins inside his coat, did not look contented, but no other gentlemen having made an offer, he had little choice. If the Elephants had died, as seemed most likely, he would have received nothing for his pains.

Presently Mr. Harrington sent me for a cart and two horses, and I ran to College Green like the wind, dodging the sledges and drays and waggons. Martin Pound, another of Mr. Harrington's grooms, had also come to Bristol. He was an old man, more than sixty years of age, and very slow, both in his actions and his wits; indeed I think perhaps he had always been slow, but age had slowed him even further. "*Elephants?*"—"Yes."—"*Two* Elephants? Mr. Harrington has bought *two Elephants?*"—"He has." The more I attempted to impress Martin with the need for haste, the slower he became. He sat on a wooden stool and shook his head in a doleful fashion, as if bemused at the extent of human folly. "*Two Elephants*? Why? Where will they live? Who is to look after them? What will they eat? How big are they?" At length he rose stiffly to his feet and hobbled toward the cart-house, but it was a good hour before we had put the horses in the shafts and returned to the quay.

The male Elephant was still alive within its crate, but its breaths came very quick and uneven, and I was sure that it lay on the point of death. The crate was nailed up, and with great difficulty and much shouting was lifted aboard the cart and bumped up the hill to College Green. Once it had been set down in the stable-yard, the cart hurried back to the quay and fetched the female Elephant.

Each crate having been placed in a separate stable, Martin and

I dismantled the boards, while Joshua and his father watched. At this moment Mrs. Harrington appeared. She was astonished at her husband's purchase, as well she might be, given his previous assurances. "Is this wise?" she cried. "Have you not considered that these animals may prove dangerous?" Putting his arm to her waist, he replied that the Elephants were no danger at present—and indeed they were in no condition to harm a flea—and that they were not rapacious and cruel, like tygers or wolves. "On the contrary, from what I hear, they are intelligent beasts, with gentle natures, who become greatly valued and loyal servants. If so in the Indies, why not here in England? Besides, they will at all times be under the care of Tom and Martin. We need have nothing to fear."

Once the two animals were settled on some straw, we cut the shackles with which they had been bound on the voyage. These shackles had chafed harshly and cut into the skin, and the wounds were discharging a foul fluid. We cleaned and dressed them as well as we could. Throughout this operation, the Elephants did not stir, and indeed for many hours they lay exhausted and asleep, while the sun came in the tops of the stable doors and shone on their wrinkled grey bodies. Sparrows chattered in the rafters, and every so often a bold sparrow might land on the ear of the stronger of the two Elephants, the female, and hop a little way over her head. The sun set, night fell; and when the succeeding day saw no change in their condition, I wondered whether they ought to be bled (and indeed my father, who was a strong advocate of bleeding, later chided me for failing to bleed them). In truth, I was not at all confident of finding a vein to open under their skins, and Martin was no help in the matter. He told me that, for his entire life, he had been a horse groom, not an Elephant groom, and that he knew nothing about Elephants, and had no desire to learn anything about Elephants, and intended to have as little as possible to do with Elephants. For all he cared, he said, I might take sole charge of the creatures. Though I too knew nothing about the care or behaviour of Elephants, I was strangely pleased by this arrangement.

As they lay like this, I had an excellent opportunity to begin my Elephant education by inspecting every inch of their bodies. Their skin was very dry, and in places looked like the bed of a dried pond, but it was softer than I had expected. Their huge ears were crinkled and stiff, and on each of their feet there sprouted a set of bony nails, the toes being concealed within the flesh. The fore-feet each had five nails, while the hind feet had four apiece, and the pads of the feet were covered in a hide so hard that it felt like horn. Their tails were thin straggling things, two feet long, and ending in tufts of hair, like the tails of oxen, which I thought unworthy of such great animals.

With some trepidation I peeled open their mouths. The tongues were fat and fleshy and there were four massive grinding teeth in each jaw, but no cutting teeth. The teeth of both the male and female were still strong and little worn, and from this, comparing them in my mind with the wear on the teeth of horses, I guessed that the Elephants were between eight and ten years old. Examining the trunks, I found that at the end of each was, not only a pair of nostrils, but also, above these nostrils, a kind of prottrusion or extension, like a finger, which is the means by which an Elephant is able to pick up tiny objects. I do not know the name for this finger, though I have often thought that it ought to have a name.

I was able to take the dimensions of both animals, which at this time were as follows:

FEMALE

From foot to foot, over the shoulder	*12 feet, 11 inches*
From the top of the shoulder, perpendicular height	*7 feet, 3 inches*
From the top of the face to the insertion of the tail	*9 feet exactly*
Trunk	*5 feet, 1 inch*
Diameter of foot	*9 inches*

MALE

From foot to foot, over the shoulder	*14 feet, 11 inches*
From the top of the shoulder, perpendicular height	*8 feet, 5 inches*
From the top of the face to the insertion of the tail	*10 feet, 2 inches*
Trunk	*5 feet, 10 inches*
Diameter of foot	*1 foot, 1 inch*

From this it may be seen that with Elephants, as is generally the case in Nature, the female is in every particular smaller than the male.

As with the Elephant which had died at sea, the tusks of the male were different in length. From base to tip, the right tusk measured thirteen inches, whereas his left tusk measured only ten inches and was somewhat blunter. This discrepancy at first seemed odd, but I later found the explanation, which is that a particular tusk is always used for digging, much as human beings use a particular hand for writing, and that this tusk is therefore gradually worn away.

Although I was unable to weigh the Elephants, I believe that each weighed about the same as a large bull, or less, for they had been starved on the voyage and their skins hung slack on their bones. As they lay asleep, little Joshua frequently visited the stables—for, like me, I believe, he had fallen in love with the Elephants—and together we would watch as their bodies rose and fell with each breath. We would rest our hands on their warm skins, or press our ears against their sides and listen to the slow beating of their hearts. Once, I remember, he asked me if the Elephants would die, and I told him that I hoped not. "They must not die," he declared in a fierce voice, "I will not allow them to die"; whereupon he knelt and began to pray for their recovery, and I knelt as well, and who can tell that our prayers did not succeed, for soon after this the stronger of the two Elephants, the female, took a long draught of water, after which she fell asleep again. The male remained on the border between Life and Death for much longer, and although he drank water on the third day it was not until more than a week had passed that he began to make a slow recovery.

After two or more weeks, both Elephants had struggled to their feet, and I was able to tempt their appetites with fresh hay and vegetables, which I bought in quantities from the Corn Market in Union Street. Once they had remembered how to eat, they ate in prodigious haste, cramming their mouths, I would say full, but an Elephant has a very capacious mouth. They liked fruits and vegetables of all kinds, including turnips, beans, and potatoes, and had an excessive fondness for carrots. I remember the great excitement they both shewed when I first placed a heap of carrots in their feeding troughs. This relish of carrots being so marked, made me speculate that the Elephants must know what carrots were; in short, that the taste of the carrots must stimulate memories of their lives in the natural state. Whether this is so I cannot say for sure; I have asked several travellers who have seen troops of wild Elephants in the Cape and the Indies, but none has ever been able to recall whether there were carrots present.

Their consumption of water was vast, amounting to a dozen barrels a day, and I also gave them fresh milk, in order to help them recover their strengths. Here I should mention that, when

Elephants drink, they do so by means of their trunks, which they use as straws, sucking up long draughts of liquid which they squirt into their mouths. I have heard it said that very young Elephants do not use their trunks, but bend down to drink directly with their mouths; whether this is true or not I do not know, but I never saw my two Elephants using their mouths to drink. However, they were clumsy, and it was not uncommon for them to knock over the pails with their feet, which when they understood an expression of surprize would cross their faces. Their pleasure in food and drink was evident, and once they had finished their meal they would demand further nourishment by waving their trunks and uttering little squeals.

One thing I quickly discovered was that their sense of smell was acute, far more acute than that of a horse; whether as sharp as that of a blood-hound I would not know, but if I entered the stables with a carrot or another tid-bit in one of my pockets, both Elephants would promptly scent it out, and the way in which their trunks greedily reached toward the pocket and, indeed, into the pocket, made me think that they could all but *see* with their trunks. This cannot be so, and yet in an Elephant the scent organ, which lies in the tip of the trunk, is so sensitive that it is akin to a third eye. Once, when the male was asleep, I made the experiment of concealing some carrots in a heap of hay, and upon awakening he instantly detected the carrots and tossed the hay aside to reach his favourite food.

I was exceedingly cautious of their strength and power, and took care not to be caught between their bodies, nor against the stable walls, when I might easily have been crushed. I kept them in view all the time; I did not once turn my back on them, or let them gain any advantage of me with their trunks, which would suddenly sway in my direction. They had suffered so much on the voyage that they might easily nurture a hatred of human beings, and I had no intention of letting them take their revenge upon me. If they felt hatred, however, they never shewed it in their eyes, which rather seemed to convey an utter weariness. The eyes of an Elephant are close-set and small, relative to the vast size of the skull, indeed, they seem to be much smaller than the eyes of horses, which appear large and globular; but they are nonetheless highly expressive.

Mr. Harrington and little Joshua regularly came to see the Elephants, and Joshua always wanted to pet them, as he did the horses; but this I strongly counselled against. However, I would hold him up to the stable doors, and then he would offer each of the great animals a carrot, which they would twitch from his hands.

"Do you think they will ever forget the experience of the voyage?" Mr. Harrington asked me once.

I answered that both dogs and horses would remember ill-treatment many years after it had happened. Mr. Harrington said he had heard from one of his acquaintances, a certain Mr. Coad, who had travelled widely in the Indies, that Elephants had infinitely superior memories to other animals, indeed, in that respect, were perhaps second only to Man, and that it was likely that some traces of their ordeal would never be lost. "Yet I believe," he continued, "that by treating them with kindness and respect, we may gradually cause these unhappy memories to dim in their minds."

Mrs. Harrington also visited. She was very nervous of the Elephants, and even more so when she saw me lifting Joshua toward them, in order to give them carrots. Her husband assured her that the boy was entirely safe, and Joshua said fiercely, "Tom will look after me!" but she remained fearful. She asked how much larger the Elephants would grow, and Mr. Harrington said he believed that they might grow a good deal more; the male would grow larger than the female. She said, "No one else owns Elephants, why should we?"—"If I had left them by the quay, they would have died."—"It might have been better if they had," she said. Mr. Harrington: "How so?" Mrs. Harrington: "Because, as they increase in size, they will grow more dangerous." Mr. Harrington: "That they may grow larger does not mean they will be more dangerous. They are peaceful enough now, are they not?"—"At the moment, they are." Mrs. Harrington looked very uncertain, however. Mr. Harrington smiled: "Would you prefer me to have bought you a little Negro boy, for a pet slave?"—"Not at all," she replied, "you know that I abhor slavery, it is a barbaric custom."—"Yet it serves a need," he answered, "and indeed most slaves are grateful to their masters, for how otherwise would they be cloathed and fed? How would they live?"—"That may or may not be, but I still do not understand what you purpose in keeping these creatures."—"I myself am not sure, but everything has a purpose. In time, they may breed."—"Why, I very much hope not," cried Mrs. Harrington, "if they are brother and sister, as you say!"—"So the Master of the *Dover* told me, but who knows?" replied Mr. Harrington. This was the first time that I had heard of the Elephants being brother and sister, or of the idea that they might breed.

The history of the Elephants before their capture is a blank, and for a long time I was not even sure whether they were from the Indies or from the Cape, though this particular doubt I later resolved when the same Mr. Coad, whom I mentioned earlier, came to see the two animals at Harrington Hall, and told me that they must come from the Indies: for in the Indies, the male grows tusks, while the female does not; however in the island of Ceylon none of the Elephants, either male or female, grows tusks, whereas in the Cape the male and the female both have tusks, though the females' are no more than short things.

I used to puzzle as to how such large creatures as Elephants could be taken into captivity. Were they caught in nets? However it was done, it seemed to me, the matter must be extremely hazardous, for if the Elephant chose to resist capture, as it must, who could stand against it? I have since heard of the ways in which they are taken prisoner in the Indies.

The first is used to capture single male Elephants, which, Mr. Coad said, are known as *tuskers*. A tame female Elephant is sent into the jungle; when she finds a herd of wild Elephants, she makes advances to one of the *tuskers*, giving him caresses with her trunk until his desires are inflamed. As he responds to her advances, she artfully leads him away from his family into some quiet nook where, as he hopes, he will achieve a conquest, and with his mind thus engrossed two young natives creep up and slip a sort of rope round his hind legs. This they wind round some sturdy tree. The wily female now moves away from the *tusker*, who on discovering the restraints on his legs flies into a terrible frenzy, roaring and trumpeting shrilly, and attempting to recover his liberty. At length, after some hours, he seems to fall into a fit of despair, but the rage soon returns, and he roars again, and tries to rip up the ground with his tusks, and then again gives himself up to despair, and so on, for several days, until the cravings of hunger and thirst subdue his temper.

The second method is, I think, the one that must have been employed with the Elephants of which I now took charge. This method involves hundreds of natives, who form a wide circle round a grazing herd in the jungle. These natives are careful not to alarm the Elephants at first, but by lighting fires and brandishing torches, they gradually persuade the herd to move in a particular direction, that is, away from all the noise and clamour, and toward a specially prepared inclosure, known in the Hindoo tongue as a *keddah*. Sometimes it may take as long as a week before the herd reaches the *keddah*. This inclosure is formed of upright and transverse beams, which make a barricade, reinforced by a deep ditch, and is in truth a series of linked inclosures, the first being large, the second smaller, the third smaller still. The barricades are concealed by thorn and bamboo, but as the Elephants approach they often grow suspicious and attempt a retreat, whereupon they are met by banging gongs and shaking rattles. Once they enter the first inclosure, a gate is shut, and then they have no choice but to advance into the second inclosure, and again the gate is shut, and at last they arrive at the third. The Elephants, by now greatly alarmed, charge and rampage, but at every point they are repelled, and they gather in a sulky group, not knowing what to do, and here remain for a day, until a small door is opened, leading into a narrow passage. Food is thrown down, enticing one of the Elephants to enter, and as he does so the door is shut. He tries to turn but there is not enough space, he tries to back out but the way is barred: he has no choice but to advance further and further, his mind whirling in terror and confusion, until he finds himself confined in a tight space. Here he is held by strong ropes, and here, while his rage subsides, that is, until it is subdued by hunger, he remains for a week or month, or longer, in the company of a man known as a *mahoot*, who will become his keeper for the rest of his life. This man never leaves the Elephant's side, and takes care of his every need; so that the Elephant comes to depend upon him, understanding his commands and doing anything to please him. Indeed, the Elephant is the man's slave, but there is this difference from many human slaves: that he serves willingly, lovingly, without questioning his position or feeling the least resentment: for, in the mind of the Elephant, his keeper, however poor or humble his station in human society, is a kind of God.

Chapter II

My two Elephants (I had begun to think of them as mine, though they were the property of Mr. Harrington) were very pleased with each other's company, and as a sign of their friendship they would entwine their trunks over the partition which divided their stables. Soon I began to feel more confident, and would let them use their trunks to explore what kind of creature I was, feeling round my neck, or my legs, or my head and face. It was a curious sensation to feel a waft of hot Elephant breath on my cheek or ear.

The stables in which the Elephants were housed faced east, and therefore received sunlight during the mornings only. One warm afternoon, I decided to let them into the yard. Being surrounded by brick walls, the yard was entirely secure, though as a precaution

I tied ropes between each of their back and front legs. My heart beat as I bent under the trunks to tie the knots, but I made a shew of bravado; for them to have detected my apprehension would have been a great error. In the yard they passed a very pleasant two hours, after which I led them back to their stables. Martin and I then took a horse and cart over the bridge to the Corn Market in order to buy fresh provisions for our charges, but we had scarcely reached the Market when one of the maids came panting toward us, crying out that the Elephants had escaped and were running through the streets. Much alarmed, I hastened back to the house, where to my great relief I found both Elephants peacefully browsing on the small weeds which grew out of the cracks between the bricks. With the lure of a few sweet carrots, I was easily able to return them to the safety of their stables.

Since I had bolted both stable doors, it was a great puzzle as to how the Elephants had broken loose. I strongly suspected that Joshua must have set them free, but when I next saw the boy, he protested his innocence. I confess that I was not entirely sure whether to believe him, which made him very cross; he stamped his foot and began to shout so loudly that Mrs. Harrington appeared and asked me what the matter was. When she heard that the Elephants had escaped, she tightened her lips and said that she had known it would happen. I promised her that they would never escape again; yet they succeeded in doing so on the very next day. I therefore set a trap, pretending to leave with the cart, but concealing myself in one of the horses' stables, with a good view of those occupied by the Elephants. Nothing happened for several minutes; then the female, who had been watching to see whether she was observed, curled up her trunk, grasped the bolt that secured the door to her stable, and slid it back in one deft motion. The male did likewise, and both animals ambled out, very pleased with themselves; at which point, I sprang from my hiding place, and drove them back to their quarters. I secured each of the stable doors with a lock, which could only be opened with a key. Both Elephants made repeated efforts to pick their locks over the coming hours; when they failed, I felt triumphant. I have defeated you, I thought to myself. Yet, soon enough, I came back from the Corn Market to find them once again in the yard, and the stable doors lying flat on the ground, torn off their hinges. The Elephants, having given up the locks, had lit upon the simple expedient of backing themselves out of their stables. They eyed me with a kind of glee, which was not at all as innocent as it pretended to be, and I gave them a severe reprimand, telling them how strongly I disapproved of their actions. They would not meet my eyes and looked uneasily away.

After this incident, I had stronger doors made, with iron bars, but it was plain that the Elephants needed proper training. However, before I had got very far with this, there was another matter to consider. Mr. Harrington and his family were returning to Thornhill for the summer months, and the Elephants had to shift also. How to move them safely over thirty miles of country was an aukward question. Martin was in favour of putting them in the same stout wooden crates which had been used to move them from the quay, and transporting them by waggon; while I argued that they should travel on foot, with their legs chained. I doubted that we would be able to persuade them into the crates, which would surely remind them of the torments that they had endured on the voyage from the Indies; and I also doubted that, if they attempted to regain their freedom, the crates would hold. Mr. Harrington, however, agreed with Martin, pointing out that, since College Green lay on the west side of Bristol, and to the north of the river, our route would necessarily take us through the centre of the city, where the streets are very narrow, and that the Elephants would be certain to attract crowds of people, causing untold havock; moreover, even when we were outside the city and in the countryside, we could not be sure that they would not take fright and bolt across the open fields. The only safe course, therefore, was to transport them in the crates.

Several days before the journey was to take place, I put the crates in the stable-yard, lining them with hay and hiding their appearance with rags and ivy. In spite of this disguise, the Elephants were not deceived; they were very wary of the open crates, and would not go near them. However, I gave them very little food, and by the third day, which was the day before we hoped to leave, the suspicions of the male had been overtaken by hunger, and he went into one of the crates and ate some hay. The female remained highly suspicious. Our difficulty was all the greater, in that the animals had to enter their crates at the same time; for, if the male saw the female being imprisoned, he would certainly take fright, and the same for the female.

Early on the morning of the journey, Martin and I had assembled a troop of helpers—some twenty strong men, from other houses on the Green—and while they stood by I laid a trail of carrots from the stables into the crates, which were piled with carrots. To my astonishment, this ruse worked as soon as I opened the stable doors; indeed it worked so quickly, both Elephants hurrying into their crates, that all of us were taken by surprize. The men rushed forward, ten to each Elephant, and held them there while iron bars were laid in place. When the Elephants understood that they had been tricked into captivity, they trumpeted in rage and distress, and I have no doubt that they would have broken out, but that the crates had been strengthened with bars, and that they were tightly confined, unable to turn or to swing their trunks. I should say here that people often believe that an Elephant's tusks are its main weapon; whereas, in truth, the trunk is far more dangerous.

Without further ado, each of the crates was loaded on to a waggon, and tightly secured with ropes; then a team of four horses was put in the shafts.

Fortune favoured us thus far, but no further: for we had scarcely left the city of Bristol behind us when the clouds opened. The rain began to pour, and the roads were soon sticky with mud, and the Elephants made a heavy load. Moreover, the horses, though strong, were frightened by the presence of the Elephants, who kept up an intermittent bellowing and trumpeting. Their cries made me desperate to cover the thirty miles as quickly as possible, in order to release them from their confinement; but we made poor progress, and as we were struggling up a steep down near Cheddar, I wondered whether we would ever reach the top. The rain pelted, and the road, which was deeply rutted, ran in chalky torrents, and the horses strained and stumbled; we dismounted, but one horse puffed and blowed so badly I thought that she would drop. As we neared the top, we met a large herd of sheep being driven to market, and their baas and bleats persuaded the Elephants to trumpet even more loudly. In the midst of this cacophony, the shepherd shouted to ask what animals we had on our waggons; on hearing that they were Elephants, he seemed as amazed as if he had been told that they were dragons. The Elephants quieted after that; and when we reached an inn at Wells, where we gave our tired horses a bait, I peered into the crate containing the *tusker*. In the lines of light shining faintly through the cracks between the boards, he stood motionless, but I caught the gleam of an eye, and I had the impression that he was looking at me. The end of his trunk slid, and blew against the crack. Within her crate, the female was equally still. I imagined the distress in their minds, and their fear that they were about to be put on another ship.

Night had already fallen with the rain still heavy when we crawled into Thornhill, passing the cottage where my family lived. We turned into Mr. Harrington's estate and drove to the stables behind the Hall. My father, whom I had not seen for over three months, was waiting with my fellow grooms, Bob Brown and Dick Shadwick. While they attended to the horses I prised open the crates, first that of the female, then that of the male. Both Elephants were dazed, and unsteady on their feet; they staggered toward each other through the puddles and bumped bodies; but I was relieved that they were alive. After I had given them a long draught of water, I led them into the cart-house, which it had been decided would be their new home. I would not allow any of the grooms, not even my father, to help, which caused some ill-feeling, but my main concern was with the comfort of the two Elephants.

Presently Mr. Harrington appeared, and with him was Joshua, carrying a lanthorn. The Elephants were standing side by side, and I remember how for one moment in the light held up by the little boy they seemed to shrink back, their trunks drooping from their faces, while their shadows flung against the rough whitewashed wall at the back of the cart-house merged to form a single dark shadow creature with a double trunk, which swayed and stretched to the slightest movement of the lanthorn. Mr. Harrington asked me how the Elephants did, and I told him that they did very well, though they were greatly unsettled by the journey.

That night I slept with them at the cart-house. In the morning, I left them in the care of my father, and went to see my mother, whom I was glad to find in good health. She told me that my brother, despite his head-aches, had been given work in the gardens at Harrington Hall, and when I learnt this I felt very grateful to

Mr. Harrington. However, she was frightened that I was in charge of two Elephants, and kept telling me to take care of myself, for, she cried out, wringing her hands, she could not bear it if I were torn to pieces and eaten alive. From this remark I discovered that she believed Elephants to be animals of great ferocity, who used their vast tusks like swords to slaughter their prey, having been told as much by Mrs. Perry, a withered old woman who was one of our close neighbours in Thornhill. Since my mother held Mrs. Perry to be an infallible authority on all matters political, historical, geo-graphical, moral, and scientific, although in her entire life she had probably never ventured more than a dozen miles from Thornhill, I had the greatest difficulty in persuading her (my mother, that is) that, on the contrary, Elephants were gentle as cows, though ten times as intelligent, and ate only vegetable matter. When I invited her to see for herself, she said that she did not dare, it was more than her life was worth; she was sure that she would be eaten. With my father's help, however, I prevailed on her to come. She gazed at the female, and then at the male, before saying, "Tom, if it is so gentle, why does it have tusks?" This question has often puzzled me, and I confess that I do not know the answer. Al-though it may be that, in the wild, the tusks are sometimes used as weapons, I am sure that they are chiefly employed for peaceful purposes, digging for roots and unearthing shrubs and trees, in which service they are very valuable.

It was about this time that I gave names to the Elephants, just as I used to name certain horses when I was a boy. The male I named Timothy, after my own father, while the female I called Jenny, a name that I had always happened to like. However, I did not tell anyone these names but kept them private, in case they exposed me to ridicule.

The rain having passed on, I allowed the Elephants out of the cart-house. At Harrington Hall, unlike in Bristol, the yard received sun for much of the day, and they enjoyed its heat, moving so that its rays angled on to the broad expanse of their grey backs. As they stood like this, with their back legs roped together, I took the opportunity to wash and scrub them, using a stiff brush, and this Jenny suffered me to do with great patience; however, when I came to Timothy, his trunk knocked the brush from my hands and tossed it toward his sister, and when I went to retrieve it, she flicked it away. This mischief shewed how far they had recovered their spirits after the journey from Bristol, and during the succeeding days they began to play any number of tricks. One of my daily tasks was to dig out the dung that had accumulated in the cart-house, taking it in a barrow to a large pit by the kitchen garden, while my father watched the Elephants to see that they behaved. (I may mention here that Elephant dung, being somewhat lighter and dryer than horse dung, is of great value in the garden.) When, after one of these trips, I returned to the yard, I heard my father shouting, and found that Timothy had seized the spade with his trunk, and was swinging it to and fro with such force that, had it connected with my father's head, it might well have knocked out his brains. I reprimanded him in as severe a voice as I could muster, but he was annoyed, and sent the spade flying through the air. I pretended to be very angry, and slapped his flank with the palm of my hand, an action which hurt me a great deal more than it can have hurt him.

It was clear that I needed to press on with their training, and I began to teach them certain signs and sounds. They regarded me attentively, for when they did well I praised them loudly and rewarded them with carrots or fruit. When they did badly, I shook my head and reproved them by wagging a finger, but this was seldom necessary. They learnt quickly, much more quickly

than horses; indeed, it was remarkable how fast we went, so much
so that I often wondered whether they had not already received
some training in the Indies. One reason for their speed was that
they imitated each other. While they watched me, awaiting the
next order, and often anticipating it before it was given, they also
watched each other.

Within a matter of days they were willing to walk forward, to
stop, to turn to the left and right, and to walk backward. I then
taught them to kneel. Among the differences between horses and
Elephants is that, while a horse has three bones in its leg, an Elephant has only two; thus the horse, when kneeling, brings his
hind legs under his body, while the Elephant lets his go behind
him, like those of a human being.

All this training I did either in the cart-house or in the yard,
and all the time I kept their front and back legs roped. In addition, I made a kind of harness, which I attached to their upper
bodies, tying it under their bellies and drawing it between their
front legs.

My next step was to teach them to lie down. This proved more
difficult, for although Elephants will lie down to sleep at night,
for an hour or two, this runs counter to their natural inclinations,
which are to stay on their feet; for when on the ground they cannot
rise quickly to their feet and are all but defenceless, unable to use
their tusks or trunks to defend themselves against any enemies. For
this reason it took many hours of teaching before I could persuade
them to do my bidding. I took care never to shew my emotions
but to remain entirely patient, in the certainty that my will would
in the end prove the greater, as eventually proved the case. It was
Jenny who first yielded, dropping to her knees and tilting her body
to one side so that she fell, crumpling, to the ground; whereupon
I praised her loudly and rewarded her with food, and the sight of

this convinced Timothy to do likewise. As they lay in the dusty yard, breathing slowly, with the spring sun on their bodies, I felt a great sense of satisfaction that two such creatures, the most powerful beasts in the animal kingdom, should have bowed to my will; and also some regret that neither my father nor my fellow grooms, who were busy exercising the horses, had witnessed this singular event. The succeeding day I took care to repeat the feat when Bob and Dick were watching, hoping to impress them mightily, but to my disappointment they said nothing and feigned complete indifference.

However, when I gave a demonstration of the Elephants' progress to Mr. Harrington, he expressed his astonishment and pleasure. "But, Tom," he went on, "you should not be doing this alone. Each Elephant should surely have his own groom. Why is Martin not helping? Or Dick?"—"Sir," I said, feeling somewhat uneasy, "it is easier by myself. The Elephants prefer a single keeper."—"They do, do they? Both of them? They have clearly expressed their preference for a single keeper?"—"Yes, Sir. And my father helps me."—"If you say so," said Mr. Harrington, who was perhaps a little surprised, "but pray, Tom, how have they expressed this preference?"—"Sir," I said, "they refuse to obey the other grooms. They will not obey them."—"They will not obey them?"—"No, Sir. They refuse. They pretend to be deaf. They will only obey me."

While this was true enough, it was also true that none of my fellow grooms ever attempted to make friends with the Elephants, or ever offered them any tokens of affection. At the time, I could not easily understand this, but now I think that it derived partly from fear, and partly from resentment at the extent to which the Elephants drew attention away from the horses. Mr. Harrington made no secret of the fact that he was more interested in the Elephants than the horses. My father, moreover, being head groom, felt that the Elephants disrupted the smooth running of the stable-yard. Here I should also mention the curious antipathy which exists between horses and Elephants. Even before the horses in Mr. Harrington's stables had seen the two Elephants, they smelt them; and, not liking what they smelt, became agitated. They were more difficult to handle; they stamped, and neighed, and these symptoms became all the more pronounced when the Elephants began to squeal and trumpet. Soon enough, the horses set eyes on the Elephants, and this frightened them so much that several sweated and shivered uncontrollably, and refused to eat. It seems that all horses are frightened of Elephants. Quite why there is such antipathy is not for me to say, but there is a fixity, an intensity, in an Elephant's beady stare which strikes terror into the heart of the bravest horse.

After this conversation, Mr. Harrington seemed to accept that I should be sole keeper of the Elephants; at least, he never mentioned the matter again. For this, I believe, I have to thank Mr. Coad, who visited the Elephants, and who told Mr. Harrington of the personal attachments which, in the Indies, form between Elephants and their *mahoot*s. Indeed Mr. Coad, when talking to Mr. Harrington, always referred to me by this curious word, *mahoot*.

Mr. Coad was a gentleman of middle age, originally from Lancashire, and his character was plainly expressed by the rugged, wrinkled appearance of his face, somewhat like that of an ancient bulldog. When he delivered his opinion on any matter concerning the Elephants—which he generally did with his legs astride, and hands on his hips—he did so in a tone which seemed to say that anyone foolish enough to challenge him should expect a sharp bite. Nonetheless, much of what he had to say I found very interesting indeed.

In the Indies, he said, the Elephants were employed by the

princely rulers to execute criminals, which they accomplished by trampling their bodies, or breaking their limbs, or impaling them on their tusks, according to the direction of their *mahoot*s. At the invitation of the Prince of Udaipur, Mr. Coad had witnessed the execution of a man who had been found guilty of ravishing a young girl. Hands tied behind his back, eyes blind-folded, he knelt on the dusty ground and awaited his fate, while the Elephant, a *tusker*, slowly advanced with its *mahoot* on its neck. It halted before the kneeling man and, at a word of command, lashed out with its trunk. The guilty man fell, uttering a single cry, which was promptly silenced as the Elephant stood on him with one of its fore-feet and crushed his chest. As an act of completion, the Elephant swept the body into the air, raising it to a height of six or seven feet, before dashing it to the ground and driving a tusk through the neck. At this point, the execution was over; the *tusker* backed away, and the relations of the dead man were allowed to claim the body. What was impressive, said Mr. Coad, was the solemn manner in which this execution was carried out, the Elephant obeying its *mahoot*'s instructions to the letter, and acting, so far as he could judge, as the perfect agent of human justice. "It is infinitely preferable to the sordid hangings that we have in England," he told Mr. Harrington. This account of the execution haunted me for many nights, and sometimes haunts me even now: I picture the kneeling man, I enter his mind and hear the slow tread of the approaching Elephant, like the approach of Death itself, and I listen with terror for the faint swish of the trunk, the last sound that I shall ever hear.

In the Indies, said Mr. Coad, it is considered a great honour for an Elephant to be appointed an executioner. Other Elephants work in such tasks as plowing, pulling carriages, and hauling heavy loads of wood and rock, much like draught horses and oxen in England, though the loads that they draw are far heavier. A token of their great strength is that they sometimes also help with the launching of ships.

Other pieces of intelligence, which may be of interest to the reader, are as follows:

That, when wild, Elephants feed chiefly on grass, leaves, bark, and fruit; among their favourite foods being a crescent-shaped fruit with a tough green skin, known as a banana;

That wild Elephants sometimes break into the corn fields, committing terrible ravages, and have to be driven out by the natives;

That Elephants have long memories, and if subject to injury or insult will look to revenge themselves, even for years afterward;

That, when Elephants come to mate, they do so with the utmost secrecy, retiring to a dense thicket; which is a sign of their great modesty; and that after mating, both animals retire to the nearest body of water, to wash themselves;

That the period of time necessary for a *mahoot* to train an Elephant is generally reckoned to be between six months and one year;

That the females are more tractable than the males; however, both sexes are subject to abrupt fluctuations in mood, in which Elephants who have always displayed gentleness will, without warning, turn angry and stubborn;

That, in the Indies, unlike in the Cape, the Elephants are never shot for their ivory; however, when a male proves unruly or wayward, his tusks may be sawn off;

That this operation, which would seem impossible, is accomplished after letting the Elephant drink quantities of the local liquor, which quickly reduce him to a state of utter insensibility.

Mr. Coad went on to tell Mr. Harrington that, in the Indies, the *mahoot*s were able to enforce their rule over their charges by

employing an iron spike, known as an *ankus,* and he strongly advised me to get myself such a spike. He said that at the root of all
obedience was fear; this principle was universal, and had equal application to the government of human society, for if people did not
fear their rulers, it was in their natures to rebel. Mr. Harrington
said that this was undoubtedly true: "Tom, you must have one of
these spikes." I asked Mr. Coad how the spike was used, and he
said the *mahoot* would either press the point into the skin on the
back of the Elephant's ear, or bring it down more or less hard on
the skull. A blow which would split open a man's head, said Mr.
Coad, was, to an Elephant, which has a skull like a rock, no more
than a light tap of remonstrance.

At his and Mr. Harrington's urging, I did get myself such a
spike, which I used a few times, though I felt a reluctance to use
it over-much, believing that it were generally better to work by
consent than fear, and so to expel the elements of ferocity in their
natures. This is true of all animals, that they may easily be ruined
by harsh treatment at a young age. A dog savagely beaten as a
puppy lives the rest of its life in a kind of cringing terror. A fine,
mettlesome young horse, whipped and lashed into subjection, loses
its spirit and becomes a worthless jade. I found that wearing the
ankus on a string round my neck, so that the Elephants could see
it, was generally enough to persuade them into obedience.

Early one day in May, I was sufficiently confident to lead the
Elephants out of the yard and into the grounds. It was a fine sunny
day, and, although I kept their legs roped, they frisked and rolled
on their backs, very like horses or cattle which have been confined
all winter. My pleasure in watching them was tinged with apprehension that, when I ordered them back to the stables, they would
ignore me; however, at a single clap of my hands, they turned attentively, and, at another clap, they rambled toward me.

Encouraged by their obedience, I made the experiment of taking the Elephants to an old copse which lay on the side of a hill, about a mile from the Hall. I led them on ropes attached to their harnesses. At the start, we walked along the track in a leisurely fashion, the Elephants feeding on the vegetation on either side, but as we drew near the copse they scented what lay ahead and quickened their pace, so that I found myself forced into a run. The hazels in the copse were in new leaf, while the ground was thick with blue-bells, and the air full of perfume. Greatly excited, and making little squeals and rumbles of pleasure, the Elephants grazed through the blue-bells, their trunks flying out to latch on to hazel branches, which they dragged and tore down and stuffed into their mouths. Throstles and other birds sang loudly, and the sun shone in lances through the leaves. It was now that I first saw Timothy use his tusk in the way that I have already described, driving it deep into the soil to lever up a young oak.

Among the blue-bells were many thin paths, made by badgers, and presently the Elephants found their holes, which had lately been dug out, with fresh mounds of earth heaped outside the entrances, and scattered blue-bells (which badgers use to line their homes). Timothy and Jenny sniffed loudly at the entrances to the holes, no doubt scenting the badgers, and making strong noises of disgust—indeed, they inserted their trunks a small distance *down* the holes—I, meanwhile, felt a fresh anxiety, lest the ground, having been mined, might collapse under the weight of the Elephants. I called them to me, and we moved down a slope where the blue-bells gave way to a snowy spread of ramsons. The Elephants' feet squeaked on the leaves, crushing them and making them smell strongly. However, instead of feeding on the ramsons, the Elephants hurried through them, making for a pond surrounded by willow and rush, and well known to me as a particular haunt of toads. As a boy, in late winter, I often used to visit it to collect the neck-laces of their spawn, or to watch the chaotic frenzy of their mating, when twenty or more glistening males would struggle to clamber on one unfortunate female. Now, in early summer, the pond was full of young toads, and as the Elephants waded in they swam frantically out of the way, while moor-hen scuttled for the cover of the rushes, and a pair of duck took flight. Having scooped up quantities of foul-smelling mud, which they splattered on their backs and flanks, the Elephants began to squirt water at each other in great jets, using their trunks like cannons. The sun made rain-bows through the spray, and the mud dribbled down their flanks. They were like unruly children, and indeed, as they wrestled with their trunks, or pushed, heads locked together, each heaving to dislodge the other and grunting with the strain, I thought that they were like human children in Elephant form.

When, at length, I clapped my hands and summoned them out of the pond, they declined to hear, and continued with their sport. I shouted threats, and even brandished the *ankus*. They pretended not to notice, and this angered me, for I could think of no easy way to force them out of the water unless I myself waded in, which with the mud smelling so foul I was loath to do. I was obliged to wait for upwards of an hour while they wallowed and splashed away. In the end I resorted to cunning, concealing myself behind a tree, and in their curiosity to discover my whereabouts they splashed out of the water. Having caught their ropes, I gave the Elephants a severe reprimand, and though either could have knocked me down with the twitch of a trunk they heard me out and seemed to shrink back and repent. As we left the copse, we met a party of wood men, whose alarm at the sight of two drip-ping, mud-soaked Elephants, draped in green weed, was so great that they flung down their tools and took to their heels.

We made many subsequent visits to this spot and I never again had any difficulty in making the Elephants leave the water; in part, I think, because I used to reward them with sugar or a carrot, but also because they were anxious not to incur my displeasure. The wood men grew to understand the innocent and peaceable character of the Elephants, and as word of our trips spread through the neighbourhood we often had company in the shape of boys and girls, who would run ahead or follow us, flitting through the trees, or peeping from a tree trunk, caught between apprehension and curiosity. A few children were bold enough to come closer; among these was a little maid no more than five years old, who approached very timidly one day. At her approach, Jenny and Timothy raised their heads, staring, so I signalled to them to stand still and walked over to the maid, who was holding some dry sticks of wood. Her name was Margaret Porter; she was the daughter of Robert Porter, a wheelwright. When I asked her if she knew what these great creatures were called, she shook her head. I said, "They are called Elephants and they are very noble and wise creatures, who come from far away across the sea." She put down her sticks and bravely took my hand and we walked toward the two Elephants, who were side by side. "Are you not at all afraid?" I asked. "No," she replied, though she held my hand very tightly. To her they must have seemed as lofty as the giants which Gulliver meets in the land of Brobdingnag. I said to the Elephants, "May I present you my very good friend, Margaret?" and two trunks slid through the air and began to explore her head and arms with the utmost politeness. She hardly knew, I think, whether to laugh or cry; at first she giggled, and then, forgetting her sticks, ran off as fast as her legs could take her. But she came back on other days, and soon became a favourite with the Elephants.

Another of their favourites was Lizzy Tindall, a girl of my own age who lived in Thornhill. She was the daughter of the tanner, George Tindall. As children, we had sometimes walked together to the school-house in Gillerton, where she had a great reputation for mischief-making; this grew from the occasion when, having cut off her hair and rubbed mud into her face, she deceived the school-master, old Mr. Gibbons, into thinking that she was a gipsy boy. Here she was successful, but on another occasion, when she claimed to have seen an angel standing in the churchyard, she was soundly whipped for lying. Now she was employed in the Hall as a maid, or spider-brusher, as she called herself, which she found much less entertaining, and when she had time she would steal away, to chat with the grooms or stroke the horses, or to feed sugar to the Elephants. There was always a good supply of sugar in the kitchens, and since they loved it even more than carrots they became very affectionate toward her; indeed, on one occasion, Timothy became too forward, his trunk slipping from Lizzy's neck into her bosom. She drew my attention to what he was doing, whereupon I told her to push the trunk out of the way, which she did, pat pat, but soon enough, back came the trunk. "Tom!" she cried, "is this not deliberate! What a saucy Elephant!" Indeed, he was perfectly innocent and had no idea of the liberty which he was taking, and I said so; whereupon she tossed her hair (which, when she took off her cap, now hung half-way down her back), and laughed, "I am not so sure, look at him! Look, Tom!" and it was true that the Elephant continued to rout round. But there was a reason for this, as I soon discovered, which was that she had hidden a piece of sugar in her bosom, to test him out.

While the Elephants held Lizzy and Margaret as particular friends, there were other people whom they regarded less favourably. Among these were my fellow grooms, Bob Brown and Dick Shadwick. I had once been on good terms with Dick, who was my elder by no more than three years, but since the arrival of the Elephants he seemed to have turned against me. At the time my voice had not yet broken and was still piping and shrill, and whenever he met me he would squeak like a mouse. This feeble joke afforded him vast quantities of amusement. I ignored him, but I could not stand idly by when he and Bob persecuted the Elephants. Bob used to divert himself by tossing the Elephants stones or pebbles, and sometimes they were deceived enough to take these offerings into their mouths, though they would generally spit them out soon enough. When I asked him to stop, he laughed. "If they are foolish enough to eat stones, let them do so," he said, and this filled me with indignation, for my father had often told me of a race-horse which had choked after it was purged with too large a ball. The ball had lodged deep in the horse's gullet, and all efforts to retrieve it with an iron instrument having failed, the animal suffered a miserable death.

I found that my father did not greatly want to hear about Bob's behaviour, and indeed he attempted to dismiss it as a mere prank, whereupon I interrupted, "Father, a prank that could end with the death of the Elephants."—"Well," said he, with great reluctance, for he hated arguments, "I will talk with him." My father went and talked to Bob. A short time later, Bob came up to me: "Tom," he said, "forgive me—I am sorry for the stones—and to shew this I should like to give the Elephants an apple each." There was a mocking smile on his face, and before I could prevent him he had held out two small green apples. Both Elephants took their apples and put them in their mouths; but while Timothy ground his to pulp, Jenny spat hers out and with it a nail. I was very angry and told Bob what a fool he was. "A fool?" says he, sneering, "who are you to call me a fool? A stable-boy!" I said that, if the Elephants were to die as a result of his apples, he would be the fool, and that, if he did such a thing again, I would tell Mr. Harrington. I had disliked him for years, ever since I had seen him set the tail of a dog on fire. Making animals suffer was one of his favourite sports. He often tormented frogs and toads, and I heard that he once poured a bottle of Aniseed over the back of a cat when the hounds were running, and they clapped on the drag and tore it to shreds.

One thing which I learnt from Mr. Coad was that, in the Indies, the captive Elephants were regularly ridden like horses, and I was resolved to try my luck in this respect, though the difficulties seemed formidable, and I could not imagine how it was done. None of the horses' saddles was broad enough for an Elephant's back, and mounting only seemed possible if the Elephant were to kneel or lie down, or to stand still while a ladder was placed against its side. What perplexed me most was how the rider, once perched aloft, directed his steed. Horses, with their sensitive mouths, are directed largely by means of the bit and bridle and the reins, and perhaps, I said to myself, Elephants equally have sensitive mouths, but it would take a strange bit and bridle to fit on an Elephant. Even if such a bridle could be fitted, looping under the trunk, and even if the Elephant were willing to accept the bit, would anyone hauling on the reins be strong enough to steer such a powerful beast? I had the *ankus* as a means of chastisement, but what if the Elephant were so maddened by the rider's presence on its back that it chose to charge away? What if it chose to unseat its rider by rolling on to its back, as horses do when they do not like being mounted? To be rolled upon by an Elephant would surely be fatal. I thought a little further, and saw that an Elephant, if it so wished, might use its trunk to knock the rider from the saddle. My father, with whom I talked this over, felt that the venture was too dangerous to be hazarded; however, I secretly decided to disregard his advice.

With this in mind, I made a rough saddle out of ropes, and fastened it on Jenny's back, tying it under her stomach. Although she submitted to this readily enough, within a few minutes her trunk was feeling over the knot and soon enough she had it untied. I tied it again, this time much more firmly, and when she attempted to undo it she failed; but Timothy proceeded to untie it for her. This is no good, I said to myself, and tied it once more, this time with the tightest of knots. Next I made a sign telling her to kneel, which she did, and I was able to climb on—although, as I clung on her back, I found myself unable to make her stand up. "Stand up! Stand up!" She remained kneeling, for in my foolishness I had forgotten that she could only obey me when she could see me.

I therefore had to teach my Elephants to understand human speech, by which I mean not the full range of speech, merely particular words and phrases. Again they were excellent pupils, listening to me with great attention, much as a young dog, anxious to please, will cock his ears and listen to every sound which falls from his master's lips. Within a month I felt ready to hazard another attempt at riding. This time Jenny rose, and now I was eight or ten feet high, leaning over the ridges of her spine, clutching at ropes, and with my legs splayed horribly by the breadth of her back. Bob and Dick were watching; so was Lizzy, who cried up anxiously asking me if I was all right, and I was about to reply when Bob rammed a hot iron into Jenny's fundament, whereupon she began to lumber forward. Being unable to grip with my legs, as one would grip a horse, and with the saddle not altogether as secure as I had thought it to be, I lost my balance, and slid over the cliff of her back. Though I put my hands out to break my fall, the pain travelled up my arms and into my elbows. As I lay on the ground, Lizzy rounded on Bob, saying that I might have broke my neck, but he laughed in her face; not for long, however, because Timothy, who had been eyeing these events, swung his trunk and knocked him sprawling. He picked himself up and went away cursing and vowing revenge. I was grateful to Timothy for administering such a swift rebuke; but my elbows hurt, and within half an hour my right elbow was swelling. I tried to make light of the pain, by pretending that it was merely a bruise, but that night I could scarcely sleep, and I knew that I must have broke a bone in my elbow. While it healed I supported it by means of a cloth knotted round my neck.

When Mr. Harrington heard of my failure, he wrote to Mr. Coad, who kindly drew a sketch of Elephant-riding in the Indies. It shewed a male Elephant, with long tusks, walking in a grove of palm trees. This Elephant was carrying an entire company of passengers, seated in a wooden platform like a broad boat. Such platforms are known in the Hindoo as *howdars*. In the sketch, the Elephant's keeper, the *mahoot*, was seated not on the *howdar* but on his neck, with his bare feet propped on the bony curves of the Elephant's ears. This was such an obvious solution to my difficulties that I cursed myself for not thinking of it before and, in spite of the pain in my arm, I took off my shoes and then and there climbed on to Jenny's neck. I found that, at the narrow junction of the neck, my position was wonderfully comfortable and secure. I could, like the *mahoot*, rest my feet on her ears, or, if I preferred, I could drop my feet and brace myself with my legs against the sides of her neck. When, by chance, she put down her head, I felt myself in danger of pitching forward and sliding down her trunk, but this was a danger to which I soon accustomed myself; and from this point on I rode the Elephants every day, and what was marvellous and almost incredible, found that I could control them well enough without use of bits or bridles, whips or spurs, or of the *ankus*, merely by the power of speech.

Chapter III

During the second summer that the Elephants spent at Harrington Hall we had a period of very hot dry weather which lasted over a month and a half. This both pleased and displeased the farmers, for while it helped ripen the corn it was torture to the sheep on the downs, and their thin cries of distress filled the air. Every pond having shrunk to nothing but a muddy stew, I took the Elephants through the corn fields to a river about three miles away. The river was shallow, the water coming no more than halfway up the Elephants' legs, but they played in it for many joyful hours, shooting water at each other and hauling up quantities of weed, which they flung high in the air.

There came a day of thunder, heard at a distance of many miles, but drawing steadily closer. Now the Elephants became restive, flapping their ears to keep off the clouds of thunder-flies which plagued their eyes, and as the sky darkened, and the growls and rumbles of thunder grew louder, I put them in the cart-house. I attempted to soothe their emotions by talking in a soft voice and stroking their trunks. No animal likes thunder, and the horses were also anxious, while all the birds fell silent. Flashes lit the sky, and the first huge drops began to splash down; then, after a brief pause, when the storm seemed to draw breath, the rain fell in a torrent, pounding the roof of the cart-house with a deafening noise and spurting as it hit the ground. On a sudden the door flew open and in burst Lizzy, her hair dripping. I gave her a horse-blanket to wrap round her shoulders and sat beside her on a heap of straw. "You do not mind me being here?" she inquired, squeezing her hair and looking at me with her dark eyes.—"Not at all, why should I? How is Mrs. Harrington today?"—"Mrs. Harrington has bought herself a new dress and is very pleased with herself," she said, and took off her shoes. "O, I am soaked! How dark it is! How is your elbow?"—"My elbow?" I was surprised; I had forgotten my elbow. "It is mended, but still a little stiff." I bent it slowly, while she watched; then she drew back her sleeve and shewed her own arm, which was very soft and fair in comparison to mine. Her hair dripped on to my arm, and she brushed it off, and let her hand linger on my arm, and then I thought that I should kiss her, indeed, that she would like me to kiss her; but I was too shy, and afraid that, if I did, she would make some joke at my expense. Even so, I might have plucked up courage and kissed her, but the Elephants chose to interrupt us, their trunks sliding over our shoulders and joining our hands. The storm continued for more than an hour; when it was at an end, a band of brilliant yellow light shone from under the dark cloud which was moving away to the east. I let the Elephants into the yard, and they splashed and trampled through the puddles with great relish.

This storm was one of the very few times that I saw the Elephants agitated. Although they started at loud noises, for instance when pheasants burst from the undergrowth, or ring doves clattered with smacking wings from the thickets, they were for the most part very placid and even-tempered. However, on one occasion, when we were riding along a track, Timothy came to an abrupt halt and gave a sharp trumpet. At the same moment he stiffened his trunk and pointed: upon which I, leaning over his head and following its line, saw a large viper coiled in the bracken. I urged him on, but he would not budge, nor would Jenny, who was following close behind, and we had to wait until the viper, perhaps conscious of danger, uncoiled itself and slid away. I conclude from this, that both Elephants knew, either by a kind of instinct or because they had seen snakes in the Indies, that snakes were poisonous, which was remarkable, though even more remarkable, to my mind, was that whenever we passed that same spot, both Elephants remembered the viper and checked stride to see whether it was still there.

In the autumn we sometimes met herds of village pigs, rooting for mast. The Elephants did not like pigs, and would hurl pieces of wood, or stones at them, with great accuracy and force. These pigs soon learnt to avoid us, and whenever we drew near would flee in squealing terror. There were also occasions when we unexpectedly encountered horses. On a day of hard frost, as we were walking through a field of bean stubble, we heard the sound of the chase, and presently the hounds came pouring toward us, hot on the drag and barking furiously. They streamed past, pursued by the horses with their riders who, as always, were shouting and tally-hoing in a state of great excitement. Neither of the Elephants was in the least disturbed by the commotion; but one black mare, upon seeing the Elephants, was so unnerved that it shied and threw its rider, a heavily built gentleman by the name of Dr. Chisholm. Dr. Chisholm lived in Gillerton; he was well known both for his love of food and for his fiery temper. His foot now being caught in the stirrup, he was dragged some way through the mire before the horse came to a halt. Picking himself up, he turned on me in a fury, what the d-v-l did I mean parading my d—ned Elephants here, getting in the way of the chase, et cetera.—I respectfully replied that I was sorry, I had not known that the chase would be coming this way, to which Dr. Chisholm retorted that in that case I must be deaf. He remounted and galloped off.

I was a good deal troubled by this matter, and feared that Dr. Chisholm would complain to Mr. Harrington. I heard no more of it. However, before long, I had occasion to remember the incident and to wonder about its consequences.

The whole of January 1768 was exceedingly cold, with a bitter north wind, and heavy falls of snow. Every morning, as my father and I walked from Thornhill to the Hall, we came upon the bodies of thrushes and blackbirds frozen stiff, and every evening the sun, sinking through a trench of violet, seemed the colour of blood. Several of the horses having fallen ill with a contagious distemper, I became afraid for the safety of the Elephants who, without the protection of a coat of hair, or fur, were exposed to the full rigour of the cold; and though I kept them in the cart-house, and wrapped them in horse-blankets, they were listless and miserable. I could understand the depression of their spirits, for they were used to the heat of the Indies. When the cold deepened, a fine powdery snow blowing through the edges of the door, I lit two small stoves, though it worried me perpetually that the Elephants might knock a stove over, and set fire to the straw. For this reason I stayed with them all night, rising from my bed to stoke the fires, or to give the embers a puff with the bellows.

My father confidently expected the weather to change with the new moon, which fell I think sometime after the middle of the month, and indeed there began a thaw shortly afterward; however, soon the cold returned harder than ever, with the same piercing wind. Mr. Harrington had not gone to Bristol, for Mrs. Harrington was about to give birth; and I remember that, to test the depth of the cold, he carried out an experiment, placing three glasses of different liquids in the open air: the glass of water froze in six minutes, hard enough to bear a five-shilling piece upon it; the glass of port wine froze in two hours, and the glass of brandy in six hours. By now this persistent weather was becoming a serious matter for farmers, even worse than the summer's drought. Mr. Harrington's barns were well provisioned with hay, but many farmers had little or no hay left and could not afford to buy more, prices being so high; moreover, in the fields the turnips had frozen to solid blocks, which left the sheep without food. People prayed for milder weather, however, when the thaw came, in the middle of February, the turnips had rotted in the ground and were pulpy and worthless, and many sheep died of starvation.

Before this thaw both Elephants did fall ill, as I had feared. The first to sicken was Timothy, whom I found with his head hanging and eyes closed, and when I offered him a carrot he declined. Soon Jenny too fell ill, and when both animals lay down, I became very afraid that they had lain down to die. With my father's help I opened their mouths, and poured cordials of milk, peppermint, and honey down their throats. The horses had been bled, as a matter of course, and my father was in favour of bleeding the Elephants; a suitable vein, he believed, lay in the roots of each ear. I was reluctant to bleed, for fear that it would be impossible to stanch the flow; however, my father urging strongly, I gave way. We bled Timothy first, and hit the vein at once. The blood was dark and very rich, and we succeeded in drawing off a full three pints of blood. When we came to Jenny, the first blow missed the vein, but we struck with the second, and though her blood was less rich and flowed sluggishly we took two pints. I should mention here the old story that the blood of an Elephant is colder than that of any other animal, but this is entirely untrue, it is as warm as that of a horse.

After this, there was little more that we could do. My father left, but I stayed with them. Sometimes I rested my hand against one or other of their chests to feel that their great hearts were still thundering away, and sometimes I talked to them, which, while helping them not at all, seemed to relieve my anxiety. To keep out the chill I let no one into the cart-house save for my father and Mr. Harrington, and Joshua, who made me kneel and say another prayer on their behalf.

Soon after their recovery, my father fell ill. First, he complained of pains shooting through his legs, next, that he was hot and giddy. Since he had always enjoyed good health, I was surprized but not greatly concerned, for, as I say, I was still thinking of the Elephants. He went home and, taking to his bed, sank into a fever. This being the middle of the day, my mother became very alarmed, and began to think of fetching the doctor—the same Dr. Chisholm whom I mentioned earlier—however, before doing so, she consulted Mrs. Perry, as she did on every matter. Mrs. Perry bustled up and, looking at my father, declared that the fever was not serious, she would stake her life on it being no more than a severe cold with a touch of ague. All this I had from Jim, my brother, who was at home, for in such weather there was little to be done in the gardens. As the afternoon wore on, my father continued to decline, and in the evening, despite Mrs. Perry's repeated reassurances, my mother sent my brother through the snow to Gillerton, where Dr. Chisholm lived. Dr. Chisholm being at table, Jim was told to wait. More than two hours passed before Dr. Chisholm appeared—patting his mouth with a napkin—to ask what the matter was. My brother told him.—"And what is your father's name? Ah yes—he is the father of the Elephant keeper, is he not? Well, let us hope he is not ill with the dreaded Elephant Fever. I cannot come now, young man, but I shall come to him later."

My brother returning home, gave this message to my mother: "Dr. Chisholm is coming later."—"But could he not come at once?"—"No, he is at table, but he will come later. He says that Father may have Elephant Fever." My mother, very frightened, cried out, "What is that?" Upon which my brother told her, that it was a special disease which human beings caught from Elephants.

Since I had stayed the night at the cart-house, I knew none of this; however, shortly before day-break, Jim appeared, and told me about my father's Elephant Fever and that I must come home, bringing a piece of one of Timothy's tusks. It seems that Mrs. Perry now believed my father would only be saved if he were given a medicinal potion made of powdered tusk. This was utter folly, I did not believe a word of it; even if it were true, Timothy would not have stood idly by and allowed me to saw off his tusk. Jim then mentioned that, as he had returned through the snow from Gillerton, he had been followed by a light. I asked, what sort of light; he did not know, but it was a dancing light, like a will o' the wisp. I said to myself, it is probably no more than the frozen crust of snow glistening in the light of the young moon; but I knew that Jim believed it to be an omen of our father's death.

I hurried home. My father lay in the icy bed-room, and while my mother moaned and shook, Mrs. Perry held sway, muttering spells and incantations. "I knew it would happen. The Elephants! The Elephants! Where is the tusk?" When I said that I had not brought any tusk, my mother begged me to run back and fetch some, for my father's life hung by a thread. I told her that I could not do so, that the Elephant was the property of Mr. Harrington; whereupon she cried out that I must ask Mr. Harrington. I did what I could to calm her and then attended to my father, who was burning hot, and in the absence of Dr. Chisholm, who had still not visited, I resolved to bleed him. Having fetched a knife, I laid bare his arm. "It will do no good!" cried Mrs. Perry, "he has Elephant Fever!" and my mother wailed that I was not a doctor, that we must wait for the doctor. "For how long? We cannot wait," I said.—"We must wait!"—"But if we wait—the longer we wait— we cannot wait."

We waited a few minutes, during which I felt my father's pulse, which was running very fast and intermittent, and I then said that I did not think we should delay any longer, that he must be bled, and I stretched out his arm. However, my mother cried out, "O! I hear him! O! He is come!" running to the window and scratching at the frost flakes; but she was mistaken. "O, Tom, you must go and fetch him!"—"But Jim has been!"—"Then where is he? Why has he not come? Why? O! O!" for my poor father had given a kind of low groan, and she flung herself in agonies over the bed. "O! Timothy! You must not leave me! You must not!" As I stood back, knife in hand, I noticed Jim's wan face and wondered whether, when he had spoken to Dr. Chisholm, he had conveyed with suffi- cient force the desperate nature of my father's condition. Yet there was another suspicion which crossed my mind, that the doctor had decided to ignore my father's illness, on account of what had happened with the Elephants when he was hunting. However, this may be to do Dr. Chisholm an injustice, for he did indeed arrive at the cottage about noon, though by then it was too late. It seems that he had been urgently called to attend to a gentleman by the name of Mr. Rogers, who had slipped in the snow and bruised an ankle.

I will pass over the melancholy details of my father's death. His burial had to be delayed for two weeks, the ground being as hard as stone, even a pick would not penetrate it; during this period he lay stiff and frozen in his bed. My poor mother was greatly distracted and would not enter the room on any account; nor would she allow a single fire to be lit in the cottage, despite the extreme cold, and when Jim and I came to carry him down the stairs, she cried, "O, do not hurt him!" After the burial, she begged me not to go on working any longer with the Elephants, for fear that I would catch the same deadly Elephant Fever. Indeed, she was certain that I would catch it. She said, through her tears, that she had known from the beginning that the Elephants were dangerous and that no good would come of them; for an angel had warned Mrs. Perry in a dream, and Mrs. Perry had warned my mother, and my mother had warned me and my father, but neither of us would pay any heed, and now the best husband anyone had ever had was dead and cold, and I would die too, that was all but certain, and she would be left with Jim, who was no help to anyone, and she did not know what she would do. I attempted to reassure her; but she was deaf to all consolation, crying out that it did not matter what happened to her, since she would not be alive for much longer.

The story that the Elephants had been the cause of my father's death was quickly spread by wagging tongues; chiefly, no doubt, that belonging to Mrs. Perry, but by others too; so that for a time it was generally believed that even to go near the Elephants was dangerous, while to breathe in a single particle of their breaths (which, in the frosty air, billowed from their mouths in clouds) was fatal. They were seen as walking contagions, and shunned by everyone but me; indeed, I too was widely shunned, with people saying that, if I had only cut off a piece of Timothy's tusk, my father would still be alive, and that I could not have loved him enough. This was a most unjust charge, for I had loved my father as faithfully as any son could have done. I was greatly troubled on my own account, but also on that of the Elephants: when I looked at them and indeed, when they looked at me, with their sad, wrinkled eyes, I felt a kind of horror. How will you survive, I thought, with such a deadly reputation? At the same time, there was something that made me doubt—not that Elephant Fever existed, but that it could have led to my father's death. I questioned my brother Jim, who repeated to me the exact words used by Dr. Chisholm: "Let us hope he is not ill with the dreaded Elephant Fever." I said to Jim, "Then we do not know for certain that he died of Elephant Fever." Jim agreed that we did not know for certain.

One Sunday after church, about three weeks after my father's burial, I plucked up enough courage to ask Dr. Chisholm. He was with his wife and another lady, walking out of the churchyard. I waited for his approach.—"Excuse me, Sir, if you have a moment, Sir, may I speak with you?" He muttered an apology to the ladies.— "Yes, young man?"—"Relating to my father's death."—"I am sorry, who was your father?"—"Timothy Page."—"Timothy Page?"— "Yes, Sir. He died three weeks ago. He was buried over there." The snow on the top of the grave had melted, and the mound of earth that marked my father's resting place was a dark brown. "Ah yes, to be sure," he said, and with some impatience, "Well; what is it?" Whereupon I asked, whether it was certain that my father had died from Elephant Fever and, if so, whether other people might catch the same fever from the Elephants. "What? What? Elephant Fever? Stuff and nonsense! What gave you that foolish notion?" I stammered: "Sir, I understood from my brother—I understood from my brother that my father had Elephant Fever, Sir,"—

"By no means," he repeated, "your father died from a Scarlet Fever."
I would have asked further questions—but with the ladies listening I felt constrained and aukward, and I thanked him and left.

My mother was waiting outside the churchyard. When she
heard what Dr. Chisholm had said, she was very upset, and refused
to believe me, or him; that is, she refused to believe that he had said
what I told her he had said. She remained convinced that my father
had been killed by Elephant Fever, and that I would die too, and
that she would be turned out of the cottage by Mr. Harrington, and
end up a pauper. Again she implored me to give up the Elephants. I
said to her, "But, if I do not look after them, who will?" She replied,
that was no concern of hers, and asked me to have pity on her, for
she would not live long. Some days later, Mr. Harrington assured
me that I need not worry about my mother, he would support her
and let her remain in the cottage. "By the by, Tom," said he, "Lizzy
tells me that there is a strange story going around, about some disease known as Elephant Fever—you may like to know that I have
spoken to Dr. Chisholm, and Mr. Coad, both of whom have assured me that no such disease exists." This was a great relief to me,
although it did not shake my mother's convictions a single jot.

My father's death meant that Bob Brown was now head groom
at Harrington Hall, and I trusted neither him, nor Dick Shadwick, to help with the Elephants. Martin was too old, and too
feeble, and Jim, my brother, too timid. However, when I needed
assistance, I was sometimes able to call on Lizzy. She was very
busy in the Hall, for Mrs. Harrington had given birth to twins
and Lizzy had to help the old nurse in addition to her spider-
brushing. However, she slipped away often enough. Her motives
in visiting the cart-house were perhaps as much to do with me as
the Elephants, for she and I were now sweet-hearts and spent as
much time together as we dared.

Mr. Harrington often asked how much the Elephants had grown, and on March 1st, 1768, Lizzy and I measured their dimensions, which were now as follows:

FEMALE

From foot to foot, over the shoulder	*13 feet, 8 inches*
From the top of the shoulder, perpendicular height	*8 feet, exactly*
From the top of the face to the insertion of the tail	*9 feet, 5 inches*
Trunk	*5 feet, 4 inches*
Diameter of foot	*10 inches*

MALE

From foot to foot, over the shoulder	*15 feet, 10 inches*
From the top of the shoulder, perpendicular height	*9 feet, 6 inches*
From the top of the face to the insertion of the tail	*11 feet, 1 inch*
Trunk	*6 feet, 2 inches*
Diameter of foot	*1 foot, 2 inches*
Right tusk	*19 inches*
Left tusk	*16 inches*

From a comparison between these measurements, and those taken soon after the Elephants arrived in England, two years earlier, it will be seen that both animals had grown considerably. Each of Timothy's tusks was longer by a full six inches, and this enabled me to make a fresh calculation of his age; for if the tusks had grown consistently at an annual rate of three inches since he was born, it followed that he was no more than six years old. However, there is some mystery here, for Mr. Coad told me that Timothy was much older, perhaps as old as twelve or thirteen, which I think was probably much closer to the truth.

That Timothy was now reaching the age of maturity was clear from the behaviour of his male member, which for much of the time he kept concealed, but which at other times, and without warning, would swell to a well nigh unbelievable size. This club, of a dark purplish or ruby hue, was perhaps three feet in length when fully engorged, although its crooked shape distorted its length. Thus hampered, he walked in an aukward fashion, his back legs wider than usual, the tip of the club dragging the ground and dribbling with urine, leaving a track like that of a snake, and sending up a plume of dust, so that it looked as if it was smoking. It was inevitable that this gave rise to much comment and curiosity. His engorgement first appeared on a warm, rainy morning in April, 1768, when he was standing in the yard and I was cleaning out the cart-house. I heard shouts of merriment from my fellow grooms, and when I saw what amused them so much, I laughed as well, though I was also embarrassed. Word spread quickly, and soon various gardeners appeared, holding their rakes and forks and spades, followed by several servants from the Hall, who put their hands to their mouths and giggled and pointed and made ribald observations. I did not feel that it was altogether proper to make a spectacle of the *tusker*, when he was so encumbered, and ordered him back in his quarters; he obeyed me but, I think, with great reluctance. Once the door was secured he reared up, trumpeting loudly, and backing into the walls of the cart-house.

In the succeeding week, this phenomenon of engorgement occurred persistently, and he became more and more restless and self-willed. Indeed, his character, which had formerly been mild and obedient, seemed to undergo a sea-change. With Jenny, he was truculent and irritable, pushing and shoving, sniffing her rump, and making persistent attempts to court and board, though she was unwilling to accept his attentions; and when I remonstrated with him, his eyes seemed to fill with a mixture of anger and defiance. I resolved to purge him, and made up three large balls of Rhubarb and Senna; but here my difficulties were at a beginning. In the matter of giving balls of physic to a horse, my father did not agree with the old idea that an iron should be used, except in cases of great necessity; for the horse quickly becomes terrified at the sight of the iron and has to be blind-folded on future occasions. Instead, my father had taught me a gentler practice: that, the horse's mouth having been opened, and the tongue drawn to one side, the ball should be delivered by hand and placed on the root of the tongue; then, the tongue being released and the hand withdrawn, the horse's head should be raised, to ease the passage of the ball down the gullet. If the ball remains stubbornly lodged in the gullet, the horse's head should be raised further, and some water given.

Even if I were to enlist the help of Lizzy or the other grooms, this practice was not one which could be used with Timothy, for he was in far too high a temper to allow his mouth to be opened against his will. Hoping to disguise the smell, I smeared a ball with sweet oil and offered it to him as a tid-bit, but he snorted with the utmost contempt; and when I offered him the physic in a pail of sugared water, he kicked it aside. After this, I wondered whether to keep him confined, and yet to have deprived him of daily exercise, at a time of year when the woods and copses were a feast of vegetation, might have made him even less manageable. I confess that I was not sure what more to do, and without my father to hand lacked anyone who could give me sound advice. However, whether my father would have been of much help in the matter, must be doubted; for his experience related to horses, while the male Elephant is a far more dangerous and terrifying creature than a horse, and has a behaviour entirely of its own, as I shall describe.

Toward the end of that week, we set off for a large, tangled copse owned by Mr. Harrington, and lying on the far side of Thornhill. The air was still and calm, and with the sun's rays dispersing a thin white mist, which hung lightly over the fields, it promised to be a fine day. Birds were singing gaily, and when we reached the copse I seem to remember hearing several nightingales in full song, for although some people in their ignorance think nightingales only sing at night they often do so by day. This particular copse was for some reason always more haunted by nightingales than any other around Thornhill. However, it was plain that Timothy's mind was running only on one thing, and as Jenny was feeding he made many determined attempts to mount her. When she rejected his advances, he threw back his head and trumpeted so loudly that the trees seemed to shiver, the air vibrating in waves of sound. He kept up this fit of roaring for at least five minutes, after which he wrenched at thick branches, tearing them off their trunks and breaking them into fragments. None of this seemed to make any impression on Jenny, who affected not to notice and continued to feed, nor on the nightingales, which went on singing lustily from the depths of the thicket. At length Timothy seemed to calm down, though he remained engorged and full of resentment; his ears flapped wildly, and his club swung to and fro, spraying jets of fluid.

We were returning through the village when the usual pack of mungrel-curs surged out to give us their noisy greeting. They were an unruly mob, often pursuing us to the end of the village, the limit of their territory. In the past, the Elephants had always ignored them, treating them with an amused disdain—as a pair of giants might treat a beetle—however, on this particular day, one of these dogs, a small white mungrel with a curling tail, which clearly saw itself as the leader of the pack, summoned up its reserves of courage and, yapping wildly, put in a charge which took it between Timothy's legs. Scarcely breaking stride, he bent his head and, with a violent swing of his trunk, sent the dog flying through the air. It travelled a full twenty yards before striking the side of the churchyard wall. I drew the Elephants to a halt, dismounted, and went over to the wretched dog, which was not moving; the force of the blow had broke its back. Returning to the *tusker*, I stood before him and ordered him to kneel; he refused. "Kneel down! Kneel down!" I shouted, but he would not kneel, though he knew the command well enough. His eyes were simmering.

I had never been afraid of him before, but at that moment, I believe, as he towered over me, his ears spread wide, my life hung in the balance. Something within him had changed: he had forgotten, or nearly forgotten, that I was his keeper, and instead saw me as a stranger. I did not dare shew my fear, but lifted the *ankus*, which I wore on a string round my neck, and held it before his eyes like a cross. "Kneel down! Kneel!" I roared. "Kneel—Timothy, kneel!" and either my words, or the sight of the *ankus*, pierced the fog which clouded his brain, and he knelt, to my very great relief, as may be imagined. I reproved him sternly, telling him that he ought to behave himself better, that he must control his passions, how otherwise could he be trusted? Although he might be irritated by the dogs, this was (I said) no reason to resort to violence. I have no doubt that he knew that I was displeased, for he appeared to listen carefully, his trunk drooping, his head depressed; and suddenly he keeled to his side and lay in the dust, the very picture of contrition.

A pretty piece of play-acting, I said to myself; yet his behaviour alarmed me a good deal, for though he had obeyed me this once, would he do so again? Disinclined to offer him another chance of ending my life, I resolved to keep him safe in the cart-house until his temper improved. To my surprize, he entered the cart-house willingly enough; yet, within the space of an hour, the fit was upon him again, and he began to squeal and trumpet in a fury, backing into the walls and tugging at the beams with his trunk. It is hard to convey, to anyone who has not witnessed it, the power and strength of a male Elephant, even of one who is still not fully grown, like Timothy. The cart-house was built of good stone, but it trembled at the violence of his attacks, and unless I acted swiftly its destruction was inevitable. Moreover, if he ran loose in such a dangerous temper, he would be well nigh impossible to re-capture. In this desperate situation, I remembered something that Mr. Coad had mentioned, about the use of liquor to pacify angry Elephants. I ran to the cellars and, with the help of some other servants, fetched several casks of rum, and these I succeeded in introducing to the cart-house, though with great difficulty. The first cask, he kicked over, without understanding what it was; the second and third he drank readily enough, and as the spirit worked on him he grew calmer and fell into a daze. I was now able to slip chains round his legs, and to lead him out of the cart-house and into the grounds, where I tied him to the trunk of a large elm tree and left him to recover his senses.

This was not the end of the matter; for the dog belonged, as I discovered, to the vicar, the Reverend Amey, who had recently come to Thornhill. He was a pompous turkey-cock of a man, not above thirty years of age but already bald; and when he learnt of the accident he flapped his miserable wings and stalked up to the Hall. By ill fortune, Mr. Harrington was away in Bristol; instead, therefore, he unburthened himself to Mrs. Harrington, who sent Lizzy to tell me that, since the Elephants had become so unman-ageable, they should be confined until Mr. Harrington returned. "Both Elephants?" I said to her (for it seemed unfair to punish

Jenny, who was innocent of any wrong-doing), "why both?"—
"Because Mrs. Harrington says so, Tom. You know she hates the
Elephants." I had not known this; indeed, I found it hard to imagine that anyone could hate the Elephants; and I asked Lizzy why.
She gave a shrug. "I do not know why; maybe she thinks they are
ugly. Especially now," she added.—"Now? Why now?" I asked.
"You mean because of Timothy?" She gave a mischievous smile. "It
is monstrous, is it not? It is four times as big as a horse's. Do you
think we should measure it, for Mr. Harrington?"

The other grooms, who relished every opportunity to damage
my interests, were full of glee at what had happened, prophesying
that Timothy's tusks would be cut off, or that he would be gelded,
or sold; thus I waited with some dread for Mr. Harrington's return,
which was not expected for another ten days. In the meantime,
Timothy remained chained to the elm, and threatened violence
to all who approached. His club continued to dribble urine, and
a strange black fluid, which I had never seen before, oozed from
two spots on either side of his face, between his eyes and ears, and
ran glistening down his cheeks. Often he lowered his head, and
pressed the points of his tusks against the trunk of the tree, at
which the Ooze (as I came to call it) flowed even more copiously.
This Ooze had a harsh, sweet smell, somewhat like hot tar. He ate
very little, spurning the carrots which I threw at him, and scarcely
seemed to drink, although at other times he drank more than fifteen gallons a day.

These signs were so remarkable that I began to ask myself
whether he might have some kind of an illness. My father once
mentioned an old horse disease, known as Wild-Fire; the exact
symptoms I could not remember, but the remedy was a ridiculous
brew of live toads, moles, swallows' dung, rags, and the soles of
some old shoes, to be cooked in an earth pot, and stamped into

a fine powder. When I opened my father's copy of Markham's *Maister-Peece*, I could find no mention of Wild-Fire; however, in Chapter XXXI, old Markham addresses the subject of frenzy and madness in a horse, which frenzy and madness he maintains are caused by naughty blood infecting, at its most extreme, not only the heart and brain, but also the panicles; that possible remedies may be bleeding, gelding, and piercing the skin of his head with a hot iron, in order to let out the ill humours. In addition, Markham gives his own cure, which is to make the horse swallow hard hen's dung, or drink the root of some plant known as Virga Pastoris stamped in water; as to the ordering of the horse, he advises that the stable should be quiet, but not close, and the horse's food limited to warm mashes of malt and water.

How much value this was to me in treating Timothy may be imagined, for I scarcely dared advance within the range of his chain, and the prospect of forcing him to swallow hen's dung or to drink some soothing medicine (when I did not even know what plant was signified by Virga Pastoris), let alone piercing his skull with a hot iron, was not to be contemplated. Besides, although he was without doubt in the grip of a peculiar frenzy, I was by no means convinced that it was the same kind of frenzy described by Markham. An Elephant and a horse are such very different creatures, there is no reason to suppose that the illnesses suffered by one are the same or similar to the illnesses suffered by the other; and nowhere in *Maister-Peece* could I see any reference to the strange fluid which oozed down the sides of Timothy's face, or to the engorgement of his club.

When Mr. Harrington returned, he came to see me with a stern face. "Tom," he said, "I am told that our Elephants have put an end to the vicar's dog." I explained that this was untrue; that the female was entirely innocent, and that it was the fault not of the male, but of his inflamed condition, which had led him to act against his true nature. Moreover, I added, the dog had been very provoking. Mr. Harrington looked at me. "I see that you are in a fair way to becoming a lawyer."—"Sir, forgive me, but since he is in a state of temporary madness, he cannot be held responsible!"—"And the Reverend Amey must be content with that?" he inquired. I was silenced. "Well, perhaps I should reserve judgment until I have seen the accused," Mr. Harrington said.

Timothy was standing in the elm's green shade, his head hanging low as though in shame. "He appears harmless enough," Mr. Harrington remarked, "what will happen if we draw nearer?"—"I am not sure, Sir—it is hard to be sure. He is a little more amenable to Reason than he was." We did move a few feet nearer, whereupon Timothy raised his head and glared, giving a short trumpet blast. "Why—those black marks—is he bleeding?" Mr. Harrington asked.—"No, Sir, that is the fluid, the Ooze, staining his skin, I believe that is one prime cause of his discomfort."

I proceeded to describe the Elephant's symptoms, while Mr. Harrington regarded the Elephant. "And this temporary madness, as you put it, Tom, this paroxysm, this passion: you believe it to be not a sickness, but a sign of his growing maturity?"—"Yes, Sir."—"He has not been bitten by anything?"—"Bitten, Sir?" Upon which Mr. Harrington told me of a madness called, I think, hydrophobia, that is, the dread of water, which chiefly affects dogs, and how in London he had once seen such a dog, a terrier, running wild, foaming at the mouth, and attacking anyone foolish enough to approach. I said, "I am sure that he has not been bitten, Sir."—"And yet he has attacked a dog, and refuses to drink water."—"Yes, Sir. But he has not been bitten, I am sure. The dog provoked him into the attack." Mr. Harrington examined me keenly, as if to satisfy himself that I was telling the truth. "If he has been bitten,

Tom, it is fatal; one may depend on it; there is no cure on earth. I know how attached you have become to the Elephants, but for his own sake it would be better to take pity on him and shoot him at once."

I was so horrified by this that I could scarcely speak, save to stammer once more that he had not been bitten and that I believed his madness to be a temporary storm, which would abate soon enough. "How soon is soon?" asked Mr. Harrington. "How long will he have to stay chained to this tree?" This was the question which I had been asking myself, of course. I answered, more out of hope than anything else, that I thought that the Ooze would dry up by the next full moon, which was a fortnight hence. Mr. Harrington nodded. "I hope you are right, Tom. I will write to Mr. Coad and inquire whether he has ever heard of this behaviour. But as and when he does recover, I think that it would be wise to avoid taking him or the female through the village, in order to avoid any further provocation. I do not wish to offend the vicar unnecessarily." At this, relief surged through me. "Yes, Sir. No, Sir."

Some weeks later, Mr. Harrington told me that he had heard from Mr. Coad, and that the Elephant's behaviour was not an illness but a sign of maturity, for male Elephants, as well as females, come into season, and then are often exceedingly ill-tempered and wild. Mr. Coad, in the Indies, had seen Elephants in this very condition, and with oozing temples, and while the Elephant might remain in season for as long as two months, it would rapidly recover—"which," said Mr. Harrington, "is excellent." He proceeded to put me a series of questions. How long, in my judgment, would it be before the female would be ready to accept the advances of the male? When would she reach maturity? I answered, that, though there was, as yet, no physical sign of her coming into season, the keen interest of the male seemed to suggest that she might be nearing that point. "And how much longer do you think his tusks will grow?" Remembering the tusks of the Elephant which died upon the *Dover*, I said that I thought they would grow a good deal longer. Mr. Harrington now revealed his intentions:

"I have been thinking for some while, Tom—indeed, it has been in my mind ever since the Elephants came here—of the vast sums of money which are spent bringing ivory to this country from the Cape. It is a difficult trade—costly, uncertain, and unnecessary, for Elephants will thrive here, and breed; our climate is perfectly acceptable. Why should we not have an English supply of ivory, produced by English Elephants? What is the objection? True, Elephants consume a vast quantity of food. But the value of the ivory would more than surpass that." He paused. "These two Elephants will be the basis of the first English breeding herd, a stock from which other herds may grow."

I was filled with enthusiasm; I thought it a grand venture, and one certain to be crowned with success. I imagined herds of Elephants, descended from Jenny and Timothy, grazing the length and breadth of England. They would be the founders of a dynasty. However, I could not help wondering what would become of the male Elephants, once their tusks were removed.

"The tusks will re-grow," said Mr. Harrington. "Once they reach a certain length, they are shed, like the antlers of deer in the autumn. I am assured by Mr. Coad that quantities of tusks are often found littering the jungles. It follows that there will be no need to kill the Elephants. And Elephants, I believe, may live to two or three hundred years of age. So one may have many years of ivory to collect." Mr. Harrington was a stern man, who seldom smiled, but he smiled now. "These are valuable animals, Tom. They are the first of their kind in England. It will take time, but, you mark my words, a hundred years from now every great estate in England will have its Elephants and we shall be selling ivory to France and Spain and the rest of the world."

With these words he went away. I confess that I was somewhat surprized to learn that Elephants shed their tusks, for Timothy's tusks seemed more like teeth than antlers. Yet soon after this he did, indeed, lose several teeth, with new teeth growing in their stead; and this persuaded me that Mr. Harrington was right, and that there was a great fortune to be made in the production of ivory, which is much in demand for the manufacture of such articles as chessmen, billiard balls, piano keys, mathematical rules, and snuff-boxes.

Chapter IV

As the Ooze abated, so did Timothy's fit of madness, and soon he was in as gentle and gracious a temper as anyone could have desired. I watched him carefully, for I knew that another storm was certain to blow up before long, and I was determined not to be caught unawares. However, as the months went by, his manners continued irreproachable, and I began to forget. It then happened that, one day in the succeeding spring, he walked out of the cart-house, crashed the door behind him, and flung an empty pail across the yard. This unexpected shew of irritability was a sharp nudge to my memory, and, suspecting what was about to happen, I chained him to the elm. Next, I tethered Jenny by a rope to the same tree, in the hope that, before Timothy was overwhelmed by the Ooze, he and Jenny might proceed to the business of mating. Yet this was a great mistake on my part: for though Timothy was soon roused and ready to oblige, as his swollen, spurting member all too readily testified, Jenny was shy and prudish as an old maid, and kept backing away. He pursued her, fleeing, in circles round the tree, and as his chain and her rope shortened both animals were drawn closer and closer to the trunk, and finally brought to a halt—he, wildly trumpeting, on one side of the tree, she, squealing with fright, on the other. How to release her from this predicament without endangering myself was a nice matter, but Lizzy helped me by distracting Timothy. Whether, even if they had mated, anything would have come of it must be doubted, for Jenny had still not passed her first blood, or not that I had noticed.

It was instructive to observe Jenny's behaviour during this period. As I rode her through the grounds, she would gradually veer in the direction of the tree to which her brother was tied, in order to see how he did; having given herself this satisfaction, she would continue on her way. Strange as this must no doubt appear, I am sure that she understood why he was restrained, and also that she was grateful to be spared his violent attentions. Toward me she was exceedingly affectionate, often brushing me with her trunk, and sometimes making a peculiar sound which, for want of a better word, may be described as a kind of rumble, or purr, not unlike the purring of a very loud cat. This low purring sound is a sign of great contentment in an Elephant. There were also times when I sensed her observing me in a curious way, much as I observed her, and as our eyes joined I fancied that our very thoughts were colliding in mid air, and mingling, like invisible atoms.

I would like to say it was now that I succeeded in teaching her to sweep the yard. But, in truth, I did not teach her; she taught herself, picking up the broom one morning after I had put it down, and swishing it to and fro. I praised her loudly, and gave her a tid-bit, and this encouraged her into further sweeping, and she soon became an excellent sweeper, though her enthusiasm sometimes made her sweep too vigorously. On one occasion she broke the broom handle, which puzzled her greatly; after staring at the two pieces she attempted to fit them together and, when she failed to do so, seemed quite dejected. To teach her to sweep slowly, and gently, using the broom like a feather, took more than two weeks. When Timothy returned from the Ooze, he watched her at work, and deciding to copy her, just as she had copied me, grabbed the broom from her grasp; however, he did not understand the reason for sweeping, and made violent sweeps in the air. Jenny was upset at losing the broom, and attempted its recovery, and a short tussel ensued, which came to an end when I ordered them to give me the broom. The matter was resolved when I provided each of the Ele-phants with a broom; thereafter, each morning, they would sweep the yard in consort, raising a storm of dust.

The spell of Ooze continued a full six weeks, and was much more severe than the first. The Ooze fairly gushed down the sides of Timothy's face, and the spray from his club stained the insides of his thighs green. The tarry smell seemed to be everywhere; even at night it hung in my nostrils. Yet afterward, he again became meek and calm. I remember one day when he had a limp in his right fore-foot. I waited for Lizzy, and then, having made him lie down, brushed the dust and dirt from the pad, and spied the head of a nail. The pad of an Elephant's foot is as hard as a board, and this nail had been driven in so deep, and was so firmly embedded, that I could do nothing with my fingers to draw it out. The skin around the nail was hot to touch. I fetched a knife and tongs, and told Timothy what I intended, that is, to take away the pain in his foot. He lay entirely still, his eyes on Lizzy, who had crouched by his head, while I dug the point of the knife into the sole, in order to get sufficient purchase to draw out the nail. This nail was nearly three inches long, and must have been in the pad some time; when I drew it out, a chute of dirty fluid poured from the hole. As I performed this operation, Timothy's trunk played pat-a-cake with Lizzy's hand, and I was very grateful for her help. When I had finished, he clambered to his feet and I shewed him the nail. "Here, this is what was hurting you, you see?" Lizzy laughed: "Tom, he does not understand, you know."—"But he does understand," I said. His trunk flickered out and removed the nail from my grasp; he examined it closely and shewed it to Jenny, who took it and examined it too, before giving it back. He tossed it away, and his trunk slid round Lizzy's shoulders. "There, you see—he is thanking you," I said. She said, "Tom, he is not thanking me, he is merely being friendly. He does not speak English, you know—he does not understand English."—"He understands more than a little," I said, "he is speaking Elephant." She made an impatient gesture: "Why do you always try to make the Elephants into something they are not?" I was surprized by this question, and as I struggled for an answer, she went on to chide me for spending so much time with the Elephants. "You devote yourself to them."—"Well; but, Lizzy, they must be cared for."—"But they are not the only thing in the world that matters. You do nothing but care for them. You never leave them."—"There is no one else to care for them, what else should I do? They depend upon me. Who else is going to pull a nail out of their feet?" She tossed her head. "I am not talking about nails—but—they are animals, Tom, are they not? You keep talking of them as though they were human."—"Lizzy, they are intelligent creatures, they are more intelligent than other animals, they are interesting company."—"Are they more interesting than your own kind, more interesting than human beings?" I thought about this. "More than some, and not others, probably. They are interesting, but in a different way."

This is one conversation which I seem to remember, among several; Lizzy often harped on the same theme. It is hard to remember exactly. When did such a thing happen, and in what order? What was the weather like? What were the Elephants doing as we talked? Sometimes I can only remember scraps of conversation, or single remarks: for instance, her remark, how curious it would be if human beings had trunks for noses, and, at the same moment, getting hold of my nose and giving it a tug. Another time, she accompanied me to the copse with the nightingales, and we sat with our backs against a tree and watched the feeding Elephants. Tiny green caterpillars were dangling on fine cables in the soft air, and speckled butter-flies dancing by, and a yaffle with its bright red head and green body landed on the stump of a dead oak and drummed loudly. Suddenly she told me to shut my eyes, and when I asked why, said that I would find out, and when I asked, what would I find out, she merely laughed and said that, well then, I would never know. So I obeyed her and shut my eyes; whereupon she fed me pieces of wet sugar, which she had in her pockets. I fell to licking the sticky sugar off her palm, indeed she licked it too, with her neat tongue, and our tongues meeting we began to kiss, only to look up and discover both Elephants staring at us in astonishment.

Some weeks later, during that same summer, I had dozed off in the hay-loft above the cart-house and woke to find her standing over me. It was a bright day and she seemed to block the light. She said, "I have been watching you, Tom."

"And?"

"Who is Jenny?"

"Jenny?"

"You called out for Jenny," she said, "in your sleep."

"You must have misheard."

"I did not mishear, you called her name three times, four, very clearly."

I was reluctant to tell her who Jenny was, for fear that she would laugh. "There is no law against calling out a name."

"I know who she is, she is your sweet-heart. She is Jenny Bush."

Jenny Bush was a girl who lived in Gillerton. "She is not Jenny Bush, I promise you, Lizzy. When have you ever seen me with Jenny Bush?"

A pair of swallows had built a nest of mud and straw in the roof of the hay-loft, at the junction between a beam and the rafter. One of these birds now swept twittering through the hatch and up to the nest. "I do not believe you, who is she?"

"She is no one."

"Then why do you call out her name? And in such a tone." She mimicked. "Jenny."

"It was not like that. I was in a dream."

"Were you kissing her? What were you doing with her? Tom! Tell me."

Her face surrounded by its long dark hair was in deep shadow and I could not see her expression clearly, the light behind was so dazzling. "Jenny Bush I promise you is not my sweet-heart."

"No, but you would like her to be. That is what it means. If you have not kissed her, you would like to kiss her."

I propped myself on an elbow and shaded my eyes. "Not at all—I like to kiss you much more than her."

"Do you indeed? Then why do you not call out my name?"

"I don't know."

She gave her head a toss. "Nor I, why you should suppose you have any right to kiss me, especially after calling out Jenny Bush's name. Why should I allow you to kiss me?"

"But, Lizzy, it was not Jenny Bush's name."

"So whose was it? Tom, I am not letting you out of here unless you tell me. I will keep you a prisoner. If you tell me, I will let you kiss me. Or I may let you kiss me."

I thought that I might as well tell her as not tell her, in order to get a kiss. In truth, it seemed harmless enough. "All right, I will tell you then who she is, so long as you promise not to laugh."

"Why, so there is someone! Who is she? Have you kissed her?"

"Of course I have not! Lizzy, if you knew who she was—"

"I am waiting to be told! Why, is she very old and ugly?"

"No, she is very beautiful, but—but do you promise not to tell anyone else?"

"Why should I promise? No, I will not promise—why is it so secret?"

We went on like this for a time, while the swallows flew in and out, and in and out. At length Lizzy sat down, and said that she promised. I nodded toward the cart-house: "It is her name."

She stared at me. "What? The Elephant? The Elephant is called Jenny?"

"It is my name for her, it is what I call her in my head, privately."

She began to laugh. Her hair fell forward, then with a sweep she dragged it back. "You must take me for an idiot."

"Why, not at all, Lizzy."

"To believe that—I cannot believe it. So what is his name?" (pointing at Timothy). "Does he have a name too, in your head?"

"Timothy."

"Timothy! Timothy and Jenny!" She rocked to and fro, laughing.

Already regretting that I had told her, I protested that it was not so very odd, that dogs and horses had names, why not Elephants?

"Not human names like Timothy and Jenny. I am not at all sure whether to believe you. Can it really be true? O, I see it is. It is as bad as if it were Jenny Bush, or almost as bad. It is almost worse. So you are in love with an Elephant."

"I am not in love with her."

"So you say," she said. "But if you had heard yourself, breathing her name . . ."

I asked her about the kiss that I had been promised—since she had said that she would give me a kiss if I told her who Jenny was. But she said that she had not promised, she had only said that she might give me a kiss, and now that she knew that Jenny was one of the Elephants she was not sure whether to let me kiss her or not: for how would she know, as I kissed her, that in my head I was not kissing the Elephant? There was no reply to this, or none that I could find; though I might have answered that, by the same token, I would not know for certain what was passing through her head.

"Well," said Lizzy, and she leant forward and kissed me; and I kissed her back, and—O, the pleasures of that hour, and afterward, the gentle twittering of the swallows, and the chinks of light shining through the tiles as I picked the hay out of her hair.

Chapter V

I now come to describe the events which led to the departure of the Elephants from Harrington Hall. Although, most nights, I slept in the cart-house, I occasionally stayed with my mother at the cottage in Thornhill. Having seen my father's ghost leading a horse and cart down the street, she had become terrified of the darkness. One such night, a night of heavy rain in June, 1769, a loud knocking roused me from my first sleep, and when I opened the window and looked out a man (his name does not matter) was standing below. He gasped that I must come quickly, that the Elephants had broken loose and found their way into the gardens at the Hall. There was no doubt from the urgency of his voice that he was in earnest.

I can scarcely express the full extent of my horror at this intelligence. With their pretty flowers and tender vegetables, their neat paths and trimmed hedges, the gardens at Harrington Hall were among Mrs. Harrington's greatest delights. At the end of a grassy walk she had had a kind of bower constructed, with a wooden seat, and here she and her two babes spent hours each day. The havock that the Elephants might wreak in this little patch of paradise, their trunks grabbing and stuffing their mouths with food, filled my mind with apprehension. As I pulled on my boots I asked the man how long the Elephants had been in the gardens; he said he did not know, but that the place was in an uproar. What I could not understand was how they had got out of the cart-house, which was locked and barred, out of the yard, which was also locked, and into the gardens, which were bounded on three sides by high brick walls and on the fourth by a low ditch.

I ran to the Hall. The rain fell in sheets. Mr. Harrington was standing on the terrace above the gardens, with a gun in his hand and Joshua at his side; they were gazing into the gloom, from which came a medley of cries. Hurrying toward these sounds, I made out the hulking bodies of the Elephants, backed against a wall by an irregular semi-circle of twenty or more torches held by various servants, among them my brother, Jim; the head gardener, Mr. Judge; and my fellow groom, Dick Shadwick. These men, whose frightened faces gleamed in the glare of the sputtering torches, had armed themselves with spades and forks and staves. Twenty feet away, side by side, the Elephants were equally terrified, and with their ears spread wide, their heads reared and trunks half curled, they seemed on the point of making a fatal charge. The custom of curling its trunk before making a charge is one that every Elephant is said to observe, and with good reason, for if the trunk sustains a serious injury the Elephant is unable to feed or drink and will therefore die.

Tapping Mr. Judge on the arm, I shouted that he and the others should withdraw for their own safety. He was in a towering rage. "Tell the master to bring his gun, we can hold the b——s here till he comes."—"Mr. Judge—"—"D'you not hear me, where's the master?" and to the men: "Watch 'em, stand fast! They are turning, they are moving, stand fast, stand fast!"—"Mr. Judge, I'm telling you, you must move back!"—"Go away, you young b——! Where be the master?"

At length he saw reason, and a grumbling retreat took place, leaving me alone in the darkness. The Elephants faced me, but without the torches I could no longer see the expressions on their faces; nor did I know how much they could see of me. Who can say how well Elephants see in the dark? As well as human beings, or not so well? Or can they recognize by smell, for certainly their sense of smell is acute? I spread my arms and slowly walked toward them, singing and calling, it is I, Tom, it is merely Tom, do not worry, do not be afraid, Jenny, Timothy, you are safe. You are safe now, they will not hurt you. I love you, I love you, you are safe. Their trunks curled in friendly greeting and I raised my hands in reply. Both trunks seemed to slide round me, as if to make sure that I really was Tom, their keeper. Then, unbidden, Timothy knelt in the mud, and I climbed on his wet body and with Jenny follow-ing, her trunk resting on his back, we rode out of the gardens, while Mr. Harrington and the servants clutched their torches and weapons and watched in silence from the terrace. Their silence did not last long, for once we were gone a confused babble of shouts broke out, which pursued us all the way to the cart-house. There I attempted to settle the Elephants, though for some hours they continued to stand and tremble, twining their trunks, and listen-ing to the trickle of the rain.

Before day-break, I left them to find out how much damage they had caused. The rain had eased but the air was dank, and in the gardens every leaf dripped. Even in the half dark, it was easy enough to trace the paths taken by the Elephants from the moment that they had entered the gardens through a door in the wall; and as the light grew, it revealed a scene of trampled plants and broken bushes, some of which lay on their sides with their roots poking upwards. The puddled footprints led me into the kitchen garden, where the quantity of destruction was, if anything, even greater; lines of potatoes had been unearthed, lettices trodden to a pulp, beans and artichokes torn up and tossed aside. Mrs. Harrington's bower had escaped damage, but that was small consolation. Mr. Judge was on the terrace, his hands on his hips and his face grim and tired. I said that I was extremely sorry for what had happened, and expected a blast in return; instead he sighed, and said that it could have been worse, no one had been killed. "Was the cart-house locked?"—"And barred. And the door out of the yard."—"In that case, how did the Elephants get out?" I said that I could not tell. "Well," said Mr. Judge, with a sigh, "it were a good thing for them not to get out again, for their sakes."

Mr. Harrington also asked me, later that morning, how the Elephants had escaped, and I gave him the same answer, that I did not know, that I had left the Elephants inside the cart-house. He asked whether they might have let themselves out, and I replied that that was impossible.—"In other words," said he, "someone let them out, on purpose? Who would want to do that?" I had strong suspicions, but not a shred of proof, and I said that I did not know. He regarded me, frowning. "Tom, they do enough damage in the woods without allowing them to destroy the gardens."—"Yes, Sir." From this time on, I watched the Elephants very carefully, and scarcely left them alone, day or night, except to visit the necessary-house.

None of this might have mattered but for another unfortunate event, which happened very soon afterward, and here I admit that I was greatly to blame. About a year earlier, Joshua had begun to demand that he should be allowed to ride the Elephants. I had faithfully promised Mr. Harrington that I would never let him do so, as he well knew; however, he persisted, advancing every argument that he could muster. "I am a good rider, Tom," he would say. "You are always telling me that I ride very well. I am eight years old, you know." I would counter that riding an Elephant was altogether different from riding a pony; besides, it had been forbidden by his father. "O, but my father said that a long time ago, when I was little. He would allow me to ride now. I know he would." To this I would reply, "In which case, Joshua, you will have to gain his consent," and here the matter seemed to end. Yet, by the succeeding day, when he came for his riding lesson, he had always discovered a fresh line of attack. "I am sure my father would not mind me *sitting* on one of the Elephants, Tom. I would not be riding, I would be merely sitting. Where is the harm in that? My father said nothing about sitting, did he?" I laughed and told him that sitting and riding were nearly the same thing.—"Pooh, Tom, you are a bore. You are only a groom. Why should I take any notice of your opinion?"

Many skirmishes of this kind took place, but Joshua never succeeded in gaining the advantage, since I had given my word to Mr. Harrington. One afternoon, however, he announced that he had obtained his mother's consent.—"But not that of your father," I replied.—"My father is away in Bristol, Tom, how can I obtain his consent? My mother has agreed. It would only be for a moment, what is the objection?" I replied that I would be happier if Mrs. Harrington were to tell me to my face; whereupon he stalked off and returned minutes later, saying that he had spoken to her and she did not mind. When I again said that I would prefer it if she were to say so to my face, he grew very impatient: "Tom, she cannot come, she does not want to come, she is busy, she is dressing." At this I gave way, thinking that since his mother had given her consent, Mr. Harrington would not mind, and I made Jenny kneel down and Joshua scrambled on to her neck. "Tom, make her stand." I did so. He sat, triumphant, his feet resting on the backs of her ears. "Where shall we go? Why are there no reins?"—"We are not going anywhere."—"Why are you so dull, Tom? You are dull as a beetle," and he began to kick his feet, urging the Elephant forward and telling her to giddy-up, as one would do a horse. Jenny took no notice but stood and watched me for her instructions, and I gently led her round the yard.

Thereafter, I confess, I often let Joshua sit on Jenny's neck, and sometimes left him alone while I attended to Timothy. This proved a great mistake on my part, for, about a week after the Elephants had broken into the gardens, he fell and put his left arm out of joint. I did not see it happen, but I heard a cry, and saw him lying on the ground. He struggled to his feet, holding the arm, which was dangling at an odd angle. Having put Jenny back in her stable, I helped him to the Hall, and as I did so he begged me not to tell his mother that he had been on the Elephant. I said, "But your mother knows that you have been riding the Elephants, does she not?"—"No," he said, white-faced, "she does not. And you must not tell her, you must not, Tom, or I will kill myself." I promised that I would not say a word unless I were asked directly.

As we drew near the Hall, out came Mrs. Harrington and the nurse with the two little girls on strings, and Lizzy a step behind, and Joshua cried out that he had fallen off his pony, and had hurt his arm. While Lizzy gave me a sharp look, for she had seen Joshua riding the Elephant, Mrs. Harrington ran to Joshua's side. "How did you fall?"—"I fell off March," he replied (March, I should have said, being the name of his pony).—"You were not on one of the Elephants?"—"No, Mother."—"Tom Page, was he on an Elephant?" My expression probably said enough, and Mrs. Harrington flashed out: "O! And when I had expressly forbidden it! How could you allow it?" At this Joshua, although in great pain, burst out, "It is not Tom's fault, Mother, it is not Tom's fault, I am to blame, not Tom!" Yet Mrs. Harrington continued to reproach me in a biting tone, saying she did not know how I could be trusted any longer and that something would have to be done about the Elephants. I was greatly alarmed, but later I gave Mr. Harrington an honest account of what had happened, and after listening in his usual careful way he said that I was not to blame, except for being too quick to believe Joshua. "It has been a good lesson for him, and he has been soundly punished," he said, "but it must not happen again," and he raised his eyes to mine. "You understand me, Tom?"—"Yes, Sir."

Some days after this, on a pleasant summer's afternoon, the Elephants were grazing in a meadow not far from the Hall. Lizzy had joined me and we were lying in a patch of long grass, listening to the grasshoppers and watching the blue sky, when she began to talk about Mrs. Harrington. She said that Mrs. Harrington was now determined that the Elephants should be sold, because they were evil-minded, and a danger to the children, and would become more and more dangerous as they grew older. I replied that Mrs. Harrington was wasting her breath, that Mr. Harrington would never sell the Elephants for, on the contrary, he intended to establish a breeding herd.

"O, but Tom, that idea is long dead!" she answered. "Mr. Harrington is in two minds about the Elephants. They are a great expense, each one eats as much as twelve horses. Why should he keep them? They are no advantage to him, all they do is eat away his fortune."

"Did Mr. Harrington say that?"

"Sometimes he says one thing, sometimes the other. And Mrs. Harrington is very persistent. It preys on her. She cannot sleep. She talks of nothing else."

"What preys on her?"

"That the Elephants will escape again. That they will harm the children. Or that something else will happen."

I felt a great hatred well inside me. "Mrs. Harrington has been opposed to the Elephants from the beginning."

"She is a mother," said Lizzy. "She thinks of her children, that is all. She is afraid. Everyone is a little afraid of what the Elephants may do, even I am sometimes a little afraid. Is that so strange? When Timothy has the Ooze he is frightening."

"He is chained."

"He is still frightening. There is the possibility he will escape. If I were Mr. Harrington—" She lifted herself up and, resting on one elbow, leant over me. "Sometimes I think—" and stopped.

"What do you think?"

She answered with a shew of reluctance. "That it may be better for you when they are gone."

The world within my head began to reel. I said nothing.

"I mean only that you would not have to think about them all the time."

"I do not—but—they have to be cared for. No one else can do it."

"But you do not allow anyone else to try. Tom, your life is ruled by the Elephants. You are shackled by them, you are their slave, you have no time for anything else, or anyone else. It is like a fever. It is Elephant Fever."

"Mr. Harrington will not sell them." I pushed her aside and sat up. "He cannot sell them. He cannot. They are harmless creatures."

"Where are you going?"

"I am going to talk to them."

The Elephants were grazing on the far side of the meadow, which was so thick with dandelion globes that they seemed to be standing in a kind of summer snow. As they rambled toward me, their feet kicking up clouds of white seeds, their trunks swinging gently from side to side, I felt myself in a daze. Everyone, I said to myself, has now turned against them, my fellow grooms, my mother, Mrs. Harrington, Mr. Harrington, even Lizzy, for, indeed, none of them understands the Elephants, or tries to understand. But then, how could they begin to understand, when they do not know the Elephants, when they do not even see them properly; what they see are two ugly misshapen creatures, half-cow, half-pig, with long snouts and thick legs, who consume as much grass as twelve horses and serve no useful purpose. It was unjust to say that they might be a danger to Mrs. Harrington's little children, since they loved children. What angered me most was the charge that they were evil-minded; for, although they occasionally misbehaved, they were never malicious and I think had no conception of evil. Their faces shone with love and innocence.

Like an old woman muttering charms, I kept repeating to myself that Mr. Harrington could not sell them, he would not sell them. Yet, in what remained of that summer, it became apparent that he was indeed endeavouring to sell them, for he brought a number of gentlemen to see the Elephants, and these gentlemen asked detailed questions about their diet, habits, temper, et cetera, as they would when deciding whether to buy a horse.

With the autumn drawing on, there were fewer of these visitors, and I began to feel somewhat easier in my mind; thus, when the blow fell, I was not as prepared as I might have been.

It was an afternoon late in October; we had returned to the

cart-house after a longer trip than usual, in which the Elephants had enjoyed themselves bathing in one of the woodland pools. Mr. Harrington was waiting. There was something in his manner that alarmed me, even before he began to speak. I cannot remember his exact words, but what he began with was, that he had lately been informed that it was impossible to induce Elephants to breed in captivity, and that no one had ever succeeded in such an undertaking, either in the Cape or in the Indies. Mr. Coad had been much mistaken on this point. Indeed, said Mr. Harrington, frowning, he had placed too much reliance on Mr. Coad's advice, for it was not true that the tusks of Elephants could be harvested in large quantities. Moreover, having considered deeply, he had recognised that to bring about a union between creatures who were probably brother and sister, was repugnant, against all moral law, he could not countenance such an idea; he had been blind not to see it before. It was his duty to prevent such a union from taking place. Therefore, he had decided to sell one of the Elephants, the *tusker*, to the Earl of Ancaster, who was building a menagery on his estate at Grimsthorpe, in the County of Lincolnshire. Seeing the alarm on my face, he went on:

"I agree, Tom, it might have been better if he were to take both, but at the moment it is not possible."

"Sir, they will be lost without each other!"

"They will be puzzled for a time, but no worse. Animals are not like us, Tom; their capacities are limited; they have short memories. They live in the present, it is their curse and their blessing. They will forget each other soon enough, believe me. It is the same with dogs." I heard this with amazement, for I seemed to remember Mr. Harrington telling me that Elephants had much better memories than other animals. Nor did I understand why it would be so wrong for Jenny and Timothy to mate; after all, the offspring of pigs and sheep and dogs and horses are commonly mated. However, it would have served no purpose to have pointed this out to Mr. Harrington, who, I perceived, had merely seized on this idea as a convenient pretext. I asked him when the *tusker* would have to leave, and he said, the coming Sunday, which was just six days hence. "If you wish, I am sure, you could go too. Indeed, the Earl asked if you might, but I said that you would prefer to remain here. Consider how much easier it will be for you, with only the female to care for."

That night I lay awake, not knowing what to do. I greatly desired to accompany Timothy to Lincolnshire; but, if I were to do so, it would have left Jenny with Bob or Dick, who were her enemies. This last was a prospect too horrible to contemplate, and when I considered the characters of both Elephants, it seemed to me that Jenny's was more timid and less robust than that of Timothy. I therefore chose to stay with Jenny, but it was the hardest decision that I ever had to make. Over the succeeding days I had to build a strong crate to carry Timothy on his journey to Lincolnshire, and every nail I drove into the wood felt as though it was being driven into my heart.

I took care to build the crate out of sight of the Elephants, so that they would not become alarmed or suspicious. On the Saturday night, under cover of darkness, I and several other servants carried it quietly into the yard and set it down; after which I disguised its appearance beneath a mass of vegetation and stocked it with quantities of hay in which I hid apples and pears. Yet in the morning, when I opened the cart-house door, Timothy recognised the trap at once, and giving a sharp and agitated squeal, retreated to the other side of the yard. Nothing would persuade him to move: ears flapping, head tossing, he rejected all my blandishments until I resorted to liquor, and in this way stupefied him into submission. He was pushed and shoved into the crate by a pack of shouting servants. When the horses pulled him away, he gave a single trumpet blast, a last anguished appeal, and I confess that I felt as much sorrow as I had at the death of my father; it was like another death.

After his departure Jenny fell into a mope. Sometimes she stood in long silences, her trunk hanging limp, sometimes she trumpeted and seemed to listen for her brother's reply, which, never coming, left her very disappointed. She walked without enthusiasm, lifting each foot as though it were made of stone, dragging herself through thick air. Imagining her state of mind, and how I, in her place, would feel if the only member of my own species whom I knew in the entire world were to disappear without explanation, I endeavoured to raise her spirits by offering her tid-bits, and by taking her to her favourite places, and by letting her bathe longer than I might otherwise have done, and at nights I used to sit by her and talk softly, he will be well cared for at Grimsthorpe, he will be pampered and indulged, to be sure, in the Earl's menagery, and one day you will meet him again, indeed, there is every chance that the Earl will love him so much that he will decide to buy you, too, but whatever happens do not fear, I will stay with you, I promise. Thus I ran on, and though I wished that she could talk to me in return, relieving the weight of sorrow that lay on her aching heart, I did have the notion (which may or may not seem laughable) that she understood some part of what I was saying, or at least understood the reassurance in my voice; but all the while there would be another voice, speaking in my head, saying that I was lying: for how did I know how her brother was being treated, and was it really likely that the Earl would buy her, no it was not. That she too would be sold by Mr. Harrington seemed certain enough, at least it was anticipated by everyone. I lived in a state of dread and uncertainty.

The winter came and went. Then Mr. Harrington informed me that Lord Bidborough of Easton, in the County of Sussex, had agreed to buy her.

"He asked whether you would agree to accompany her, since you know her habits well. I said that you might prefer to remain here, that it should be your decision, whether to go or no, I would not press you either way. I have no wish to see you go, but Lord Bidborough is a wealthy man with a fine estate, and, from what I hear, has a reputation as a considerate employer. I am in no doubt that you would be treated fairly."

I said at once that I would go. Mr. Harrington nodded. "I am sure you are right, Tom. And I am sure that you will do very well."

I shall hurry over the days that remained before my departure from Harrington Hall. Suffice it, that word quickly spread, and though Bob and Dick congratulated me by tipping a pail of filthy water over my head, others offered me their best wishes. Mr. Judge said that Lord Bidborough's gardens would fare all the better for the Elephant's dung, which he would miss a good deal. As for my mother, when she heard the news she burst into tears, and wringing her hands, said, that she would never see me again and that she rued the day I had set eyes on the Elephants, which had brought nothing but bad luck, and had killed my father, whose death, it seemed, she still blamed on Elephant Fever. "And what of poor Lizzy? You will break her heart." I flew into a rage: what of poor Lizzy, it was none of her business, there had never been any understanding between Lizzy and me as regards marriage, if that was what she meant. She went on wailing about the heartlessness of men who trifled with the affections of girls without any heed for the consequences. In truth, I did feel somewhat uneasy on Lizzy's account.

She had come running to the cart-house, panting for breath. "I have heard—is it true? Tom? Mrs. Harrington told me—tell me it is not true?"

"What is true or not true?"

"That you are leaving—you and the Elephant—you are going hundreds of miles away."

"Yes; she has been bought by Lord Bidborough, of Easton, in Sussex."

"But, Tom, *you* have not been bought," she said. "Lord Bidborough has bought the Elephant, not you."

"Lizzy, I have been looking after her for over three years. No other keeper will understand her. She needs me to look after her."

"She will find another keeper, there is no doubt. She will find another keeper. If you go to Sussex I will never see you again."

"It is not hundreds of miles. I will come back to Thornhill, I am sure. I promise you, Lizzy, I will come back."

"When?" she asked. "When? You will never come back, Tom. I know you will never come back."

She was trembling and shaking, and she uttered these words with great force and passion. I confess that I was altogether taken aback. I had never been entirely sure, I think, how much she felt for me; although we were sweet-hearts, I had sometimes wondered whether she was playing a sort of game. I now perceived that she was very much in earnest, which pleased me; and yet if love was on her side, it seemed to me, Reason was altogether on mine. Lord Bidborough had asked me to go to Easton, Mr. Harrington had made no attempt to dissuade me from going, and it was by no means certain that any other keeper would know how to care for Jenny. Who could tell how she might be treated?

Again I promised that I would come back to Thornhill, but I said that it was too late to stop me from going to Sussex, the matter was settled. I then walked across the yard to a small store, from which I dragged down a sack of carrots. She followed at my heels, pleading. "Tom, you cannot tie yourself for ever to an Elephant. You cannot spend the rest of your life caring for an Elephant."— "Why not?"—"Because you cannot, it is unnatural. She is only an Elephant."

At this, my mind began to burn. *Only an Elephant.* As if a creature as noble and brave as an Elephant, as fine and beautiful and intelligent as an Elephant, were worth no more than a common frog, or bird, or beetle, or rat. I gazed at her, the sack of carrots in my hand. "When you say she is only an Elephant, you mean that she does not matter, when weighed in the scales. She does not matter, she is unimportant. But that is not what I believe."

"You believe she is worth more than a human being," Lizzy said in an accusing tone.

"Sometimes I do," I said coldly, and her lip began to quiver and she turned from me, weeping.

She hoped, I am sure, that I would take her in my arms and say that I loved her and would stay at Harrington, abandoning Jenny, who was *only an Elephant.* Or perhaps she hoped that she could come with me to Easton as my wife, and indeed, had she not said that fatal phrase, *only an Elephant,* so it might have turned out. But those three words angered me more than I can say, and I pushed past her and tipped the carrots into Jenny's trough, and what do I remember after that? A roaring in my ears, a blackness in my vision—it pains me now to think that we parted thus; I can scarcely bear to think of it. The reader may judge me harshly, if he chooses, and yet, was I not in the right? Is it not evident, that an Elephant is of more value than many human beings?

Jenny and I bid farewell to Harrington Hall on a fine day in the spring of the year 1770, with the trees snowy with blossom. I was one month short of my seventeenth birthday. Before our departure, I shook hands with my brother, Jim, and told him to care for my mother, who was red-eyed with weeping. As a present she gave me a number of my father's possessions, including his best hat, which I clapped on my head, and his copies of Markham's *Maister-Peece* and *Gulliver's Travels*, which I packed in a small bag. I also took my leave of Joshua, who clasped my hand and said that he would always remember me, come what may. He was even more white-faced than when he had put his arm out of joint. Mr. Harrington, by his side, wished me well and thanked me for my service. "I shall always be grateful to you, Sir," I said; and I meant it sincerely. I later learnt that he had sold Jenny for the sum of three hundred guineas, making an excellent profit.

Chapter VI

The journey from Somersetshire to Easton took four days.
Our progress would have been quicker, but in every parish
we were met by groups of children, like detachments of soldiers
sallying forth to meet an army. Once they had ascertained that the
Elephant was in no way dangerous, they ran beside us shouting
questions, or raced to fetch their mothers and fathers and their
aged relations, who came out of their houses and cottages and
plied us with dainties and sweet-meats and other refreshments.
Sometimes word of our approach flew in advance of us, and Jenny
was greeted like a Queen by the pealing of church bells. All this
noise and excitement made me apprehensive, but she was calm and
good-humoured, and seemed to enjoy the attentions of the crowds.
We stayed the first night at The Antelope, in Sherborne. On the

morning of the second day we travelled through a country of soft grassy fields, greatly alarming its cows, which kicked up their legs and ran away. We were again delayed in every village, but in the afternoon we climbed a high down, and made good progress along the drove. Toward the end of the day, we approached the city of Salisbury, with its shining spire, and leaving the down crossed a big river at a ford.

I thought it best to avoid Salisbury itself, and we stayed at a solitary inn, the name of which I cannot remember, but in the middle of the night I was awoken by trumpeting—I ran out, wearing nothing but a shirt, and found three drunken rogues in the act of breaking into Jenny's stable, with the intention of stealing her, though they denied anything of the sort. After this, I thought it best to watch over her, but the stable was so small I could not find anywhere to put down my head and I had to sit in the yard. It was a fine starry night, though very cold when the dew came on, but I wrapped my great coat round me and was comfortable enough. On the third day we passed Winchester and reached Petersfield, staying at The Hand And Glove, and here the landlord, a cheery fellow, brought the Elephant quantities of potatoes, and several pails of ale, each of which she drank with great gusto, putting her trunk into the pail and draining it in a single draught. Thereafter, I fell into conversation with a hoary-headed old man who, on learning my destination, said that he knew Easton well. When I asked him whether the house and grounds were as beautiful as I had heard, he replied, that they had once been so; and when I endeavoured to find out what he meant by this, he said, that I would see for myself soon enough. Extracting any information from him proved hard work, however, after supplying him with ale, his tongue was loosened, and he let me know that Lord Bidborough had been improving his entire estate, according to the fashion; that people from villages for many miles round, and also a regiment of soldiers, had been employed to dig lakes and build temples, and erect an Obelisk. "It is known as Improvements," he said, making it clear that he, at least, did not consider it an improvement on what had been there before. Since I had never heard of an Obelisk, I asked him what it was; he replied, that it was a tall pillar, a spike, built of stone, rising to a point. "Though," he went on, in a grumbling tone, "what the *point* is of your Obelisk— what good it do to anyone—that I can't say—but then"—and he swung his pot in the direction of Jenny's trunk—"what is the *point* of that thing?" I told him that the trunk of an Elephant had many purposes. "In that case," he answered, "an Obelisk may have many purposes, too—all I know is, all the lords and ladies round here is having them built. No park is complete without its Obelisk, believe me. It is the fashion."

The succeeding morning, one of Lord Bidborough's grooms rode out to meet us. His name was John Finch, and he had been in Lord Bidborough's employ for twelve years. His title was that of Groom to the Stranger's Horse: that is, he was to care for any horses belonging to ladies and gentlemen staying in the mansion. He was dressed in his Lordship's claret and green livery. He told me that Lord Bidborough was a most considerate nobleman, of about sixty-five years, while Lady Bidborough was somewhat younger, being his third wife. From his first wife he had a daughter, Elizabeth, who was now married to Lord Parham, of Dicker, Sussex; from his second, a son, Mr. Charles Singleton (Singleton being his family name), at present travelling in Italy and Germany, and a daughter, Miss Anne Singleton, aged fourteen.

Finch told me that Lord Bidborough's Improvements, by which I mean the changes to the Easton estate, had been in train for nearly two years. The first stage of the work, which had already been completed, had seen the creation of a lake, with the earth being used to throw up hills and mounds. I was astonished by this and asked how big the hills were. "Well," said he, "they are proper hills." After this, he said, thousands of young trees had been planted in clumps and groves and walks, and an Obelisk had been erected at the far end of a long avenue of lime trees. A stone temple, dedicated to the goddess Diana, was being built on a hill-ock to one side of the lake.

All this greatly heightened my eagerness to reach Easton, in which sentiment I was matched by Jenny, who strode along at such a speed that Finch had to canter his mare to keep pace. When we arrived, turning through the entrance gates and riding along the drive, I found myself craning my neck for a glimpse of the man-sion, but a slight rise, which has since been smoothed away, hid it from view. However, once we had reached the top of the rise we saw it before us. In my head I had formed a picture of a grand mansion in grey stone, perched on an eminence, and so it was; but beyond it lay the lake, which in size far exceeded my imagination. It was surrounded by a vast expanse of dark, shimmering mud. Within the park, hundreds of labourers were at work, some plant-ing trees, some building the temple, others moving cart-loads of earth or stone, and when these labourers caught sight of the Ele-phant, the nearest, then those further away and finally the whole army, stopped their work, and sent up a ragged chorus of cries and cheers, which gladdened my heart.

Finch led the way round the mansion to the stable-yard, which was at least four times as big as the yard at Harrington Hall, and here I dismounted. While the horses, stabled along three sides of the yard, whinnied uneasily at Jenny's presence, the grooms brought her hay and water, for which she was very grateful. Soon there appeared other servants in livery—maids, gardeners, pages, all consumed with curiosity, none having seen an Elephant before. However, they fell back at the entrance of an elderly gentleman, wearing a dark green coat, green britches, and a club-wig, and carrying a thin stick with a silver handle; this was Lord Bidborough, who turned out to be as kind and courteous as Finch had described. He shook me by the hand, asked after my journey, and said how pleased he was to welcome an Elephant to Easton. "She is a most remarkable creature, and I look forward to making her acquaintance more fully," he said in a voice full of warmth. He was accompanied by his daughter, Miss Anne Singleton, and by his favourite dog, a brown and white setter who stood by his legs and watched his every move. Later that day, or the next, I was given a suit of livery and I remember that when I had put it on I felt very proud to count myself his Lordship's servant.

The stables along the fourth side of the yard had been turned into one, in order to provide accommodation for the Elephant; however, her presence disturbed and unsettled the horses to such a degree that, after two days, we moved to a coach-house. Although this was very pleasant, Jenny drooped, and lost her appetite, much as she did after Timothy's departure for Lincolnshire. Once or twice she stamped with a fore-foot; another time she trumpeted loudly, and seemed to spread her ears for a reply. At the time, I thought that she was weary from the journey; however, since then, it has occurred to me, remembering the urgency with which she strode toward Easton, that she may have been suffering from disappointment, having hoped that she was travelling to meet her brother. During this melancholy period his Lordship several times came to see the Elephant, and asked me many questions about her health and behaviour, which I did my best to answer accurately. With him he always had his dog, and I remember that he introduced the dog to Jenny much as if he were introducing two human beings: "Argos, pay attention, if you will, I should very much like you to meet the Easton Elephant"—at which Argos, a very amiable and sober animal, turned his mournful eyes from Lord Bidborough to Jenny, and then back to his Lordship. The devotion of Argos to his master is such that he is said to sleep in a box at the foot of his Lordship's bed.

When Jenny's spirits shewed no improvement after a week, I resolved to bleed her, which she allowed me to do without the least objection. Having taken three pints of blood, I gave her a drink of egg yolks mixed with Aniseed, half a dram of powdered Turmarick, and a penny worth of Treacle; after which she recovered her appetite and began to take a keen interest in her surroundings.

Both she and I were eager to explore the park, which we soon discovered to be very fine and spacious; the distance round it being more than ten miles in all. Within its bounds live more than a hundred head of deer, of a kind which I had not seen before; they are smaller than roe deer but very pretty, with spotted coats, and are not hunted, but kept solely for their beauty. The lime avenue begins below the mansion and runs past the lake to the Obelisk, which stands on a grassy knoll with a prospect over a wide expanse of Sussex. Near at hand are deep, secluded valleys, wooded with hazel, ash, and oak, and brimming with the songs of birds; beyond, fields, pastures, villages, and hamlets, and beyond all else the thin line of the sea.

These wooded valleys were a great delight to Jenny in her first summer at Easton. Arriving at dawn, when they were still held in blue shadow, she would plunge into their midst, and root and tear and feast and forage with such pleasure that it made my heart lift. The birds would begin to sing, and the rising sun to penetrate the wood, dispersing the moisture and whitening the dust between the branches. Sometimes she would glance round to assure herself that I was still there; and sometimes I would play a game, hiding behind a trunk, whereupon she would give a short, questioning squeal, are you there, Tom? and I would step into view, I am here, I am here. I often used to ask myself what she would do if, as an experiment, I had slipped away. Would she have made her way back to the coach-house, like a faithful dog? Or would she have continued to browse through the woods, following the valleys until she reached the sea?

One sunny morning, as we rode back to the coach-house, I saw the grooms riding a string of horses toward us. In order to avoid them, I took the Elephant down the terrace which runs along the side of the mansion, and a window opened above our heads and Lord Bidborough looked out in his night-cap. "Good morning, Tom; good morning, Madam," he said. ("Madam" is often how his Lordship addresses the Elephant, just as he addresses Argos as "Sir"; indeed, I think he must be among the most courteous of noblemen to have ever lived.) He asked where we had been, and how the Elephant fared, and I thanked him and said that she was in very good spirits. I ordered Jenny to stretch her trunk toward him, which she did, and taking his Lordship's hand she shook it gently. His Lordship seemed so pleased that ever since then I have made a point of riding that way, and his Lordship will often look out of his bed-chamber and give us good morning.

Here I should describe the mansion, which was built in the year 1749 and has upwards of fifty rooms, or so I am told by the foot-men, though there is a disagreement as to the exact figure. Fifty-five? Fifty-eight? Fifty-nine? It is said that no one knows the answer, even Mrs. Eakins, the house-keeper; the rooms are impossible to count exactly, every attempt produces a different number. Among them is the long room which runs by the terrace; it has a marble floor and is decorated with looking glasses and pale statues of gods and goddesses from Ancient Greece and Rome. Another room is the Library, which contains so many thousands of books that the walls are altogether hidden. Most of the rooms I have never seen, but once, soon after I came to Easton, when his Lordship and Ladyship were away, I was very bold and, pretending to take a wrong turn out of the servants' quarters, walked down a corridor into a circular hall, which rose to a domed ceiling. An open door brought me past an armour-clad knight, and into a huge saloon full of chairs and settees; the ceiling was painted with angels and arch-angels, and on the walls were various portraits of ladies and gentlemen in gold frames. One I think was a portrait of his Lordship as a young man, when he still had a full head of dark hair; there was a spaniel at his feet, and he looked very noble and handsome. Another portrait shewed her Ladyship, or it may have been one of his Lordship's previous wives, in a long silk dress. This room was so wonderful that I could have lingered for hours but was afraid of being discovered, and left quickly.

As we rode round the park, Jenny used to gaze toward the lake, and made several attempts to persuade me to ride her in that direction. Knowing her love of bathing, something which, I believe, all Elephants share, I sought his Lordship's permission to allow her into the lake, and he not only raised no objection, but also said that he would like to witness such a singular event. Lady Bidborough too decided to watch. One afternoon, therefore, I led Jenny down to the lake. It had been flooded only a few weeks earlier, and the water was still very turbid and confused. I motioned her forward, whereupon she waded in, deeper and deeper: to her knees, her shoulders, her back. At this point, I was sure that she would stop, but to my consternation she continued until she was entirely submerged, save for her trunk, which she held above the surface of the water and used as a breathing tube. By watching this waving snake of a trunk, I was able to follow her progress as she swam round the lake. She remained underwater for more than two minutes, and when she surfaced did so on the far side of the lake, which puzzled her greatly. She swung round, saw me standing by his Lordship and her Ladyship, and swam toward us, again submerging herself and using her trunk as a breathing tube. Whether Elephants generally swim in this fashion, or whether it is some peculiar habit which she has discovered for herself, I cannot say, but both his Lordship and her Ladyship pronounced themselves delighted.

It was not long after this first bathe that his Lordship asked me whether the Elephant might be willing to carry passengers on her back. I replied that she would be honoured, and that same day I got me some ash-wood and a saw, and began to build a proper Hindoo *howdar*, very like the one I had seen in Mr. Coad's sketch. I made the *howdar* large enough for eight people, four seats facing in the direction of the Elephant's head and four in the direction of her tail. This *howdar* is secured with a tight girth and crupper, while a ladder is strapped to the Elephant's side, enabling passengers to mount and dismount with ease, though his Lordship prefers to be hoisted into his seat by the Elephant herself.

Later, I made a much smaller *howdar*, a kind of padded chair, for his Lordship's personal use. His Lordship suffers badly from Gout, indeed his Gout is now much worse than it was, and he often uses the Elephant to inspect the Improvements in the park. He maintains that travelling by Elephant in this small, padded *howdar*, which he calls his *throne*, is altogether more comfortable than riding on a horse. The Elephant takes great pleasure in being able to serve his Lordship in this way.

When I arrived at Easton, as I have already mentioned, the lake was surrounded by wet mud, but by the succeeding summer a green carpet of grass made it hard to remember how dull and brown the scene had been before, and indeed the lake, which is shaped with a series of graceful curves, looked as natural as if it had existed in the days of Adam. This beautiful lake is fed at one end by a small river, and there is something wonderful in the fact that such a river, even smaller than the river in which the Ele-phants used to bathe in Somersetshire, should be able to create such a large body of water. The same river issues from the other end and flows for a short distance before plunging over a rocky precipice into a deep pool. Behind this Cascade is a pine-wood, which contains a rude wooden house known as the Hermitage, and here a man known as the Hermit lives and contemplates Life. Nearby is the Grotto, which is presently being built out of rocks and boulders brought from some quarry in Derbyshire. Its walls and ceilings are to be decorated with glass and shells, while its floor will be a mosaick of pebbles.

It was in our second summer at Easton that his Lordship gave orders for an Elephant House to be erected to the west of the man-sion. An airy, tall building, with high windows which give good light and excellent ventilation, it contains a hay-loft and a small room in which I sleep. It has its own walled yard, with a large stone mounting block in one corner. An arch-way leads toward the lake and the temple; in the head of this arch-way is set a tablet bearing the date 1772. In the spring of that year Jenny and I moved into this fine building, and have lived here ever since in a state of great contentment, for which I would like to express my gratitude to my noble master, Lord Bidborough.

Part II

Sussex, 1773

May 30th

Last night I thought that I had finished writing the History of the Elephant, and as I put down the pen my imagination carried me straightway to London, where I seemed to see Dr. Goldsmith and several other men of science and letters lost in admiration of the book. With this fond idea I retired to bed; and now am I again at my desk; for, having read over the History, I find that it is far from finished, and that the writing is rough and clumsy and full of faults. There is surely much more to be said about the Elephant's life here at Easton, while the account of her time in Somersetshire is altogether wrong. How is it that Lizzy Tindall bulks in it so large, when I scarcely intended to give her a single mention? Either she has sailed into the History against my will, or my thoughts and my pen have run away with each other on a private adventure.

Indeed, the more that I have read, the more certain I am that I shall have to re-write what I have written, and that therefore I shall need to apply to Mr. Bridge for fresh supplies of ink and paper. I have already visited Mr. Bridge once, for this purpose. I went to his room on the ground floor of the mansion; he was sat at his desk, with the door wide open. I knocked, he looked up, saw me, looked down again and pretended to study some papers. I waited for a full minute and again rapped my knuckles on the door; whereupon, after giving me a sour look which extended from my head to my boots (no doubt in case they were covered in Elephant dung), he consented to hear my request. After which: "What is the purpose of this?"—"I am writing a History of the Elephant." A grunt of disdain. "Does his Lordship know of this History?"—"He does; it was he who asked me to write it." Another grunt. "How many sheets do you require?"—"Twenty, if you please. And three quills." Reaching into a drawer, he gave me ten sheets of paper and a single quill. "That should be sufficient."

Mr. Bridge is the Easton steward and is known as "the Toad," because his right cheek is disfigured by a large hairy wart, or wen. This wart is an occasional topick for lively conversation at the servants' dinner table, he has several times had it chopped off, but it is like an ash stool and soon grows back, stronger and more prominent than ever. Lately, there was a rumour that a second wart, a companion to the first, was sprouting on the back of his neck, but this is probably unfounded. However, Mr. Bridge is also toad-like in manner, for when dealing with Lord or Lady Bidborough he crawls and cringes in the most abject way; yet, with all the servants, save Mrs. Eakins, the house-keeper, he assumes a sharp, superior tone, just short of contempt. No one likes him. He is excessively hard upon me, since he knows that Lord Bidborough often visits the Elephant House, and talks to me directly—but, of course, he does not know the subject of our conversations, and this preys on him. "You are sure that his Lordship knows of this History?" he asked as I turned to go.—"I am sure," I said.

I answered confidently enough, though I have begun to fear that his Lordship may have forgotten the History. He has been away in Bath, in an attempt to find a cure for the Gout.

June 1st

Evening. As I sit at my desk I hear a noise, and see his Lordship hobble into the Elephant House with a flagon of port wine in one hand, and a stick in the other. His dog, Argos, follows at his heels. I hasten to welcome him. "Good evening, your Lordship."—"Good evening, Tom, good evening, Madam. Are you well?"—"Very well, my Lord, thank you, my Lord." At a sign from me the Elephant's trunk slides out and, taking his right hand, which holds the stick, shakes it up and down. His Lordship beams. "Ah, it does me good to see you both. Sit, Sir, Argos, sit. Over there, if you will. Thank you." The dog, following the direction of his hand, withdraws to the doorway. "Now Tom, as you may see, I have brought a little wine, which I am under instructions to take for my confounded Gout. Would you care for a glass?"—"Thank you, my Lord. I hope your Gout is better, my Lord."—"Thank you, Tom. Well, I would not say that it is altogether better, but it is no worse, despite the best efforts of my doctors to make it so. Now, what of Madam? Would she like a glass?"

I draw up a chair for his Lordship, and he pours out two glasses of wine—one for himself and one for me—and a third for the Elephant. Her trunk twirls in his direction. "Gently, Madam, gently." To an Elephant, a glass of wine is a mere drop, and in less than a quarter of a second she has drained it into her trunk and communicated it to her mouth. This delights his Lordship. "But," says he, "I wonder if we may not manage a small Improvement. Do you think, Tom, she may be persuaded to drink like a human being?" And with that, before I can stop him, he has given her the glass itself—hoping that she will hold it by the stem, so that he can fill it from the flagon. Instead of which, she promptly whisks it into her mouth, which closes shut. "Good G-d!" cries his Lordship, aghast, "Tom—stop her—Madam—she is swallowing it whole!" I step forward. "Open your mouth, please," I say, and she obeys. At first, I can see nothing of the glass—then, presto! the Elephant moves her giant tongue, and juggles it into view, gleaming, deep in her mouth. Her trunk, curling past my cheek, retrieves the glass, which she presents to me—holding it by the stem—her expression, all the while, being one of vast amusement. His Lordship is also amused. "I had been sure she would swallow it! But how well she understood you when you told her to open her mouth! It is remarkable, her power of comprehension—quite remarkable! I hope that you will put this in your History, Tom!"—"If you wish, my Lord."—"By no means, Tom—it is not what I wish, but what you wish. It is your story, not mine. Well, it is her story!"

His Lordship then asks me how the History is proceeding. At this, my heart begins to thud, and, instead of answering that I have covered nearly thirty sheets of paper, I find myself stammering that I have written only a very little.

"Tom, a little is better than nothing. I should be most interested to read what you have written, if I may."

It would be the easiest thing in the world to go into my room, and take what I have written from the table, and give it to his Lordship. And yet, at the thought of him reading my miserable words, I shy away, and answer that the History is not yet in a fit condition for his Lordship's eyes.

"Well, when it is ready, I shall be very glad to see it, believe me, Tom. I am sure that it will make excellent reading. When it is finished, perhaps it should be bound and printed. After all, she is the only Elephant in England, is she not?"

At the prospect of the History being set in print, my heart beats even stronger; but I reply that there is another Elephant, who lived with her in Somersetshire, but was sold to the Earl of Ancaster, who has a menagery on his estate at Grimsthorpe, in Lincolnshire. Lord Bidborough is surprized.

"You mean, a menagery with monkies and the like—not a pheasant menagery?"

"No, my Lord—at least—I do not know about monkies—"

"Well, well. And he has an Elephant too, does he?"

"Yes, my Lord."

"Another female?"

"No, my Lord, a male. Brother to this one."

His Lordship ponders a moment, tapping his stick on the floor. "Well, I shall write to the Earl of Ancaster. It would be interesting to compare accounts, would it not, Madam?"

This has raised my hopes that, after more than three years, I may find out about Timothy. The letter will reach Lincolnshire next week, or the week after, and a page will carry it to the Earl on a gleaming salver. I imagine a high room, flooded by pale sunshine, with a stone-vaulted ceiling; at the end of a long table an elderly man in a wig, opening the letter, reading.

June 4th

Early afternoon. His Lordship appears at the Elephant House with Lady Bidborough, Lord and Lady Seely, Mr. and Mrs. Arbuthnot, and Mr. du Quesne. In addition a frosty-faced gentleman, whom I have never seen before. "Dr. Casey" (says his Lordship), "may I present Tom Page, my Elephant Keeper—been here three years—knows more about Elephants than any man alive, though he denies it, the rogue, do you not, Tom?"—"Yes, my Lord."— "What did I tell you?" cries Lord Bidborough. "Why, he can almost speak Elephant!"

With Jenny kneeling, I fasten the *howdar*, and strap the ladder to her side. She rises and walks to the mounting block. The ladies mount first, next the gentlemen; I stand guard lest any of them fall or trip. The Elephant now coils her trunk around his Lordship and lifts him into the *howdar*—"Excellent! Thank you, Madam! Argos," he orders the dog, who is standing not far from Jenny's tail. "Further away, Sir, keep off, thank you. We do not want you in the way. That will do; thank you."

Dr. Casey, in a high, precise voice: "How long will the tour take, my Lord?"

Lord Bidborough: "Sir, that depends upon Tom here. He is the Pilot of our little ship. He may make the Elephant go faster or slower, as you desire."

Jenny swings me into position on her neck. I glance over my shoulder, to ascertain that all the members of the company are secure.

Mrs. Arbuthnot: "O, we do not care what speed we go over the Ocean so long as we go safely."

Lord Bidborough: "I can assure you, Mrs. Arbuthnot, you are safer on the back of an Elephant than you would be riding on any other animal, far safer than a horse. There is not the slightest danger of our capsizing."

Mrs. Arbuthnot: "Unless we meet a mouse. Is it not true, that Elephants are frightened of mice?"

Lord Bidborough: "I am assured by Tom that it is entirely false, Mrs. Arbuthnot. Thank Heaven, a mouse carries no terror for the Easton Elephant!"

Laughter here; out of which Dr. Casey: "In that case, my Lord, it would appear that no less a natural historian than Pliny is in the wrong. He certainly writes of Elephants being frightened of mice." He adds a few words in what I assume, in my country ignorance, to be Latin.

Lord Bidborough: "There are many curious stories in Pliny. For instance, he writes that, in Ancient Rome, there lived an Elephant which had been trained to entertain the Emperor by walking along a tight rope, which he could do not only forward but backward. And that, in Ethiopia, there existed a race of giant Elephants, as much as thirty feet high. From which I draw the conclusion, that Pliny was not always the most reliable of historians, at least with regard to Elephants. Tom, shall we proceed?"

"Yes, my Lord."

I tap Jenny's head, and at a slow, easy pace she leaves the Elephant House and begins down the gravel walk which leads to the lime avenue. Argos trots alongside.

Lady Bidborough: "My husband has become a great authority on Elephants, as you perceive, Dr. Casey."

Lord Bidborough: "By no means, by no means, I have a mere smattering of knowledge. Tom Page here is the true authority. Indeed, he is writing me a History of the Elephant!"

Lord Seely: "Gad! Well done, Tom!"

Mr. Arbuthnot: "Let us hope he will prove more reliable than Pliny! Eh, Tom?"

"I hope so, Sir."

They laugh again, Lord Seely loudly, and I feel uneasy. However, it is perfectly true that Elephants have no fear of mice, or, at least, that Jenny has no fear of mice. At the Elephant House, they nest in the hay, and run around her feet at night.

Dr. Casey: "My Lord, why does your Elephant have no tusks?"

Lord Bidborough: "She is female, Dr. Casey; that is all. Is that not so, Tom? The females are tusk-less."

"Yes, my Lord, except in the Cape, my Lord. The females in the Cape have short tusks."

Lord Bidborough: "There, what did I say? The voice of authority."

Lord Seely: "I would very much like to have a pair of tusks. They would lend me an air of distinction!"

With much laughter at this remark, we enter the lime avenue. The young leaves shimmer and flicker. In the distance, the Obelisk is a tall, dark spike, an exclamation point.

Mrs. Arbuthnot: "I heard a most curious story last week from Lady Franklyn, whom I met in Town. She told me of a woman in Gloucestershire, who lately gave birth to a baby with a tail. The tail was fully six inches long."

Mr. Arbuthnot: "Lady Franklyn told me that the tail was over a foot long. We may safely conclude, therefore, that it was an inch in length."

Lord Seely: "Excellent story! The woman in question must have had relations with an ape!"

Lady Seely: "In Gloucestershire?"

Lord Seely: "In Africa there are races that are half-man, half-monkie. The pongo is half-man half-monkie, I have read of it. The pongo that comes from the Congo. Ha ha."

Mr. Arbuthnot: "It is more probable that the entire story is an invention. It is another tale out of Pliny."

Lady Seely: "It is certainly a tail! It is the tale of a tail!"

General amusement, not shared by Mrs. Arbuthnot: "Indeed, I am sure that it must be true, for the tail was cut off—Lady Franklyn saw it with her own eyes! It was covered in white down."

Mr. Arbuthnot: "We must not doubt Lady Franklyn's veracity, but, had she seen the tail before it were cut off, attached to the baby, I should be more inclined to credit the tale! A tail covered in white down sounds uncommonly like a sheep's tail!"

Lord Bidborough: "I remember hearing—from Lord Monboddo—of a Scotsman with such a tail, which he had concealed even from his wife, who discovered it only after his death."

Lord Seely, chuckling: "Excellent!"

Dr. Casey: "One should not entirely dismiss the idea that a baby should be born with a tail, for just as certain human beings behave like animals, so their offspring will develop animal features. It is on this account that the inhabitants of foreign countries untouched by Civilization have so much coarser features, darker skin, and more hair, than the inhabitants of countries such as England. The woman need not have mated with a monkie or a Negro, merely with a man who allowed his Passions to hold sway over his Reason."

Lord Seely: "Or with a sheep—hey, Dr. Casey?" He baas loudly.

More laughter here, this time not shared by Dr. Casey.

Mrs. Arbuthnot: "O, but that reminds me of another story—did you hear—a woman in Wiltshire, who—"

Lady Seely, with a shudder: "La, I cannot believe that, I cannot. I refuse to believe it!"

Mrs. Arbuthnot: "But it is true, I have it on excellent authority!"

Mr. Arbuthnot: "What piece of fish-wife's gossip is this?"

Mrs. Arbuthnot, severely: "Mr. Arbuthnot, it is not a piece of gossip but entirely true. It is the story of a woman in Wiltshire—in the Town of Hungerford—a woman whose breast was infected with a Cancer—"

Lady Seely: "I cannot believe it, I declare, I refuse to believe it."

Mrs. Arbuthnot: "—who applied a toad to the infection; whereupon the toad began to give suck, and, swelling and changing colour, until it was a brilliant butter-yellow, dropped off; and since the swelling was reduced, the woman applied another toad, and the same thing happened, and another and another, until the Cancer had been entirely sucked away!"

Mr. Arbuthnot: "I heard this story. It appears that the toads, as they suckled, seemed to enjoy themselves."

Lord Seely, with a loud laugh: "Gad, I am sure they did!"

Lady Seely: "I declare, I could not bring myself to do such a thing, even if I had a Cancer. There is something so vile and hideous about a toad. It is the most deformed and disgusting animal in the entire Creation."

Lord Bidborough: "Is it not possible that to a toad other toads may possess great beauty?"

Lady Seely: "That may be so, but I am very glad that I was made a human being, and not a common toad! To spend one's life crawling in dank, gloomy holes would be unendurable!"

Lord Seely: "Have you considered that someone might keep you as a pet? I heard of a family that kept a toad as a pet for thirty years. They would bring it to the table and feed it maggots from a pot of bran. They said it was a most amiable creature."

When we reach the Obelisk, I halt the Elephant and set up the ladder, allowing the party to dismount. The sky has clouded and the woods are dark and green, the birds quiet but for a trilling lark and the cries of a distant hawk. A gusting wind ruffles the grasses. Jenny ambles to the nearest bushes, eases herself, and snatches at a tangle of vegetation, cramming it hastily into her mouth like a child with a pie, and giving me a look of guilty pleasure. On a sudden she raises her head to stare down a woodland path. Following her gaze, I see little Alice King walking toward us. One of Jenny's great favourites, she is a young maid with dark hair and shining eyes. She is carrying a basket filled with shells, which she has collected from the sea-shore. "Do you have some pretty ones?" I inquire, and she nods shyly. "They are for the Grotto, Tom." Her father is Robert King, the mason, who is working on the Grotto. Jenny's trunk sidles over her hair.

When the ladies and gentlemen return from their walk they are deep in conversation.

Lady Bidborough: "Dr. Casey, was there not once a parrot that cried 'fire' during a conflagration one night, and so saved all the members of the household, who were asleep, from burning? No one had taught it to say 'fire,' but it knew the word, and its application. It was counted a hero."

Dr. Casey: "Is it not as likely that the parrot, alarmed by the smoke and flames, began to squawk loudly, as would be only natural, and that these indistinct squawks were, in the general confusion, interpreted as the word 'fire'?"

Mrs. Arbuthnot: "I heard of a parrot that could speak fluent Milton. Do you remember, Mr. Arbuthnot? Mrs. Urquart was telling us of it, it belonged to one of her cousins."

Mr. Arbuthnot: "If I remember correctly, Mr. Urquart told me that Mrs. Urquart's cousin believed the parrot was Milton himself, transmogrified by the Devil!"

Lord Bidborough: "Dr. Casey, what you say about parrots may be true. But what of dogs and horses? What of Elephants? An Elephant is, of all animals, commonly thought to be among the most reasonable; will you not allow my Elephant some sparks of Reason?"

Dr. Casey: "Elephants are good at imitation, and can perform certain tricks, my Lord, there is no doubt. That an Elephant seems to be capable of Reason does not necessarily make it so, however."

Lord Bidborough: "Yet my observations of this Elephant, Dr. Casey, have convinced me that she possesses Reason. I have seen her do certain things that she could not have done, without some powers of reasoning."

Lord Seely: "Dogs are d—ned clever creatures. I have a little bitch at the moment who is stuffed with brains."

Dr. Casey, very courteous: "My Lord, while dogs and Elephants may seem to shew signs of Reason, their behaviour is driven solely by Instinct. It is a matter of Theology. Reason was given by God to Man alone, in order to distinguish him from the rest of Creation. It is Reason that enables Man to rule over and conquer the passions, which are part of his baser, brutish nature."

Mr. Arbuthnot: "I do not dispute the theological point, Dr. Casey, and yet, as Lord Seely says, dogs are remarkably clever. When Odysseus returned from Troy, Homer tells us, only his dog was able to recognise him. Would you say that was mere instinct? Surely one must allow the dog the power of memory."

Lord Bidborough: "Indeed, the original Argos!"

Dr. Casey: "A dog may well possess the rudiments of memory, but memory is not the same as Reason. The mind of an animal is essentially passive; it is like a harp, on which the winds of instinct will sometimes play and make what may sound like music, but it is not true music. By contrast, the mind of a human being is active;

it too is like a harp, and we understand it as such and may play it at will."

Lord Seely: "Dr. Casey, I declare I wish I could shew you this bitch of mine, I venture to suggest you might change your mind."

Any further words on this subject are prevented by Lady Seely, saying, "I do hope we will have time to visit the new Hermit."— "O, on no account must we miss the Hermit!" Mrs. Arbuthnot echoes, "Dr. Casey, as a philosopher, you will be entertained by the Hermit, believe me. He is a wonderful Hermit!" Dr. Casey answers that he looks forward to it very much.

The party climbs back aboard the Elephant, and we ride to the temple, where the marble statue of the goddess, standing with her bow drawn, is much admired. "Diana the Huntress, goddess of the moon," says Dr. Casey, and striking a worthy pose he declaims in Latin, or Greek, for all I know. "True indeed," says Mr. du Quesne with a sigh; "Bravo," cries Lord Seely.

We make for the Hermitage, entering the pine-wood. The wind dies away, stirring only the tops of the pines, which sigh like the sea. Some tiny birds twitter, a squirrel hurries over the litter of dead needles. The Hermit's house lies deep in the wood, and is held in permanent shade. At its entrance sits the Hermit; on our approach, he looks up quickly before bending his head over the Bible. He is clad in black, and has long, unkempt hair and a long beard. "A melancholy sight," remarks Dr. Casey. Lord Bidborough says, "Well, he is a simple man, whom I am told has suffered many tragedies. Now he lives in solitude and contemplation, shunning all society. Draw closer, Tom." I press Jenny's head with a finger, and she moves slowly closer, lifting a low branch with her trunk. The Hermit remains still as the statue, and seems not to notice us. "Will he not speak?" asks Mr. du Quesne in a whisper. Lady Seely: "No, he never speaks." Mr. du Quesne: "Never?" Lady Seely: "He has taken a vow of absolute silence. He subsists on a diet of roots and berries."

A fly buzzes round Jenny's eyes; she flaps her ears. Wood ants crawl over the pine needles. Mr. du Quesne asks if he may dismount. "By all means," says his Lordship; whereupon Mr. du Quesne clambers from the *howdar*, and walks up to the Hermit, who is studying a page of his Bible. "The Book of Job," announces Mr. du Quesne; and he reads, in a shaking, doleful voice: "Man that is born of a Woman is of a few days, and full of Trouble. He cometh forth like a Flower, and is cut down: he fleeth also as a Shadow, and continueth not."—"Gad—a most excellent Hermit," remarks Lord Seely.

The truth of the matter is that the Bible-reading is a sham, since the Hermit cannot read. He is a man by the name of Isaac Simmons, who lives in Easton village. He and his wife have seven children. He has a bad leg and is a Hermit merely because he can find no other employment.

June 5th

Evening. Lord Bidborough hobbles into the Elephant House, Argos a step behind. "Ah, Tom, I am glad to find you here." In his hand he has his flagon of port wine. "No, Sir," he tells Argos, "wine would not suit your digestion. Why, you don't agree. Here you are, then, Sir, if you will." The dog sniffs the wine, wrinkles his nose, and turns aside. "What did I tell you?" his Lordship remarks in a pleased voice, pouring out the usual three glasses and setting the flagon on the floor. "Stay there, Sir," he tells the flagon. "Well now, Tom, what was your opinion of our discussion the other day?"

"In respect of what, my Lord?"

"Why, in respect of the rationality of animals. And of the distinctions between Man and the brutes."

Sometimes I cannot tell whether his Lordship means me to speak or not, and I remain silent. He continues, in his dry voice: "Dr. Casey is a learned man, but I confess that, for my part, I am not convinced that the differences between humans and the higher animals are as great as he asserts. He will not allow—will not even allow—the possibility that animals are able to think for themselves. Yet, look at Argos. He is annoyed, he feels banished, he is sulking. Or, look at her"—he indicates the Elephant. "She is thinking at this very moment! She is asking herself, whether I will give her another glass—are you not, Madam?"

I glance at Jenny, who is in a mischievous temper. Her eyes move from Lord Bidborough to the flagon of wine; shift momentarily to me; return to the flagon. Her trunk advances, tentatively, as though shaping itself into a question.

"Surely the problem—the entire problem of our relations with the rest of the animal kingdom—comes down to language! Dr. Casey would deny animals any independently conceived thoughts; whereas, I maintain, they are as full of thoughts as we, but are unable to express them in a form that we human beings can easily comprehend. They cannot speak our language; but, then, nor can we speak their language. Is not this the true gulf that lies between us? It is an abyss, a chasm, but one of incomprehension, not of thought or feeling or rationality!" Lord Bidborough contemplates the Elephant. "It is absurd to deny her a large portion of Reason. She is more rational than many human beings; indeed, in her own

Elephant way, I believe, she is something of a philosopher—are you not, Madam? If only she could speak for herself—she and Dr. Casey would have an interesting debate!"

I say nothing, fearing to interrupt the course of his Lordship's thoughts; but Jenny's trunk gently curls round his stick. "No, Madam, no. Unhand that stick, if you please. That is my stick." She eyes me; I make a sign; she unhands the stick. "Thank you, Madam. I am very grateful to you." Now, however, her trunk whisks and flicks the wig off Lord Bidborough's head and into the air. "Hey!"—"I am sorry, my Lord," and at my sign she retrieves the wig and plants it on his head back to front, with the tail falling over his nose. "Not at all," he says, obviously amused, and rearranging the wig, "she is bored, she finds our discussion tedious, does she not, and attempts to divert herself. It illustrates my point exactly. You know, Tom, among the distinctions that Dr. Casey would draw to divide us from the animal kingdom is that of humour. Animals are supposed to lack a sense of humour, to be incapable of laughter. But does not a creature like an Elephant laugh? Clearly she does not express her laughter as we do; but why should we therefore conclude that she does not laugh, or is incapable of laughter?"

"I believe she laughs, my Lord. She laughs with her eyes. And sometimes with her trunk."

"I am sure that you are right, Tom. But what is the opposing argument? Dr. Casey would argue that, for laughter to be true laughter, it must come from the mouth. Against which, an Elephant would argue, would it not—were it able to argue—that our laughter is not true laughter!—Hmmm." His Lordship taps his stick against his side, and gives a swing of his gouty leg. "The other day you mentioned, did you not, Tom, the Earl of Ancaster's Elephant? Did they—the two Elephants—it may sound like a curious question—did they ever communicate with each other?

Did you ever gain the impression that they were talking to each other?"

"Often, my Lord. Many times."

"Well, I am sure they did; all animals do, with their own kind. But in their own way!" His Lordship looks from Jenny to Argos, and back again. "I once heard of an Elephant that could count up to ten—do you think it possible that Madam might learn to count?"

"I am not sure, my Lord. I could try to teach her, if you like."

"Well, well . . . whatever else, she is an excellent creature. How old do you think she is, Tom?"

"My Lord, I believe that she was probably born around seventeen fifty-five."

"So she is eighteen. And how long will she live? How long does an Elephant live?"

"I do not know, my Lord. A gentleman by the name of Mr. Coad once told me that Elephants could live for two hundred years."

"Yes, that is what Pliny says, so it is probably untrue. Still, it is a strange thought, is it not? Two hundred long years. Why should Elephants be allowed two hundred years? We have sixty or seventy, eighty if we are very fortunate, while a horse dies in twenty, a dog in fifteen, and a may-fly has to cram its life into the span of a single day. In the morning it is born, in the afternoon it lays its eggs, by evening it is dead. And so the world goes. There is no rhyme nor reason to it at all. How old are you, Tom?"

"Twenty, my Lord."

"You are not married?"

"No, my Lord."

He nods. "You live a solitary life here, you are almost like the Hermit. But then I suppose you have the other servants to talk to."

"And the Elephant, my Lord," but Lord Bidborough seems not to hear. He says:

"My son is twenty-two, you know, G-d bless him. He will return soon, from abroad, I hope."

I wait, expecting him to say some more, when Jenny stretches out her trunk to the flagon of wine and, having removed the stopple with a quick twist, begins to bring it to her mouth. I prevent her, and order her to give me the flagon, which she does, though with a look of great reproach; while Lord Bidborough shakes his head in amazement, declaring that he has never seen the like and that she is the most intelligent creature in existence: "I wish that Dr. Casey had been here—what a pity! This is proof that she can reason! If only he had been here!"

As a reward, he pours Jenny another glass. Then, leaning on his stick: "You know, Tom, it occurs to me, we ought to have her portrait taken. She would make a fine portrait, would she not?" He surveys her huge form and, with a smile, bows slightly. "Madam, you shall be immortalised in oils. What do you say to that, hey?"

With this, his Lordship hobbles goutily away, Argos his shadow.

June 12th—25th

His Lordship is away in London. Mrs. Eakins says that he is expected to be away for upwards of two weeks, searching for a cure for the Gout. These are two weeks longer to wait for news of Timothy. Every day I see the post-boy with his packet of letters, and I wonder whether it may include one from the Earl of Ancaster. We must be patient, I say to Jenny, we must not hope for too much, we must not hope, though it is difficult not to hope, or to imagine, that London itself may contain the Earl of Ancaster, and that he and Lord Bidborough will meet at some coffee-house. As the two elderly noblemen sit together, in red leather chairs, I perch between them like a pet magpie and, cocking my head this way and that, hear every word of their conversation.

—I understand that you possess an Elephant, begins his Lordship—I do indeed, replies the Earl, a most excellent handsome creature, he lives at Grimsthorpe; he is a great joy to me and to all who meet him!—Lord Bidborough: I, too, own an Elephant, a female—the sister to your Elephant, I am told!—The Earl: Why, I did not know he had a sister. How interesting! How does your Elephant?—Lord Bidborough: Very well, thank you—she is in very good health and excellent spirits—(he pauses here to sip a glass of port wine)—it would be a fine thing if the Elephants were to meet, would it not—imagine how pleased they would be to see each other again!—The Earl (fired with enthusiasm): I agree—indeed—a splendid idea—we must set this in train immediately! Would you prefer to bring your Elephant to Grimsthorpe, or should I bring mine to Easton?

Until his Lordship's return, I have been attempting to teach the Elephant to count—that is (for she is able to count naturally, I am sure), I have been attempting to teach her to express her counting by stamping. Thus I hold a carrot before her eyes.—Jenny, you can see this—you know what it is, do you not? She blinks slowly.—What is it? It is a carrot, Tom.—That is right, it is a carrot, how many carrots is it?—How many?—Yes. It is one carrot, is it not, Jenny? A single carrot. Now lift your leg and stamp, once.—Why, Tom?—I should like you to.—Which leg am I meant to lift, Tom? The right or the left?—Well—it does not matter—either leg. She does not exactly stamp, but flexes her left fore-leg.—Good, that is excellent. Now look—and I hold up another carrot. How many carrots am I holding up now?—Tom, you are holding up two carrots. And you have three more, hidden behind your back, in your other hand. What is the purpose of this game?—It is not a game, Jenny—the idea is to teach you to count, like a human being.—What is counting?—Counting, Jenny—it is very useful to be able to count from one to ten. And it will greatly please his Lordship. Now, as you say, I have two carrots in my hand—but, if I give you one, how many do I have left?—Why will it please his Lordship?—It will please his Lordship, because . . . I notice the sly look in her eyes. O, never mind, Jenny. It will please his Lordship because it will shew him how intelligent you are; it will demonstrate that the differences between human beings and animals are not so great as some folk believe. Jenny pops one of the carrots into her mouth.—Is it so important? May I have another carrot, please, Tom?

We have been practising this for four days, and I cannot say that we have made any great progress. It is not that she cannot count, but that she cannot see the point of stamping; and, indeed, I think that she is probably right. After all, if she were able to stamp her way up to ten, what would it mean? Today, after another failure, I begin to rack my brains and ask, what can we humans do which animals cannot? What can I do that Jenny cannot? Well, I think, I can cook food. I can dress myself, and mend my cloaths when they are torn, but there is little else, save for shooting a gun, angling, playing cards, sailing ships, and riding a horse (though this last is ridiculous, for an Elephant's inability to ride a horse can scarcely be held as a lack of accomplishment on the part of the Elephant, any more than a human's inability to ride a beetle or a toad). Besides—I say to myself—how easily the question may be changed. What can we humans not do that animals can? To which I answer: Why, we cannot swim like a fish, we cannot dig like a mole, we cannot fly like a bird; we cannot follow a scent like a dog, we cannot see in the dark like an owl. Yet, because we claim to have Reason, we say that we are vastly superior.

It seems to me, therefore, that I should not be attempting to make an Elephant think like a human being; instead, I should be attempting to learn how to think like an Elephant, although what that means, what that would mean, I have scarcely any idea.

THE GOSSIP IN THE SERVANTS' quarters concerns Lord and Lady Bidborough's lovely daughter, Anne Singleton, who is now seventeen, and Mr. Church, who is one of her Admirers. Mr. Church is handsome, or at least is accounted handsome by half of the maids, while the other half maintain that he is anything but handsome. I have no opinion on the matter, save to observe that his chin cannot have ever felt more than the lightest touch of a razor, and that his wig is so white it almost dazzles. It sits on his head like a patch of crisply curled snow. However, his looks do not matter as much as his wealth, for he has lately inherited an estate of more than two thousand acres near Horsham, in the County of Surrey, and the question is whether the beautiful surroundings of Easton, conjoined to the beauty of Anne herself, will persuade him into a further conjoining, that is, into a proposal of marriage.

Twice now Miss Singleton and Mr. Church have arrived at the Elephant House and asked to be taken on a tour of the park. Twice I have put the *howdar* on the Elephant's back and watched as Miss Singleton and Mr. Church mounted the ladder and settled into their seats: she at the back of the *howdar,* facing forward, he at the front, facing back. Yet, as we ride out, a silence falls; a pool of silence, which grows to a lake, an ocean, a waste of emptiness;

at length, as our voyage threatens to become unendurable, Mr. Church clears his clogged throat:

"Hem—Miss Singleton—how fine the limes appear today!" Miss Singleton: "They do, do they not—very fine—exceptionally fine—I have never seen them look so fine!" Mr. Church: "How long ago were they planted?" Miss Singleton: "It is no more than three years ago." Mr. Church: "They have done very well, to have grown so fast—it is remarkable. They will look even finer in fifty years." Miss Singleton: "I am sure they will." Mr. Church: "In a century, they will be finer still. They will be magnificent." A long pause ensues, after which Miss Singleton: "Is that a crow or a raven?" Mr. Church: "I think—I think it must be a crow." Miss Singleton: "I hate crows, they are such evil birds." Mr. Church (fervently): "I declare, I hate them too, indeed I should not mind if all the crows in the world were shot." Miss Singleton: "And yet I have a curious affection for rooks." Mr. Church: "I could not agree with you more, rooks are the most amiable birds."

Another pause, even longer than the first, is again broken by Miss Singleton: "O, do you hear the cuckow, Mr. Church? I heard, the other day—a most interesting piece of information— that cuckows call in different notes in different counties; so in Kent a cuckow may cuckow in A flat, in Surrey in A sharp, in Hampshire in B flat, and so on. Here in Sussex it calls in B." Mr. Church: "When I return to Horsham, I shall have to listen out for the Surrey cuckow." Miss Singleton (anxiously): "You are not planning to leave Easton soon?" Mr. Church: "Not—not for a few days, I hope. I should be sorry to leave before your father's return. Do you know when he is expected?" Miss Singleton: "It is still not certain. He is likely to be away some days longer, I believe."

Again a silence, this time broken by Mr. Church: "I hear from her Ladyship that your brother, Charles, is returning shortly, from

Italy." Miss Singleton: "He is, it is true." Mr. Church: "I look forward greatly to meeting him." Miss Singleton: "I hope that you will like him." Mr. Church: "As he is your brother, I cannot fail to like him very much indeed." Miss Singleton: "My father and mother hope that Travel will have been an improving influence upon him. You yourself have never thought of travelling, Mr. Church?" Mr. Church: "I—" Miss Singleton (hastily): "O, please forgive me—I do not mean that you need Improvement, or that you ought to travel! Merely that, if I were a man, I feel sure that I should be curious about the world! And yet, why is there any need to go abroad? After all, one can travel easily enough through novels!"

Mr. Church (after a long pause, and in a low, gloomy voice): "I am grateful to you, Miss Singleton—indeed I am grateful—for saying that I do not need improvement—although, of course, I am all too conscious of my defects." Miss Singleton: "O, Mr. Church, believe me, I am certain that you have no defects!" Mr. Church: "It is kind of you to say so—hem, Miss Singleton—I fear that, if I were to travel, my heart would remain here in England." Miss Singleton (with a gasp): "O, mine would remain here too!"

At this point, I felt certain that Mr. Church would propose. However, there followed a silence broken only by the gently creaking stays of the *howdar*.

This was the full extent of their conversation on their first journey; the second was even emptier. After the second, three of the maids, Susan, Poll, and Fat Ellie, flew into the Elephant House, impatient to hear about the tour. Susan is one of the house-maids; she is about twenty-three years of age, but has the sense of someone much older. Poll and Fat Ellie are much younger, no more than fifteen, and work in the kitchens.

I gave them a short account of proceedings, to which they listened with open mouths. "If only he were not such a milk-sop of a man," they said. "He is all manners and no passion. He is as cold as a statue." This reminded me of Dr. Casey's remark, that it is Reason which enables Man to rule over and conquer his passions, but when I said as much they laughed at me. "What I mean," I stammered, "is that although Mr. Church appears cold, he is very hot underneath." They laughed again. "What do you know about it all, Tom?" Susan asked.

Whether Mr. Church marries Miss Singleton is of no concern to me, but surely he needs to ask permission of his Lordship before making his proposal. Nothing will be resolved until his Lordship's return from London.

THE DAYS DRAG SLOWLY BY. His Lordship has still not returned. When will he return? asks Jenny, gazing at me. I do not know, I tell her. Tomorrow, or the day after, or the day after that.—And then we will hear about Timothy?—Yes, I am sure. I am sure.

In his Lordship's absence, I have been busy at my desk. I am writing, or attempting to write, a Dedication to his Lordship. I have written this twice, thrice, a dozen times, without success. I try the word *remarkable*—and immediately find myself thinking that, instead, I should have written *admirable*. Surely *admirable* carries precisely the right shade of meaning for my purpose? I strike out *remarkable* and write *admirable*—but at once I see that *admirable* is not right at all! No, the word that I should have used, is *excellent*, for it is one of his Lordship's favourite words, and *admirable* is therefore tossed aside in favour of *excellent*. Five minutes later, I have re-considered again: the weather-cock is veering toward its original position, and I am now beginning to think that *remarkable* is, after all, the word which I need—unless, perhaps, it is some other word which is hiding in a thicket of my mind. Well then, I plunge into the thicket—beat through the undergrowth with a stick—and flush out *magnificent*. It is like this all the time: at every turn, to change the metaphor, there are possible words, and phrases, and expressions eagerly lining up before me, like labourers at a day-fair, all of them begging to be hired. How many ways there are of writing the same thing! How hard it is to write when every thought turns to Timothy!

I must finish the History soon, I know; yet I am no longer sure where it should finish. It must be brought up to the Present. But where does the Present stop? A month ago—a week—a second? Or next week? O, if the History were to conclude with Timothy's arrival at Easton, with him and Jenny, greeting each other, after so long apart, why, that would be the perfect end.

June 27th

Yesterday afternoon Lord Bidborough's carriage rattled up the drive, and this morning Jenny and I stood under the window of his bed-chamber, and he looked out in his night-cap. "Good day, Madam!"—"Good morning, your Lordship!"—"Good morning, Tom! A fine morning! I shall be coming to see you later, if I may."

Soon he hobbles in, very gouty, and stamping hard—one of his London doctors, it seems, having told him that the cause of his Gout lies in poor circulation of the blood, which has clotted in the offending toe, and that, to disperse the clot, he must, therefore, stamp his right foot regularly, however much it hurts—indeed, the more it hurts, the better, for the pain is a sign of the clot being disturbed. Nonetheless, he is in an excellent temper on account of his son, Charles, who is now back in England. "He is expected here soon enough, and is very eager to have a ride upon the Elephant, if she is willing to carry him." I—thinking all the while of Timothy—answer that she will be honoured. Lord Bidborough nods, and stamps his foot, wincing in pain, and rousing Jenny's interest (she stares at him, puzzled, as though wondering whether he, too, is under some compulsion to count carrots). "No, I do not have any food, you greedy creature" (for her trunk is twitching around his pockets). "Madam, desist!"

His Lordship then tells me how, in Town, he attended a meeting of the Royal Society, "which as you may know, Tom, is the pre-eminent scientific body in the kingdom," and there again met Dr. Goldsmith, who confided in him that he was preparing a vast work, a history of the whole of animated nature, including both the animal and vegetable kingdoms. "He is very interested in using your History of the Elephant in his work."

I say proudly, "My Lord, I have written a Dedication."

"A Dedication?" My master cocks his head. "You believe it requires a Dedication, Tom?"

"I—I am not sure, my Lord. Do you think that it should not have one? I will leave it out."

"No, no, Tom. Whatever you wish. A Dedication is not, I would have thought, strictly necessary, in a work of this kind—the History of an Elephant. On the other hand, provided that it is to the point, it can do no harm."

"Thank you, my Lord."

His Lordship frowns. "Perhaps I should look at this Dedication, Tom, if I may."

Having fetched it, I wait with great anxiety as he fastens a pair of spectacles on his nose and begins to read:

To The Very Noble Lord Bidborough of Easton

> *My Lord, I hereby respectfully dedicate this Work of Natural History, which describes the Life of a Most Remarkable Creature, in the Hope that, in some small Measure, it may contribute to the Store of Human Knowledge. Were the Subject of this History able to speak her Heart, it must not be doubted, that she would wish to Trumpet her very great Gratitude to your Lordship for his Generosity and Kindness in taking her under his Protection; in the Absence of which Capacity for Expression, that Task is left to the Pen of the Author, who is honoured to be able to write himself, your Lordship's humble and obedient Servant, Thomas Page, Elephant Keeper.*

"Excellent," he says. "Excellent indeed! Though there is no need for the 'very.'"

"My Lord?"

"The noble Lord Bidborough is sufficient. There is no need to ennoble me any further."

"No, my Lord. Thank you, my Lord. Also, my Lord, with re-spect to the title of the History . . . I was thinking of giving it the title, 'The True History of an Elephant.'"

"'The True History of an Elephant'? Very good."

"I also considered 'The Natural History of an Elephant.' Or, 'The Life and History of the Elephant.' Or, 'Observations on an Elephant,' my Lord."

"Well . . . well . . . ," His Lordship hems and havers, "any one of them will do very well, I should say. 'The True History' is perhaps the best title. We do not want anyone to think that it is a novel, do we?" He stamps up and down the Elephant House like a sentry. "Have you ever read a novel, Tom? My daughter seems to do nothing else."

"I have read *Gulliver's Travels,* my Lord. And *Pilgrim's Progress.*"

"The *Pilgrim's Progress*? Ah yes, I remember, you mentioned it before, did you not? Well, I do not know whether *The Pilgrim's Progress* is exactly a novel, or *Gulliver's Travels,* for that matter. *Gulliver* is more a catalogue of adventures, is it not? But, pray, I am interested—what was your opinion of *Gulliver's Travels*?"

"My opinion, my Lord?"

"Did you find the book entertaining, or instructive? Was it an improving work?"

When I first read *Gulliver's Travels,* when I was about eight, or ten, I loved the story, and believed every word to be true—indeed, I believed that I was Lemuel Gulliver himself. Who has not sometimes imagined himself into another person, or country, or walk of life, or even into another age? However, unwilling to advance an opinion with which my master may disagree, I answer that I found it entertaining enough, and particularly enjoyed the final part of the book in which Gulliver visited a land ruled by intelligent horses.

"You approved of that, did you?" his Lordship dryly asks.

"Yes, my Lord."

"You would like to be ruled by horses?"

His Lordship's expression seems to say that he himself does not approve of that part at all. I am confused.

"Human beings have their faults, G-d knows," he says, "but they are not all so irredeemably bad as the author of *Gulliver's Travels* would have us believe. If we lived with horses as our masters, would the world be a better place? Or dogs? I fancy dogs might turn tyrannical." He muses a moment. "However, Tom, I expect you would prefer to live in a land ruled by Elephants."

"Yes, my Lord"—the vision of a land ruled by Elephants springs to my mind, and I answer with sudden certainty—"I am sure Elephants would be kinder, and gentler, than human beings, my Lord. The country would be more peaceful. There would be less quarrelling and fighting, and lying and cheating."

"So we would have a Parliament of Elephants, to pass laws over us? And we would be their slaves, to do their bidding?"

"Yes, my Lord, but, my Lord, it would be different—we would be their friends. They would treat us with kindness and respect."

Despite his Gout, Lord Bidborough laughs. "Tom, I fear that the world would be hard-pressed to manage without any servants at all! Who would harvest the crops? Who would build the buildings, or cook food? I fancy that we might have to press some monkeys or baboons into service. However, I grant you, it is an admirable idea. The Country of the Elephants! What would be the morals"—(stamp)—"customs"—(stamp)—"religion"—(stamp)— "of such an imaginary country?"

I reply that I do not know, but that, with respect to religion, there is a story that Elephants sometimes worship the moon, ceremoniously washing themselves in lakes and rivers in order to purify their souls.

"You know, Tom, that not everyone will admit that animals have souls, or any spiritual faculty?"

"Yes, my Lord, but I think they are wrong."

"I likewise," agrees his Lordship. "If animals do not have immortal souls, it must follow that there is no place for them in Heaven, and I would be very sorry indeed if Heaven were to contain no birds or animals. Or dogs. I cannot believe it." He goes on sentry duty again. "In *Gulliver*, Tom, what is it the human beings are called by the horses?"

"Yahoos, my Lord. The horses are Houyhnhnms."

"Yahoos and Houyhnhnms. And Gulliver is able to converse with the Houyhnhnms, is he not? Well, well. Novels are strange things, built on weak premises, and stuffed full of improbabilities and contrivances." He gazes at Jenny. "You know, Tom, I have occasionally toyed with the notion that an Elephant is somewhat like a novel."

I try to think how an Elephant could possibly, in any form, resemble a novel.

"Those ears—those legs—the trunk—she is such an irrational beast! She is a collection of improbabilities! If no one in England had ever seen, or heard of, an Elephant, and a traveller were to describe a quadruped with a nose more than four feet long, legs like tree-trunks, hairs like wires, and a whip of a tail, would anyone believe him? He would be roundly condemned as a liar; he would be laughed to scorn." His Lordship affectionately pats Jenny on the flank. "If G-d is the Author of all things, as we are led to believe, it is curious to wonder what kind of temper He must have been in when He resolved to write the Story of the Elephant. Well, Tom, when you have finished the History, I would very much like to see it. I am sure that it will make excellent reading."

"Thank you, my Lord."

"Hmmm." Further stamping. "D—n this toe. I wonder whether it might help if you were to set yourself a date by which it should be finished. I do not mean to hurry you, but if it had to be finished by, say, the end of July? A month hence. Could you manage that? It need not be as long as *Gulliver's Travels,* you know. Well. Good day to you both."

"My Lord?"

He turns an inquiring face upon me, and I stammer: "I was wondering, my Lord, whether, by any chance, there had been a reply from Lincolnshire, my Lord."

This question, running across the current of his thoughts, catches his Lordship amidships. "Lincolnshire?"

"In connection with"—(I nearly lose my head and say "Timothy")—"in connection with, if you remember, my Lord, I mentioned to you"—(my tongue tying itself in knots)—"in connection with the other Elephant, the male, my Lord. From the Earl of Ancaster."

"Oh, yes," says he. "Well, I certainly wrote to the Earl, did I not? But no, Tom, there has been no reply yet, to my knowledge. I or Mr. Bridge will let you know when one comes."

"Thank you, my Lord." Then I venture even further, though my emotion is such that I can scarcely express myself. "It has occurred to me, my Lord, that, if it were possible, it would be a fine thing, if the Elephants were to meet again."

"And how would that be managed, hey? You think we should invite the Earl of Ancaster to bring his Elephant here from Lincolnshire!?"

"It was merely a thought, my Lord."

"No, no, I am not saying that it is not possible. I agree that it might be instructive. But, Tom, Lincolnshire is some distance from Sussex, is it not?"

I fall silent.

"Well," says his Lordship, giving a last stamp, "we must first wait for the Earl's letter. I do not know the Earl, save by reputation."

My mind is wound up like a clock. Every hour brings the Earl's letter nearer, with its intelligence of Timothy. Why has the letter not arrived? Is the Earl sick, is he abroad? Has his letter gone astray?

I cannot sleep. I climb from my bed and look out of the window. The moon is not to be seen, lurking behind a large dark cloud that seems trimmed with silver; it glows brighter and brighter, it bursts forth in its full radiance and bathes the sleeping grounds. Black trees float like seed-heads over the grey land, the land has no substance. Is Jenny awake? I turn, and look into the heart of the Elephant House. The moon-light shines at a slant through the windows; her left side catches the light, her right lies in indistinct shadow. I cannot see whether she is awake, or asleep, or dreaming. Is she dreaming? You may tell when Elephants dream—they are like dogs—by the flicker of their eyelids, by the twitches that jerk their bodies like invisible wires. What they dream of is another question. Does Jenny dream of Timothy, of Harrington Hall? Or do the arms of her dreams reach further back, across the ocean, to the Indies?

Jenny, I say—Jenny, are you dreaming? Are you awake? Yes, Tom, she replies, I am awake.—What are you doing?—I am thinking, Tom. I say, Jenny, do you remember Timothy, your brother? She seems to raise her head from the floor. Yes, Tom, of course I remember Timothy, it was not so long ago, a mere three years, I remember him well. We lived together at Harrington Hall.—Jenny, I say, we are hoping to have news of him soon. Lord Bidborough has written to the Earl of Ancaster. We shall hear how he does in Lincolnshire. Jenny says, He is a good man, Lord Bidborough.—Yes, I say, he is a good man, a great man. At the thought of his Lordship's greatness a feeling of warm contentment seems to spread through me.

I think of Timothy all the time. I think of him snorting and trumpeting, playing in the stream, tearing up roots with his tusk. I think how patiently he lay on the ground while I took the rusty nail from the great pad of his fore-foot. I think of the moment when I treacherously persuaded him into the crate, of the expression on his face when he understood that he had been tricked. I think of the confusion that he must have felt on his release, among strangers. Then I comfort myself by imagining him under the same moon that shines here. His tusks will have grown over the past three years. I imagine his ivory tusks, moon-coloured, curving into the moon-light.

July 4th

A letter comes this morning: not from the Earl of Ancaster, but from my mother. Who wrote it for her, I do not know. It is the first letter from her for upwards of a year and tells me that my brother, Jim, has given up his work as a gardener and is gone to sea on one of Mr. Harrington's ships. He left for Bristol in February, and she is full of gloom. *Now with your Father gone and Jim at Sea and you with your Ellyfents I have no one else in the World and am very desolet and do not expect to live many Months so fare thee well my son Tom.* This is such nonsense and I have written back to tell her so, though the news about Jim is astonishing. He was always so shy and timid, with his head-aches, that to think of him now, travelling the world like Gulliver, and seeing porpoises, mermaids, whales, and I don't know what else—for, by now, he may be halfway to Africa—it is scarcely believable.

The letter also contains a supposedly infallible cure for the Gout, given to my mother by Mrs. Perry; and for that reason—Mrs. Perry, I mean—I resolve not to mention it to his Lordship.

However, when I see him this afternoon he is in such pain that I change my mind.

"An infallible cure, hey? Well, I should be very glad to hear of it, Tom, though I hope it does not involve cupping, or purging?"

"No, my Lord."

"No hot baths, or cold baths? And it is not one of Dr. James's Powders?"

"No, my Lord, at least—it is a matter of"—I bring this out with a certain shame-facedness—"the flesh of a viper."

Despite his pain, Lord Bidborough laughs more than I think I have ever known. Tears spring in his eyes. "Indeed? A viper? Pray, is the viper dead, or alive?"

"O, it is dead, my Lord."

"Do I have to hang it round my neck?"

"No, my Lord. I am told that a portion of raw flesh should be rubbed on the affected joint, twice a day."

His Lordship continues to laugh. "Well, Tom, I have tried so many remedies, none of which has done the slightest good, that I am now at the stage where viper's flesh may be my only chance. You are sure it will not bring me bad luck?"

"No, my Lord—that is, yes, my Lord, so long as it is fresh."

"Ha! What if it is not fresh?"

I am silent.

"You know," he says, "I foresee one problem with this cure—I do not have a ready stock of fresh vipers."

I promise to look for one.

"Thank you, Tom. Viper's flesh, hey? And if it does not work, I shall cut off my big toe, and have done with it!"

When the sun comes out I go a viper-hunting. I find my viper easily enough, basking on a grass bank, and beat it to death with a stone. As I return, I meet Isaac the Hermit; he is bathing below the Cascade, in a deep pool thick with white foam, but clambers out and limps toward me. Water streams from his beard while a strand of green weed coils round his neck, though the rest of his body is very white in the sunlight. He dries himself on his rags, and I ask him how he likes it in the wood as a Hermit, whereupon he tells me, with many curses, that he likes it not at all: that in the winter he nearly died of cold, that even in summer the pine-wood is dark and clammy; that he is plagued by black ants and biting flies; that his hut leaks in the rain; that he has nothing to do all day but sit and stare at the Bible; that he has been told by Mr. Bridge that he will be discharged if he ever lights a fire. "Are you allowed to bathe?" I ask. Squeezing out his beard he answers, "No," and grins, "nor fish neither. What is that thing?"—"A viper—for his Lordship's Gout." He responds: "That'll do no good. He should try bathing in the sea." So I say, "Why don't you tell him?"—to which he replies: "Tell his Lordship? Why should I tell him? I don't owe him any favours. Besides, I can't speak—I've taken a vow of silence, haven't I? If I open my mouth even for a yawn, I'll be discharged." This last is uttered in a voice of great bitterness, and Isaac proceeds to rail against the miseries of his life and how for playing the part of a Hermit he is paid a mere four pounds a year, which is no more than any of the maids. He says that he leads a dog's life, and would not be a Hermit for another winter, not on any account, but would prefer to starve in a ditch.

His words about playing a part remind me of something that has been puzzling me, ever since the visit with Dr. Casey and Mr. du Quesne: whether Lord Bidborough knows that he is a sham. Isaac gives me a cunning look. "A sham? What does that mean, a sham?" I explain: "That it is a pretence, a lie, a story; that you are playing a part, that you are not a true Hermit." He replies that of course Lord Bidborough knows that it is a pretence, and Lord and

Lady Seely too; he is sure of it. "I am here for shew, that's all. As are you and your Elephant. We are their slaves. They can do with us what they will, curse them."

Not being sure how to deliver the viper to Lord Bidborough, I carry it into the servants' quarters, where I meet Poll and Fat Ellie, who screech and flee down a corridor, and I chase after them, hissing, and waving the creature, and encounter Mrs. Eakins, who puts on a very stern face and tells me not to frighten her girls. She says that it is best to take the snake to Mr. Bridge, who will no doubt give it to his Lordship.

Upon this advice I go straightway to Mr. Bridge. At the sight of a snake dangling over my arm, he flies into an instant rage. What do I mean by bringing that object into the mansion? Is it some prank? As he rants on, never allowing me a single word of explanation, his Lordship enters the room. "Why, is that my viper, Tom? Thank you very much; I am most grateful to you." Mr. Bridge is exceedingly out of countenance, to my great satisfaction.

July 9th

Lord Bidborough's son and heir, Mr. Charles Singleton, yesterday arrived at Easton after nearly four years abroad, to general rejoicing, and this afternoon came to the Elephant House. With him Lord and Lady Bidborough, Miss Singleton, and Mr. Church.

His Lordship, who is on crutches, and with his foot wrapped in bandages, says, "Now, Charles, this is Tom Page, you remember I was telling you he can speak Elephant—though he says he can't, I believe not a word of it—go on, Tom, make her shake his hand," and I sign to Jenny, who promptly puts out her trunk and shakes Mr. Singleton's right hand. He is fashionably dressed, in an embroidered red waistcoat, white silk cravat, and velvet breeches, and very handsome, and I am struck by his very great resemblance to his Lordship. "I undertake that Tom will answer any question you care to ask about Elephants," declares his Lordship, and Mr. Singleton says that he is very glad to meet me. "No doubt I shall be posing him some questions in due time, as: what did the Elephant say to the Rhinoceros, what did the Rhinoceros reply, and who was the winner?" I am so thrown by this sally that I do not answer. "There, you see," he says triumphantly, "I have found him out already." There is much laughter at this. Jenny's trunk sways slightly from side to side. "Take my advice," says his Lordship, "and don't ask why the Elephant has no tusks." Mr. Singleton smiles: "Why, now I am determined to learn why she has no tusks, but I will not ask, I shall hazard a guess instead." He looks at Jenny. "Either she has them concealed inside her cheeks—but that I doubt—or they have been sawn off, and made into billiard balls—but then there would be stumps, I fancy." He walks round to her tail end. "I perceive that she is a cow—is that not the correct term for a female Elephant? May that be the explanation?" Lord Bidborough laughs again, while Lady Bidborough and Miss Singleton clap their hands. Mr. Singleton says, with great modesty: "It was not so very difficult. I have seen Elephants before."—"In Italy?" asks Lord Bidborough.—"Yes, in Rome," comes the reply, "the Pope always rides on one, for preference, when he goes on his parades around the city. He is nervous of horses, or so people say." Miss Singleton: "Why?" Mr. Singleton: "Why, for several reasons—because he is a coward, and because he holds that horses are Protestant and consequently will not obey him." At this, again much laughter.

They are all in a very witty mood. When Lord Bidborough, who is naturally eager to shew off the changes he has made at Easton, proposes a tour of the park—"For" (he says to his son), "I would greatly value your opinion on what has been done in your absence," Mr. Singleton replies that he will do his best to answer honestly; at which Lady Bidborough says, "Charles, pray, do not be too honest—your father's toe may not be able to bear too much criticising of his Improvements."—"Nonsense," replies his Lordship, "my toe always values an honest opinion. Although, as regards the toe itself, I confess, so many false and contrary opinions have been passed about it in the past weeks, it has grown a little tender." Mr. Singleton replies that he has the greatest respect for the paternal toe: he esteems it highly, and proposes to pray every night on its behalf to the Patron Saint of Toes, Saint Toadibus—"who sitteth on the right Toe of the Father." Lord Bidborough chuckles: "Well, your prayers may do more good than any of the Pills and Powders I have been given. There are as many remedies for the Gout as there are quack doctors, and all of them useless. I have tried everything." Mr. Singleton: "Pray, Sir, what colour is your urine? Is it a fine Amber, or Honey, or Straw? Is it clear, or cloudy? What is its perfume? That will be ten guineas, if you please." Lord Bidborough laughs once more: "Let us begin the tour." Here even Mr. Church manages a feeble witticism, "I hope it will be the short tour, not the grand tour," and when Miss Singleton smiles he is sufficiently emboldened to continue: "I am not sure that we have time for the whole of Italy and Switzerland this afternoon."

I draw Jenny alongside the mounting block and they climb aboard; however, his Lordship chooses to be lifted by Jenny, and as she lowers him his foot strikes the side of the *howdar*. He lets out a cry of pain. This makes her Ladyship anxious: "You are not well enough for this, you ought to be a-bed."—"I am perfectly well," his Lordship replies in an irritated voice, "it is nothing much. It will pass. Thank you, Tom" (for I have passed him his crutches). Meanwhile Mr. Singleton, still affecting to be a doctor, asks him to describe the nature of the pain. "The pain? It is like having one's toe gnawed by a dog."—"Indeed? What breed of dog, Sir? Spaniel? Grey-hound? Mastiff?"—"The breed is immaterial."— "Well, Sir, your remedy is to hang the dog, forthwith! Twenty guineas!"—"You ought to be a-bed," repeats Lady Bidborough.— "Nonsense—nonsense—I do not propose to be ruled by my toe!"

Throughout this gouty conversation I have been waiting to hear whether his Lordship will mention the viper, which he now proceeds to do. "I have been anointing my toe with viper's flesh, on Tom's advice." Mr. Singleton gives a sharp laugh: "Viper's flesh?" and, addressing me: "Are you an authority on Medicine as well as Elephants?"—"No, Sir," I explain, "it is an ancient Somerset-shire remedy, given me by my mother."—"Who is," he says, "no doubt, equally ancient, and a witch of high renown. I have heard of the witches of Somerset. There are seven such hags, and they all deserve burning. Father, you may shortly expect the toe to turn black, and drop off." Lord Bidborough, greatly amused, confesses that he does not care greatly if it does drop off; indeed, he would be pleased. "I am sick of the thing, Charles. I have immersed myself in the waters at Bath until I am half-drowned. I have taken the Duke of Portland's Powder, and Dr. James's Powder. I have even attempted Dr. Cheyne's milk and vegetable diet."—"For less than two weeks!" protests her Ladyship. His Lordship ignores this, saying that the only remedies he has found to be the slightest good are wine and brandy.—"And yet every physician since Hippocrates has advised abstinence from wine in cases of Gout," Lady Bidborough points out in a tart voice. Lord Bidborough: "Which shews, does it not, how worthless they all are? When it comes to wine I prefer to take the opinion of St. Paul." Her Ladyship now begins: "Dr. Cadogan—" but his Lordship cuts in swiftly: "That quack!"—"Dr. Cadogan," her Ladyship resumes, "strongly advises abstinence from wine. He maintains that there are three causes of the Gout: intemperance, indolence, and vexation. The first leads to the second, the second to the third." His Lordship gives a bark of contempt: "And thus he succeeds in vexing all those who suffer from Gout, and thereby making their condition worse!" His irritation draws a small silence, which his daughter breaks: "Why, Father, what did St. Paul say?"—"To avoid excess, my dear girl," Lord Bidborough tells her. "Too much wine is bad for the constitution, but a little is excellent." Mr. Singleton: "How interesting, I did not know that St. Paul was such a great physician! Did he have divine authority for his opinion? We may be certain that Tom's witch of a mother has Satan on her side, to support the viper: what of St. Paul?"

There is further laughter here, and I am greatly relieved when the conversation turns to the park. Pointing his crutch this way and that, Lord Bidborough explains why the temple has been sited there, and not there; why this grove has been planted there, and not here; why the lake has been shaped as it is, to lead the eye onward: everything having been done for a reason, the various parts composed to make a harmonious whole. Mr. Singleton declares that everything is admirable; he cannot conceive how anything could have been done better, it is a work of genius. "The genius lies in the character of the country," replies his Lordship; "all I have done is helped it to find its voice, when previously it was dumb." Mr. Singleton says, "Indeed, Father—you have made it sing. It is the Opera of Easton," and he bursts into song, which is received with applause. When we reach the Grotto we find Robert King, hard at work mortaring shells and minerals into the walls and ceilings.

Sitting outside in a patch of long grass, is little Alice, his daughter; she talks to me and Jenny while the party enters the Grotto. I ask her if she has gathered any more shells, and she opens her hand. Three tiny gold shells lie in her palm. "Why," I exclaim, "they are blackamoors' teeth!" for that is the name they are called in Somersetshire. Alice looks doubtful. "Tom, are they really blackamoors' teeth?" No, I tell her, they are shells—it is merely a name. Glancing at me with her bright, twelve-year-old eyes, she says that she hopes to find enough of them to make a neck-lace. "If you do," I say, "I should very much like to see you wearing it."

As we are talking like this, the party comes out of the Grotto— Mr. Church holding his head, having hit it on some jagged piece of rock. "It is nothing, a mere bump, I assure you, a nothing," he is saying in answer to Miss Singleton's solicitous inquiries, but she insists on removing his wig and examining the injury: "O, but it is enormous—it is swelling—I can feel it—" This in a voice of great anxiety. Mr. Church: "I assure you, Miss Singleton—it is nothing." Miss Singleton: "But it is enormous! Do you feel faint?" Mr. Church: "I confess, a trifle." Miss Singleton: "Let me hold it—there—" drawing his head toward her and pressing the heel of her palm against the bump, "O, it is a great egg, I hope I am not pressing too hard, is it not very painful?" Mr. Church: "Not at all—ahem—thank you—indeed—I am most grateful—" This tender moment does not pass unnoticed by Lord or Lady Bidborough, who exchange significant glances; nor by Mr. Singleton, who makes some amused remark to his Lordship, which I fail to catch, though I think it relates to the possibility that Mr. Church's bump may, if pressed hard, produce a swelling elsewhere in his anatomy.

Afterward we are moving through the gloom of the pine-wood to the Hermitage, when I notice Isaac behind us, limping through the trees, and, in order to give him time to reach his hut unobserved, I turn Jenny from the path and take a circuitous route. We startle a party of deer. At a bark from one of the hinds they bound away, before halting to stare from a distance. Their little tails twitch on their pale bodies. When we come to the Hermitage, Isaac is sat over the Bible. "Did I not see this fellow a few minutes back," asks Mr. Singleton, "running through the woods? I am sure of it. Hermit? Do you hear me? Why were you not at your post? Hermit! Hermit!" and snatching a pine cone from a branch he flings it at Isaac, striking him on the side of the head. Lord Bidborough smiles broadly: "Come, Charles, come, this is not fair to the poor man—he is deaf and dumb, we should not torment him," to which Mr. Singleton retorts that he does not believe that the Hermit is deaf, and throws another cone, which bounces off the Bible. Isaac rises to his feet and, with a shew of outraged dignity, drags his bad leg into the hut. "You see," Lady Bidborough tells Mr. Singleton, "you have offended him mortally," and yet even she is laughing.

In these high spirits we return to the Elephant House; here they dismount, and I am about to take down the *howdar* when Lord Bidborough swings back on his crutches.

"Oh, by the by, Tom, I had clean forgot, the painter will be starting shortly. I have asked him to make some preparatory sketches. Also, I have received a reply from the Earl of Ancaster, I have it here—" standing on his left foot and pulling out his letter-case. "I am afraid that the information may disappoint you somewhat."

"My Lord?"

"He no longer has the Elephant; he tells me that he was obliged to sell it, very shortly after it reached Lincolnshire."

I repeat, like a village dolt: "He sold it?"

"However, all is not lost. He sold it to Lord Luttershall, who

lives in Northamptonshire, at Langley. I once met Lord Luttershall, in Town; an excellent gentleman, with very refined sensibil-
ity. I shall get Bridge to write to him."

Until this moment, the possibility of Timothy having been sold
has never entered into my head. I stammer out: "My Lord, did
the Earl of Ancaster—in his letter, did he say why he sold the
Elephant?"

"Why, not exactly—well, what does he say?" Lord Bidborough
fastens his spectacles on his nose. "Let me see—merely that, for
particular considerations—hmmm—which he does not specify—
he was obliged to abandon the notion of a menagery. No other
reason is given." He puts the letter back in the letter-case. "Well,
well, we shall see what happens."

"Thank you, my Lord."

He seems to have finished, but then adds: "You know, Tom, I
have been thinking over your idea of uniting the two Elephants—
you say that they are brother and sister?"

"Yes, my Lord."

"Well." His Lordship smiles. "There is nothing better than a
family re-union. Perhaps it will be possible to arrange, in some
way. Who knows? Lord Luttershall may even be willing to sell his
Elephant."

On this note he swings away. My heart is bounding like a deer.
I say to Jenny, Jenny, is this not wonderful news? Timothy is in
Northamptonshire: which is not so far away as Lincolnshire: and
Lord Bidborough will buy him from Lord Luttershall, and we will
see him again. She says, we must not hope, we must not hope
too much, Tom. We do not know, for certain, that he is still in
Northamptonshire. Lord Luttershall may have sold him to someone else, who may have sold him to someone else. We must not
hope. Then she turns from me, her deep-set eyes falling away, as

though reluctant to meet my gaze, as though sensing that something is not right. I say to her, Jenny, why, what is the matter, what is wrong?—I do not know, she answers.—There is nothing wrong, I say.—I do not know, Tom, she says, I do not know, but it is not good to hope too much.

Her unease makes me uneasy. What does she sense that I do not sense? How much does she understand?

July 12th

In the stables I find John Finch and tell him—I cannot contain myself, I am so full of the possibility—that his Lordship has resolved to buy another Elephant. Finch is currying Mr. Singleton's horse. He whistles. "Is that true? Another one? Where is it now?"—"The Elephant? He is in Northamptonshire, at Langley." I ask him how many miles Northamptonshire is from Sussex, but he does not know. "When are you fetching it?" he asks. I confess that this question is not very welcome, for it forces me to admit that his Lordship has not yet bought the Elephant.

Finch then asks for my opinion of Mr. Singleton. I reply that I have nothing to say against him. "But not much in his favour," he observes. Staying on the side of caution, I point out that I scarcely know him, but that he seems a great wit, and that everyone speaks highly of him. This is true: all the maids admire him prodigiously, and say how much more of a man he is than Mr. Church (and with justification, for, having failed to propose to Miss Singleton, Mr. Church has retired, abject, to Horsham).

A long silence follows. At length Finch says, "Tom, you've been here three years. I've been here fifteen. I knew his character when he was a boy."

When I try to discover what he means by this, he shrugs. I am already beginning to understand, however, for yesterday afternoon I took Mr. Singleton and two other young gentlemen, Mr. Partridge and Mr. Huntly, on a tour of the park, in the course of which I learnt Mr. Singleton's true opinions concerning his father's Improvements. The Obelisk, which he calls the Spike, he admires, but the lake is the wrong shape, while the Cascade is a feeble trickle in comparison with the great torrents gushing from the Alps; and though the temple is pleasant enough, the statue of Diana is a poor imitation of one in Rome. I cannot say how much this irritated me. Mr. Singleton's greatest derision was reserved for the Hermitage, where he and his friends had some fine sport, creeping up on poor Isaac as he lay fast asleep, and tugging on his beard to see whether it was real or not. Isaac, in an anguished voice, howled at them to leave him alone, which they answered with taunting applause. "The Hermit is not so dumb after all!" Mr. Singleton remarked.

This is merely the beginning, for that night the three young gentlemen come into the Elephant House, singing catches and rolling a barrel of strong beer. They broach it and draw off a full pail, which they offer to Jenny. She is delighted and drains it at once, whereupon they re-fill the pail and she drains it again. I see that they hope to make her drunk, but what can I do to stop them? Silently I watch as they fill a third pail. "Why so grave?" Mr. Singleton chides me. "Why the sad face?"—"Sir, she is not used to quantities of beer. If she becomes drunk, I cannot answer for her behaviour." He seizes on this reply like a dog with a rat. "O—you cannot answer—but why should you answer? Tell me, Tom, whose

Elephant is it? Is it yours? Do you pay for its keep?"—"Sir, she is your father's Elephant."—"Indeed," says he, "and my father gives her wine, does he not? Let her drink her fill." Then he takes a new tack. "I understand that you are writing a History of the Elephant. Is it long, is it short? Is it more than one page? His name is Tom Page, so we must count on one page, at least. How does it go, I wonder?" He throws out a hand, and declaims: "'The Natural History of the Elephant,' by Thomas Page. 'From Antiquity to The Present.' The Elephant is a Creature which surpasses all other animals in size and ugliness. It has four legs, and a probbossis known as a trunk, and is scared of mice. The End." I bite my tongue. "Not a word?" says he.—"Sir, I beg your pardon, I have nothing to say."—"Nothing to say?" he mimicks. "Well, that is most uncivil of you, Tom. We are truly disappointed, are we not? We are mortified with disappointment." As they laugh at this, Jenny releases a long fire-brand of a fart. "Hark," says Mr. Singleton, "the voice of the Elephant! She speaks! She talks!"—"She is expressing her love of good English ale!" declares Mr. Huntly, and Mr. Partridge continues, "Now we have heard the thunder, I hope we will not have too much rain." Mr. Singleton: "I hope Tom will not omit to mention the Fart in his History!" This makes them laugh even louder. They slap and prod the Elephant like a prize-pig, and give her more beer. After a time they go away in high spirits, and leave me very angry.

July 14th

Today I meet the painter, Mr. John Sanders, a man of uncertain age, thirty in the shade, fifty in the sun, with bad teeth, an unhealthy complexion, and hair faded ginger in colour and unevenly scraped across his pate, like the coat of a mangy fox. He is afflicted by perpetual sneezes and coughs, which he blames on the country air, and is much given to snuff, in consequence of which his cloaths are stained dark brown. He is consistently ill-tempered, and we have scarcely exchanged a civil word.

He begins by ordering me to stand with the Elephant on the grassy slope below the Elephant House. Here he sets up his easel, but, the ground being uneven, cannot find the right place, and when he has finally got it set, says that we are not standing exactly where he told us to stand, that we must move this way (motioning with his hand). I move Jenny forward about two paces, but this is far too far; I move her back one pace but this is not far enough; I move her back to the original place but he remains dissatisfied. Again we move a pace, then another; finally he takes out his pen. At this moment, the breeze (it is a breezy, windy, gusty day) rises, and the easel topples to the ground with a crash. Mr. Sanders curses, sets it aright, and glares. "D-v-l take it, this is no good, I cannot work here."

Thus we retire to the yard of the Elephant House, where there is more shelter, and for some time he sketches away, fortifying himself with frequent pinches of snuff and barking instructions. I am to sit on her neck. I am to dismount, and stand by her trunk. I am to raise my left hand toward her, I am to look into her face. As I comply with this last command, my eyes meet those of Jenny.

What are we doing? she asks, why are we standing here?—We are standing here, I tell her, so that this gentleman may take your portrait for his Lordship.—If you say so, Tom, but it is very tedious, how much longer will he be?—I do not know.—Is this what his Lordship meant when he said I should be immortalised in oils?—It is, yes, though he is merely sketching at present.—Well, she says, it is very tedious.

We remain frozen like this for a small eternity of time, during which, save for an occasional twitch of her trunk and the flickers of her eye-lashes, Jenny scarcely moves a muscle. Mr. Sanders then looks up. "How did it lose its tusks?" he demands.

Why does everyone ask this question? Why must people think that an Elephant without tusks is incomplete, like a man who has only one eye or one leg? Concealing my irritation, though perhaps not very well, I explain that she has not lost her tusks; that since she is female, and from the Indies, she does not grow tusks. Mr. Sanders is evidently displeased by this.

At noon, he releases us for an hour; at one o'clock, he resumes his sketching. He is as uncivil as ever, and issues so many contrary instructions that I find myself saying that an Elephant is not some piece of furniture; to which he replies, that it would be easier if she were a piece of furniture. I ignore this, and politely ask whether I may see his work; he informs me that I will not be able to understand it. My curiosity is aroused, and when, soon afterward, he retires into a thicket to answer the call of Nature, I seize my opportunity and glance at the sketch-book. To my astonishment, he has made the Elephant gigantic—she stands a full thirty feet high, as tall as the Obelisk, as massive as one of Pliny's Ethiopian monsters! Her ears as big as rhubarb leaves—her eyes, glowing like red-hot Coals—and, most remarkable of all, a pair of monstrous tusks! I turn a page: here is another sketch, also shewing her with tusks, and with her head flung up in a strange, unnatural posture.

As I blink at this, Mr. Sanders struggles out of the thicket, buttoning his breeches and cursing that he has been stung by a nettle. Where he has been stung, he does not say, though it is clearly in a tender spot. "Where is a dock? What the d-v-l are you doing?" I say, "You have given her tusks!" He answers (furiously rubbing within his breeches), "Why the d-v-l should she not have tusks? What right have you to say whether she should have tusks or not? Go back to your station." I am so indignant that I cannot prevent myself from arguing: "But, Mr. Sanders, she does not have tusks! It will not be a true portrait! It will be a lie!" He gives a scornful laugh. "What do you know of Art? The keeper of an Elephant! You presume to tell me—"—"I am not presuming, but—"—"Where is a dock? Why the d-v-l are there never any docks when you want one?"

I bite my tongue while he hunts for a dock, without success. At length, calming himself with several pinches of snuff (and sneezing prodigiously, venting showers of spray), he resumes his sketching. I stand in silence by the Elephant, though my thoughts are far from silent. If his portrait gives Jenny tusks, I mutter indignantly to myself, why then, how can it be a portrait of Jenny? It cannot; it will be a portrait of another Elephant, an Elephant that has never existed, a sham Elephant. Then I think that it will be all right: for he will shew his sketches to Lord Bidborough, who will certainly order him to paint Jenny as she is. Mr. Sanders too is thinking on what has passed, for he looks up and says in a calmer voice: "It is a vulgar error to believe that the Artist is a mere imitator, a copyist, holding up a glass to Nature. Instead he selects, he invents, he sweetens, he beautifies. He *improves* on Nature."

"Mr. Sanders, I do not claim to know anything of Art; but why is it an Improvement to provide her with tusks? She has no tusks; that is the truth of the matter. You may as well give her stripes, or fur, or wings."

The painter gives a bark of derision. "You believe his Lordship would thank me for a portrait of an Elephant with wings?"

"Nor will he thank you to see his Elephant turned into a monster with tusks."

"Then, if he prefers, Master Page, I shall paint her without tusks. I care not a fart." He puts down his pen. "I once took the likeness of a daughter of the Marquis of Granby. A repulsive girl with fat lips, a skin pitted by the pox, and a curious squint. When I had done with her, the squint was gone, her skin was smooth as cream, and her lips were a perfect rose-bud. Did the Marquis object? To him, it was an exact likeness, and he asked me to turn his other daughters into similar beauties, for ten guineas apiece. If I were to represent the world in its true character, with all its blots and blemishes, do you suppose I would get much work?"

I say to myself, it is a lie to portray an Elephant with tusks when she has no tusks. It is a lie, just as it would be a lie if I were to fill The History of the Elephant with untrue stories. However, I keep silent, not wanting to pursue a pointless cause. As Mr. Sanders sketches away, another idea strikes me, and I ask him whether he has ever worked at Langley, in Northamptonshire, the seat of Lord Luttershall—hoping that he may have some news of Timothy—but Mr. Sanders says that he has never been to Langley.

Evening. Lord Bidborough comes to the Elephant House. "How goes it with Mr. what-d'ye-call him, the painter?"

"My Lord, he has been drawing the Elephant with tusks."

"Tusks? Ha! Upon what grounds?"

"He maintains that they are a vast Improvement, my Lord."

"Indeed! I shall study his Improvements with interest," he replies.

July 16th

Mr. Sanders, having shewn his sketches to Lord Bidborough, and been instructed to remove the tusks, has begun to paint Jenny in oils. This morning we are standing for him in the yard of the Elephant House when Mr. Singleton appears in the archway. He gives us a brusk good day, which we return. "Thank you," says he. "Now, if it is not too inconvenient, Mr. Painter, I should like you to rest your brushes while I borrow this animal for a short time."

I assume that he wants to ride in his Lordship's throne, but no: his intention is to sit on Jenny's neck. "Sir," I say, "she is not accustomed to strangers." He replies in a pleasant voice: "She will accustom herself soon enough, and then I will no longer be a stranger, will I? My father has ridden her often enough, I am sure."

"No, Sir."

"No? Pray, why not?"

"He has never asked to, Sir."

"Indeed? I cannot believe that it is much more difficult to ride an Elephant than a horse."

I attempt to explain that it is not a matter of skill, but that, while a horse may be controlled by means of the bit and bridle, an Elephant is different; that the rider's control, if it can be so described, lies to a great extent in the Elephant's willingness to be controlled; that there needs must be a contract of mutual understanding, between the Elephant and her rider—

"What is that?" he interrupts.

"Sir, it is an *ankus*."

"Which you use, do you not, to chastise the Elephant, when it refuses to obey?"

I tell him that I scarcely ever have cause to use the *ankus,* since the Elephant understands me well enough; I merely wear it, as a token of Authority—

"Well, now, I shall wear it, for the same reason, and no doubt she will understand me."

He holds out his hand, and I take it off my neck and give it to him. "Now I should like to mount, if I may. Pray, tell her to lift me into the saddle."

He raises his hands, and I sign to Jenny. However, instead of placing him on her neck, she holds him in mid-air. Mr. Singleton glares. "D—n—what is happening?"

"Sir, she is uncertain what to do."

"Well, tell her what to do. This is intolerable."

I give the sign; whereupon she uncoils her trunk and lets him fall to the ground. He stumbles and picks himself up, breathing rather heavily. "I understood that this creature obeyed you."

I look at Jenny: her eyes are lowered, she seems as demure and innocent as you would like. She must have misunderstood, I say.

"Make her kneel," orders Mr. Singleton. "I will mount by myself."

He climbs on to her neck and tells me to order her to rise. I do so, and she obeys. He sits there, legs dangling. "Well then, giddy-up, d—n you!" and urges her with his knees. "Walk, will you? Walk! Why is she not walking? What is wrong with the beast?" He kicks his heels against the sides of her neck. "What do you do to make her walk? What is the command?"

I reach out my hand to Jenny's trunk, and begin to lead her out of the yard. However, Mr. Singleton tells me to step aside, saying that he does not want me to lead, that he is capable of riding by himself. He speaks in such a sharp, peremptory voice that there is no purpose in arguing. I step aside. "How fast will she gallop?" he inquires. "I have heard it said that an Elephant may gallop as fast as a horse, if not faster."

"I am not sure, Sir."

"You disappoint me. My father assured me that you could answer all questions about Elephants."

"Sir, I have never had any occasion to make her gallop. I do not know whether Elephants are able to gallop."

"Well, maybe I shall find out." Again he falls to urging Jenny with his boots. "Walk! Giddy-up! Walk, will you?" When she does not move, he raises the *ankus* and brings it down on her skull. It makes a dull, wooden thud. "Walk, d—n you! Well, you shall be punished, if you will not even walk," and the *ankus* thuds again. She shakes her head. He gives her a third blow, and she sinks down and rolls over, pitching him on to the stones. Though he springs up nimbly enough, his breeches are streaked with dirt.

He stands with his hands on his hips. "Well, Master Page, I perceive what kind of character she has. Only you may ride her. That is what I am meant to understand by her behaviour, is it not? No one else is permitted, save as a passenger."

He hands me the *ankus* and strides proudly away, whereupon I turn on Jenny, who has risen to her feet, and ask her to explain herself. She listens, swinging her trunk from side to side, her eyes shifting uneasily.

Mr. Sanders, who has been a spectator of the entire scene, throws back his head and gives a savage laugh.

Later I watch Mr. Singleton spurring his horse across the park, its hooves flinging up clods.

July 21st

His Lordship is unwell. Last night he had a bad fall; as he descended a flight of stairs, on his crutches, either his legs gave way, or one of the crutches slipped on the stone. How serious his condition is I do not know. When I spoke to Mrs. Eakins early this morning she said that he was in no danger, that a doctor had bled him and that he was resting peacefully, but later I happened to walk into the kitchen yard where Poll and Fat Ellie were plucking some black turkies. Their hands were covered in blood and feathers. They told me that his Lordship had had a Paralytic Fit, and that there were no less than three doctors at his bedside, and that Lady Parham, his daughter from his first marriage, had been sent for. What is a Paralytic Fit? Poll says, with a smirk, that he is unable to speak, or to move his legs. "If his Lordship dies," says Fat Ellie, wiping her bloody hands on her skirts, "Mr. Singleton will be our lord and master."

Lord Bidborough's illness has put Mr. Sanders in a low, grumbling temper. He tells me of a commission that he once had, to paint the favourite hound of some gentleman in Essex. Shortly before he, that is, Mr. Sanders, was due to begin work, the gentleman was struck down by an Apoplexy which rendered him insensible; his debts, which had previously been concealed, then came to light, and the commission was withdrawn. Mr. Sanders was left badly out of pocket. "If Lord Bidborough dies, I may be paid, or I may not," he concludes in a despondent tone, and begins to talk about his wife and four children, who live in the Surrey village of Streatham, and depend upon him for their entire existence.

I assure him that there is no question of his Lordship's life being in danger. He says: "Are you a doctor, now, or an Elephant keeper?"

If his Lordship dies, if Mr. Singleton becomes the new Lord Bidborough, what then? Will Mr. Singleton be willing to buy Timothy from Lord Luttershall? Will he even want to keep Jenny?

July 22nd

Mrs. Eakins reports that his Lordship has been bled again, and, as a result, has recovered somewhat. This has relieved me a little of my anxiety, and yet I am now troubled by the thought that, while he lies a-bed, the letter may have arrived from Northamptonshire. Even now, it may be on Mr. Bridge's desk, waiting to be opened. Indeed, it may already have been opened and read by Mr. Bridge!

I pluck up courage, and visit the Toad. He is dozing, elbows up, chin resting on his palms, squashing his fat face. When I knock, he fails to wake. On his desk are some papers, half-hidden. I wait, cough; he does not stir. I tip-toe toward the desk. Among the papers I can see a letter, with a crimson seal. The seal is very big; I am sure it is a nobleman's seal. However, Mr. Bridge cannot be as deeply asleep as he seems, for without warning his eyes spring open and he sits upright. The pressure of his hands has turned his chin bright red. "What the d-v-l are you doing here?" I am sorry to disturb him, I say, but I would be grateful for more sheets of paper. "Again? What? How dare you come in here? How many sheets this time?"—"Ten will suffice," I reply, whereupon he thumbs out six and gives me good day. I stand my ground. "Mr. Bridge, I wonder whether, by any chance, his Lordship has received a letter from Lord Luttershall, in Northamptonshire." He answers that any letter addressed to his Lordship is none of my concern. "Good day to you now, be off."

I consult Jenny. She asks whether I am sure that it is the letter. I say, I think it is the letter. It may be the letter.—But you are not entirely sure? she asks. No, I am not entirely sure, how can I be sure? But I have resolved to steal the letter. She gazes at me, blinking. Mrs. Eakins locks all the doors. How will you get in?—I will find a way in, I will force a window. She flaps her ears. It is not a good idea, she says, it is far too dangerous. The Toad does not like you, he never has. If you are discovered, you will be discharged, or worse. Even if the letter is from Lord Luttershall, who knows whether it will have any news of Timothy? Why was he sold so quickly by the Earl of Ancaster? Why did the Earl of Ancaster say that he was *obliged* to sell him?—I do not know, I tell her, but perhaps he found the Expense too great.—Or perhaps it was the Ooze, she says, and gazes so seriously at me that I feel frightened.

Should I try to steal the letter? I imagine myself by the mansion at night, standing in the shadow of its walls, taking off my boots. I force a window, climb in, listen. There are no sounds; everyone is deep asleep. Carefully I feel my way past dark furniture, watched only by the eyes of the ladies and gentlemen hanging on the walls. My ears are straining so hard that the skin seems tight on my face; and when I turn a corner, when I find myself greeted by the pale form of a marble goddess, or by the figure of the armoured knight, his visor shut, his breast-plate, greaves, and sword faintly gleaming, one of my knee-caps begins to jump up and down. Yet I move on, trembling, down one corridor and then another, and reach Mr. Bridge's room. I wait, my hand on the handle of the door. Mr. Bridge is sleeping in the adjacent chamber; his slow, wheezing snores rise and fall. Quiet as a mouse, I turn the handle. It opens. In I steal, fumble through the darkness to the desk; find the letter, put it in my pocket, and hurry away. I slip back through the mansion, climb out of the window, and run triumphant back to the Elephant House. Jenny, lying in the straw, raises her head.—Where have you been, Tom?—Nowhere.—Where have you been?—Go to sleep.

I take the letter to my bed-room, light a candle, use the blade of my pocket knife to lift the seal. Opening the letter, I read what? Why, that Lord Luttershall is delighted to hear from Lord Bidborough, that Lord Luttershall will gladly sell his Elephant to his Lordship.

How easy it is to imagine oneself into happiness! Yet that same imagination also supplies a dozen ways in which I fail to steal the letter. I fail to force the window. Or, I force the window but fail to find Mr. Bridge's room. Or, I do find his room, but the door is locked. Or, I find his room, and the door is unlocked, but as I pick up the letter he wakes. Or, blundering in the darkness, I crash into some piece of furniture, and the alarm is raised, and I am discovered behind a curtain by Mrs. Eakins, or Mr. Singleton. If that were to happen, what could I possibly say in my defence? Jenny is right, it is too dangerous; there is nothing to do but wait.

July 25th

His Lordship is said to have made a further recovery, though he remains deprived of speech. I have seen him once only, and from a distance, in a bath-chair, attended by her Ladyship and the faithful.

Argos. Meanwhile Mr. Singleton's two friends, Mr. Huntly and Mr. Partridge, are again staying at Easton. Last night they came to the Elephant House, and with them Poll and Fat Ellie. Poll flirted her impudent eyes at Mr. Partridge, while Ellie could do nothing but admire Mr. Singleton with ogling attention. How it would all have ended I do not know, but Mrs. Eakins appeared and promptly whisked both girls away to the safety of their beds.

Afterward, the gentlemen began to talk in low, easy voices about horses, and horse-breeding and betting. I could not hear much; however, Mr. Partridge suddenly exclaimed: "Done! Two hundred guineas!" and Mr. Singleton addressed me: "Tom Page One Page? Mr. Partridge and I are resolved to hold a race between the Elephant and a horse, in order to determine which is the faster, as a scientific experiment. He believes that the horse will easily win, while I favour the Elephant. You will be jockey of the Elephant, Tom Page One Page—since you are the only man alive capable of riding the creature"—this in a sarcastick voice—"while Mr. Partridge will ride the horse."—"Yes, Sir," I replied, and they began to talk about billiards.

This race is now set to take place for Friday. Mr. Partridge has declined the mounts in Lord Bidborough's stables and is gone to fetch his best thorough-bred. Everyone has been laying bets, and Finch has warned me to keep a close watch on the Elephant, since he has heard that an attempt will be made to give her a dose of poison. The general opinion is that the Elephant has little chance of winning the race: she will lumber like a cart-horse, and be easily out-stripped by the horse. I cannot tell. I am not even certain whether Jenny will agree to run. What if she refuses? This afternoon I take her to the lime avenue, and endeavour to persuade her into a run. Elephants do not trot like horses; instead, when they need to make speed, they move their legs more quickly. She manages what might be called a short canter, before ambling to a halt. Tom, why do you want me to run? she asks, it is a warm afternoon, let us go to the lake. I say, There is to be a running race, between you and a horse.—When is the race? she inquires.—Friday. She swings her trunk. In that case I shall run on Friday, if I must. Now, Tom, may we go to the lake, please, I would like to bathe.

We go to the lake. As she swims, no doubt frightening any number of fish, for his Lordship has stocked the lake with carp, I am joined by Mr. Sanders, the painter. "The Portrait is finished," he announces in a gruff voice. Wishing to myself, that I could say the same of the History, I ask him whether he is pleased; by which I mean, pleased that it is finished. However, he takes me to mean, is he pleased with it as a work of Art? "You may see it if you wish," he says. "No one else has seen it yet." I understand, then, that he greatly wants to shew me the Portrait, indeed, it is for that reason he has come to join me by the lake, to issue me with an invitation. I say that I would very much like to see it.

Later, therefore, I do indeed go to Mr. Sanders's room. The Portrait is propped on a large easel and smelling strongly of spirit. Mr. Sanders waits, scratching his teeth, and patting his brow with a green handkerchief.

My mouth opens and shuts like a baby bird; I cannot think what to say. The Portrait shews the Elephant to one side of the lime avenue, with the temple on the right and the mansion in the background. I, her keeper, am nowhere to be seen, but Lord Bidborough is standing by her trunk, offering her a bright red apple. This apple is too red, and the limes are too green, and the sky is too blue. As for Jenny, she has no tusks, thank G-d, but is still enormous, a veritable Colossus, and there is something wrong in the shape of her fore-legs, which are too thick and short, and in the curve of her trunk, which looks like a misshapen trumpet, and in the tilt of her head and the cast of her expression. In short, she is unreal, improbable, an invention.

I tell Mr. Sanders that he has caught the Elephant's likeness perfectly.

"You think so?"

"I do. Most certainly. It is excellent."

"It will look better when it is varnished, of course. And framed."

"It is excellent already."

Mr. Sanders does not seem to want to believe me, however. "I had great difficulties with the tail," he says. "The tail was a Challenge."

The tail? The tail is a rope. But there is nothing wrong, I hope, in a certain species of lying, and whatever the faults of the Portrait, I have come to like Mr. Sanders. Over the past few days he has become much more talkative, offering me occasional pinches of his snuff, and certain glimpses into his life as a travelling painter (or, as he styles himself, "Artist"). Until about five years ago, he was much in demand for his portraits; the flow of commissions then became more and more irregular, and finally dried up; after which, to support his family, he had to resort to giving lessons in water-colour to young ladies who had no talent whatever, save in chattering of their latest beaux. The drought ended when a Mr. Peters of East Grinstead, Sussex, asked him to do a portrait in oils of Hercules, the famous cockerel. ("You have heard of Hercules?" Mr. Sanders asks, anxiously; to which I reply, lying again, that everyone has heard of Hercules.)

At first, Mr. Sanders was not sure whether to accept the commission of Hercules. "Then I thought to myself, it was a Challenge. An Artistic Challenge." Since which, he has faced many such Challenges. Two months ago, he was in Oswestry, taking the likeness of a vast pig, which, having been stuffed and crammed with pies and puddings, had swelled to such a corpulent size that it could scarcely move; two months before that, in Devon, taking the portrait of a champion bull. This is the story of Mr. Sanders's life. He is angry that he is obliged to resort to animals, which he does not consider proper subjects for his Art; he consoles himself by thinking of them as Challenges; at the same time, he is proud of the skill with which these portraits are executed. He exists some-where between the hope that one day his merit will be recognised, that he will be acclaimed as a great Artist; and the fear that he will find himself without work and fall into the pit of penury, dragging his family with him.

"I think it admirable," I say. "Have you considered Argos—his Lordship's dog?"

"For a portrait?" Mr. Sanders pulls a wry face. "It has probably already been done."

I tell him that there is another Elephant, presently owned by Lord Luttershall, in Northamptonshire, which his Lordship has resolved to buy and bring to Easton. When his Lordship has fully recovered, I say, he will surely want to have its Portrait taken.

"If he recovers," Mr. Sanders answers, gloomily.

July 26th

After midnight, voices in the darkness. Remembering Finch's warning, I pull on my cloaths and run into the yard. Mr. Single-ton is standing there, a bottle in his hand. "Tom Page One Page?" The moon shines low in the sky. "It is such a fine night that we are resolved to take a short tour on the Elephant."—"Now, Sir?"—"If it is not inconvenient," in a curt voice. At this moment I see Mr. Huntly in the shadows, and with him Fat Ellie. There is no sign of Poll.

I fetch the *howdar,* strap it on Jenny's back, and lead her to the mounting block. Ellie is badly drunk, indeed can scarcely walk, and Mr. Huntly has to help her on board. "So you have never been on an Elephant before?" Mr. Singleton asks her. When she does not reply, he puts the question again. "Have you never ridden on an Elephant?"—"No, Sir, never," she replies, with a giggle.—"And how do you find it?" is his next inquiry.—"Very pleasant, Sir, thank you."—"Well, we shall go to see the Spike." She asks what the Spike is. "Why, my dear, it is the Obelisk, of course, and it will look very fine and picturesque by moon-light. Maybe we will hear a nightingale." Small chance of that, I think to myself, for nightingales have not been singing these six weeks past.

As we travel down the lime avenue, the moon flings the shadows of the trees in blotches over the ground. The two gentlemen talk in low voices, and from Ellie there comes the occasional squeal; glancing over my shoulder, I see her slumped against Mr. Huntly, who is taking a long swigg from a bottle. This glance earns me a rebuke from Mr. Singleton, who is in an impatient mood. "Can we not go faster?" I give Jenny her orders, and she strides along at a great pace. Her ears are wide, her trunk half-coiled, and I can sense her excitement in the night air.

The Obelisk lies far ahead, black against the pearl-grey of the sky. We are not half-way there, however, when the gentlemen change their minds and tell me to take them to the Cascade. A little way further and they have begun to argue, with Mr. Huntly saying that they ought to go back. "Why?" says Mr. Singleton. Mr. Huntly: "Is it not obvious?" Mr. Singleton: "You may go back if you like." Mr. Huntly: "Singleton, you know that this is no d—n good. Look at her, she is cut. She is beyond anything. Stop the Elephant." Mr. Singleton: "This is my d—ned Elephant, not yours." Mr. Huntly: "I am going back. I am not a party to this." Mr. Singleton: "Go back then, if you will."

The argument continues for several minutes, and finally Mr. Huntly jumps off. In the half-dark he misjudges the drop and falls aukwardly, but picks himself up with a curse and walks away.

We go on, not as fast as before; Jenny seems less certain of herself. Mr. Singleton talks to Ellie in a calm, pleasant voice, while she mumbles her replies. "You are a sweet girl, even if you are a Fat Ellie-phant. You do not mind me calling you the Ellie-phant, do you? It is my pet name for you. It suits you perfectly." More of this. Then a gasp: "You see, I promised to shew you the Spike—what do you say? Is it not a fine prospect?" and though I dare not turn my head I somehow divine that he has unbuttoned his breeches. "Come now, it is not so strange, is it now? You are a country girl. It will not bite you." She says nothing, and in an attempt to rouse her, for she is barely sensible, he slaps her face. At the second or third slap, I turn. With her hair tight in one hand he has pulled back her head so that her mouth gapes, her buck-teeth shine, her eyes start. "Sir," I say.— "What? D—n you, did I not tell you to look ahead?"—"Yes, Sir."

We reach the Cascade. Here he orders me to stop. I do so, wishing with all my heart that I had forgot to strap on the ladder.

I set up the ladder and Mr. Singleton carries Ellie down. He puts her on her feet, she falls in a heap; he lifts her up again. "Come, my dear, let us have a walk, come now, there is nothing to fear." Though she seems to resist, he is determined, and catches her arm. She casts a wild imploring glance at me. They cross a stretch of moon-light and disappear into the darkness of the pine-wood.

The moon shines brightly, the air is altogether still; when I listen, I can hear nothing above the steady roar of the Cascade. Every second is as long as a minute. I ride Jenny to the very edge of the trees. I wait, picturing the darkness within. Jenny's trunk snakes back to find me. What is happening, Tom?—I do not know.—Where have they gone?—Jenny, I do not know, be quiet.

A stag with a heavy set of antlers trots into view, very pale in the moon-light, and moving with a strange kind of stiffness which seems to denote its agitation. Then Mr. Singleton appears. He shouts something I cannot hear, and makes off on foot. I dismount, leave Jenny by herself, enter the darkness. Ellie is sprawling on the ground. She is moaning. I try to lift her, she cannot walk. I carry her out. Half her cloaths have been torn from her body. I help her dress, help her into the *howdar*. As we ride back to the mansion, she shivers and retches.

When we reach the Elephant House she speaks for the first time, in a distracted voice, saying that she cannot sleep in the servants' quarters, that the doors are locked. "Where then?" I ask. She is silent. "Where is my shoe?"—"Your *shoe*?"—"My shoe—I have lost my shoe."

I offer her my bed in the Elephant House. She stumbles inside. I lift the *howdar* off Jenny's back, and, finding it covered in vomit, wash it clean.

When I wake at dawn, Ellie is still asleep. I leave her, and ride Jenny through the park, tracing the same course which we followed in the night. The sun is rising into a blue sky layered with trails of misty cloud, while the limes are bright with green leaves. The air seems full of singing birds. I think, our lives are divided into darkness and light, night and day; in one we lie asleep, at the mercy of our dreams, which carry us where they will; in the other we tell ourselves that we are awake, and hope to control our actions. Now, though I seem awake, my head spins, I feel I am still dreaming; in the brilliance of the morning everything is so fresh and clean that I can scarcely believe what happened in the night. By the Cascade I come upon Isaac, crouched in the cover of some reeds, fishing; beside him, in the long grass, a silver fish, flopping and gasping.

The missing shoe lies in a patch of dandelion, on the edge of the wood. Jenny sniffs with her trunk. What is this?—It is Fat Ellie's shoe.—What is it doing here?—It does not matter; pick it up, give it to me. She does so. Tom, what happened to Fat Ellie?—It does not matter.

We return to the Elephant House, and find that Ellie has gone. I give Jenny her broom and she sweeps violently.

In the afternoon I am stood in the shallows of the lake, scrubbing Jenny's flanks, when Mr. Singleton rides up. To my astonishment, he makes no reference to Ellie, merely putting to me a series of inquiries about the race. At the end he says, "Tom, I find that I have been guilty of baiting you, and I should like to apologise; it was not done with any malice, and I sincerely hope you will forgive me; as a token of which—" and from a coat pocket he pulls three guineas. Three guineas! I understand well enough, that I am required to keep silent. Should I keep silent? What would be gained by telling the truth? What would be lost?

July 27th

I meet Susan hanging some wet cloaths by the laundry. I have Ellie's shoe in my hand. "Susan—where is Ellie?" I ask. She turns round, sees me, and bursts into tears. "Leave me alone—I am not speaking to you." Puzzled, I ask her what it is that I have done wrong. She refuses to reply, but again tells me to leave her alone. "Where is Ellie?" I say. "Will you give her this?" (meaning the shoe)—"Then it is true!" she cries. I say, "What is true?"—"It is true that she spent the night at the Elephant House! O, I do not want to know!"

I tell her the truth. I tell her that Ellie did indeed spend the night at the Elephant House, but I also tell her why Ellie spent the night at the Elephant House. I tell her what happened in the park with Mr. Singleton. She listens, without looking at me.

Then:

"Why did you do nothing to save her?"

"What could I have done?"

"You are a man. You could have done something, I am sure. Instead you helped him."

"What could I have done?"

"You could have stopped him."

"If I had refused to obey him, I would have been discharged, and there would have been no one to care for the Elephant."

She shakes her head. "Tom, his Lordship would never allow you to be discharged."

"His Lordship is ill," I say.

"You could have done something," she repeats, and turning her back on me she continues to hang up the cloaths. Among them, a pair of Mr. Singleton's velvet breeches, which dangle, agape, dripping.

JENNY IS PLAYING WITH SOME HAY. She is not hungry, but is amusing herself by tossing lumps of hay into the air, and watching them fall through a band of sun-light.

But, Tom, she begins, you are entirely innocent, are you not?

Yes, I agree, I am innocent.

Mr. Singleton is the guilty one, is he not? He is guilty.

Yes, he is guilty.

Then I do not understand. Why is Susan blaming you?

She blames me, Jenny, because she thinks that I should have stopped him.

How would you have stopped him?

I do not know.

What has happened to Ellie's shoe?

Susan has undertaken to give it to her.

Jenny blows into the hay with her trunk. She draws a heap of hay together and blows it apart. Why will Ellie not tell the truth? she asks. Why does she not accuse Mr. Singleton?

Probably she is afraid. She thinks she will not be believed. People will think she is lying. Not John Finch, but other people, they will assume that she is lying. And it is very probable that she too has been given some money by Mr. Singleton.

Jenny's trunk slips round my neck. Tom, you are entirely innocent, she repeats.

I do not feel entirely innocent. Because I did nothing to save her? No, not for that reason; but because after the attack, when Ellie was lying in my bed in the Elephant House, I wanted to join her. I stood by the bed and looked into her dull face. Her lips moved, her breath came short and warm. I leant over her, I sensed the heat of her body, I drank the heat of her breath. My blood rose. I longed to climb into the bed and, whether she consented or no, to renew the assault which Mr. Singleton had begun. In the swelling darkness I felt like Mr. Singleton, dragging her into the trees, tearing off her cloaths, ignoring her pleas for mercy.

It was the Ooze, Tom; that is all.

Perhaps. Who knows? But then the question comes, what is the difference between him and me? What he did, I, or some black part of my male nature, a part which remains deep in cover, would like to have done. What is the difference? Jenny?

Reluctantly, she lifts her head from her game with the hay.— The difference is plain enough: you did not climb into the bed.

Only because I lacked courage, I answer her, because I feared the consequences. That aside, there is no difference between us.

Tom, it does not matter why you did not climb into the bed. What matters is that you did not climb in. Another difference between you and Mr. Singleton is this. He is the son of Lord Bidborough, and heir to one of England's greatest estates. You are the son of a groom, an Elephant keeper, and heir to nothing.

I remember Susan's words.—I am a man, I tell her. I am a human being.

She gazes at me, expressionless, a pale stalk hanging from the tip of her trunk.—What is a human being?

What is a human being, and what is a brute? Dr. Casey's distinctions have never seemed that clear to me. I wonder to myself: does Jenny believe that she is a human being? Or that I am an Elephant? Sometimes I think one thing, sometimes the other; sometimes I believe she supposes that I am both man and Elephant.

There is a dream which I have had, more than once. In this dream, I am an Elephant in a hot country. I can see my long trunk, I can feel the weight of the tusks. I reach up with my trunk, and latch on to the branch of a tree; I drag it to the ground and stuff its leaves and fruits into my mouth. There are other Elephants near me, including Jenny, also feasting. As we move through the jungles we meet grey monkeys swinging through the trees, and deadly crocodiles lying in the rivers, and lions lurking in the thick grasses. We come to a watering hole, its sides slippery with mud.

With the rest of the herd I wade in, submerging myself and breathing through my trunk. As we clamber out, with Jenny ahead of me, the Ooze burns from my temples, and between my hind legs my long club stiffens and hardens and begins to smoke. Advancing toward Jenny, trumpeting, I curl my trunk along her back. She lumbers forward, her ears flapping. I pursue her, scattering the other Elephants. She breaks into a trot, but I am hard behind, a roaring beast. I drive her into a quiet part of the jungle, hemming her in a green, creeper-walled chamber from which she cannot escape. There she stands, patiently, while I board. When I discharge, it is a bolt of lightning which strikes the sky into flames, and I imagine that she will bear my children, who will be both Elephant and Human, and that they will have the minds of human beings but the bodies of Elephants. Then I wake in the darkness, and lie horrified that my mind should have given birth to such an unnatural story.

July 29th

Today I prepare Jenny to run against Mr. Partridge's thoroughbred. I wash her, and brush her, and I allow her to eat only a little. Over her back I spread a green and claret cloth, his Lordship's colours. She is in a merry mood, but I still do not know whether she will run. Will you run? I ask her.—I expect so, Tom, she says calmly. Even so, I am not sure whether she will run.

At noon, I ride her out of the Elephant House and toward the lime avenue. A large crowd has gathered, for all of his Lordship's servants—gardeners, woodmen, grooms, maids, pages—have been given permission to watch the race. There are cheers and shouts. Among the maids, I notice Fat Ellie. Her face, full and blotchy as the moon, seems to stare at me. Poll is standing at her side.

His Lordship is sat in his bath-chair, in the shade of a lime tree, attended by her Ladyship, Lord and Lady Seely, Miss Singleton, and several other ladies and gentlemen. Mr. Singleton detaches himself from this little contingent. "I am counting on you, Tom Page. How is the Elephant?"—"Very well, Sir," I reply.

It is a warm day. Mr. Partridge has already trotted his horse to the start of the race, by the lake. This horse is a creature thin as a toast-rack, and twitching with nerves; at the mere sight of the Elephant it frets and chafes, and as we draw closer it bucks wildly. Mr. Partridge is wearing spurs, and carrying a heavy whip. He curses the horse, and hauls so hard on the reins that its head is forced up, its eyes widened by fear. I remember Ellie's bulging eyes, forced open by Mr. Singleton.

Over the next couple of minutes the toast-rack becomes more and more agitated. It breaks into a thick sweat; its mouth is bleeding. Mr. Partridge wrenches its head to face the course. "Come; let us begin," he says impatiently. A horn is to be blown by one of the pages, to start the race. He is about to raise it to his lips when Jenny's tail stiffens, and the usual copious stream pours forth; she follows up with a further thudding evacuation, the smell of which is enough to send the horse into a frenzy. The page gives a blast on his horn, and Mr. Partridge digs in his spurs. The horse rears upwards, flings him to the ground, and careers in altogether the wrong direction. Thus Jenny strides triumphant down the lime avenue.

At the end of the course I ride up to his Lordship, in his bath-chair. He struggles to speak to me, but the right side of his mouth is twisted or frozen, and although some sounds come out, I cannot understand them as words. It is painful to watch him struggle so. His feet, which rest on cushions, are bare, and for the first time I see his gouty toe, very red and swollen, and covered in bumps. He is not wearing a wig, and the shadows of the leaves flicker uncertainly on his grey hair. When Jenny, unbidden, stretches out her trunk and takes his hand, his eyes seem to meet mine, and I feel sure that I shall never have as good a master again.

August 10th

The days slip by. The weather is hot and heavy, with no wind. For two evenings now we have heard distant thunder, but there has been no rain. Mr. Sanders has left Easton, while Mr. Church has returned from Horsham and, unlocking at last the secrets of his heart, has proposed marriage to Miss Singleton. She has refused him. There has been general astonishment, but it seems that delay has proved fatal to his chances, her affections having transferred themselves to the person of Mr. Huntly. It matters very little, for his Lordship has had another fit, this more serious than the first. He has been bled and cupped many times, but is no longer able to make any sounds at all; to communicate his wishes, he can flutter one of his hands, no more. He lies a-bed, eyes open, staring at the flies on the ceiling, while the maids tip-toe past his bed-chamber, and talk in whispers. The doctors come and go.

The lake is a glass; the air ripples in the heat. The park is pale as paper. The deer stay in the shade, their little tails twitching. In the fields beyond the park the farmers will be soon beginning the harvest; they will be harvesting, too, in the fields of Northamptonshire, around Langley. When shall I see Timothy again?

I find Susan. I ask whether she may be able to do me a small favour. "Why, it will depend on the favour," she says, with a quick smile, whereupon I tell her that there is a letter on the Toad's desk, with a crimson seal, that I am very anxious to see. "A letter about what?"—"The Elephant's brother."—"A brother? O—you mean another Elephant. And you would like me to steal the letter? What will I have in return?" I offer her three guineas, and she laughs. "Three guineas!"

I laugh too. "Tom," she says, "I will do it for a kiss." So I give her a kiss, and she says that she will look for the letter tonight. I thank her very much.

Evening. More thunder. The storm draws closer, the sky darkens with high, towering clouds. As Jenny and I wait in the Elephant House she grows restless. It is only thunder, I tell her. It will not hurt you—I do not like thunder, she says, when will Susan have the letter?—Not yet, not yet. It is too early. There is another clap of thunder, and as it dies away I see from her expression that she is listening. What is it?—Someone is coming. I can hear nothing, but the hearing of Elephants is much more acute than that of humans. Jenny, are you certain?—I am certain, Tom. Someone is coming. I listen: perhaps Susan has the letter already.

It is Mr. Singleton. If I am startled to see him, I am much more alarmed at the sight of little Alice King by his side. He greets me: "Ah, Tom, you know Alice, I am sure. We have come for a ride on the Elephant."—"Sir, if you please," Alice says, "I should be getting back home, it is late, my father will be wondering where I am."—"Well then," he replies, "the Elephant will carry you home. Tom, put on the *howdar*, if you will." Her eyes watch him doubtfully. "I assure you, Alice, there is nothing to fear. You will enjoy a ride on the *howdar*. You will be like a beautiful Indian princess. Is that not so, Tom?"

I say nothing, but at the thought that I am again destined to serve as his accomplice a wave of abhorrence rises within me. As I strap on the *howdar* I think of Susan: *You could have done something*. I tighten the girth and glance at Jenny. What should I do?—You must stop him, she says.—How?—I do not know. You must do something.

They climb aboard. I do not strap on the ladder, but Mr Singleton notices. "Tom, you have forgot the ladder."—"Yes, Sir."

Scarcely have we left the yard before he remarks that it is a shame to have such a short ride, would she not like to see the Obelisk? "I would, Sir, but my parents will be anxious," she answers. "I would prefer to go home, Sir, if it's the same to you." He replies in a pleasant voice that it is not all the same to him; that, when he has such a beautiful companion, with such perfect looks, the looks of an Indian princess, he can on no account agree to take her straight home, it would be a sin against Nature. "Have you ever heard the story of the Princess and the Tyger?"

"No, Sir," says she.

"Well, I shall tell you it, if you like. It is a story from the Indies. Steer for the temple, Tom. Well, the Princess, who was the most beautiful Princess in the whole of the Indies, was walking alone one day, through the jungles—you know what a jungle is? it is an Indian word for a thick forest—when she met a ferocious Tyger. It was the biggest Tyger that she had ever seen, and it sprang out and roared at her. She turned to run—however, the Tyger could run much faster than the Princess, and soon he caught her. He was about to eat her, for he was very hungry, when he understood how beautiful she was, and indeed he felt himself falling in love with her. He agreed not to kill her, on condition that she would kiss him, ten times, as he directed. The Princess was a little frightened, but thought to herself, if I do not kiss him, what will happen? I will be killed and eaten. So she said: 'Where do I kiss you first?'—'Why, on the cheek,' said the Tyger, and she kissed him on his whiskery cheek. Then she asked where she should kiss him next, and he told her, on the mouth, and she kissed him on the mouth. What do you think of the story? How do you think it ends?"

"I do not know, Sir. How did they understand each other?"

"The Tyger could speak human, I suppose," he answers, a trifle impatiently. "Or the Princess could speak Tyger. It is of no great importance. The fact is, they did indeed understand each other very well, just as you understand me, you know. But, let us pretend," he continues, "that you are the Princess, and I am the Tyger, and that I have caught you, like so"—turning my head, I see him lean toward her, putting a hand round her waist—"and am about to eat you up. So you must kiss me, is that agreed, my pretty one, starting with the cheek." He offers her his cheek, which she kisses. "And now on the lips, if you please."

"I should prefer not to, Sir."

"Why, it is merely a make-believe. And it will help us to discover how the story ends—though I am sure that it will end with the Princess falling in love with the Tyger. Is that not how all the best stories end? D-v-l take it, Tom—where are we going? Did you not hear me? Steer for the temple."

"Sir," I say, "I think it may be coming on to rain." This is true enough: the thunder has become louder and more persistent.

"Well then," he replies, "the temple will be an excellent place in which to shelter."

I ignore him. I press hard on Jenny's head, ordering her to go faster; she responds at once, putting on her best pace. "What the d-v-l! Are you deaf? I tell you, steer for the temple!" He curses me, and strikes out several times, but at the speed we are travelling there is little he can do. Alice clings to the sides of the *howdar* like a passenger in a rough sea, while Mr. Singleton continues to shout and rant. "Stop the Elephant! D—n you! If you do not stop you will be discharged!"

We are rushing along the drive and through the park gates. Ahead of us lies the safety of Easton village.

I stop the Elephant by Alice's little cottage and jump down. Her father, Robert, is by the door; I lift Alice down and hand her into his safe keeping. Mr. Singleton has also dismounted. He faces me. "Give me that thing—I shall ride this beast back myself." He reaches for the *ankus*, which is as usual hanging on a leather string round my neck. "Let me have that."—"Sir, I cannot allow you to have it."—"Indeed?" he says with a sneer, and grabs it so hard that the string snaps. With a back-stroke he flings it into my face, catching my nose and knocking me to the ground. "I shall see you discharged in the morning. I am sure we shall have no difficulty in finding another Elephant keeper."

So saying, he clambers on to the *howdar* and brings the *ankus* down on Jenny's skull like a hammer. "Walk, d—n you!" She shakes her head. "Walk! Walk!" He hammers furiously. On a sudden, she strides away.

I shout at Robert to keep Alice within doors, and then I run after Jenny and Mr. Singleton. Darkness has fallen, and in the gloom I soon lose sight of them. When I arrive at the Elephant House, I find it empty. My nose is strangely benumbed; I touch it with my fingers and feel warm blood and broken bone. I stand under the arch-way, reflecting on my fate. In the morning I will be summoned to Mr. Bridge's room, and discharged from his Lordship's service. I will be parted from Jenny, and she will be left alone. I will never see her again. Our story is at an end.

By now the storm is very nearly overhead and the rain has begun to fall. The lightning continues, and as each flash holds the park in a blue glare, my eyes travel from the temple to the lake, and along the lime avenue, and back and forth. Then the flash fades, and the thunder breaks. In the space between two of these thunder-claps I seem to hear a shrill, high-pitched trumpeting sound, very like a scream, not unlike the angry roars that Timothy sometimes used to make when he had the Ooze. I listen, staring in the dark. The rain is falling in a torrent. A second scream pierces the night, and judging that it comes from somewhere near the temple, I start in that direction. Yet my ears have deceived me, for when I reach the temple neither Jenny nor Mr. Singleton is there. Where, I wonder, has he taken her? Or where has she taken him?

I run back to the Elephant House. My nose has now begun to sing with pain; I walk up and down, trying to compose myself, trying to quell my anxiety. The minutes pass; the storm is moving on, leaving behind a heavy darkness; I hear nothing. Again, I set out to find her. I walk down the lime avenue to the Obelisk; I walk back, calling her name. Then I see her standing in long grass, a black shape by the edge of the lake. At my approach, she raises her head. Although the *howdar* is still on her back, there is no sign of Mr. Singleton. Her trunk curls round my shoulder, and breathes against my ear. "Where is he?" I ask. "What has happened?" Her eyes are hollows of darkness. "Jenny," I repeat. "Where is he? Has he gone? Let us go back to the Elephant House."

Instead, she uses her trunk to coax me round the lake. I let her lead, and follow until she stops. We are near the Cascade. Her head hangs, and her entire body seems to tremble. She will not take another step. "What is it? Jenny?" Her trunk nudges me onward. I am beginning to guess, and yet, even so, I do not see Mr. Singleton until I stumble upon him. He is half-way down the slope which leads to the pool. In the darkness, all I can make out are indistinct patches of pale light marked by his cravat and breeches. "Sir? Mr. Singleton?" He makes no sound, or none I can hear above the roar of the water. We are so close as to be within range of the drifting spray. Bending down, stretching out an uncertain hand to the patch of dark above the cravat, my fingers close upon something as soft and wet as clay, in the form of his nose, or rather, the two nostrils. From this touch I recoil, before forcing myself to feel again, whereupon I touch his lips, and my fingers, brushing against and moving the bottom lip, seem to enter his mouth. My fingers are already sticky with my own blood, but this circumstance fills me with more terror than I can easily describe, for even as a boy I never liked to touch dead things, out of a superstitious fear that, in some strange manner, that which killed them might kill me. The body of a murdered man would bleed afresh if it were approached by the murderer, or so my mother used to say. While I dread Mr. Singleton in the state of death, I dread even more the thought that at any moment he may stir and spring to life, reaching up with his arms and pulling me upon him in a deadly embrace.

I take his boots and drag him some way up the slope, after which I unbutton his shirt and slide a hand inside, laying it flat on his chest. The skin is still warm, and I think that I feel the flutter of a heart-beat; but here I am mistaken, for it is my own heart beating through my hand. "Jenny," I say. "What happened? Did you kill him? Did he fall off or did you kill him?"

Her ears are wide, her face an inky blot. She will not reply, and yet I seem to know how Mr. Singleton died: either he fell

off, or she knocked him off with her trunk, and as he lay on the
ground, she knelt and crushed his chest. Is that not how Elephants
execute condemned men in the Indies? But now Jenny coils her
trunk round my body, swings me through the night air and places
me on the back of her neck. Her trunk presents me with the cold
metal of the *ankus,* which must have been lying somewhere in the
grass. What does this mean? That she accepts my right to own the
ankus, to be her keeper? Or that she is admitting to the murder
and asking for punishment?

Whatever the reason, she is striding away, not back to the Elephant House, but past the pine-wood and on to the Obelisk. The
air pours by, I have never known her move at such a speed. Once
we reach the Obelisk, she continues at the same headlong pace
into the darkness of the woods.

The deeper we go, the deeper the darkness grows. As we crash
through the trees it is all I can do to stay on her neck, for she pays
no heed to branches. I shout at her to stop, but she does not hear,
and I have to shout again and again before she draws to a halt.
Her body heaves beneath me. "Jenny, where are we going?" She
charges on.

The woods thin. She slows. She finds a winding track which
brings us into pale meadows. The heavens have cleared, the sky is
a fisherman's net of stars holed by black clouds. A herd of sleeping
cows rises in panic and rushes through a sudden blast of moon, and
the same moon lights the silver body of a river, edged by willows.
Jenny topples down its crumbling banks, enters its molten body,
and joins the current, following each twist and curve. Sometimes
it narrows, and we are wading through deep pools; sometimes it
grows broader, and we splash over tongues of gleaming shingle.
Again I ask her where we are going, and now she replies that she
does not know. Soon, however, I hear a long murmuring sound,

something like the wind in the pines, and the air begins to smell fresh and salty. We are on a pale shore, sprinkled with frills of seaweed. Drifts of shells crack under Jenny's feet.

I dismount. At the land's edge the waves come in and break, one after the other; lines of dark flowers opening into a sudden white blossom, bursting into cascades of petals which slide to our feet, dark and white, and vanish.

Jenny waves her trunk, questing. "Tom, what lake is this?"

"This is not a lake, but the sea."

"What is the sea?"

What is the sea? Is the sea a strange kind of land in flux? Or is the land a kind of sea that has set like wax?

"It is a house for fishes and eels," I answer. "As the land is a house for men and Elephants."

"I remember this smell," she says. "It was on the ship that brought me and Timothy to this country."

Amid the sounds of the breaking waves I hear a cry, a wail that fades into nothing; it seems to come from inside my head. We are alone, Jenny and Tom, the Elephant and her keeper, with the land behind us and the sea in front. We are the only beings in the world, Man and Elephant. Two misshapen creatures, with arms, legs, appendages, prottuberances.

"Do you remember the voyage?" I ask.

"O, Tom, it was dark and terrible, and endless. It was full of fear. I cannot talk about it."

"Yet you endured."

"I endured by contracting my being into a hard knot. I endured by holding to my memory of what life had been like before."

A crab scuttles over the dim silk of the sand. A third creature, no more fantastical than the other two.

"What was it like before? What do you remember?"

She does not answer.

The moon has withdrawn behind a cloud. Cold water swirls round my ankles, fingering. I feel her great, breathing body at my side.

"Shall we go back?" I ask her.

"To Easton?"

"To the Indies. If we walk along the coast, we shall eventually reach Portsmouth, where there are plenty of ships. I would take care of you on the voyage."

She again makes no reply; I turn to face her.

"Jenny, it would not be like the last time, with the sailors. I would not allow it—we would be together. We would endure together."

"We would die together."

"We would not die. Jenny, we would not die! We would endure! And then, then—!"

She regards me, blinking slowly. Criss-crossed by wrinkles, her face is a book of doubts. "We cannot simply leave. You forget, Tom. You forget that I am owned. I am not a free being, but the property of his Lordship. We would be apprehended, and you would be charged with stealing me. What is the penalty for stealing an Elephant?"

The gallows. Transportation for life. Imprisonment. I turn to the ocean. The moon shines on the black water.

"We cannot stay on this beach for ever."

"We shall return to Easton," she says.

"If we return to Easton, I shall be charged with killing Mr. Singleton."

"Not at all, Tom. Why will you be suspected? Mr. Singleton died of an unfortunate accident."

I cannot think. My entire face feels as though it has been torn apart. My nose scarcely exists as a nose.

"Jenny, what shall we do?"

"We shall return to Easton," she repeats, very firmly. "We shall return to Easton, and perhaps we will be able to go to Lord Luttershall."

At these words I am suddenly glad. "Yes, we will go to Lord Luttershall's, and see Timothy again, and everything will be all right."

I kneel to wash my bloody face. As I lean forward, cupping the sea in my hands, the *ankus* dangles from my neck, and since I never liked the thing, I slip it off and throw it away.

Slowly we return to Easton. The woods are dank and heavy with moisture. We reach the Obelisk; the park is still dark, but the sky has begun to lighten. The last owls are hooting their farewells to the night, a redbreast twitters the first notes of the day.

A dew has fallen; I think of the dead man, wet with dew and spray, lying in the thunder of the Cascade. Jenny is right: there is no reason for anyone ever to know the truth of his death. He fell from the Elephant, that will be enough.

At the Elephant House, a small figure is waiting in the yard: Susan.

"Where have you been?" she cries. "Tom? O, Tom, Tom, what has happened to your face?"

"A branch."

"A branch?" She puts a hand to her mouth. "Your nose—your cheek—it is ripped open—it is horrible—horrible!"

"It was a branch, Susan, a hawthorn branch. It will mend."

"I have been waiting for you, Tom. I have been waiting here all night, not knowing where you were. Where have you been? I have the letter. If you read it now, I will take it back before Mr. Bridge wakes."

"Have you read it?"

"I have looked at it. The seal was already broken."

"And?"

She hesitates. In that hesitation I feel a pang of fear.

"Tom, you must read it yourself."

She hands me the letter. In the yard it is too dark, but I take it through the arch-way, and read in the light of dawn.

My Lord,

I am grateful to you for your letter and for your best wishes for my health and that of my wife. You inquire about the Elephant which came here from the Earl of Ancaster's estate at Grimsthorpe in Lincolnshire. This unhappy beast reached Langley in the Spring of 1772, and was placed in a coach-house, which had been prepared for its reception. Here it was attended by two grooms, whom I had appointed to care for its needs, and who did their best to make it comfortable; yet, from the start, despite the assurances which I had received concerning its good nature, it displayed an uncertain and vicious temper, trumpeting loudly, spurning all overtures of friendship, and threatening violence to any who approached closely. Though its legs were tightly manacled, it was judged too dangerous to be allowed out of its quarters; indeed, no one durst enter its quarters for fear of being attacked; and at times it would charge the walls of its enclosure, striking them with colossal force, recoiling with its brains dazed. I myself witnessed these charges, and can vouch for the ferocity of its behaviour. There was then a period in which, though its manner remained sullen, it grew calmer; which encouraged the grooms to renew their overtures. I had been assured that it had been broken to ride, but I fear that this must have been incorrect, for when one of the grooms attempted to mount the creature, lowering himself on to its back from the beams of the coach-house, it flew into a rage and bucked like a wild bull, and had the man not been sup-

ported by a harness, there can be little doubt that he would have lost his life. For their own safety, the grooms resolved to blind-fold the Elephant, something which I understand they achieved only at great hazard, and after numerous attempts, by stupefying it with strong liquor. However, once the Elephant had recovered its senses, it swiftly removed the blind-fold with its trunk. I believe that some discussion took place among the grooms, as to whether its trunk should be trussed, until they understood that this would have left it unable to feed itself. Orders were given for the making of a large leather hood. The Elephant having been given a fresh quantity of liquor, this hood was slipped over its head, and secured round the neck. Frustrated by its inability to remove the hood, and finding itself in a perpetual darkness, the animal fell into a condition of listless despair, occasionally reviving enough to renew its attempts to beat out its brains. It refused to eat, contemptuously tossing aside the hay which it was offered. I was at this point consulted. Seeing the wretched condition of the animal, and of its quarters, which were by then deep in ordure, I resolved that the hood should be removed. My hope was that the Elephant would respond with gratitude. This was, I regret to say, a fond ambition, for as soon as its sight was restored it seized hold of one of the beams of the coach-house and, with an incredible display of strength, pulled down the roof; following which, it broke down the door and, dragging its manacles, ran screaming through the grounds, to the general terror. A large body of men, armed with muskets, swords, and pitch-forks, was assembled in order to capture the Elephant. These men courageously strove to force the creature back to its quarters, but its temper was so high and its behaviour so alarming that they succeeded only in driving it further away. They finally surrounded it near the chapel; but when the Elephant understood that its liberty was threatened, it

made a charge—whereupon one of the men, bravely standing his
ground, used his hanger to lop off the bottom part of the trunk.
At this, the animal gave a terrible groaning cry, which is hard
to describe, save to say that it was almost human in its quality.
It shook what remained of its trunk, scattering showers of blood,
and as an act of mercy, for it was greatly distressed, I gave orders
for it to be shot. Rifles were promptly fetched from the house,
while the Elephant was held at bay. The first ball, which was
fired into a crease below the creature's blade-bone, in an attempt
to find its heart, seemed to make no significant impression; nor
did a second and third, which were fired into the same spot. At
the fourth, however, the creature stood still, as if stunned by some
internal blow, before sinking slowly to its haunches; yet it contin-
ued to hold up its head, and to my astonishment its eyes seemed
to weep tears of pain or sorrow, which trickled down its cheeks.
Eleven further balls were discharged into its skull before, with a
last groan, it toppled to its side, and expired. In attempting to
account for the Elephant's behaviour, I had its body anatomised
by Mr. Edward Deacon, surgeon, of Conduit Street, London; as
a result of which, two circumstances came to light, first, that the
shorter of the tusks was infected at its base with a large and puru-
lent Abscess; in other words, the creature was suffering from the
Tooth-ache, which must have caused it great pain; and, second,
that the Brain itself was infected, for the Glands to the front of the
skull were distended to the size of cannon-balls, and flooded with
liquid. According to an account given by the grooms, this liquid
gushed incessantly from the creature's lower Temples during the
last days of its life. Whether these facts provide more than a par-
tial explanation for the Elephant's violent actions, I cannot say; I
fear that its ingrained nature was so set against humankind that
it stood no chance of Redemption, but this may be to do the animal

*an injustice. The carcass was buried in the grounds of the chapel.
The skull (somewhat damaged) I still have, along with the tusks,
one measuring twenty-two and the other eighteen inches.*

*I greatly regret that I have had to render your Lordship such
a sorry tale; however, I am glad to learn that your Elephant is
well . . .*

I can read no further. I stumble back into the yard, and hand
the letter to Susan, who says something, I forget what. My mind
is full of uncontrolled pictures. The blindfold, the hood, the slash
of the sword, the spray of blood. O Timothy, my Timothy, how
could they do this to you? Why did it happen? Why was I not
there to protect you? As I fall weeping to the ground, I feel the
pressure of Jenny's leg against my arms. "It will be all right, Tom,"
she says, loud and clear, "it will be all right."

I look up, astonished; she is watching me with her sad, sagging
eyes. "It is not all right," I say, "it is not all right, it is all wrong, it
can never be right."—"No," she says, speaking even more clearly,
as clearly as any human being ever spoke, "believe me, Tom, trust
me—it will be all right." And she bows her head, and lays her
heavy trunk in my lap.

November 2nd

For more than a week it has been raining. The leaves have fallen
from the limes; they lie grey and blackening below the bare
branches. The park is a sponge. A solitary heron hunches by the

lake, while a stag gives a distant bellow. I put my hat on my head and hurry from the Elephant House to the stables.

John Finch is sat on a bench in one of the stables. He is polishing a stirrup-iron with a soft cloth. He looks weary, but he has not been discharged, or not yet. "You will be leaving soon," he says. "Tomorrow," I tell him, taking off my hat, and he nods. "Where is it you are going?"—"Worcestershire."

A few weeks ago, this stable would have held his Lordship's horse, but it has been sold, as have several more horses. Indeed, lately there have been rumours that the entire estate may be sold. Whether this is so, no one knows, not even Mr. Bridge. Neither her Ladyship nor Miss Singleton has been seen at Easton since the day after his Lordship's funeral, when they left for London.

I might ask John Finch if he has heard anything about the future of the estate, but from his expression I sense that he would prefer not to talk about the future. I am of the same mind. It is easier to sit in a dry stable, to polish bits and stirrup-irons, to rub oil into saddles and bridles, to pretend that everything will go on as it has always gone on. His Lordship is not dead, we are not going to Worcestershire, Timothy is well, my nose is as perfect as it ever was. No, it is not perfect, but it is improving steadily; that is what I tell anyone who asks. In truth, the nose continues to trouble me; it throbs and burns, and fluid dribbles from the base, and, if I sneeze, pain shoots through my entire body. I breathe through my mouth. Some parts of the skin on the nose remain dead to touch, and I have scarcely any sense of smell; while this last may indeed improve, the nose will never recover its former appearance. It hangs to one side of my face like a red trunk with a gaping eye, and strangers start at the sight of it, and seem either frightened, or fascinated. I am lucky not to have been blinded, for the hook of the *ankus* missed my right eye by a mere half inch.

Finch knows, I am sure—all the servants seem to know—that my nose was injured not by a hawthorn branch, but by a blow from Mr. Singleton. I suspect that, in addition, he guesses Mr. Singleton's death to be far from a simple accident, a man falling from an Elephant on a dark night; but he has never asked me directly. Now, on my last day at Easton, in the quiet of the stable, I am tempted to tell him the truth. This temptation is easily resisted, however. It is not that I do not trust Finch to keep a secret, for he has always seemed to me a very private man, but that I myself do not know the truth with complete certainty. No one save Jenny knows, and she refuses to tell me, although I have asked her often enough. "Tom, why does it matter?" she says quietly. "I have forgotten." I do not believe her, of course. How can she have forgotten that night?

"There is pleasant country in Worcestershire?" John Finch inquires.

"I hope so. I have never been there."

"What do you know of your new master?"

"Mr. Davies? He is a timber merchant. I know nothing else."

Finch glances up from his polishing. "A timber merchant?"

"Yes."

"Why does a timber merchant want an Elephant? To haul timber?"

"I do not know."

His eyes study me. "Well," says he, "I must wish you luck."

"Thank you."

I leave him to his work, and walk toward the servants' quarters, with the intention of saying farewell to Susan and the other maids. A thrush lands before me, a snail in its beak; I watch as it hops to a stone, and hammers the shell into pieces.

Beyond the terrace I see Argos, staring along the drive, waiting for his master. His tail is down. Poor Argos; since the death of his Lordship he has been a lost soul, a shadow without its body. I call to him, "Argos? Argos?" and his head jerks in my direction, and jerks away. When I walk up and put an arm round him—his coat is wet, he has been here a while—he ignores me entirely. I am the wrong man. I am not his Lordship. Even so, I am happy to keep him company, to wait by his side. "Argos, you are a good dog," I say. His Lordship once talked of his hope that there would be dogs in heaven. Perhaps his Lordship is waiting for Argos, just as Argos is waiting for his Lordship.

As I stand here, I think of the three happy years that Jenny and I have spent at Easton. I think of the park, the lake, and the Elephant House, which we will be leaving tomorrow at dawn; and indeed, it feels as though we have already left this paradise, that the beauties of Easton lie somewhere in our pasts, that we are hauling cart-loads of timber through the muddy lanes of Worcestershire. I also think of Gulliver, who hoped to stay for ever in the Land of the Houyhnhnms, and found himself banished. Yet I cannot remember why he was banished. Had he committed some crime, or was there some other reason? I stand in the rain, failing to remember, facing the empty drive, with the dog pressed against my leg. The rain is not heavy; it falls softly, in sheets of tissue. I walk on, to the servants' quarters.

Part III

London, 1793

1

The monkie sits, legs crossed, smoking his pipe, eyes closed in ecstasy as the fumes intoxicate his brain; the bear rests on his haunches and scratches fleas. Jenny stands and watches, blinking slowly, thinking—though what she thinks of her life here, I do not know. I have asked her many times; she will not say. That is, she will not give me what I believe to be a true answer. What she always says is that we are here, that there is nowhere else that we can go, since she, like the other animals, is owned by Mr. Cross.

"What if you were not owned by Mr. Cross?"

"Tom, there is no prospect of anyone buying me."

"But what if the Menagery were to shut down?"

This is far from unlikely. Mr. Cross has made it clear, upon any number of occasions, that the Menagery is a commercial affair and that, if it does not make enough money to cover its costs, it will be brought to an end. In which case, she will be sold again, if someone is willing to buy her.

She says, "Tom, if I am sold to someone else, then I am sold to someone else. If it happens, it happens. If not, not. There are many possibilities."

We have now been six years with Cross's Famous Menagery. For the first, it was located at Gravesend; for the next, in St. Albans; for the last four, in London. During these years, many animals in the Menagery have died, for various reasons which I will not set out here, except to say that it does not seem to suit every species of animal to be kept in close confinement and put on display for twelve hours every day. Among these animals are a zebra, a hyena, an eagle, a giraffe, a porcupine, and a series of man-eating lions, since Mr. Cross holds that, in order to draw in the crowds, a proper Menagery must have a ferocious lion, for preference, one that roars loudly. When a lion dies, he engages some merchant to procure him another.

The lion at present in the Menagery does not roar, to Mr. Cross's chagrin. The merchant told him that he was a Roarer, and a Man-Eater; however, he is, or has become, a sad, owl-faced creature, with hollow cheeks and staring eyes, and a mangy, thread-bare coat. Nonetheless, a notice is displayed, which reads: *Man-Eating Lion. Beware,* and the wall at the back of the cage is covered with the painting of a bloody-jawed lion, standing over the body of its unfortunate victim. People sometimes inquire of me, or Mr. Scott, how many humans the Man-Eater has eaten. Dozens, we reply. Hundreds. In truth, we do not know whether he has ever tasted human flesh. Perhaps, years ago, in another country, in another life. His present diet consists, for the most part, of horse bones, which he gnaws moaning, on account of his rotten teeth. He will not last many weeks more.

Mr. Cross likes every creature in the Menagery to have a history. The small brown bear, which lives in the cage next to the Man-Eater, is said to have been found in a mountainous cave in Russia, in confirmation of which the wall painting has Bruin lurking in a gloomy cave, among the snow-clad peaks. The next cage—Pray, Sir, let me walk you this way—contains a large, striped snake, known as the Prince of Wales, supposedly from the swamps of Madagascar. Whatever it may do in the Madagascan swamps, here it sleeps much of the time, waking only to eat dead rats and live mice; the latter, even after having been swallowed, may be seen struggling within its digestive coils. We then come upon the little monkie, Stephen, with a face like that of a human child, but horribly wrinkled in anxiety. He mops and mows, and attempts to hide from the publick gaze by burying his face in his hands. His right hand is a claw; no one knows why, but Mr. Cross has devised for him a complicated tale in which he was rescued at sea, being the sole survivor from a Spanish privateer loaded with treasure, and there, Sir, behold the scene itself, in which he survives on the vast ocean, clinging to a single spar among the billows.

Last of all, we encounter Jenny, whom Mr. Cross has given the name of "The Empress." The notice outside her cage reads: *Formerly owned by various members of the English nobility, The Empress descends from a line of Royal Elephants. She began her life a hundred and fifty years ago in the court of an Indian prince, whom she often carried on tyger-hunting expeditions, displaying great bravery. She was captured after a long battle and brought to Europe . . .* The painting shews her deep in the Indian jungles, the prince seated on her back in a golden throne, and a ferocious, snarling Bengal tyger at her feet.

When I protested to Mr. Cross that very little of this was true, he smiled at my innocence. "You think that we should say that she is two hundred years old? Tom, people like stories. So long as the stories are possible, it does not matter whether they are true or false."

Her true history is that she is about thirty-two years of age, and has spent much of that time in England. Her first owner was Mr. Harrington, of Somerset, who sold her to Lord Bidborough, of Easton, Sussex; after his death she was sold to Mr. Davies of Worcester, who found the cost of her maintenance too great to bear and was therefore obliged to sell her to Mr. Hockaday of Monmouth; he, too, could not bear the expense, and sold her to Sir John Fortescue of Northampton, who killed himself after losing his fortunes in a wild speculation. It was after this that she was bought by Mr. Gilbert Cross for his Famous Menagery.

My fellow keeper at the Menagery is Mr. Sam Scott. We share lodgings above a barber's in White Horse Yard, off Drury Lane; he sleeps there one night, while I stay at the Menagery, or the other way round. We do not divide the animals up between us, but it is understood that Jenny is my particular responsibility.

The Menagery is situated in the Strand, to the north of the river. It opens at ten o'clock every morning, and remains open until ten o'clock at night. We are at our busiest on Sunday after-noons, though we are not nearly as busy as we once were. Then, everyone was eager to see the animals, and fashionable ladies and gentlemen waited in a line which stretched as far as Catherine Street. The novelty has worn off, however, and there are entire afternoons now-a-days when we may have only ten or twenty visi-tors. Lately, to persuade more people to pay their shilling apiece for the privilege of entering, Mr. Cross hired a fire-eater. He was a Negro. Long tongues of flame poured from his mouth, and his skin glistened like a black pond. Except for the snake, all the ani-mals were frightened, especially Stephen, who shrank back cower-ing and gibbering, an arm over his eyes, a most pathetick sight.

This ruse did not succeed in drawing a crowd. The truth is that, in a restless city, we no longer excite much curiosity, we are a stale attraction.

"Do you think," I ask Mr. Scott, "that the Menagery is certain to close?"

"Most likely," he answers, without the least visible concern, and puffing his pipe. Mr. Scott is a great lover of tobacco, holding (like many folk) that it serves as a defence against the infections that spread through the city; for which reason, out of prudence, I too now smoke a pipe.

In the first few weeks of living here, I was so anxious that I scarcely ever left Jenny's side. However, at the urging of Mr. Scott, who undertook to watch over the Elephant during my absence, I put on my coat and ventured further into the city. In my country imagination, I had formed two pictures of London: one, consisting of elegant buildings and wide, sunlit streets, full of clubs and coffee-houses in which gentlemen discussed weighty affairs of state; the other, consisting of taverns, whore-houses, and dark alleys inhabited by thieves and murderers. These pictures are true enough; what I had not imagined, what I soon discovered, was that the city has many other pictures. I had not imagined that, the streets being paved, there would be a perpetual din of iron wheels, continuing long into the night; nor had I imagined the hourly calls of the watch-men, which serve no obvious purpose except to wreck the smooth passage of sleep; nor the noxious air, which gives me a constant cough and dry throat; nor the stenches which rise and attack the senses during the heat of summer; nor the dark, murky fogs of winter which steal silently up the river and settle on the city for days, turning noon to the semblance of dusk, and bringing fevers and agues. Nor had I imagined that there could be such vast numbers of people, hurrying this way and that, each engaged upon his or her own secret business. Often, I would do no more than stand on some street corner and watch the bustle in a kind of open-mouthed amazement, wondering where such a person was going, where he came from, what his affairs were. Every man and woman seemed the embodiment of a walking story, in which only a few sentences, or words, were visible, the rest hidden in a peculiar kind of fog; while snatches of conversation, floating to my ears, intrigued me so much that, more than once, I followed in a vain attempt to hear more.

This daze was complicated by fear: not so much the fear of being set upon and robbed, or of being pick-pocketed, though that did frighten me enough to make me walk about with my hands stuck in my pockets, as the fear of losing my way in the endless streets. In the summer months, as often as not, I would go to St. James Park, or across the river to the Vauxhall Gardens, where the temples and groves and bowers reminded me of Easton; indeed, every leaf on every tree, and every blade of grass, seemed a friend. I remember hearing how, not many years ago, there was a nightingale which sang at Vauxhall, every summer's night, from the thickness of a bush along the Grand Walk. This bird, or, rather, the song of this bird, became famous; people came from far and wide to hear its music, which began without fail as twilight fell and continued long into the night. Courting couples, in particular, would stand and listen, entranced. When I heard this tale, I was thrilled at the thought of such a bird making its home in the city, which, but for caged larks and gold-finches, is mainly populated by hordes of thieving, chattering sparrows, and as I strolled down the Grand Walk I would wonder whether it was in this or that bush that the bird had sung, and tell myself that, if a nightingale once lived here, then a nightingale might live here again. A fond idea: for soon I learnt, from Mr. Scott, that the nightingale was a man, skilled at imitating the bird's song, who had been hired by the proprietor of the Gardens to lurk in a bush and attract visitors, each one paying his or her shilling, in the same way that Mr. Cross had hired the fire-eater. However, this story puzzled me. Was it truly possible that people believed that they were hearing a nightingale?

Mr. Scott, who was packing his pipe, a matter over which he takes a great deal of care, did not answer for a moment. "It's a nice question," he said at last. "I grant you, it would seem easier to have put a cage-bird in there, if it could have been prevailed upon to sing every night. They sing well enough in captivity, I believe. Still, maybe a man was thought to be more reliable."

"But, surely," I replied, sticking to my point, "no one was truly deceived. No one could imitate a nightingale!"

"It may be that some folk were truly deceived, and it may be that some were not."

"But there the man was, piping and whistling away! Those who were not deceived, or who suspected that it was not a nightingale, which must have been most people, surely—why did they not look into the bush, and discover the deception?"

Mr. Scott struck a flint and lit his pipe. "Ah, well, there, you see, I don't know; but I would guess that a second man was employed, supposedly to protect the nightingale from being disturbed, but really to prevent people from inquiring into the truth. But, probably, Tom, they wanted to be deceived."

This startled me. "Why?"

"If their minds were on the business of courtship, they might prefer to believe that it was a true nightingale."

"But, if they wanted to be deceived, if they knew that they wanted to be deceived, they must have known that they were being deceived, and therefore they could not have been deceived."

"Yet they were, it seems." He took a puff on his pipe. "Now, I don't go to the play-house, it is of no interest to me, but people do go, all the time. Now, if they're watching something happen on the stage, such as a man being killed, do they believe that he is truly being killed? I'd say not. They allow themselves to be deceived into believing that he has been killed, though they must know that he is still alive, like you or me. Same with the nightingale. They believe it and they don't believe it, at the same time." Another puff. "Would you say that most people who visit the Menagery truly believe our little monkie survived a ship-wreck?"

During the winter, the Gardens are closed, but in those early days I drew comfort from the river, imagining how the water that flowed under my eyes had once flowed through fields, and below the outstretched arms of willows. One such day, an evening, after walking along the Strand to the Devil Tavern at Temple Bar, I heard a familiar sound and, looking up, saw a party of duck flying high, following the river's course to the west. The sun had set, but fiery fragments still glowed like fading embers along the breadth of the sky, into which the duck were flying in the shape of a V, and their faint calls were such music to my ears, I can scarcely begin to describe the emotions that passed through my mind. I watched until the duck were specks, or less than specks; and long after they were gone, my imagination pursued them through the night, until I seemed to see them circle and bank, and wheel, above the calm circle of a moon-lit pond. This pond was not any pond, but one which I had known some twenty years before in Somersetshire, a pond which was indeed frequented by duck, and in which the Elephants had sometimes bathed, when I worked at Harrington Hall; there, with a series of gentle splashes, I let them come to rest on the gleaming, shivering, stilling water. It was probably a different evening, though in my memory it seems the same, when I stood at the same spot by the river. The tide was low, exposing the thick slime of the river's banks, along which some women were scavenging for fire-wood or other valuables. Among them, a couple of rats skipped and scurried; they have no fear of humans. On the river itself, a broad-bottomed boat was being slowly rowed against the current, so that it remained in the same spot, while a boatman probed the bed with his long, hooked pole. After some minutes, the rower shipped his oars, allowing the boat to move a few feet downstream, where the man with the pole tried again. There are many craft that ply up and down the river, and though I had probably seen such boats before, I had never paid them any attention, or bothered to ask myself what they were doing. Now, however, the man with the pole gave a cry, and, drawing a dark shape from the waters, hauled it aboard. At this, a man standing near me turned to his neighbour and said, "That's the third this week."

I watched as the boat made for the wooden jetty at Temple Bar. It tied up to one of the jetty's thin legs, exposed by the low tide. The glistening body, lain on the pebbles, seemed not quite human, as though it might have been that of a monkie, or a seal, or not a body at all, until I made out the thick hair, and the dangled arm.

This fishing for the dead, as I have since learnt, is a regular occupation. Bodies of men, women, sometimes of little babes, are dragged from the river's black depths; occasionally, I am told, a woman is drawn up with her babe still held to her breast. Ten corpses were discovered last month; eight, the month before; thirteen, the month before that. No one knows who these people once were, and why they are found in such numbers, but there are stories, there are always stories; they swirl round the city on invisible currents. One story says, these are people so far sunk in misery that they have thrown themselves off the bridges, though they must know that, by so doing, they will forfeit all chance of heaven.

Another story holds that they have been murdered, though for what reason is again unclear. Either story may be true, or both, or neither; meanwhile, the city goes heedlessly on with its own life, as the river does too. The city and the river are perfect images of the other, violent, treacherous, powerful, and curiously alluring.

In those early weeks, I sometimes used to find myself searching the crowd in the forlorn hope of seeing the face of someone whom I could claim as an acquaintance, however slight. I never saw anyone, with any certainty; but, once, as I walked quickly over Black Friars Bridge, I persuaded myself that I had seen someone I knew, from Somersetshire, who was walking alone in the opposite direction. My footsteps took me on, while I told myself that it could not be her, for why would she be here, in London—I could think of no possible reason—however, as I drew near the end of the bridge, the feeling grew upon me that it had been her, or might have been, and with the image of her face before me I turned and hurried back. However, she had disappeared, and I put her out of my mind.

That same year, however, in the summer, as I was walking through some ill-lit streets to the north of Cow Cross, I saw or thought I saw her again. She wore a shawl, and stood deep in shadow, at the meeting of two streets. For some time, I watched her from across the street, but could not clearly see her face. A man came up and spoke to her, and they went away together down a dark alley. I went back to the Menagery in a state of great uncertainty.

When my mother had written to me at Easton, she had never once mentioned Lizzy Tindall, though her letters had often carried information about other people in the village. Was it possible that Lizzy could have come to London? Was it possible? It was possible.

"Do you remember Lizzy?" I asked Jenny.

"Lizzy? Of course I do. Little Lizzy Tindall," Jenny replied.

"I think I have seen her."

Jenny eyed me, surprized.

"I think I may have seen her. But I am not sure."

"Are you sure, Tom, that it was not her ghost that you saw?"

I thought about this, for, certainly, there are said to be ghosts in the city, as there are in the countryside; they are seen, especially, during the winter fogs. Whether they are really ghosts, I do not know; nor, indeed, what a ghost is, if such a thing exists. An unhappy spirit, disturbed from its lodging, or an unsettled possibility floating through the mind? My mother, in her grief after my father's death, used to say that she saw his ghost, leading a horse past our cottage; but no one else ever saw this strange apparition. What did she see? Nothing, or something?

The next evening, I returned to the same spot, and waited. When she appeared, she had the same shawl over her face, and whether it was Lizzy or not I could not tell. In the gloom I could scarcely see her at all. I said: "Lizzy? Is it you? I am Tom. You are Lizzy, are you not? Lizzy Tindall? I am Tom Page."

I reached up to her shawl, but she stepped back, as if fearing a blow, as Stephen the monkie does at the Menagery.

"I mean you no harm," I said. "Believe me. To be sure—are you not Lizzy Tindall, from Thornhill? You worked for Mr. Harrington, you remember? At Harrington Hall?"

"Where's that?"

"In Somersetshire, in the west country, as you know, Lizzy." I persisted: "I know you are Lizzy. I am Tom. Do you not remember me? We were sweet-hearts. You may not recognise me, I had an accident to my nose."

She did not reply, but led me down the alley, which was called

Frying Pan Alley. The further we advanced, the darker it grew, and the more narrow, and for a moment I was afraid that I was being led into an ambush; many a man has been lured into an alley in order to be robbed of his money and cloaths, or worse. We turned through a low doorway, into a room, where an aged crone, huddled in an elbow chair, counted money by the light of a guttering candle. Beside her lay a huge dog, which rose to its feet and barked loudly. Pursued by these barks, I followed Lizzy up a flight of creaking stairs which seemed to continue longer than was possible; finally we arrived at the very top of the house, in a space as dark as pitch. I could not see even my hand in front of my face.

"Can we not light a candle?"

"I have no candles."

"No rush-lights?" I stared about me. "Is there no window?"

"Here? No."

Her voice was low, and soft, the accent not west country but that of a Londoner. But, I said to myself, it is like the plumage of birds; according to our surroundings, we adapt and change. If she had lived in London for some years, it was only natural that she should speak like her fellow citizens.

"You are Lizzy, are you not? Tell me you are Lizzy Tindall."

"If you want me to be Lizzy Tindall, I do not mind."

"No. No, I want you to be Lizzy Tindall, because you *are* Lizzy Tindall. I know you are Lizzy Tindall. Why deny the truth? You must know who you are."

"Why then, I do not deny it. I am Lizzy Tindall, indeed," she said indifferently.

I persisted. "Of Thornhill, in Somersetshire."

"As you say," she said with a sigh. "I am Lizzy Tindall, your Lizzy Tindall, your own sweet-heart, from Thornhill. What else do I need to be?"

"I need you to believe that you really are Lizzy Tindall, for, I assure you, without a doubt, you are."

"And I am, so I am," she said.

I continued to doubt, however. "There are no candles or rushes, anywhere?"

"No—I have told you. Why do you not believe me?"

She was standing, or so I guessed from her voice, about six feet in front of me. I moved toward her, my hands outstretched, fumbling in the blackness and encountering nothing, though I barked my shin on the sharp edge of the bed.

"Where have you gone?"

She gave a low, impudent laugh. "I have gone nowhere, I am here, I am waiting."

With a sweep of a hand I caught her and held her down. She pleaded with me and cried out for help, no doubt thinking that I was about to harm her, however I clamped my hand over her neck. Once she was still, I explored every inch of her face—her eyes, her lips, her nose, her ears, her chin, her mouth. The image of her familiar features rose in my mind like a dark mirror: yes, surely, there could be no doubt, she was Lizzy. Yet a question remained. I lifted my hand.

"How did you come to London? What made you leave Harrington?"

"Please let me go."

"I will not harm you, I have told you. But I must know why you left Harrington Hall. Answer me."

There was a silence before she spoke. "Why, to find you, Tom," and putting my hand aside she sat up, and ran her fingers through my hair, "it was so cruel of you to leave me, my heart was a-breaking."

At this I yielded, and pulled her to me. She did not smell of the country; it was as if her entire body had drawn into it the city's smoke-filled, grimy essence; yet, in the dark, I found it easy enough to imagine that we were, not in this mean little garret, but back in the hay-loft, with the swallows chittering in their nests.

I went away; however, I soon returned, night after night, up the same blind alley, through the same low doorway. The old woman was always in her chair, though for all the notice she took of me I myself might have been a ghost; yet the dog came to know me and, instead of barking, would fawn about my legs, sniffing at the smells of the Menagery and accompanying me up the endless stairs to the garret. Once, as Lizzy and I were lost in passion, it stole into the room and began a frenzy of licking at the soles of my feet. I say Lizzy, for, at every visit, the strength of my desire to make her into Lizzy succeeded more completely. Very soon she began to re-member Harrington Hall and Thornhill, and Mr. and Mrs. Har-rington and little Joshua, and Bob Brown and Dick Shadwick and even Mr. Gibbons, our venerable school-master at Gillerton, and how she had tricked him into believing that she was a gipsy boy. She remembered everyone and everything. How this happened I cannot say for certain, but I think that, without knowing it, I must have been her tutor. One night, between caresses, I would gently remind her of the thunder-storm, when she took shelter in the cart-house; the next, she would murmur, "O, Tom, do you not remember that thunder-storm, when I was longing for you to kiss me, and you did not?"—"I was still very young," I found myself answering, "I longed to kiss you, but I was afraid."—"What were you afraid of?"—"I am not sure . . . I was afraid that you would be angry."—"O, Tom, I could never be angry with you." The succeed-ing night, I might ask, whether she remembered the day in the hay-loft when we became true lovers, and in due time she would remember that well enough, just as she would remember when I fell off Timothy and broke my elbow, or when the Elephants escaped into Mrs. Harrington's garden. "Such a night," she would say, "I thought they would be killed . . ."—"So did I—you remember the rain?"—"I do . . . how it poured . . ." So we carried on. Once, as I lowered myself into her body, she gave a gasp. "Why, it is nearly as big as Timothy's."

How strange this was! I do not think that she was lying, or not lying simply; indeed, I am sure that a part of her truly came to believe that she might be Lizzy Tindall, that she was Lizzy Tindall; as for me, I had no doubts, for beneath her Cockney I allowed myself to hear a Somersetshire accent discovering itself again, and this seemed a kind of proof. It is true that, when I met her in the street, I made no attempt to remove her shawl, which I might have done; indeed, that I always avoided looking at her too closely, for fear of being un-deceived. Yet one night, as we coupled in the impenetrable darkness, my ears seemed to catch the cry of a baby, not very loud but altogether distinct and close by, and when I paused to listen the cry came again, even closer.

"What is that baby?"

"What baby, Tom?"

"I heard a baby—there is a baby in the room!"

"There is no baby in here. Tom, please, there is no baby in here. It must have been a cat."

"A cat?"

"Or a rat—in the roof—they have their litters—"

"But there it is again—listen! It is a baby, not a rat!"

She attempted to pull me to her, to drag me back to the bed, but I was determined to find the baby which, I thought, she had stored in some secret place. As I hunted about, I came upon the stub of a candle, which, having my tinder-box with me, I proceeded to light. She struggled to prevent me, throwing herself forward and clinging to me; at last, however, it was lit. The flame gathered its strength and drew itself up, illuminating the bare cabin of the room with its broken plaster walls and sloping roof and rotten floor, on which the dog lay, mouth hanging open, exposing a tongue marked by inky stains. A ragged curtain hung in a corner. When I swept it aside, there lay not a baby, but a wooden doll, a child's toy, with flaxen hair and painted lips and eyes. Filled with a strange fear, I turned, and now, as the candle lit Lizzy's naked body— the flaccid skin of her stomach, the lolling breasts, the harsh lines that hooped her mouth, the trickling blood—for, in our struggle, my arm must have caught her a blow—my fear doubled and re-doubled. She was like one of the dead women pulled from the river at Temple Bar. Quickly I blew out the flame, and attacked with a ferocity that made her struggle and cry out, knowing that it was necessary to destroy what the candle had revealed. In this way, I seemed able to return her to being Lizzy.

When I told Jenny, that I had found Lizzy Tindall, after all these years, living in London, she said, "It is a good story, Tom, it is a good story." Sensing her doubt, I said, "You will see her soon, Jenny; I will bring her here, to meet you. You will see."

At which she looked away, uneasily.

Lizzy seemed altogether reluctant to come to the Menagery; though I urged her many times she always made excuses: either she was busy, or it was a long way to the Strand, or something else. "The Elephant would like to see you again," I would say.—"O, the Elephant . . . there is really an Elephant, is there, Tom?"—"Of course—you remember the Elephant—" She stroked my cheek. "Yes, yes, Tom, I do remember—I remember very well—but I want to be sure, you know, that it is the same Elephant—I would not like to come all the way to the Strand, for a different Ele-phant—"

I think that, perhaps, she did not believe in the existence of the Elephant; however, late one hot summer's afternoon, she appeared wearing a blue silk dress and a jewelled neck-lace. She had an ostrich feather in her hair and a trail of perfume, and her face was thickly daubed with paint. I felt shy and aukward, both because she looked so different and because at that very moment I was applying oil of Turpentine to the bear, in order to kill some of the multitude of fleas which live in his fur, and my hands stank of the oil. I introduced her to Mr. Scott—"Very pleased to meet you, Madam," he said with a bow, and a blush—whereupon Mr. Cross sprang from his booth at the entrance to the Menagery, shining with sweat and cramming a crooked wig over his balding head (though what am I to talk, for much of my hair, too, is falling out). Having kissed her by the hand, he appointed himself her escorte. "Madam, if you will permit me, I shall be delighted to shew you the Menagery." Upon which, he led her round the animals, telling one fantastick story after another: how, for instance, at risk to life and limb, he had personally captured the Man-Eater, in a jungle, as it was about to devour another victim. "Appearances are deceptive . . . if you were to enter the cage now, I can assure you, Madam, there is no doubt, you would be lucky to escape alive."

This might have been comical, but I could tell that Lizzy was embarrassed at Mr. Cross's fawning behaviour, and, in truth, so was I. I had dreamed of the moment when Lizzy and Jenny would see each other again. Now here was Mr. Cross to contend with, getting in the way, holding her arm.

When we reached the Elephant, as he was embarking on another improbable tale, this one about Jenny's royal ancestry, I wanted to interrupt him, to say that Lizzy had met the Elephant before, years ago, that we came from the same village in the west country; but the words seemed to stick in my throat. Instead, I watched Jenny's expression (I could not see Lizzy's, because she was in front of me), eagerly hoping that she would shew some sign of recognition, even of joy, at a familiar face. She did not. Her expression remained impassive.

"She is very good at playing the drum," Mr. Cross announced. "She learnt that, in the Indies, at the royal court, where she was brought up a hundred and fifty years ago. Tom, make the Empress play the drum, will you?"

I signed to her, and Jenny, picking up the stick with her trunk, struck the drum twice: bang bang.

Mr. Cross was pleased. "There! Have you ever seen an Elephant play the drum before, Madam?"

"I have not," said she, turning her face so that she was speaking as much to me as to him. "No, I have not. I have never seen an Elephant in my entire life. It is—she is—a very—a very fine creature."

"The Empress is the only Elephant in Europe," declared Mr. Cross, who led her on to look at the monkie. I followed, my brain burning like a furnace, scarcely able to believe my ears. That she had never seen an Elephant before? We had talked about the Elephants so many times! "Fifteen days at sea," Mr. Cross was proudly saying. "Fifteen days, Madam, I assure you, before he was washed up on shore, more dead than alive. A true miracle."

When Lizzy had seen the animals, she was about to go; but before she did so she gave me her hand. "Farewell, Tom. I am sorry, believe me." These words, and the tone of open pity in which they were uttered, confounded me entirely, and before I could say a word she was gone, disappearing with a swirl of her dress into the busy street, leaving behind the memory of her perfume. Mr. Cross and Mr. Scott were convulsed with laughter, but I paid them no heed, which served to increase their mirth tenfold. Jenny would not meet my eyes.

While I was angry with Jenny, and with Mr. Cross and Mr. Scott—and indeed with myself—I was most of all angry with Lizzy. I could not understand why she should have denied herself, and I was determined to make her admit to the truth. That night, after the Menagery had closed, and with Mr. Scott looking after the animals, I walked up to Cow Cross. There was no sign of her where she generally stood, but I went up the alley and the old crone was nodding in her wormy chair, her apron spread with money, and beside her the dog. I climbed the creaking stairs, and called Lizzy's name, for I had convinced myself that she was there. No reply came, but I seemed to hear a rustle. I doubted; moved forward, arms outstretched; and groping in the darkness, over the bed, my hands closed on the wooden doll. I flung it aside and, in a sudden rage, clattered down the stairs to the old woman. "What is her name? Tell me her name!"—"Whose name, Sir?"—"Up the stairs! Her name! You must know her name!" I took her by the shoulders, meaning to shake the name out of her. "What is her name?"—"Name? I don't know."—"Her name!" Coins scattered and fell. "Her name is Lizzy Tindall, is that not so? Tell me her name is Lizzy Tindall!" She shrieked and cackled like a goose. "Why ask, if you know already?" I rushed out.

That night, and many others, I spent hunting Lizzy round the city. I would first visit the house in Frying Pan Alley, and when that proved fruitless try the stews of Turnmill Street, stopping at each gaggle of whores to inquire whether they knew of a certain Lizzy Tindall; whereupon one of the party, a raddled hag dressed as a dairy-maid, might reply that she knew her very well, why, she had seen her that very afternoon along the Ratcliff Highway, and if I went to such-and-such an address I would be certain to find her. Thence I would hurry, my hopes raised, but no one at that address had ever heard her name, and I would return to the same whores who, at the sight of me, would burst into peals of laughter. "Why, Sir, you have just missed her, she was here not ten minutes ago, asking after you"; and now I would be directed to another whore-house, in Long Acre, where some hideous, carbuncled, bandy-legged jade whose withered dugs hung to her waist and whose skin stank of old fish would take my arm and claim to be Lizzy Tindall, or Lizzy Tindall's twin. Night after night this game repeated itself. The thought that Lizzy was hiding in some nook or cranny, and that I would eventually run her to earth, drove me on, and once when I came to the house in Frying Pan Alley the old woman attempted to prevent me from mounting the stairs, and this convinced me that I had found her at last. I thrust the beldam aside and, seizing her candle, charged up and burst into the room; whereupon a tangle of flesh resolved itself into one spluttering gentleman and three naked beauties, none of whom I recognised. I made my sincere apologies, and withdrew.

As the summer wore on—I cannot say exactly when, but at some point—the cold truth began to dawn: that she had not been Lizzy Tindall, and had never been, and that the story we had created, and which seemed so real, had been nothing but a sham. Indeed, I had known this all along, or should have done: for my Lizzy, the Lizzy who had helped measure the dimensions of the Elephants as they lay in the yard at Harrington Hall, would by now be twenty years older than the silky, smoky, perfumed creature of the city who had visited the Menagery. Yet in some curious way I had truly believed that she was Lizzy.

As Mr. Scott says: it is possible to believe and not to believe something at the same time.

In the weeks after this, I flew into a violent rage, which overwhelmed all my powers of Reason. I became a scoundrel, a villain; no word is strong enough. God forgive me, but every night was the same: it made no difference whom I chose from the armies of whores plying their constant trade, and from these lowly creatures I sought refuge in drink and more drink, so that there were times when, stumbling from tavern to whore-house, and whore-house to tavern, my senses were so befogged and befuddled that I had no idea where I was, or even who I was; had I been asked my name, I would have been lost for a reply. Twice I was robbed in the streets. Somehow I always seemed to find my way back to my bed in the Menagery, or to White Horse Yard, where I would wake in the morning to the first snips of the barber's scissors. The barber is Mr. Pounce; he is a fat, cheery man who not only cuts hair but also draws teeth, upon request; indeed, he once drew one of mine, which I thought as rotten as those of the Man-Eater, but which, as it turned out, was still well rooted. As he wrenched at my jaws, trying to assert a grip with the forcipes, he grunted with effort, and the sweat sprang on his forehead, while I was in such agonies that I nearly fainted; yet I welcomed the pain, telling myself that it was a punishment for my foul and dissolute way of life and that, once the tooth was out, I would reform my behaviour and become a hermit. My resolution failed; the day saw my rage grow and grow until, by night-fall, it was again an un-governable force.

What is there in my nature that brings on these spasms? It would be easy enough to talk of brutish appetites, and of animal spirits, and indeed, I am sure, there was something of the Ooze about my behaviour. It would have been better if I had been chained to a tree and fed nothing but bread and water. But there is something in human depravity which, I think, far exceeds any-thing to be seen in the behaviour of animals.

At length I caught a severe infection, which distressed me greatly, and laid me low for several weeks. Thus the storm blew out, and I found myself sailing in calmer waters; indeed, though it may seem strange to say, the city itself seemed a calmer place. The hubbub, the noise, the coming and going of strangers, the eternal procession of chaises and drays and carriages of every kind, all this ceased to bewilder me, and became part and parcel of life. It must have been about then that Mr. Scott first remarked that, if the Menagery stayed here much longer, I would turn into "a true Londoner," a prophecy he has since repeated several times.

I wonder. If to be a true Londoner is to think of London as one's true home, the root of one's being, I doubt that I ever will think of myself in that way. I am country born and bred, even if the countryside, with its fields and woods, has come to seem a foreign land, another Indies, radiant with colour but curiously indistinct and uncertain. When did I last catch the call of a cuckow, floating and fading among the snows of the hawthorns? When did I last hear the blind river of a nightingale's song, bubbling and sobbing in the darkness? And, indeed, if I were to hear a nightingale, would I now be sure that it was a true nightingale, not a man hidden in a bush?

I tell myself that this is a great city, some say the greatest city that the world has ever known; but it is a hard place to live, for all that. I have never been pinched by the cold as I have in London. That is, the winter when my father died may have been colder; but it did not *feel* as cold; the reason chiefly being, I believe, that the cold in Somersetshire is a dry, thin cold, which invigorates the senses and draws the vapours out of the land, whereas in London the cold is damp and raw and clogged with infection.—Onion, Sir, your Honour, pray, try this raw onion—it is an excellent foil to the cold, and will infallibly warm any body in a trice. Why,

Madam, thank you kindly—I am most grateful—but when it comes to the business of keeping the extremities warm, I should prefer a few sticks of good fire-wood to a barrowful of onions. Yet there is scarcely any fire-wood here. Instead, the city depends on sea-coal, which is a feeble, spluttering, popping, crackling thing, and, besides, not always easy to get, for everyone wants coal in cold weather, and supplies run low. Short of fuel, Mr. Scott and I heat the Menagery by burning the dried dung of the animals. Jenny's dung seems to burn best, and the smell is far from unpleasant; but the stoves never give off enough heat, and the animals suffer. Bruin the bear has a thick fur, and dozes; and the snake curls into a stone, and Jenny, wrapped in blankets which cover her back and neck, and straw tied in bundles round her legs, stands and endures. Mr. Scott has given Stephen an ancient great coat; it is far too big for him, so that his head almost disappears beneath the collar, but it must provide some warmth. Teeth chattering loudly, and racked by coughs, he huddles in a corner and strokes his withered hand. Meanwhile, the lion moans.

Two winters ago, the river froze over, from bank to bank, all the way from Putney Bridge down to Redriff, and the ice was so thick that people set up booths selling gin and gingerbread and other wares. Fires were lit, and sheep and oxen roasted on spits. As the crowds grew, Mr. Cross conceived the excellent commercial idea of exhibiting the Man-Eater on the ice. Loaded in a hired cart, he was taken down to the river's edge. When the horses felt their hooves slipping on the frozen sheet, they began to panic, and might have bolted had I not been there to calm them, for Mr. Scott has no skill with horses. The lion stayed the entire day on the ice, groaning with pain and licking his paws, which as his spittle froze would have soon been cased in ice if Mr. Scott had not come to his aid. He returned very sad and shrunken. I dread the winters.

Yet spring and early summer, when breezes waft the scents of the country into the city, are harder still for me; then I feel that London is, like the Prince of Wales, a snake, and that I am one of the mice which it is in the process of swallowing and digesting, by slow convulsions. Struggle as I may, there is no escape.

2

If living here is so strange for me, I ask myself, what must it be like for Jenny?

When I look at her now, she seems her usual, easy, good-natured self, and when I talk to her, she replies in her usual, easy, good-natured way. But it is not, it cannot be, good for her to live in such a small cage, measuring a mere twenty feet by fifteen feet, or for her never to see the sky, or feel the warm sun on her back. Her skin is too dry, her joints ache even more than my elbow, her mind is dulled into a lethargy. How I long to be able to take her into some meadows, where she can stretch her stiffening limbs; or into some woodland nook, where she can roam and feed on fresh green leaves! How I long to watch her bathe again; to watch her thunder into some cool river, or lake, or pond! It is not possible.

The distance to the river is less than a quarter of a mile, but who would bathe in that stinking vat of poisons, the city's sluice, of which even to drink a mouthful is fatal, or so people say? Yet, even if the river were crystal clear, I could not lead her into the streets without causing a commotion, and even if I could lead her into the streets without causing a commotion, I would not have the permission of Mr. Cross. No, it is not possible.

"It is not possible," says Jenny. "I am owned. I am the property of Mr. Cross. I am content, Tom."

"I do not believe that you are content. How can you be content?"

"There are worse places to live."

"But this is a prison!"

"It may seem like a prison, but it is not a prison in my head. In my head I am free enough. I see the people who come into the Menagery, and as they watch me, I watch them. I smell their scents, and imagine their lives."

"But you cannot go outside. As you say, it is not possible. That is the truth."

"It is tolerable, Tom. We are together. I like the stories you tell me, from outside. Last night, what was it like?"

"It was cold," I say. "The wind was from the east. People walked with their hands in their pockets and their heads down, not talking."

"What was the sky like? Could you see the moon?"

She often asks me this; she likes to hear about the moon.

"The sky was clear," I reply, "though there were a few dark clouds. The moon was waning, but still large. It rose gracefully behind the buildings and shone brightly. The clouds were dark, but the moon whitened their edges. Late in the evening, I looked up and a halo of light surrounded the moon."

"Is that not a sure sign of bad weather?"

"It is said to be. My father believed it to be so."

I tell her of a tavern yard, in which men cheer and shout at two bewhiskered rats, which having been set to fight each other, are locked together, neither daring to open its jaws, and how they roll over the stones; I tell her of the music drifting from a great house in which a ball is taking place, and the lacquered carriages which wait outside, attended by liveried foot-men, and the horses stamping their hooves; I tell her of a small fire, in the flicker of which an urchin, barefoot, and no more than eight or nine years old, crouches over a baby wrapped in a bundle of rags.

"Where was their mother? Why do they not go home, on such a night?"

"I am not sure whether they have a home, Jenny. They may be lost."

"But what will become of them?"

"I do not know."

She gives me her innocent gaze. "Why can they not live in the great house, where the ball was taking place?"

"The world is not like that. It is not possible."

What is possible, and what is not possible. It is possible that, on a certain cold night, beautiful ladies and handsome gentlemen should glide over a ball-room floor; yet it is not possible that, on the same night, a shivering child and a baby should find shelter. It is possible that a certain Elephant should live in a small dark Menagery, and that she should be able to converse with her keeper, just as it is also possible that the sun exists to shine and to heat this world; yet it does not seem possible that the same Elephant should be allowed to walk out of the Menagery, and to feel the warm sun on her back.

In the day, I bring her hay and carrots, turnips and other vegetables from the Market. I bring her tid-bits of gingerbread and sugar and liquorice; and sometimes a tub of ale, which she loves; I scrub her skin, and I pick off fleas, and clean between her toes. At night I settle her to sleep, and twice a year, in the spring and autumn, she allows me to give her a gentle purge, to clear the impurities from her digestion. Yet I wonder, who is keeping whom? Am I keeping Jenny, or is she keeping me?

"We are keeping each other, Tom," she assures me. "We are keeping each other. It is tolerable."

If we knew how long we would have to stay in the city, it would be more tolerable. If we knew that, in a year's time, we would be going to York, or Southampton, it would be more tolerable, and it would be more tolerable if we knew that the Menagery would have to close down, that we would be sold, though we might be sold into even worse conditions than here. What is so hard to bear is the prospect of no prospect, of living here always, of living here and dying here, like the giraffe. O, the poor giraffe! How well I remember that hot, heavy August day, when the flies were thick, and how she seemed unable to stand, and tottered on wabbling legs. Mr. Scott and I tried to support her, he on one side, I on the other, our arms up-raised; and, for a moment, we seemed to be succeeding. Then her joints gave way, and she fell with a crash into the dust. What did she think, in those last moments, as her eyes grew dull and her life ebbed away? Did she know what was happening? Did the other animals, who saw the dead giraffe as it was dragged past their cages—did they know what had happened? It is said that, along with human beings, the only creatures that have a fore-knowledge of death are Elephants. Indeed, it is said that, in the Indies, Elephants have their own burial places, sacred groves littered with the bleached bones of their dead relations; but this may be another story. I have never asked Jenny. Nor have I ever asked her what she thinks of the twice-weekly cart-load of horse-bones which Mr. Scott and I shovel into sacks and store at the back of the Menagery. Perhaps she knows that they are bones, that they once joined other bones to form the frames of creatures with soft skin and warm blood, and sinews and veins, and beating hearts, and that such creatures breathed, fed, slept, woke, walked, trotted, pranced, cantered, galloped, and flew over hedges and ditches on sun-lit mornings. Yet perhaps she does not know; or perhaps she prefers not to know. It is better not to ask.

Soon after the death of the giraffe I became alarmed about Jenny's future; indeed as I lay awake at night, listening to her long, rumbling snores, I could think of little else. One moment I would picture her falling to her knees, toppling to her side, and dying like the giraffe; the next, I myself had died, and she was left alone, lost and friendless, a shrunken version of her real self. This was a worse prospect, for then she would be at the mercy of the savage world of those human beings who believe that animals have no capacity either to reason or to feel, and may therefore be treated as objects. Yet there was another, much brighter possibility, that she would be bought by some wealthy gentleman with a large estate, another Lord Bidborough, in whose generous care she would enjoy a true freedom. Which gentleman, Tom? Is it likely? How many gentlemen can afford the vast expense of an Elephant?

I had no answer to these questions until one night when a quiet voice whispered, as if in a dream, Why, Tom, wake up—have you forgotten Mr. Harrington's son, little Joshua, and how much he loved the Elephants? By now he must be a grown man, and if, as is possible, his father has died, and he is now in charge of Harrington Hall, well then, surely . . . and in an instant my mind, leaping ahead, told me that he had already agreed to buy the Elephant, and that I had found a means of escape from the Menagery, and from London. Our story, which seemed to have come to a halt, would begin again. We would live again at Harrington Hall, where we were so happy, and all would be well.

Thus I began to compose a letter. *To Mr. Joshua Harrington, Esquire. Sir, You will remember that, many years ago—Sir, Many years ago—Sir, You may remember that, more than twenty years ago, your father owned a pair of young Elephants, of which I was their keeper—Sir, more than twenty years ago, I had the honour to serve your father, Mr. John Harrington, as his Elephant Keeper. It may interest you to know that one of these Elephants is still alive, the female—that one of these Elephants, the female, is still alive, though her present situation in London, in a Menagery—in a stinking Menagery, is far from ideal and stirs the compassion of all who see her—but this is not true—in a stinking Menagery, exposed to publick view, is far from ideal for such a noble, intelligent creature, and—*

And what? Something stopped me—the memory of Lord Luttershall's letter, the fear that, were I to send such an epistle, the answer, if indeed I received an answer, would be another blow in the face. *Dear Mr. Page, I regret to inform you that Mr. Joshua Harrington was drowned at sea, five years ago. Dear Mr. Page, I regret to inform you that Harrington Hall is now owned by Lord and Lady B—. Dear Mr. Page, I regret to inform you that Mr. Joshua Harrington, though remembering the Elephant well, would not be interested in its purchase. Dear Mr. Page, I write on behalf of Mr. Harrington, who is presently in the Barbadoes . . .* there were a dozen replies which seemed more likely than the one I wanted.

I therefore attempted to suppress the idea; indeed, I did suppress it, though it remained in my mind as a little piece of hope which I would take from its cupboard and nibble now and then, like a mouse with a piece of cheese. So matters stood until last summer, when Mr. Cross decided that, in order to revive the fortunes of the Menagery, a fight should be held between the lion and the bear. This fight was held on May Day, at ten o'clock in the evening, by special licence from the authorities. Over the preceding weeks, Mr. Cross took it upon himself to teach the bear to feign death. Encouraged by the salutary exercise of the whip on his snout, Bruin soon learnt this simple lesson, and at the first twitch would topple over and lie on his back with his eyes closed— Mr. Cross's idea being that, after some minutes of sparring, the lion would win the fight and be proclaimed the victor. Mr. Scott and I were sent to stick bills round the city, in order to advertise the event; and, as we did so, I remember saying to Mr. Scott, that I feared that the fight would end badly, by which I meant that one of the animals would be injured. "End?" said he. "For my part, I shall be greatly surprized if it even begins."

In the event, his prediction proved accurate. A crowd of more than a hundred red-faced men, many of whom seemed drunk, and all of whom had placed bets either on the bear or the lion, pressed into the Menagery at the appointed hour. Torches having been lit, both animals were led into the same cage, and there they stood (Mr. Scott by the bear, I by the lion), as Mr. Cross proceeded to introduce them to the spectators, comparing them to the heroes of antiquity. The bear he proclaimed to be none other than Hector; the lion, Achilles; but little enough of his speech could be heard above the shouts of the crowd, and soon he stepped aside. The fight would then have commenced; unfortunately, both combatants being so cowed by the noise and the torches, neither was willing to come to terms. On one side of the cage stood the little bear, his head down, his mind in a state of utter confusion, while on the other side the Man-Eater had sunk to the floor, to which he had been glued by fear. Straddling his body, I attempted to haul him to his feet, but as soon as I did so, he fell back; whereupon Mr. Cross, alarmed by the rising temper of the crowd, pushed me aside and seized a torch—his intention being to frighten the Man-Eater into fighting. He succeeded in setting fire to the tail of the poor animal, who, giving a frantic howl and rising to his feet, fled across the cage, where the bear had already chosen to play dead and was flat on his back with his eyes shut. Most members of the crowd laughed and jeered, I think at Mr. Cross as much as at the animals. I quickly took pity on the Man-Eater, leading him back to his cage, where he lay in darkness and misery, with his tail still smoking.

This spectacle filled me with such loathing and disgust that I again began to entertain thoughts of Harrington Hall, though my aversion to writing a letter remained as strong as ever. One afternoon later in the summer, when Mr. Scott and I were drinking tea, I turned to him for advice.

"How old would he be, this Joshua Harrington?"

"Thirty years old. But it is perfectly possible that he is abroad, or dead. Or that his father is still alive."

"And there's no one else in this village—what's it called?"

"Thornhill."

"There's no one else in Thornhill who'd be able to give you any information?"

"No one. But it is a day-dream. Mr. Cross would never sell the Elephant."

"Old Gilbert? He'd sell anything if the price was high enough. If I were in your position, Tom, I'd write the letter. Or I'd apply in person."

"You would apply in person?"

Mr. Scott considered. "I believe I would. A letter he might throw away without another thought, but if he were to see your face, after so many years, it'd be bound to touch his heart. Wouldn't it now? Now, how long would it take you to get there? Two days?"

"Two days, or three. And the same to return."

"Well then, five days in all. I'll look after the Empress for you. She'll be all right." He drew the dish of tea to his mouth.

"You don't think she'll pine?"

"Pine? She may droop a little, that's true. But she'll be all right. I'll look after her. I'll sleep here."

I was not sure, however. To leave Jenny, for five or six long days and nights, when I had never left her for even one day and night, would not be easy. It was certain that she would pine; indeed, already I seemed to see her standing in the darkness, listening for my return. I had, moreover, another fear, one which had grown since the fight between the lion and the bear, that the Menagery might somehow be set on fire, and the animals burnt alive. There are plenty of house-fires in the city, generally in the winter, sometimes because people fail to have their chimneys swept as they ought, or for other reasons. I remember that, in my first year in London, a mansion in Holborn was razed to its foundations after a servant girl fell asleep over a candle.

Despite all this, I was inclined to go. For one thing, it occurred to me, I might learn something of my brother, of whom, to my regret, I had had no intelligence for fifteen years. In a letter, written not long before she died, but which I have somehow lost, my dear mother said that she had heard from another sea-man, a Captain Fitzpatrick, who having met Jim near Cochin, in the Indies, reported that he had had all manner of adventures, having been ship-wrecked, and chased by cannibals, and captured by pirates; but, having survived these calamities, was in a fair way to making his fortune. Another traveller's tale, of doubtful worth, I thought. Why, for all I knew, Jim was here, in London; the city is crowded with former sailors. We might have sat in the same tavern, drunk from the same mug, enjoyed the same whores. Nonetheless, I told myself, it was also possible that he now lived back in Thornhill.

"Five days?" asked Jenny.

"You will be safe with Mr. Scott."

"And at night?"

"He will stay the night here, with you all. You will be safe."

She was silent, her trunk twisting slowly, forming and un-forming question-marks.

"It is not Mr. Scott," she said.

"What then? You do not want me to go!"

"I have no opinion."

"No—I can tell—you do not want me to go."

There was a long pause, during which she walked to the back of her cage and rubbed her hind-quarters against the picture of the Indian prince. "Tom, what do you imagine you will find, when you arrive in Thornhill?"

"What do I imagine? I do not imagine anything."

"What are you hoping to find?"

"I am hoping to learn whether Joshua is now in charge of the estate, and, if so, whether he may be willing to buy you off Mr. Cross. And perhaps gain some intelligence of Jim. That is all."

She gazed frankly into my face. "You are not hoping to meet Lizzy Tindall?"

"Lizzy Tindall?" It was true that somewhere, in my picture of Thornhill, I seemed to see the little cottage where the Tindalls once lived, and where, God knew, she might live still. However, that Jenny had divined this secret, which I thought I had kept private, vexed me greatly. "I can assure you, I have no particular intention of meeting her."

She blinked slowly, but said nothing, as though doubting me.

I began to rebel. "If we happen to meet, is there any harm done? Why should we not meet? Jenny! What reason do you have?"

"There is no reason."

"In that case, why do you ask? Are you jealous?"

"Jealous?" She tossed her head. "I am no more than a half-reasoning animal."

A half-reasoning animal, indeed! I stared, and if she were human, I believe, she would have been covered in blushes. "Why—the truth is, Jenny, you are jealous!"

"The truth is," she retorted hotly, "I do not want you to be hurt. But I am only an Elephant."

This was, as she well knew, the very phrase that Lizzy herself had once used, and I was so annoyed that I left her without another word. I busied myself in filling the lion's water-trough and sweeping up his dung. He did not stir, even when the broom brushed his whiskers. Well, Sir, I said to him, give me your advice. Jenny says, or thinks, that I should not go back to Thornhill, on the grounds that I might meet Lizzy Tindall, but this is a distraction, it is not the main point at issue, which is to meet Joshua Harrington and thereby escape the present situation. Now, Sir, what is your considered opinion? The lion yawned and yawned again, revealing four ginger stumps in his jaws. I am too tired, he seemed to say, leave me alone. My tail hurts, my bones ache. I need to sleep.

Over the next few days, Jenny beamed the entire force of her affections upon Mr. Scott. Whenever she saw him, at least when I was watching, she would trumpet with pleasure and hurry forward. "The Empress is in a good mood," he remarked. "I don't know what's come over her lately. Here—stop that, will you—steady, steady now," for she was wafting hot air into one of his ears. I, by contrast, was treated with a shew of cold civility. She pretended not to hear me, and when she did, pretended not to understand.

"Jenny, what is happening?" I said at last.

She turned toward me. "What is happening?"

"Why are you behaving like this?"

"I beg your pardon?"

I repeated the question. "You and Mr. Scott. I am not entirely blind. What are you attempting to achieve?"

"I am not attempting to achieve anything." Her expression was one of extraordinary innocence, while her tone was nothing short of haughty. "I happen to enjoy Mr. Scott's company."

"Indeed, so I perceive, you make that very plain."

"Why," she flapped her ears, in apparent consternation, "am I not allowed to talk to Mr. Scott? I am sorry, I did not know."

"This is nonsense, as you know very well. You cannot talk to Mr. Scott, and Mr. Scott cannot talk to you."

"Why?"

"Because he cannot!" I said impatiently. "Jenny!"

"I am sorry, Tom. I thought that you had finished. What is it?"

"You are being ridiculous. All this is intended to prevent me from going back to Thornhill. I understand, it is transparent. You are jealous of Lizzy Tindall."

"Not at all, Tom," she said smoothly. "I am not at all opposed to you going back to Thornhill, and leaving me with Mr. Scott. He is a man of many excellent qualities, as you have told me yourself. We will rub along very well together, I am sure. I shall teach him to talk to me."

"O, this is impossible!" I cried. "Yes, I am going back to Thornhill, though not to see Lizzy Tindall, but in the hope that it may enable us to leave this damp, flea-ridden pit of horrors. Are you content to stay here for ever?"

"I am only an Elephant," she repeated. "It is not my decision. Stay away as long as you like. I shall be content here with Mr. Scott as my keeper."

Why, how provoking this was! In her resolve to keep me by her side, she had determined to make me jealous of Mr. Scott!

Our dispute continued for longer than I care to remember, through the autumn and into the winter. At times I felt angry with her; at others, with myself, for being swayed by her female behaviour, which seemed more human than Elephant. I said to myself, am I being so very un-reasonable, when this is our best hope of escape? She does not understand; all she can see are the five days that I will be away, and a groundless fear that I will never return; she is unable or refuses to look into the darkness which lies ahead if we do not escape from the Menagery. It was true, I knew, or I think I knew, that there was a certain risk in what I proposed; at risk was the hope itself, the little piece of cheese on which I liked to nibble. However, it seemed to me that at some point I would have to put the hope to the test, to discover whether it was worth anything; and, that being so, the better sooner than later. To delay gained me nothing: better to know the truth now, than to feed on a falsehood.

3

It was a dark day in February when, my heart full of foreboding, I finally caught the Coach for Bath. The passage of every dull mile, rattling me further from Jenny, made me feel that the thread which held us together was being stretched thinner and thinner to the point of breaking, and when the Coach stopped at the Castle in Marlborough I was in half a mind to return at once. I reproached myself for cowardice: having come this far, I told myself, I must go on for Jenny's sake. Yet I was resolved to make my journey as brief as possible; indeed I had solemnly promised both Jenny and Mr. Scott that I would be back in London by the Saturday, that is not five but four days hence (though Mr. Scott had urged me to stay away longer, if necessary).

Once in Bath, therefore, I did not linger a single moment

but set forth at once on foot, though the day was well advanced. Having climbed the brow of the hill which looks over the city, I asked a man who stood by an inn, The Bear, whether the road before me was the one which led to Wells (for I knew that, once I was near Wells, I should be able to find my way easily enough to Glastonbury and thence to Thornhill). He answered that there were two roads which led in that direction, and either would do; but, he added, after about six miles I would come to a fork, and there I should be sure to take the right prong, else I should go completely out of my way. I thanked him and took the road, which led me on to a high open plain marked by a few stone walls and thorn bushes. Not having been abroad in such wild country for so many years, and without Jenny at my side, I wondered whether I would have been wiser to have spent the night at The Bear, especially when the possibility of footpads, cut-purses, and other ruffians came into my head; moreover, I began to doubt whether I was on the right road, despite what the man had told me; there had been something about his face which lacked conviction. As darkness fell apace, this doubt grew, for there was no moon and I could not see the way clearly, and though I watched for the fork which the man had mentioned, I never found it. The road seemed to turn too much to the south, when I needed to go further west, and when it plunged into a dark wood my confidence deserted me entirely. However, I pressed on, and made out the dim shape of a mile-stone, and my fingers, fumbling over its mossy face, seemed to trace the letters WELLS XVIII, which put me in better heart. Thereafter I looked for every mile-stone, counting my steps.

It had been my intention to march through the night, for the sooner I reached Thornhill, the sooner I would be able to return to London. I made good progress, however toward the end of the night the rain fell and my legs began to ache, and, the distance between each mile-stone growing greater and greater, I allowed myself the luxury of a rest in the lee of an old stone barn, where I eased myself and lit a pipe. I had brought a loaf of bread with me, and now I ate some, reserving the remainder for my journey back. While I was sheltering by the barn I heard voices and two or three men rode close by, but did not see me, to my relief. Toward daybreak, I drew near Wells, and within an hour having struck on a lucky road came to a particular sheepfold which I recognised, and so knew that I was back in my home country. My steps quickened, and finally I stood on the top of the down above Gillerton.

In the distance lay the grey shape of Harrington Hall and, somewhat nearer, the little cottages of Thornhill clustered round the tower of the church, and the beloved woods and fields and ponds which my imagination had haunted for so long. The rain had stopped, and below the pale of the dawn sky hundreds of rooks and daws were flying in long black straggling lines, borne on the currents of the wind; and as they drew nearer, uttering their familiar caws and chacks, O what a pleasant, friendly greeting this was, or ought to have been! Yet, at the thought of entering the village, of meeting someone who might know me, I was filled with a nameless apprehension, which left me sick in the pit of my stomach. Indeed, soon enough, as I descended the sunken cart track which leads off the down, I did meet a shepherd, a young man, who leant on his crook and eyed me narrowly. Mustering my reserves of courage I left the down and walked through Gillerton, and began along the lane to Thornhill. Hundreds of times, and without the slightest sense of fear, I had trod this same lane, so why did my feet weigh so heavily? Why did I feel that I was walking to my death?

As I entered the village, two barefoot children were trying to catch a hen which had run into the street, while a young woman, in a dark smock, was stooping at the well. My legs carried me onward; I saw a bowed old woman shuffling along with a load of sticks on her back and I knew at once that she was Mrs. Perry, though I could scarcely believe that the old witch was still alive. I recognised no one else; nor did anyone give any sign of recognising me, though I was much stared at. I thought, I am a stranger here now, I am a stranger, though I am not a stranger. The village seemed to have changed, but I could not tell how it had changed. Perhaps it is still the same, only I have changed, I said to myself, but I was not sure.

The Hall, at least, seemed much as I remembered, and I waited in the grounds with my back against a tree to see whether anyone might come out. In my mind I had told myself how, if Joshua rode toward me, I would step out of cover and salute him, at which point he would stop and I would make myself known, and I rehearsed the words that I would say. An hour or two passed, and a small herd of spotted deer grazed near me, and a yaffle gave a loud laugh as it flew past, but no one came out of the Hall. At last I heard the sound of an axe, and making my way in that direction I found a white-haired old man and two boys about ten years of age, standing beneath the same elm tree to which, long ago, I had chained Timothy when he had the Ooze. They were chopping up a giant limb, brought down by some gale. This ancient was Mr. Judge, who had once been head gardener at the Hall. I approached, and asked him, whether he could tell me anything about Harrington Hall, however he was deaf and I had to repeat the question several times before he understood. Leaning on the haft of his axe and scowling, he demanded what it was I wanted to know, and I said, who owned it now, who owned the estate, to which he replied that it was owned by Mr. Harrington, the squire. "Why do you want to know?"

"You do not recognise me, Mr. Judge?"

His face was very red and mottled under his white hair. "No; should I?"

When I told him my name he staggered. "Tom Page? Tom Page? Son of Timothy Page, the groom?"

"The same."

"Well I'll be d—ned!" He peered at me, suspicious, with rheumy eyes. "You were the lad with the Elephants!"

"The same, I was."

"Well! I don't know!" He turned to the boys. "Did you know that? There were Elephants once, up at the Hall. Two Elephants! Monsters!" He raised a hand to shew how big the Elephants had been.

The boys gazed to the height of the elm. "Yes, Gran'fer," one replied in a piping voice; however, he and his brother exchanged a sly, smirking glance which said as plain as a pike-staff that they did not believe him.

"It is true," I said to them. "I still care for one of the Elephants, in London."

Mr. Judge gave a grunt. "Anywhere's better than here, as you've likely heard."

"Why so?"

"Why? Why? The master! The Squire!"

"Mr. Harrington?"

"Bearing down on poor people!" In a voice of indignation, Mr. Judge told me how wages had gone down, and prices had gone up, and rents, and no one was allowed to collect wood any longer, even in winter, or take their pigs or cows on the commons, even though it had been their right to do so since the days of Adam. "It's our right to graze on the commons!" he said angrily. "It's an Englishman's right! No one keeps a cow now, as there's nowhere to graze it."

"What then do people do for milk?"

"Milk? No one drinks milk! No one drinks it! Or they do buy it, but the price of milk . . ." Even redder in the face, he kicked at the axe. "Same with butter! And cheese! And meat! He thinks we're horses, he thinks we ought to live on oats and water! He's a tyrant!"

"Is this Mr. Joshua Harrington, or his father, John Harrington?"

"The father?—He's dead. No, the son, worse luck, the son. You wouldn't remember him. He treats us like slaves."

"I do remember him, I do, Mr. Judge."

He muttered a curse. "There's more misery here I'd say than in any other village in the whole of England."

The rest of the conversation I cannot recall very clearly, my mind was so over-thrown. That Joshua, who had been such a sweet boy, should have grown into a tyrant—how was this possible? When did the corruption set in? As I walked back through the village, I went into the churchyard to visit my father's grave, and found that at the head of the grave a large stone had been erected to my father's memory, and to the memory of my mother, who had been laid to rest in the same plot seven years earlier. This stone could only have been erected by Jim, and it raised my hopes that he might now be living in the village; and thus I made my way to the old cottage where he and I were born. In London I had often pictured it but always in spring and summer, not as now, in the dead days of winter, with the thatch rotten and mouldy. A he-goat with a sleak white beard raised its head and fixed me with its mad eyes.

A little girl answered the door, and called for her mother, who soon appeared. She was a woman of about thirty-five with a tired face and red nose. "O, but it is Tom Page!" she cried, wiping her wet hands on her apron. "Annie, run and fetch your father and tell him it is Tom Page, who used to look after the Elephants!" It turned out that her name was Margaret Edwards, but I had known her as Margaret Porter, the daughter of Robert Porter, who was the wheelwright in Thornhill when I was a boy.

She asked me into the cottage, which was very cold and shabby, with no sign of a fire and only a few sticks of furniture. At her invitation I sat on a stool, which rocked on the uneven floor. I could scarcely believe where I was. "Did you not once live here?" Margaret asked.—"I did, indeed."—"I am sorry there is no fire— what happened to the Elephants?" When I told her that one was still alive, and living in London, her face broke into smiles. "After so long!" she exclaimed, "O, I am pleased!"—"Well, they are long-lived creatures." As we were talking, her husband came into the room. A stocky man with one wall eye, John Edwards was some years younger than Margaret and did not remember the Elephants, though he could remember being told about them. He seemed chiefly interested in the question whether London was truly such a sink of vice and corruption as people said, with dozens of har-lots and jezebels on every street-corner. When I informed him that there were indeed harlots, and jezebels—returning the phrase without amendment—he gave a low, lecher's laugh. "I knew it! Heh! Heh! What be they like?" I replied that such women were probably the same the world over. He leant greedily forward, fixing me with his wall eye. "They be sometimes known as hackneys, be n't they? Seein' as how they be for hire. Heh, heh! What be the fare?"—"About six pence, generally."—"Six pence!" said he, and gave his leg some hearty slaps, while Margaret merely smiled. The little girl crouched on her haunches and stared.

At length they asked what brought me back to Thornhill, and being reluctant to divulge my main purpose, for fear of looking foolish, I mentioned Jim; but they had heard nothing of him lately, though they remembered that he had been in the village some time after my mother had died. "Weren't he Master of some ship?" John asked. I said that I did not know. "O, he were—the ship's name—what were it called?"—"It was the *Fortune*," Margaret said.—"That were it—the *Fortune*! Trading out of Bristol!"—"The *Fortune* is one of Mr. Harrington's ships," said Margaret. "He was the Master, your brother. And may be still, very likely. He was very well dressed." She spoke of him in very respectful terms, as if he had become a gentleman.

I confess that I found this intelligence strangely painful. To learn that the brother whom I knew, or thought I knew, who could neither read nor write, and who suffered from such head-aches he could scarcely stir abroad for two or three days at a stretch, was now in sole charge of a great ship and its crew, to whose members he would issue orders which would be obeyed forthwith, and that this ship sailed, no doubt, all round the world, was entirely unexpected. He was my one and only living relation, and I had always counted upon meeting him again at some point in our lives, and renewing our friendship; for, certainly, we had been friends as well as brothers. Yet now, as the Master of the *Fortune*, he seemed a stranger, and I wondered what, if chance were to bring us together, he would say to me.

I went on to ask John and Margaret about Mr. Harrington, and here they had a great deal to say, much of it confirming Mr. Judge's account. It seems that, soon after his father's death, Joshua Harrington fell under the sway of some new agricultural ideas, which persuaded him to inclose the common land, supposedly to improve it; however, the effect had been to deprive many people of a large part of their livelihoods. Those with a trade were barely able to make ends meet, while those without, that is, the ordinary villagers, no longer had land on which to graze their cows, or pigs or sheep, as they were used; nor were they allowed to gather firewood or brush, nor even to glean after the harvest. I suggested that Mr. Harrington did not, perhaps, understand the sufferings which his Improvements had caused; at which Margaret said bitterly, "O, he understands well enough, but he has no heart. If you were to cut him open, you would find a hole where his heart ought to be."

As these words sunk into me, I understood that there was no longer any point in applying to Mr. Harrington, and that my hopes were in vain. Before leaving John and Margaret, however, I cautiously inquired about Lizzy Tindall.

"Lizzy Tindall?" asked John. "Who would that be now?"

"Why, you silly man, he means Anne's daughter," Margaret said, "only she is not Lizzy Tindall now, she is poor Mrs. Shadwick."

"Shadwick?"

"She lives in Gillerton now. She will be pleased to see you, I am sure."

This was another and much harder blow for which, I confess, I had not been prepared. Dick Shadwick! Memories of the many indignities that I and Jenny had suffered at his hands came back to me.

As soon as I could, I thanked them and walked away. My road now lay through Gillerton, and while I had no desire to meet Dick again, I retained a strong curiosity with regard to Lizzy. If I might only set eyes on her for a moment, or exchange a few brief words, I thought, I would be satisfied for ever.

A woman whom I asked for directions mumbled, "You be n't her husband, be you?" When I replied that I was not, that I was merely an old acquaintance, she said—"If she be n't at home, you may find her at work, most like." I wondered whether she meant at the Hall, imagining that Lizzy must still work there, but the woman pointed me far across the fields, toward a little hazel copse.

In the days of my youth a path had led straight over the fields to the copse; now a quickset hedge blocked the way. I squeezed through its thorns and crossed the next part of the field. This had lately been put to the plow, and after the rain the earth stuck to my boots in clods, but the wind was behind and blew me along like a ship. Once I had pushed through a second line of quickset I saw a party of labourers digging a long ditch around a part of the copse, for what purpose I do not know. Waist-deep in the ditch were some twenty or more men, women, and children, bending and straightening to throw up loads of what seemed to be as much water as earth. All were much the same brown hue as the ditch itself, as if the mud ran through their veins. I approached a woman in the nearer part of the ditch, and asked if she could tell me whether Mrs. Shadwick were here, whereupon she called to another woman, "Betty! Betty!" and Betty put down her spade and climbed from the ditch. "He be wanting Lizzy Shadwick!" Betty looked eagerly at me. "It is about Dick, is it? You have seen him?" I replied, to her obvious disappointment, that I had not, I knew nothing of Dick, but that I used to know Lizzy from many years earlier, when I worked at the Hall. At this she said, "You cannot be Tom Page." I was greatly surprised that this woman Betty, whom I had never seen in my life, should know my name. "I am."—"She has spoken of you, sometimes, and the Elephants." In both her voice and manner she seemed less than friendly, and when I asked if Lizzy were present, Betty at first made no reply. Then she said: "It will be a great shock to her, you must be gentle."

She turned on her heel and walked some way along the ditch. I followed, wondering which of the diggers was Lizzy. Betty stopped at a toiling figure, dark with mud. "Lizzy dear, stop that now, it is someone you know, it is someone come to see you."

The woman looked up, and yes, it was Lizzy, it was Lizzy indeed, I knew at once, it could be no one else; yet how pinched and hollowed her face had become! Her eyes started from their sockets. "Lizzy," said I, "it is I, Tom Page, how do you do?" and leant forward to give her my hand, to help her from the ditch, but she ignored it and began to laugh. There was something in this laugh which cut me to the quick. It was not like her old laugh. "Why, you are never Tom Page!" she said scornfully. "I would know if you were Tom!"

"I am Tom, I am, Lizzy. I assure you."

"Lizzy dear," said Betty, "he may be Tom, you know, only changed."

However much I had changed, it could not have been as much as she had changed. I scarcely know how to describe what she was like, her cloaths little better than rags and dripping with mud, her hair tangled and grey and matted. But it was not the externals of her appearance which troubled me as much as what lay beneath.

She took my hand in her muddy hand and I pulled her sliding from the ditch. The mud streamed from her boots and the lower part of her shanks. She drew very close, until her face was no more than three inches from mine.

"No, you are not Tom," she declared. "You are too old."

"We are both older, Lizzy, that is all. And I once had a mishap with my nose."

"Your nose?" She laughed again, and reached out a hand, as if to touch it, but stopped short. "Who did it? A man or a woman?"

"It was a man."

"Not Dick?"

"No, it was not Dick, it was no one you know."

"Dick is my husband," she said earnestly, "in sickness and health, for richer for poorer, till death us do part. That is true, is it not? They say it is true. For richer for poorer, in sickness and health."

"Indeed, it is true."

"Then why is he not here? If it were true, he would be here, wouldn't he?"

Betty spoke. "He be returning soon, Lizzy dear. He be returning on the first ship, soon as he be able, it is certain."

"No no," she replied, "you are mistaken, Betty, he will never come back. He will never come back, he has wed one of the native women. He has a little baby son."

"'Tis not true, Lizzy, 'tis not true."

"You are lying; I have seen the letter."

"'Tis not true, I promise you."

This was entirely obscure. I waited, and presently Lizzy returned her gaze to me. "Why then," she said, "maybe you are Tom Page, and you have come back. Have you come to dig? You will need a spade, you know. You cannot dig a ditch without a spade. Unless you do use your bare hands."

My heart was ready to burst. "I have come to see you, Lizzy. Will you walk this way?"

"Walk this way?" She tossed her head, in something like her old manner. "You are not my husband, are you?"

After some coaxing, however, she allowed me to lead her into the copse, beyond the ears of Betty and the other labourers. This copse was one which she and I had sometimes visited with the Elephants; now, as we stood among the hazels, with little patches of snow-drops at our feet, I would have liked to have revived Lizzy's memories of those happier days, but my tongue clove to the roof of my mouth. The wind cut between us, the trees gave no shelter. I asked her about her husband.

"Dick?" she said faintly.

"Yes; where is he?"

She gave a hopeless gesture with one hand. "You are looking for Dick?"

"No," I said. "No, Lizzy, I have come to ask for your forgiveness. For what I did to you, I must ask your forgiveness."

She gave a quick, nervous laugh. "And what did you do to me, Tom? What did you do?"

"It was in the stable, shortly before I left for Easton."

Between the hazels I could see that the labourers had abandoned their digging and were gathered together staring at us, no doubt hoping to glean some scraps of our conversation.

"Lizzy, do you not remember—before I left for Easton, with the female Elephant, what happened?"

She passed a muddy hand across her face, as though brushing away a spider's web. "I do remember the Elephants very well."

"One is still alive, the female. I still care for her."

"Not at the Hall. There are no Elephants at the Hall now."

"No, not at the Hall, but in London. But you do not remember what happened when I left?"

"What happened, Tom?" Her voice was quiet, her face attentive. "What was it you did to me?"

"I struck you."

"And why did you strike me, Tom?"

Under the heat of her question I felt myself flush, despite the chill of the wind. I did not want to answer. How, in truth, should I have answered? How could I have answered? That it had been the Ooze? But I did not think it had been the Ooze. That I had wanted to hurt her? Perhaps. But why I had wanted to hurt her, I cannot truly say. Why does any man act thus, and not thus? Is it because he is acting according to or against his own nature?

"I do not know, Lizzy, but it was a bad thing to do, it was wrong of me, which is why I now beg for your forgiveness."

"Then I do forgive you," she said simply. "It was nothing, Tom. But you did break my heart, you know, for choosing the Elephant over me, and that was what broke my heart, and I have not forgotten, I have never forgotten. You did go away and leave me behind. That was why I—why Dick—" She checked, and raised her eyes to mine. She was trembling. "You live in London now. It is very fine, people say."

"London is very big, and noisy," I said.

"The Elephant is well, I hope?"

"She is well enough, in the circumstances. She is a very wise creature."

There followed a short silence in which neither of us was able to speak. Her eyes were very large, and I felt that, as I looked into them, I was truly looking into her heart. She then said something but in such a low voice that I was unable to hear.

"I beg your pardon?"

"You and your wife, you have children?"

"No. She is—that is—no, we have no children."

She gave a piteous smile, and lowered her eyes to the snow-drops, which seemed very white against the dark mud clinging to her legs and boots. I touched her elbow and said, I am not sure what I said, but I led her trembling out of the copse. We made our farewells by the ditch. "I am glad the Elephant is well," she said in a bright voice, "Yes, I am very glad she is well, even though she were the cause of it all. She had a name, I know."

"Jenny," I said.

"Jenny. I remember. I remember. I remember." She lifted her

spade and, using it as a support, eased herself into the ditch. The next moment she was digging as if I no longer existed, or had gone long ago.

I trudged along the ditch as far as Betty. She told me that, three winters earlier, that same winter when the Thames froze in London, there had been a great deal of hardship in Somersetshire, with many poor families starving. Dick Shadwick had been caught in the act of stealing a deer from the grounds of Harrington Hall, as a result of which he had been transported for seven years to the other end of the world. I asked whether it was true that he had taken another wife. "That is what Lizzy imagines, but whether it is true . . . but it makes no difference if it is true or not, they never come back," she replied.—"Then I am very sorry for her. Why did she not go with him?" Betty said that it was a long voyage, and dangerous, and she had two young children. "And now?" I asked, dreading the answer, which was that both had died. When I repeated that I was very sorry, Betty looked at me with plain hostility. "Well you may be, Mr. Page. She is a gentle soul, and has suffered much."

Thus condemned I plodded away, the wind stiff in my face and the clods sticking to my boots like leg-irons. It was now late afternoon, but my only desire was to return to Jenny's side, and I walked through the night for about six hours until weariness overtook me, and with a hard rain commencing to fall I took shelter under a bush. Here I attempted to sleep, but could not put thoughts of Lizzy out of my head. The rain trickled through the thorns and my mind was so full of horrid ideas that I leapt up and started to run through the darkness, without exercising the least caution; twice, thrice, half a dozen times I tripped and lost my footing and fell into puddles, only to pick myself up again and run on. About five miles from Bath, as I panted along, I was set on by three robbers, armed with knives and cudgels, who sprang out of the night. I tried to flee, but they caught me and one felled me with a blow to the head. When I recovered my senses I was lying in the mire; they had taken my great coat, which contained not only my pipe and tobacco and the half loaf of bread, but also my purse, and inside it the five shillings on which I had been counting for the Coach. In addition they had relieved me of some teeth, and my face was very much swollen and bruised.

With my head throbbing, and cloaths thick with mud, I staggered into Bath, where for a day and a half I attempted to persuade people to lend me the fare, but in the condition I was everyone thought me a common beggar. One young lady with a kind face would I believe have taken pity on me, but that a fat crow of a Parson loudly ordered me away, declaring that my story as he put it was plainly nothing but a packet of lies. This made me even angrier; I stood my ground and let him know that, if he so desired, I was willing to take my oath on the Bible that every word I had uttered was true, whereupon he fastened a claw on the lady's arm and drew her away. So much for Christian charity, I muttered to myself with great bitterness. There were others to whom I applied, and one man was good enough to give me six pence, three of which I spent on a loaf of bread and a mug of ale, reserving three for further eventualities; thus I bade farewell to the city of Bath and set out on foot for London, the distance being no more than ninety or a hundred miles.

I walked through the day, and for the night found an old barn, somewhere short of Marlborough, where no one disturbed me and I was warm and comfortable though very troubled in my mind. The succeeding day being Saturday, which was the day that I had promised Jenny I would return, I walked on. Several coaches passed me travelling to London and as they rattled into the distance I cursed my ill-fortune. The wind blew steady from the north and cut me to the bone. Near the town of Hungerford I entered an inn, the John of Gaunt, where I drank a mug of ale and warmed myself at the fire; as I did so, the inn-keeper decided to engage me in conversation, inquiring whether I had got my swollen face from too much winking at women (for by this time I could scarcely see out of one eye). When he heard of my mishap, he said that I was lucky to have escaped with my life, the robbers in these parts being so notorious. Indeed he would not travel alone in the hours of darkness for any consideration; why, only two weeks earlier, two servants to Lady Finey, riding at night from Amesbury to Hungerford without any escorte, had lost their fingers and thumbs. Startled, I asked what he meant, whereupon he explained, with a beaming face, that it was a common superstition among thieves that a severed finger (which they kept in a leather pouch around their neck) protected them from harm when they were busy with their evil deeds. Such fingers were known as robbers' candles. I was not sure whether to believe him and may have looked confused. "O, it's well known—but you do not come from these parts, I can tell," he went on, and this remark threw me into further confusion, for where indeed did I come from? Three days earlier, I would have said without hesitation that I came from Somersetshire; now I no longer knew.

That night, with the inn-keeper's warnings fresh in my mind, I hunted for another barn or place of safety, but could find none, and was obliged to take refuge in a wood; not having my great coat to keep me warm, I heaped myself with dry leaves, but to little avail. The night growing steadily colder, the cloud clearing and the stars shining between the black branches, the wind blowing hard from the north, my teeth (such that I had left) chattered loudly, and I gave up any attempt at sleep. Better to die on my feet than freeze to death on my side, curled like a wood-louse, I thought. I walked very circumspectly; every bush and tree seemed loaded with danger and as I thought of the severed fingers I kept my hands in a tight clench.

On the Sunday morning I was very stiff, and my shoes were falling apart and within them my heels were cut and bleeding, but every step I took was another step nearer Jenny, and this thought bore me up. My spirits further revived when I sat on a bank eating my last scrap of bread, and the peals of some tower church began to float over the wet fields, and the sun peeped out its face behind the clouds. I took this as a sign that Fortune now favoured me, and this proved true enough, for while going along a straight piece of road I was over-taken by a man in a cart who, seeing my exhaustion, carried me more than twenty-five miles, though I was asleep for much of the way. He set me down near the Great Park at Windsor; so it was that on the evening of the Sunday I came to the river, and saw ahead of me the buildings of London town, and thus I returned to the Menagery, where to my joy I found that Jenny was safe and well. The moment when I opened the door and saw her again I shall never forget; her trunk stretched toward me and gave a purring vibration, and her eyes gleamed with pleasure and curiosity.

"Tom! You are back!"

I tried to smile, but my swollen face would scarcely let me. "I am back, I am back, and I am very glad to see you."

"I knew you would come back today," she said. "I knew you were coming."

"How could you know?"

"Last night you were very cold. I could tell. This morning I felt you coming nearer and nearer. I have been expecting you for the past hour." The tip of her purring trunk drifted over my cloaths. "You have been in mud."

"The mire."

"It is a good smell." The trunk, moving upwards, brushed my lips. "What happened? Did you meet little Joshua?"

"No." On a sudden I felt more weary than I believe I ever felt in my entire life. I took her trunk and wound it round my neck.

She waited. "What then? Did you learn anything of your brother? Where is your coat?"

"O, Jenny, Jenny . . . I will tell you later."

"Tell me later then, Tom. For now, it is good that you are back here. I have been thinking of you, all the time."

"You are the most wonderful Elephant. You are the most wonderful friend, my true friend, my only true friend."

"You are my Tom," she answered, simply. "Tom Page, Tom Page."

4

The price of this little Jaunt was that I fell into a Fever which kept me tossing and sweating in my bed for days, in which I scarcely knew whether I was in London or Somersetshire, or some other country. At the height of it I was beset by a strange fear that Jenny was merely a figment of my imagination, and that neither she nor the Menagery existed or had ever existed. When I attempted to argue that I knew she existed, as much as I myself existed, a voice, speaking within my head, asked how I knew, and when I replied, I know because I know, because I saw her lately, the voice said, you think you saw her but in truth you did not see her, she is part of your imagination. I cried out, but I did see her, I am certain of it, I talked to her, and the voice answered, very severely, you did not talk to her, Tom Page, no human being can talk with an animal, it is against all natural law. And who are you? I asked—at which the voice fell silent, and I felt better, and sank into an uneasy dream in which I found myself back in the Strand, outside the Menagery. The doors were locked and bolted against me; and though I hammered with my fists and shouted, no one would let me in. Why, I asked myself, will no one let me in, and instantly I saw a ladder, which was propped against the side of the building. I climbed it, and in this way reached a small and dusty hatch, which I opened with some difficulty, using a strange crooked lever. This gave me a view over the Menagery, in which Mr. Scott sat on Jenny's neck and rode her round her cage. So I understood that Mr. Scott was now her keeper, and I was for ever shut out from Jenny's love.

My mother always held that dreams were a form of prophecy, which I do not believe, but do not entirely disbelieve either; and in my fevered state this terrible dream made a great impression on me. As I lay in bed, one moment burning hot and the next shaking with cold, I convinced myself that it was indeed true, and that Mr. Scott had deliberately persuaded me to visit Somersetshire with the sole aim of making himself Jenny's keeper in my absence. I could not help recalling all the little signs of affection which she had shewn toward him, how on this occasion she had followed him everywhere with her eyes, how on another she had wrapped her trunk round his neck and drawn it gently over his cheek. What a fool I had been to leave them alone!

I must have again fallen asleep, for when I woke there was darkness outside and a strange clamour in the street. Listening to this clamour, and wondering at its cause, I heard the words *fire* and *Strand*, and a sudden conviction took hold of me that the Menagery was ablaze. Springing from my bed I ran to the window. A red flickering glow hung over the roof-tops, and in my imagination I seemed to see the flames as they rippled up the walls and spread along the beams, leaping to light the tinder-dry grass of the Man-Eater's mane and the straw which lapped Jenny's legs.

Bare-foot, and wearing nothing but a night-shirt, I ran into White Horse Yard and down Drury Lane, and as I reached the Strand I smelt the smoke. The fire turned out to be some way short of the Menagery, with several houses ablaze, among them a well-known whore-house which I myself had visited more than a few times. A number of whores stood outside, in various states of dishevelment, coughing and choking and gaping at the fire as it raged and crackled. Men were running to and fro with pails of water which they tossed on to the flames, but in truth nothing could be done to tame the blaze; the heat was so intense that it was impossible to approach very near without being roasted alive. This proved a blessing, however, for on a sudden a fiery truss which had been dangling by a thread from an upper storey crashed to the stones in a shower of sparks. One man, struck on the shoulder, fell burning to the ground; water was instantly poured over him and the fire extinguished, though his cloaths continued to smoke. Another man, with a blackened face and wild eyes, ran hither and thither crying hoarsely for his wife, or maybe his daughter. Meanwhile the occupants of the adjacent houses, fearing the spread of the fire, were hurriedly carrying chests and tables and the rest of their possessions into the street.

I had the same fear with regard to the Menagery, yet outside its doors I met Mr. Scott smoking a pipe in his usual calm way. Later he chuckled as he told me how astonished he was to see me clad in nothing but a thin night-shirt, and that in my Fever I shrieked and babbled that the animals must be brought out, they would all be burnt alive, there was not a moment to be lost, et cetera. When he attempted to reason with me, pointing out that the wind was taking the flames in another direction, I cursed him and swung a fist at his head, and ran into the Menagery, where I attempted to lead Jenny from her cage. I remember none of this, only that I woke in daylight to find myself lying in a bed of straw, covered in the monkie's great coat, and Jenny watching me.

The Fever passed, but for a long while afterward I was unable to tell Jenny about my journey to Harrington Hall. When I did at last manage to speak on the subject, I made no mention of Lizzy Tindall. I cannot forget her dark face, she haunts me even now: she rises like a ghost from the wet ditch and stares at me with an expression which says, louder than any words, Take me with you to London now, Dick will never return, take me with you to London. What should I have said? What could I have said? She is married, even if her husband has abandoned her; it would not be possible to bring her here. And yet that face, those eyes . . . it was a mistake to go back. I reproach myself greatly for having done so.

My spirits in those days were further lowered by the concerts, which are another of Mr. Cross's desperate schemes to revive the fortunes of the Menagery.—Concerts, pray? *Animal* concerts?—Yes, Sir, indeed—though it must be added, in all conscience, with regard to the Truth (and, please note, the capital T), that they contain no music.—No music, why, how can a concert be a concert if it has no music? Explain yourself!—Well, Sir, by your leave, I shall do what I can.

It was about a month after I had returned from Somersetshire that Mr. Cross came into the Menagery with a cheap fiddle. Mr. Scott and I should teach the monkie to play some tunes, he said, to accompany the Empress on her drum, while Bruin the bear should learn to dance in time. "Rule Britannia," played by a monkie and an Elephant, with a dancing bear, would be sure to draw in the crowds.

Teaching Jenny to hit the drum with a stick was easy enough; she mastered it in a matter of minutes. Instructing Stephen to play the fiddle was much more difficult. During that first lesson, we succeeded in putting the bow into Stephen's left hand (it had to be the left, for the right, as I mentioned, is withered to a dead bird's claw); however, he had no idea why he was being asked to hold the bow, and, as soon as we stepped away, he let it fall to the floor. I picked it up, replaced it in his hand, folding his bony fingers below mine; at which, Mr. Scott knelt before us, offering the fiddle, and I began to guide the bow over the gut. The sound frightened the little monkie: his mouth opened wide, and his scraggy body shook and trembled. However, it was a kind of progress, and as a reward Mr. Scott decided to give him a pipe of tobacco, lifting it to his lips. I was sure that he would be burnt, and indeed, as soon as he breathed in the hot smoke, he choked and fell gasping to the floor.

Since then, Stephen has advanced on the fiddle to the extent that he will hold the bow without dropping it, and will scrape and saw at the fiddle, so long as Mr. Scott or I hold the fiddle and guide the bow. The bow saws thin air more often than not, and when it touches the gut, the noise is a wild, horrible caterwauling. The art of fiddle-playing is so far beyond his capabilities that, if he were taught for the rest of eternity, he would never play anything like "Rule Britannia." However, to my great surprize, he has entirely mastered the art of pipe-smoking, and sits for hours with the pipe between his lips, even when it is empty of tobacco. The pipe has become his pet, his passion, his reason for living: if you try to take it from him, in order to fill it with tobacco, he refuses—runs to the corner of his prison and hides it behind his back, where he squats, baring his teeth in a pitiful threat. "Come, Sir—come, Stephen—don't be so naughty—put away those fierce teeth, Sir, and hand over your pipe. I insist, Stephen." Mr. Scott laughs loudly, and indeed I laugh too; Stephen's anguish is so human, it is hard not to laugh. Sometimes we let him keep it, yet other times we get it off him, prising it from his tight fingers: whereupon he howls and shrieks, flinging himself to the ground. We fill it with a few sprigs of tobacco, and hand it back. "Stephen—here—see, your pipe—have it back." Sunk in misery, he will not open his eyes. "Stephen—here—" Then he looks up, and in an instant his little face is transformed from misery to joy. And why should Stephen, whose life contains so much fear, not have this simple pleasure?

As for Bruin, he is as good at dancing as Stephen is at playing the violin; which is to say that he does not dance at all, but understands that he is supposed to do something, and when the cacophony begins, therefore, he lies on the ground and rolls from side to side, grimacing hideously, and collecting straw and dung in his fur. He does this because he hopes to please us, and so to be rewarded with a lump of sugar or some other tid-bit, and also because he is afraid. So he rolls, and Stephen scrapes the violin, and Jenny bangs the drum, and people laugh, and Mr. Cross is delighted, and rubs his hands in glee; while I, steering Stephen's bony arm, and watching this sorry spectacle, imagine the lives which these creatures might have had, among their own kind, if they had never been captured. Bright pictures of jungles and mountains and plains float through my mind, like sunlit clouds. It is a vision almost too much to bear; my eyes prickle in shame: for even as I write, "among their own kind," I feel a kinship with these creatures. We inhabit the same world; we breathe the same air, beneath the same sky. We have two eyes, two ears, teeth, a brain, a heart. We are born into a state of helplessness; we grow, and learn to fend for ourselves; we feel pleasure and pain; we grow old and die. Why do philosophers always look for differences instead of likenesses? A flea makes no great distinction in its choice of living quarters: it prefers a bear, but will cheerfully take ship on a monkie or lion or Elephant, or a human being.

Shortly after the end of one of these concerts, I was cleaning between Jenny's toes with a small brush when I heard my name. Looking up, I saw a stooping, elderly man in a coat and hat. "Tom," he said, "it is Tom, isn't it? Tom Page? How are you now? I thought it must be you. Why," for I was at a loss, "don't you recognise me? You remember—I was at Easton—years ago—did a portrait of the Elephant. John Sanders." He took off his hat, which glistened with rain-drops, and I recognised him then, of course; though the foxy tinge to his hair had entirely faded away, and he seemed somewhat smaller than I had remembered, an air of snuff still clung to him. He shook me warmly by the hand. "Yes, I'd heard that there was an Elephant here," he said, "and I'd meant to call in. I thought that it must be the same one."

He asked what had happened to me, after the death of Lord Bidborough and the sale of the estate at Easton, and I told him how the Elephant had been sold from one owner to another, down the years, until she was finally bought by Mr. Cross.

"So you stayed with the creature? Thick and thin?"

"I did."

He seemed to reflect. "And what does your wife think of London town?"

"I am not married."

"Well, and why should you be? When you marry, you're no longer a free man, believe me." He called to his wife, who was watching Mr. Scott toss the snake a mouse: "Edith—come over here—I was right—it is the same Elephant!"

Mrs. Sanders, a stout, burly woman, with a heavy brown umbrella which made a puddle on to the floor, said that she was very pleased to make my acquaintance, having heard all sorts of stories about the Elephant from her husband. "Told me he was nearly trampled alive, once—didn't you, John?"

"I was scared all the time, to tell the truth," Mr. Sanders replied. "Every moment that I was painting. It wasn't in a cage, like this—it was standing in the open! There was only Tom keeping it off me! I tell you, my hand shook like a leaf. O, it was a miracle that I ever finished that painting! I've often wondered what happened to it."

"John, it's always like that," said Mrs. Sanders. "You've done so many portraits, and you never know where any of them are, do you?"

"But it was a good portrait, that one," he answered her. "One of the best I ever did, I'd say; could be the best. At least, the only one that I ever did of an Elephant. I shouldn't mind seeing it again, though I don't suppose I ever will."

There came a loud howl from the monkie. I begged their pardon, and went to see what the matter was. It turned out that Stephen had dropped his pipe, which had shattered. He sat over the broken pieces, rocking to and fro with grief and giving small wails and sobs, like a child whose toy has been broken. Tears coursed down his wrinkled cheeks. "Stephen? Stephen. It is only a pipe. I will get you another pipe." He did not understand; instead, thinking that I was going to steal the remains of the pipe, he gathered them together and retreated to brood in the furthest corner of the cage.

I took out my pipe, put it on the floor, and, leaving him to recover his composure, returned to Mr. and Mrs. Sanders. We talked for ten or fifteen minutes, and I asked him how the Art was progressing. He replied that he was "still grubbing in the same soil," though it had become no easier to find work. There were fallow patches. The fashions in painting had changed; the animal work had largely dried up, and everyone now was interested in landskips. So, he had become a landskip painter, producing views of ruined abbeys and castles, and sunsets and lakes.

"Do you know Richmond Castle, in Yorkshire? I did that recently. Jervaux Abbey. I take what comes along. If I was asked to do more animals, I wouldn't refuse."

"He never refuses anything," Mrs. Sanders put in. "Do you, John? Why, you ought to do one of the animals here. Look at that lion. It's asking to have its portrait taken!"

We glanced round. The Man-Eater, chewing one of his paws, looked utterly dejected.

"You could do it if you wanted," Mrs. Sanders said. "You could do better than whoever did those daubs." By "daubs," she meant the pictures on the walls of the Menagery. "Much better," she added.

Mr. Sanders did not speak for a moment. "It would be a Challenge, certainly," he conceded at last. "An Artistic Challenge. To take the likeness of a lion. The King of the Beasts."

"It would be a Feather in your Hat," she told him. "A proper Feather."

Mr. Sanders regarded his hat with an expression of some doubt, turning it in his hands.

"John, now we're here, you may as well ask," Mrs. Sanders urged. "It never does any harm, asking. If you don't ask, you'll never know."

I directed him to Mr. Cross, who was sat in his little booth. While he was there, Mrs. Sanders talked of their children. They seemed to be doing well enough. Of their daughters, one was married, with two children, while the other had lately been widowed, but was bearing up and recovering her spirits at home with them. As for their sons, the elder was employed by a bank in the city, and the younger was a school-master in Highgate. On balance, she was glad that neither had decided to follow in their father's footsteps as an Artist. "It's not easy, Art," she told me. "It's not like people think. You can't depend on it, with assurance. There's not sufficient security."

Mr. Sanders came back soon enough. He seemed relieved that Mr. Cross had declined to commission a portrait of the lion. "I wouldn't really have wanted to do it. I wouldn't have done it. I've finished with animals."

"Well, you were right to ask," Mrs. Sanders said firmly. "But tell Mr. Page about the death-masks."

"O," said Mr. Sanders, "that's the latest," and mentioned the name of some rich gentleman, Sir John F—, an alderman of the City of London, whose mask he had taken recently. "It's not hard, once you know how. You take the first impression in plaster-of-paris, before casting in bronze. I'm hoping it'll build up. Word of mouth, that's how these things work. I've thought about advertising, but it's expensive."

"Practised on me at the start, he did—didn't you, John?" Mrs. Sanders gave a joyous laugh. "I felt half-dead! Plaster up my nostrils!"

Mr. Sanders nodded, and confessed, in a tone of slight melancholy: "It's not what I ever expected to be doing—death-masks. They're not what you'd call Art."

"You have to take what Life gives, John," Mrs. Sanders said, rallying him. "You can't always pick and choose. We do very nicely for ourselves. We're very fortunate, compared to many."

They lived in the country, about eight miles south of London, in the village of Streatham. Mrs. Sanders gave me their address, and said that, if I could escape, I would be very welcome to join them for Sunday dinner, and to bring my wife. "He is not married," Mr. Sanders corrected. "In that case," said Mrs. Sanders, "he is very welcome to bring himself."

I thanked her, but said that, since I had to look after the Elephant, it was impossible to leave on a Sunday, it being our busiest day of the week.

Mrs. Sanders looked at Jenny, who was calmly waiting for me to finish my conversation. "Surely you can leave the creature for half a day? Can't someone else take care of it?"

She pressed me so hard that, eventually, I went to Mr. Cross, and, to my dismay, he raised no strong objection. Thus it was agreed that I would visit them on the next Sunday but one, arriving about noon. Mrs. Sanders said, that she would roast a joint of meat, if that was agreeable to me. I replied that it was very agreeable.

"That's easy, then," said she. "We shall look forward to your company. O, it's good meeting up with old friends, isn't it, John?"

"It is, indeed," Mr. Sanders agreed, with a faint smile.

After he and Mrs. Sanders had gone, I found little Stephen smoking his new pipe—his eyes closed in what I took to be an ecstasy, though his expression was that of a soul in torment. I left him, and returned to Jenny, who held out the little brush which I had been using on her toes. "Tom?"

"Jenny, Mr. and Mrs. Sanders have invited me to Sunday dinner. Should I go?"

"Why, of course you should go, Tom, if you would like to."

"It would mean leaving you for part of the day. You would not mind? Mr. and Mrs. Sanders's daughter, who has been widowed, is living with them."

Her trunk swayed upwards. She regarded me with some anxiety.

"She may not be there," I said.

"Tom," she said seriously, "if you want to marry anyone, you must do so. I understand."

I laughed. "When I have never even met her, it is a little early to talk of marriage. She is probably ugly and sallow-skinned, and hare-lipped. Besides," and I reached out with my arms, and gazed into her eyes, "how could I marry her? O, Jenny! How could I ever marry someone else, when I am married already?"

This reply seemed to satisfy her, for her trunk reached out and affectionately brushed my ear. After which, she gave me a little tap on the side of the head, as if to reprove me for such a foolish remark.

5

In the days after this surprizing visit, I found myself thinking of Mr. and Mrs. Sanders a great deal. It seemed altogether strange that he should have said that he was frightened of Jenny, when he was at Easton; hard as I searched my memory, I could not remember him being frightened. Nor could I explain Mrs. Sanders's remark about old friends: it did not appear to me that Mr. Sanders and I had ever been true friends, or that we had even approached that condition. However, there was no doubt, that to invite me to their home for Sunday dinner was a clear offer of friendship.

Ever since the calamities of my journey to Somersetshire, I had felt a great reluctance to leave Jenny's side. However, the Sunday was a fine sunny day, and I reached Streatham in under two hours' walking, and there had a very merry time of it. Mrs.

Sanders cooked a shoulder of mutton, with capers, and potatoes in gravy, and afterward we ate gooseberry pie and a custard. I was then prevailed upon to try a pinch of Mr. Sanders's snuff, which . brought tears to my eyes and afforded the rest of the company a vast quantity of amusement; when Mrs. Sanders developed a fit of violent hiccupping, even their widowed daughter Jane, who had been very quiet, seemed to smile. Mr. Sanders later shewed me the plaster-of-paris mask which he had taken of Jane's dead husband, and this I greatly admired.

I walked back to the Menagery feeling much revived, and that very evening began to hunt for the History of the Elephant, which I wrote at Easton. At first, I could not find it, and became greatly agitated, lest it had been stolen. Who would want to steal such a worthless thing? Yet it meant more than a little something to me, both because of the many hours I had spent writing, all that time ago, and because of the memories which it contained. At length, I did find it, to my relief, though I also found that the ink had faded badly, and that a beetle had feasted on the sheets, devouring letters and even entire words, and tunnelling nearly to the end, where Death was written in the shape of its grey, flattened, snub-nosed skeleton.

This, I said to myself, is the History of the Beetle, within the History of the Elephant.

As I sat and turned its tattered pages, all kinds of curious thoughts ran through my head. Despite its title, the History no longer seemed to contain as much truth as it might have done. Certain things (it said) had happened; but they seemed as improbable as the adventures of Gulliver. Did I, Tom Page, truly once meet two Elephants, along with a dead leopard, and a baboon with a white beard and blue testicles, on the quay in Bristol? Did the hand of the same Tom Page truly hold the pen that made those marks, and those, on this trembling sheet of paper? Yet, as I read on, I also thought how different my life might have been. I might have married Lizzy, and stayed in Thornhill as an ordinary groom at Harrington Hall, or she might have come with me to Easton, and we would have had sons and daughters, like Mr. and Mrs. Sanders, and lived in a little house. Or, I might have followed Timothy to Grimsthorpe, and saved him from madness. Or, I might have ignored my father's advice, and gone to sea in search of adventure, like my brother, and become a wealthy man. Another thought then crossed my mind: that I might never have gone to Bristol, all those years ago, and met Jenny and Timothy. Indeed, Jenny and Timothy might have died on the ship which brought them from the Indies, or might never have been captured and taken on board! How many possibilities we face, at every turn! I might never have been born! I might have been born an Elephant, not a human being!

I do not feel any lasting regrets, however. They arrive like passing clouds; they blow across the sky and hide the sun, and then they are gone. The past is past; as to the future, it must be left to write itself. Jenny will very likely survive me, for while it cannot be true that Elephants live as long as two hundred years, no one doubts that the span of their natural lives greatly exceeds that of human beings, and so, though it pains me to contemplate the prospect, I must believe she will find another keeper. Long before then, however—and this I also must believe—there will come a time when she and I will leave the Menagery, or when the Menagery will leave London (for certainly we cannot stay here for ever, with Mr. Cross losing money, and what remains of his hair—it is, as Mr. Scott puts it, laughing, a nice question as to which will disappear sooner, for on the latter count Mr. Cross has only three or four greasy strands left, which he proudly drags over his pate

or hides under his wig)—and we will once more find ourselves
among the nightingales.

Until then, I am attempting to follow Jenny's example, that is,
to avoid false hopes and to live in the present time, extracting what
value I can from each passing moment. A giant, whiskered rat,
tumbling through a hole in the ceiling's rotten plaster, runs across
my chest: Why, good morning, your Worship. A servant girl, leaning from a window, empties a chamber-pot, and its foul contents
splash my feet: Well, good afternoon, Madam. Two watch-men,
stopping outside the Menagery, wake me with their noisy shouting: Ah, good night to you, Gentlemen.

After all, this city has much to offer. New stories, old stories,
new versions of old stories, abound at every turn; they are part of
the common currency, traded like any other goods. A visit to the
Market supplies not only carrots and potatoes, but also the tale of
a drunken butcher who fell into a drain, and was not recovered
for ten days, and then only because his dog smelt him out, and
barked at the entrance to the drain, raising the alarm. This story is
probably untrue, or not wholly true. "It is not important. I believe
them all," Jenny says. "I like your stories, Tom. Tell me another."
So I tell her about the young woman, forced to work in a Lambeth
stew, in which line of employment she found herself accosted by
her own sweating father, whom she recognised during the act by a
prominent mole on his ear-lobe. Or, say some, another part of his
anatomy. Again, this is probably less than true, but the question
of what is or is not true now seems less important to me. It may
be true, it is possible; and on that possibility both she and I feed
with relish.

The summer has now faded, and we have sailed into autumn
weather. It drips, it drizzles, it pelts, it pours; between clouds
the sun shoots out a ray, but never for long. Leaves from distant

trees whirl through the air, and carts and carriages clatter up and down the puddled streets. Two afternoons ago, between showers, I walked up to the Market and bought a sack of apples for Jenny; and having done so, joined a small crowd which had formed in a circle around a drunken man trying to dance to an organ. He swayed and lurched, rolled his eyes and seemed to trip on the wet cobbles, but then recovered himself. People were clapping and jeering. Presently, a crippled woman, bare-foot, with scarcely a tooth in her head, broke from the circle and joined in, the man clasping her by the waist and holding her in a tight embrace. I am certain that they did not know each other; they were complete strangers. But as I watched them reeling to and fro, growing ever more breathless and giddy, I found myself remembering Mrs. Sanders's remark that one has to take what Life offers. I am sure she is right. Not to take what Life offers would be a great mistake, and taking what Life offers must be one of the secrets of happiness. Is that not what, in their own way, the two dancers were doing? And indeed, is that not what, in her own way, Jenny has taught me? If I remain uneasy, I think, it is perhaps merely because Life seems to offer different people such different things.

The drunken man and crippled woman stumbled round and round, and at last they fell in a heap, gasping. Everyone cheered and jeered, and dispersed. I went to the east of the square, in search of fresh oranges; I found none, but noticed some short blackish objects, curved in shape, on a barrow which stood beneath one of the arches. Never having seen the like before, I asked the costermonger what fruit they were. "Bananas," he told me. "Banana fruit." Startled, I remarked that I had always understood bananas to be green—for I could remember Mr. Coad saying as much, years ago—whereupon he fired up and roundly declared that they were bananas when they were taken off the *Rose*, which had landed at Deptford that very morning, after a voyage from the Indies, and since then they had not changed, they were still bananas. "And anyone who says otherwise is either a block-head or a liar," he asserted, in a pleasant tone of challenge—which I hastened to decline, saying that I was sure that, since he said they were bananas, they could be nothing else, and had never intended to suggest otherwise. This mollified him; he grew more amiable, and told me that when bananas reached these shores, after weeks at sea, they were generally rotten; however, these particular speci-mens had, against the odds, survived the voyage in reasonable con-dition. "Sailors don't like 'em," he added. "Think they bring bad luck." When I asked him about the taste of bananas, he replied that opinions varied. They had a curious taste, unlike any other fruit, being neither sweet nor sour. They had no pips, or none to speak of, and very little juice. The skin was not eaten. "You throw the skin away. The part you eats is inside the skin." Taking up a banana, and stripping back the black skin, he revealed the pale, pulpy, sweet-smelling flesh.

I bought six, even though they cost three shillings, and bore them back to the Menagery where, for once, I found a goodly number of visitors. Several were standing at Jenny's cage—among them a little boy whose eyes, at the sight of an Elephant, nearly started from his head. He was no more than three years old, I would guess, and I found myself imagining that I, like him, was seeing an Elephant for the first time. What a magnificent creature she is, I thought—so huge and grey, so calm, so wise! How could I ever regret her part in my life? Yet there was a curious expres-sion on her face, as though she was thinking about something very hard, so hard that she had not seen me.

I put down the sack of apples and invited the boy and his mother into the cage, assuring them that they would be perfectly safe. Once they were inside, I gave a banana to the boy, who held it toward the Elephant. When she took it from him and put it in her mouth, his face lit with astonished delight. Her trunk came out a second time, and coiled round his hand, and shook it.

"The Empress is thanking you," I said. "Would you like to ride on her back?"

The boy's mouth fell open—in his emotion he lost all power of speech—but his mother said, "O, Sir, that would be such a treat for him, if he could!"

In a moment, he was swung high through the air and seated on her neck. "Hold her ears, and you will be safe," I said, and the boy reached out, and clung to her ears.

He did not stay there long. She lifted him down, and he and his mother, having expressed their thanks, walked on.

"How is it," I said to Jenny, "that such a boy, so sweet and innocent and gentle, can become what most men become? What savagery is there, in human nature, waiting to emerge?"

She stared at me. "What was that fruit, Tom? Have you any more?"

Sliding my hand into the sleeve of my coat, I held up five black fingers. "Do you remember? They are bananas."

"I do remember, Tom," she said. "I remember very well."

I gave her the bananas, one by one, and she planted them in her mouth, and her pleasure was such that it made me feel very happy indeed.

It was near the end of the day. I lit my pipe.

"What were you thinking of, Jenny?" I asked. "When I came in just now. What were you thinking?"

She swung her trunk gently, and answered through a mouthful of banana. "I was not thinking, Tom. I was writing."

"Writing? Jenny, you cannot write!"

"I write in my head," she replied. "Surely, is it not true that all writing begins in the head?"

"Or in the heart. Well . . . but how many pages have you written?"

"I am not writing in pages. It is all one page." She seemed shy. "One long Page."

"What are you writing? A poem?"

"A story."

"A story? What story?"

"I am writing the True History of Tom Page, the keeper of an Elephant, who was born in the year seventeen fifty-three, in the village of Thornhill, in Somersetshire," she said.

"O!" I took my pipe from my mouth and stared curiously at her. "And where does this History end? Here? Not here, I hope?"

The end of her trunk gave an expressive twirl, this way and that. "Why, Tom, of course not; there are many possibilities," she said.

Part IV

The repository, a concrete building to the south of the River Thames, gives no clue as to its contents. In a dream I press the intercom button, speak my name; the door softly opens. I advance down a corridor, tiled with black and white squares, to the reception area. Lying on an unmanned desk is a form, for visitors; it asks for my name and address, and the purpose of my research. I tick the box marked "Private." It asks for the subject of my research; after some hesitation, I write:

"Exotic animals of the 18th century."

There is no one to give the form to. I leave it on the desk, push through another door and find myself inside the mausoleum.

Bones. The bones of birds, animals, reptiles hang in aisles like clothes in an enormous dry cleaner's. The aisles taper into the distance, a hundred, two hundred yards, further; I can't even see where they end. They disappear into a gathering gloom.

The air is very still, and dry, humidity controlled. As for the smell, that's hard to define, but it must be none other than quintessence of bone.

The floor before me slopes gently forward, so that, as I take my first steps, I have a sense of a gradual descent, and also of a sudden self-consciousness. An overhead camera is recording my progress—someone, the keeper of the temple, is watching from another room—but that can't be the reason, I'm used to CCTV. It must be the skeletons themselves. There are so many, so many more than I had anticipated, or thought possible; each species represented by dozens, even hundreds of specimens, each specimen similar to the other. In this great company, I am the only thing still alive. It feels as though the skeletons are watching.

But, also, I'm watching myself. Who am I to disturb the dead air of this ossuary? By what right am I here?

Every step seems an act of sacrilege. I wish that I had worn shoes with rubber, not leather, soles.

I walk down an aisle of tigers, servals, lions, cheetahs, cougars, members of the cat family, baring their useless teeth. I take a right turn, and come upon the mallet and truncheon and club-hammer bones of the horses and zebras, their mouths neighing silently. I continue past small fish, large fish: arrangements of spikes and needles, eyeless and finless, though some still brandish their old weapons—spears, daggers, sabres, a once fearsome armory. The further I advance into this underworld, the greater my apprehension becomes. The skeletons seem more densely packed, the aisles narrower; it's hard to move without touching the protruding bones. There's less light, too; I'm negotiating a kind of interior dusk, a layered shade, in which the only colors are tints of gray.

One could spend hours searching; one could lose one's way and disappear forever.

Yet I find the elephants easily enough; instantly recognizable, they hang in a long, lunar procession beyond the tapirs and warthogs. Their rib cages are the hooped sides of stranded ships. Their spines are lines of jagged rock on the seashore. Few have any tusks, which must have been removed, but some still have stumps embedded in the great sculptural plates of their skulls.

Attached to each skeleton is an old-fashioned luggage ticket, on which are written the identity of the species in question, the sex of the animal and the date and manner of its death. The first elephants I examine are all *Loxodonta africana*, the African elephant; but at last I reach the Asian elephants. *Elephas maximus.*

MALE, D. INDIA, 1959. SHOT

MALE, D. SIAM, 1937. SHOT

MALE, D. CEYLON, 1935. SHOT

FEMALE, D. ASSAM, 1924. SHOT

The shots ring out in my head. Shot after shot after shot after shot.

FEMALE, D. RAJASTHAN, INDIA, 1913. SHOT

BABY FEMALE, D. BURMA, 1903. SHOT

Label after label. As I walk slowly on, I realize that the skeletons have been hung in chronological sequence. The further I move along the procession, the further back in time I'm going.

Thus I arrive at the late eighteenth century, and at a single gray, dangling shape. I reach up, my heart beating, to the label tied round one of the curving ribs.

FEMALE, D. LONDON, ENGLAND, C. 1799. PNEUMONIA?

A vast face, a dune of curves, with two dark hollows for the eye sockets. Is this, was this, once, my Jenny?

No answer. But a low vibration disturbs me. What is this? Then I realize: beneath my feet, not far beneath my feet, must be an Underground line. As the trembling grows, I seem to see the train pass below me, its brightly lit carriages threading its cargo of passengers through the darkness. Men, women, children, none of them aware of what lies above, and each of their minds a little carriage of light, with its own pictures. I long to take my seat on this train, I long for the train to carry me away to the next station. But this is not where the dream is going. The vibration, having risen to a thrum, fades and dies, and again I am left in the strange twilight. I touch the skeleton with a gentle finger; it moves, and the movement transmits along the wire from which she hangs so that the next skeleton up the aisle moves too. I push again, harder now, and harder, and she sways, and a century of elephants begins to sway in unison, creaking to and fro, and for a moment it becomes nearly possible to reclothe these tatty bones in skin and flesh, to reimagine them into life. But the swaying soon subsides, like the passing train; imagination fails. If there are such things as spirits, why assume that they stay beside their bones? Surely the spirit of Jenny would be by Tom's side, roaming in the warm fields? Where else could it be?

And suddenly I am frightened. As I stand among these gaunt relics, the dream has thrown up a terrible possibility: that Tom and Jenny's love may have failed, that Tom has married Mr. and

Mrs. Sanders's widowed daughter, Jane, and that they have gone to live in a quaint, weatherboarded cottage in Kent. They have three little children, on whom Tom dotes. He works as a groom to the Reverend Andrew Gould, a fox-hunting parson. While Jenny, alone and abandoned, dies of pneumonia in the chill of some London winter.

Is it possible? It is possible.

Is it true?

LET US REFUSE TO BELIEVE this dream. Let us calmly reject this possibility and try another approach. We know—it was reported in the *Times*—that Gilbert Cross, the proprietor of Cross's Famous Menagerie, died on the tenth of February, 1794. We know that he died childless and deep in debt, and that the menagerie closed shortly afterward. A register of the animals was compiled for the purposes of the sale: it includes a bear, a monkey, a snake and a lion, but it does not include an elephant. The elephant has disappeared. How can an elephant disappear? Hard to say. But it may be worth noting that from the fourteenth to the seventeenth of February, according to the meteorological journal kept by William Bent, of Paternoster Row, much of London lay in the grip of a dense, clammy fog, during which it was apparently hard to see from one side of the street to another.

Come with me into this lost, fog-bound city. Come through the muffled streets and forgotten alleys. It is midnight on the sixteenth of February, and we are standing in the Strand, outside the menagerie. The streetlamps have been lit, but the fog traps and contains their swirling light. As we wait for something to happen, a pair of doors suddenly opens, and out come Sam Scott and Tom Page, and behind them Jenny. In the fog she seems huge. The two men say some brief words and shake hands. Then, reaching down with her trunk, she swings Tom into the damp air, lowers him onto her neck and strides in the direction of Charing Cross.

Few people witness her progress. A pair of tired watchmen, a drunkard swaying over the cobbles, two elderly prostitutes coughing in the entrance to a jeweler's shop. A horse, pulling a chaise in which a young blade caresses his new mistress after an evening at the playhouse, almost collides with the elephant; it gives a wild, frightened swerve at this ghostly juggernaut and careers away. The elephant continues, her stride quickening: past Charing Cross, down Whitehall, into Parliament Street, along Abingdon Street. Then more streets, and more, and at last she and her passenger reach the river, sliding through the fog like a dark snake.

There is a bridge over the river, and at the entrance to the bridge is a toll gate, and even in this nighttime fog there stands a solitary man, the ancient gatekeeper, the keeper to the gates of heaven. He is carrying a lantern, a globe of foggy light. As the elephant looms out of the murk he reels, raising the lantern, but by now she is moving at such a pace that she barely seems to touch the ground. With Tom crouched low on her neck, she hurtles over the bridge, forcing a way through the fog, which closes behind.

What then? Who knows? It would seem that the fog hides Tom and Jenny forever. Yet there are some old stories, which may be true, or may contain some shadows of truth, at least.

These stories relate how, one spring and early summer in the mid 1790s, a man and an elephant traveled through the green countryside of southern England and at each town and village were greeted with admiration and delight. The elephant was a female, and though her prodigious appetite and great strength were noted, what appear to have impressed people the most were her gentleness and good nature. One story describes how at dusk, near a small village, the man and elephant trundled down a track which led to a pond. At the man's command, the elephant rolled over, and lay on her side to be washed and scrubbed. This accomplished, the man sat on the bank, while the elephant splashed and bathed to her heart's content. A large moon had swum into view, and to the watching villagers it seemed as though the gleaming elephant was herself part of the moonlight.

Nowhere is the name of the man given, but according to the stories he was a native of Somersetshire, and he possessed an extraordinary ability to communicate with the elephant. It is this last detail, above all, which surely confirms that the man and the elephant were Tom and Jenny. What joy they must have taken in their escape from the city. What joy they must have felt as they walked down the quiet woodland lanes, as they crossed meadows white with lady's smock, as they trailed through fields of long, silvery grass skimmed by swallows. While the stories give no hint as to how their journey ended, the general direction of their travel would seem to have been westward, and it is at least possible that their immediate destination was the port of Bristol. Perhaps, therefore, just perhaps, some time in late May or early June 1794, Tom and Jenny took ship for the Indies.

If so, this ship must be none other than the *Fortune,* a vessel of two hundred tons, under the command of Captain James Page, Tom's brother. On its voyage it appears to us in a series of pictures: moving down the narrow muddy river and swinging toward the choppy waters of the open sea; wallowing and pitching through a thunderstorm in the Bay of Biscay; heeling and creaking and groaning along the coast of Africa. It rounds the Cape of Good Hope and enters the Straits of Madagascar, and gales buffet and toss it like a little toy. Yet, as its name suggests, this is a lucky ship; it survives all; and before it vanishes we have a last glimpse of it in its crossing of the Arabian Sea. The day is fine, the air soft as milk, the sea a pearly luminescence, and Tom and Jenny are standing on deck, side by side, by the forward rail, with Jenny's spread ears echoing the wide, rippling sails. We too are on deck; and suddenly Tom seems to catch sight of us, and murmurs something to Jenny, and both look, curious, puzzled, in our direction. Much as we would like to make some gesture, to establish communication, there is nothing that we can do. For now a sailor high in the rigging gives a loud shout, and Tom and Jenny turn away from us, and gaze over that shining sea toward the crinkled line of writing on the distant horizon.

Reading Group Guide

England, 1773: After a long voyage from the East Indies, a ship docks in Bristol, England, and rumor quickly spreads about its unusual cargo—some say a mermaid is on board. A crowd forms, hoping to catch a glimpse of the magical creature. One crate after another is unpacked: a zebra, a leopard and a baboon. There's no mermaid, but in the final two crates is something almost as magical—a pair of young elephants, in poor health but alive.

Seeing a unique opportunity, a wealthy sugar merchant purchases the elephants for his country estate and turns their care over to a young stable boy, Tom Page. Tom's family has long cared for horses, but an elephant is something altogether different. It takes time for Tom and the elephants to understand one another, but to the surprise of everyone on the estate, a remarkable bond is formed.

Questions for Discussion

1. Differences of class were an unavoidable part of life in 1800s England. How do they manifest themselves throughout the novel, both in everyday life as well as in how the characters relate to each other?

2. Do you think that Tom and Jenny spoke to each other literally?

3. Do you think it would have been possible for Tom and Lizzie to have ever had a life together? If they had stayed together, how do you think their lives might have been different?

4. What is the novel saying about the differences between animals and human beings? Do you think that humans are morally superior to animals? Or inferior? Do you think that animals like elephants are capable of moral intelligence?

5. Is the portrait the novel offers of the relationship between Tom and Jenny too sentimental? Does it seem credible to you? Is the depiction of Jenny too idealized?

6. What is the novel saying about the nature of male sexuality, especially sexual violence, both in elephants (Timothy) and human beings (Tom Page, Mr. Singleton)?

7. In the London section of the novel, Mr. Cross tells Tom Page: "So long as the stories are possible, it does not matter whether they are true or false." Do you agree? What is the novel saying about the value of stories and storytelling?

8. In the London section of the novel, Tom Page sometimes seems to lose his grip on reality; he looks back on his country childhood with a kind of disbelief, as if unsure whether it really happened. Do we sometimes also look back on our own pasts in that way?

9. Is the novel's last section too much of a surprise? In introducing a modern narrator, what is the writer suggesting about our engagement with the lives of people in the eighteenth century?

10. Which ending do you believe really happened? Is it important that a novel choose an ending, or does leaving it up to the reader to decide what happened bring one closer to the story?